The Servant's Fortune

Joanna Stephen-Ward

Also by Joanna Stephen-Ward

Vissi d'arte – A novel about love and music

Eumeralla – A family saga

The Doll Collection – A crime novel

Suspicion Points – A detective novel

The Servant's Fortune

Joanna Stephen-Ward

Popham Gardens Publishing
June 2015

Copyright © Joanna Stephen-Ward

The right of Joanna Stephen-Ward to be identified as the author of this work has been asserted in accordance with sections 77 and 78 of the Copyright Designs and Patents Act 1988.

The characters in this work are fictitious and any resemblance to actual persons, living or dead, is coincidental.

All rights reserved. No part of this publication may be reproduced, stored in a retrieval system, or transmitted in any form or by any means: electronic, mechanical, photocopying, recording, or otherwise, without written permission from the publisher.

In loving memory of:

Ethel Curnow née Stephen
Carlyle Stephen
Jack Holland

Dedicated to:

Peter my husband
Kerry Conroy my sister

Special thanks to:

Sue Lightfoot for proof reading the manuscript

Annie Morris for reading the first chapters and giving me valuable feedback

Peter Stephen-Ward for the cover photo and the title

This novel would not have been written had it not been for my cousin **Dianne Farrugia**

The Servant's Fortune is a sequel to *Eumeralla*, but can be read as a complete novel by itself. *Eumeralla* ends in February 1973. The sequel begins a few days later. Below is a list of major and pivotal characters from *Eumeralla*.

The Mitchell Family

Eleanor – born 1918 (owner of Eumeralla)
Greg – born 1916 (Eleanor's husband)
June – born 1946 (secret daughter of Ruth Lancaster & Laurence Clarkson)
Tom – born 1947

The Clarkson Family

William 1885 – 1947 (owner of Acacia until 1947. His first wife died in 1930)

Their Children

Laurence 1915 – 1965
Jonathan 1916 – 1946
Virginia – born 1918

Keith – born 1949 (Laurence's son)
Gabriella – born 1950 (Laurence's daughter)
Fiona – original name was May. (June's twin. Adopted by Virginia & Alex.)

The Lancaster Family

Margot – born 1900
David – born 1908
Alex – born 1911
Francesca 1917 – 1945
Ruth 1919 – 1973
Catriona (Tree) – born 1947 (David's daughter)
Kim – 1948 – 1973 (David's daughter)

Stefan Jovanovics (Catriona's husband)

Marriages between the Clarksons & Lancasters

William Clarkson & Margot Lancaster
Laurence Clarkson & Francesca Lancaster
Virginia Clarkson & Alex Lancaster

Part 1

The Exiles

February 1973 – April 1974

Chapter 1

February 1973

Kingower, Victoria, Australia

Stefan braced himself to enter Kim's cottage. The sight of the golden Labrador in his basket on the veranda made the task ahead more depressing. The water bowl was empty, but the other bowl was, as usual, full of food and covered in flies even though it had only been there a few hours.

Stefan patted him. 'What are we going to do with you, Toby?'

He swatted away the flies, picked up the bowls, unlocked the door and stepped inside. Weak from lack of food Toby struggled to his feet and followed him. Apart from the empty fridge and kitchen bin, which the cleaner had cleared out, the cottage was as Kim had left it at the beginning of January.

Did she have any premonition of her own death? he wondered as he threw away the dog food. Any feeling of foreboding? She can't have done or she wouldn't have ridden Devil. Why did she ride him? She knew he was dangerous.

He washed the bowls and filled one with fresh water. Excited by Kim's scent, Toby went around the cottage sniffing expectantly. Stefan wished he could have put off this chore indefinitely, but Douglas Farquhar, the new vet, was moving into the cottage at the weekend. He began with Kim's bookshelves. As many of the books were veterinary he left them. If Douglas didn't want them he could give them to a library. Kim's graduation photo in a silver frame made him more thankful that Catriona, her parents and aunt were being spared this ordeal.

He packed Kim's clothes in suitcases for the church jumble sale, and put her jodhpurs, riding boots and hat in a box to take to the tack room. When the wardrobe and chest of drawers were empty, he stripped the bed and put the sheets and pillowcase in a basket by the washing machine. Douglas would be bringing his own bedlinen, but Stefan made up the bed with clean sheets thinking that after a two-hour journey from Melbourne he might be grateful that all he had to do was unpack.

He'd thought the worst was over until he went into the room Kim had used as a study. On her desk was a diary. He thought he'd better look at it so he could decide if and when he should give it to Catriona.

> *Yippee! Catriona and Stefan are engaged,* she had written in March 1972. *Luckily for us Stefan loves it here. He's applied for a teaching post at the local school, which is becoming vacant when the history and English teacher retires.*

'Less than a year ago,' he murmured.

It felt a lot longer. So many things had happened since then – most of them bad. His infatuation with Fiona. Kim's prophecy about disaster befalling the Lancaster family. His and Catriona's marriage that had been doomed from the moment he had called her Fiona when they were making love on their honeymoon. Catriona's jealousy and misery. His discontent. Kim's death in a riding accident. Her Aunt Ruth's death from breast cancer a few weeks later. The only good thing that had happened was Catriona's pregnancy.

He felt he was prying, but could not resist the temptation to read more.

March 1972

> *Bloody Fiona. I didn't think it would be possible to hate her more than I already do. Today she came to lunch – she invited herself and wouldn't be put off. When she arrived I knew Catriona and I had been foolish to tell Stefan she was a slut. Dressed in a black polo necked jumper and black velvet trousers she looked classy. I could*

see by Stefan's surprised expression that he was expecting someone completely different.

What a scene. In the middle of lunch she showed him a newspaper cutting about her real father Jonathan Clarkson, who had been killed trying to rescue someone from a burning house. She denounced Aunty Margot as a liar for telling us that he was a coward. She also called Aunty Margot a cheat, so heaven knows what Stefan thinks about that. We'll have to tell him about Acacia. Aunty Margot didn't cheat anyone out of their inheritance. If her stepchildren hadn't been nasty to her their father would never have cut them out of his will.

He seemed mesmerized by her. She uses her beauty as a weapon. If she causes trouble between him and Catriona I'll feel like killing her. Thanks to Fiona we are all diminished in his eyes. Aunty Margot spent an hour on the phone to Aunty Ruth, who made all sorts of excuses for her. She's our aunt – she's not even related to Fiona so why does she always defend her?

'Because,' mused Stefan, 'she was her mother.'

When their true relationship had been revealed after Ruth died Catriona had been too stricken by Kim's death to react. He wondered how Kim would have greeted the revelation. A few days later she had written :

Aunty Margot's explained why she told us Fiona's real father was a coward. One of the brothers had to stay on the land – Fiona was right about that. Jonathan and his brother Laurence tossed a coin to see who would go to war and who would stay. Aunty Margot overheard the whole thing – she wasn't spying, she was reading a book in the lounge and they were near the window. The coin decided Jonathan had to go, but he told Laurence that he was frightened, so Laurence said he would go instead. Odd that he was too frightened to go to war, but ran into a burning house to save someone's life.

Not wanting anyone to suspect that he was obsessed by Fiona

Stefan had never asked why Margot had told Catriona and Kim that her stepson was a coward, and he wondered why Catriona had never told him. Perhaps with all the wedding preparations she had forgotten. It was also around that time that he was having serious doubts about marrying Catriona. On several occasions he had made excuses to stay in Melbourne at the weekends rather than go to Kingower.

June

Can't believe it! Fiona's got an identical twin. She's gone to live in Queensland with her real mother on a sheep and wheat property called Eumeralla. Hope she stays there and we never see her again. We have to invite her to Tree and Stefan's wedding. Dad said it would cause all sorts of problems if we don't, but I hope she doesn't come.

Stefan wondered if his and Catriona's wedding day would have been less of a torture for him if Fiona had been absent. With shame he recalled the way he had gazed at her while taking no interest in Catriona, apart from feeling imprisoned by marriage. He turned to September to see what Kim had written about the wedding.

Stefan turned up. I was worried that he wouldn't, because it would have been humiliating for Catriona. He looked unhappy, but when I asked him what was wrong he said he was nervous and hates being the centre of attention. He did smile as they were leaving for their honeymoon, so I hope everything will be all right.
Fiona was there, looking stunning. Odd how things turn out. I was upset when I knew she was coming, but if she hadn't I would have never met her brother Tom. We danced most of the night. He adores horses, and is interested in my work as a vet. How I wish he wasn't Fiona's brother.

I was a bastard, Stefan thought. How could I have made my

feeling so obvious? I should have made an effort, but I was consumed . . . no, that's no excuse.

He flicked through the diary until he came to October.

A wonderful holiday on Eumeralla. I'm in love with Tom. He's the most masculine man I've ever met, much more so than the softies who come from Melbourne. June is much nicer than Fiona. Tom's parents, Greg and Eleanor, made me welcome and I felt really at home with them all. I'm pleased Fiona wasn't there – although why she left is a mystery to everyone. I wish Tom wasn't her brother. Aunty Margot's worried about it too.

If she'd known Tom wasn't Fiona's brother things would have been different, Stefan thought. If she'd gone to live on Eumeralla she'd still be alive.

He closed the diary. He dared not read any more. Kim's later references to him would be scathing and derogatory and well deserved. As quickly as he could, he finished sorting out her desk. There were three letters from Tom. He put them in the diary without reading them.

The cleaner would come in tomorrow to vacuum, polish the furniture, and clean the kitchen, bathroom and windows. After putting everything in his car he went back inside. He felt dreadful when he saw that Toby was asleep in the washing basket, clearly comforted by Kim's scent. It would have been cruel to get him out, so he dragged it outside onto the veranda.

'I can't let you stay inside, Toby. If I leave the door open for you snakes might get in.' He shook out the blanket in the dog basket. 'Aunty Margot will come by later to give you some food, but I don't suppose you'll eat it.'

$$\Omega \quad \Omega \quad \Omega$$

Douglas's life was changing at a speed that left him no time to wonder if he was doing the right thing. It had started with a phone call from Catriona in the middle of January, telling him that they needed another vet to replace Kim.

'I remember you telling me last year that you'd like something more challenging than neutering pet cats and dogs,' she had said.

He had driven to Whittlesea two days later for an interview, and was offered the job immediately. An added incentive was the opportunity to live in one of the cottages on the Kingower property. Catriona's husband Stefan had shown him the cottages to see which one he preferred. Even from the outside the cottages, although the same style and size, were very different. One was painted cream with the corrugated iron roof and woodwork painted brown. The other was white with a navy roof and woodwork. Although Douglas had been on the Kingower riding treks many times, he had always stayed in the homestead with the other riders, and had only seen Catriona and Kim's cottages from a distance. They had small front gardens planted with lavender hedges and lilac trees.

'This was Catriona's,' said Stefan as he opened the navy door.

The interior was feminine, with yellow and blue floral curtains and matching upholstery on the sofa and armchairs. The walls were primrose and the woodwork white. The carved furniture looked Victorian. Catriona was tall, thin and wore her frizzy hair tied back. Her clothes were austere. She only wore dresses to weddings or balls and she rarely wore jewellery, so the romantic femininity of her decor surprised him. He would have matched this cottage to a frivolous girl who wore pretty dresses, read magazines and romantic novels and spent a lot of time shopping for clothes and make-up.

Although the same size and layout Kim's cottage was very different. The wheat coloured walls, cream carpet and upholstery and plain Scandinavian furniture were more to his taste.

'I'll have this one,' he said before he had even gone into the bedrooms.

Stefan smiled. 'It'd be my choice too. It'll be good to have at least one of the cottages occupied again. Is there any furniture you don't need?'

'No. My flat's furnished. My sister's getting a friend of hers to take my place.'

'Do you want me to leave the stereo?'

Douglas examined it. 'It's much better than mine. I'll buy it from you.'

'No. If you want it we'll leave it. What about the LPs? I think there's every album the Beatles and Rolling Stones made.'

'Fantastic, but you must let me give you something for them.'

Stefan shook his head. 'Think of them as a moving in present.'

When Douglas had finished looking around they went outside and Stefan locked the door.

Douglas looked at the empty dog basket on the veranda. 'Where's Kim's dog?'

'Her aunt's taken him for a walk. She comes every day to feed him. He drinks water, but he hardly ever eats. We took him to live with us, but he ran off and came back here – it was lucky he didn't get hit by a car – although it would have been quick and he wouldn't be suffering like he is now.'

Douglas shook his head. 'Poor creature.'

'I hope you don't miss Melbourne,' Stefan said as they walked back to the car. 'It's a completely different way of life here. It might take some getting used to.'

Douglas was not sure if he heard regret in Stefan's tone. 'Catriona's phone call came at the right time,' he said. 'Things are awkward in Melbourne at the moment. I broke up with my girlfriend a month ago and she's my sister's friend, so it'll be a relief to get away from the all the resentment. Some of my friends have booked riding weekends in two weeks, so I'll see plenty of them. Do you prefer it here?'

Stefan shrugged. 'Some things are better. Some are worse.'

'What are the worst things?'

'Everyone knows everyone else.'

'Is that bad?'

'They all know each other's business. You go shopping in Whittlesea and people stop and talk to you, and what was supposed to be a ten minute trip ends up taking an hour.'

'People are friendly then?'

Stefan nodded. 'Too friendly sometimes. You can't be anonymous here.'

'I reckon I'll like that. Who wants to be anonymous?'

Chapter 2

Sydney

February 1973

June had refused to speak for two days. She had ignored Virginia throughout the flight from Brisbane, and Fiona had been too afraid of being rebuffed to try to draw her out. She hadn't acknowledged Alex when he met them at Sydney airport, and even Fiona was getting hostile looks. As they reached the winding and hilly roads of Vaucluse Fiona hoped that June might find some pleasure in the view of the harbour, but her sullen expression stayed the same.

'We're here,' said Fiona when Alex pulled up in the driveway of their house.

June got out of the car, grabbed her suitcase from Alex when he lifted it out of the boot, and stood glowering in the front garden while she waited to go inside.

'Do you want to share a room with me or have your own?' Fiona asked her as they stood in the doorway of her old bedroom.

'I don't care. I hope we won't be here long. The sooner we're out of this horrible place the better.'

In the seven months since they had been reunited for the first time since they were babies Fiona had only ever known June in sunny moods. She found her anger intimidating, but was pleased that she had broken her silence. 'This isn't a horrible place. It's one of the most exclusive suburbs in Sydney. Look at the view. You've got to admit it's a stunning harbour.'

June went to the window. 'I'd rather see sheep, horses and grass. Yes, Fiona, it's beautiful house – your bedroom is beautiful, but I don't want to be here – I want to be on Eumeralla.'

'So do I. But we can't.'

'Everything all right?' Virginia asked from the doorway.

'No!' snapped June. 'Thanks to you it isn't.'

Virginia spoke as if she hadn't noticed June's aggression. 'Dinner will be at seven.'

'Thanks, Mum,' said Fiona.

'I can't believe you still call them Mum and Dad,' June said when Virginia left.

'They'll always be that to me.'

'If Ruth was alive, what would you call her?'

'Aunty Ruth.'

'Not mum?'

Fiona shook her head. 'If you ever see Eleanor again what will you call her?'

'Certainly not mum. But I never want to see her again anyway.'

'She didn't know Keith was your brother, Juju. It's not all her fault.'

'She lied to every one. That is her fault.'

'But she vowed never to tell.'

June turned away from the window. 'What's the point in talking about it?'

'I used to be as angry as you,' Fiona said. 'Now I know how others felt – why they found me so tiresome.'

'How do you expect me to act? I've been torn away from everything I love.'

'I know. But try and understand the circumstances. It's not as if everyone deliberately planned to destroy your life.'

June didn't reply.

'Is being angry going to change anything?' Fiona challenged. 'Is it going to make Ruth's letter a mistake? Is a miracle going to occur and you'll discover that you and Keith aren't brother and sister?'

'Is not being angry going to change anything?' June countered.

'No, but it might make things easier – '

'For Aunty Virginia maybe, but not for me.'

'Juju, you've got to think about the future – '

'Oh I think about the future all the time – a future without Keith and Eumeralla.'

'Okay. Keith can't be replaced, but Eumeralla can. And one day you'll find love again.'

'Stop trying to cheer me up – I'm not in the mood for platitudes.' June sat on one of the twin beds and put her head in her hands. 'I wish I'd never found you.'

Not attempting to hide her hurt, Fiona said, 'Thank you, June. There are other bedrooms – go and take a look at them and – '

June jumped up and threw her arms around Fiona. 'Sorry. I meant . . . I should have gone back further and said I wish we'd never been separated. Then this would never have happened.'

Fiona pulled away. 'It might have. You and Keith would have grown up together. You still might have fallen in love. Eleanor and Johnny grew up together and that didn't stop them falling in love. And if you hadn't found me where would you be now? What would you be doing?'

'I'd be on Eumeralla, of course.'

'Exactly. And your boyfriend, who you weren't all that keen on, was in Europe – '

'What's he got to do with anything?'

'Until you'd met Keith you'd never been in love.'

'So?'

'Juju, even though I was there for less than a year I loved Eumeralla, but I'd grown up in a city. I'd had lots of boyfriends and thought I was in love a few times. It was easy to meet people at the tennis club and ski club and at work. Eumeralla was your whole life. You hardly ever left it. It's so isolated. Tom only met Kim because he came to Catriona's wedding with me.'

'He'd had girlfriends. Hazel was always bringing her townie friends to visit.'

'But because of me your parents were desperate to keep you away from anywhere Keith might see you.' She saw June's mutinous look and said, 'Okay, not your parents – Eleanor and Greg. But looking at your situation clearly – you were stagnating.'

'I was happy – '

'Because you didn't know anything different. You'd scarcely mixed with anyone outside Eumeralla.'

'You lived in the city,' said June. 'And were you happy?'

'No, but – '

'There you are then.'

Fiona gave up and tried to think about all the things she had to do. She took her diary out of her bag and began to make notes. 'Tomorrow I'll go into the city and book our flights to London. Do you want to come?'

June looked at her as if she'd asked her if she wanted to jump into a fire. 'No, I don't.'

'But you'll have to get your photo taken for your passport.'

'You've got photos of yourself – use one of them.'

'I'll need your birth certificate.'

June flung her case open, rummaged through her clothes and pulled out an old brown envelope. 'There it is. Dad – I mean Greg – gave it to me before I left.' She looked at the certificate. 'Lies. It's all lies. Jonathan Clarkson wasn't my father. Eleanor Clarkson's not my mother.'

'Did Greg adopt you?'

June shrugged. 'How would I know? Everyone's lied.'

'Not Greg.'

'He did. If it hadn't been for Keith coming to Eumeralla and seeing me and thinking I was you, no one would have ever told me anything.'

'Juju, this complicates things. You'll have to get your passport and bank account and everything under the name of Clarkson not Mitchell.'

'I don't care. I'm being forced to go somewhere I don't want to go. It doesn't matter what my name is. Anyway I've never had a passport or a bank account.'

Dreading June's reply, Fiona said, 'You don't have to come to England with me, you can go to Kingower if you'd rather.'

'What would I do there?'

'Help with the riding school, the horse treks and the horses. You could live in one of the cottages and – '

'Why can't we both go to Kingower?'

Fiona hesitated, wondering where to begin. 'I can't.'

June looked puzzled. 'Why not?'

'Did you know Kim was psychic?'

'No, but there was something . . . odd . . . different about her. Not in a bad way. Red always growled and barked at strangers – we worried he was going to bite someone, but he instantly adored Kim. We couldn't believe it. He wouldn't leave her side. Toddles wouldn't either – but that's not so odd because she's much more friendly. And the horses were crazy about her too. Tom's nickname for Kim was Magic. But what's this got to do with why you can't live on Kingower?'

'It's a long story.'

'Tell me.'

'Not at the moment. Why don't you go and visit it? Once you've seen it you'll be able to make a decision.'

'What's it like?'

'Beautiful. Much more wealthy than Eumeralla. Not as big though. Only one thousand acres. They employ grooms, gardeners and a cleaner. Catriona's a year younger than us – she's a vet. She's married and expecting her first baby.'

'I thought Kim's sister's name was Tree or something.'

'That's her nickname. When Kim was little she couldn't say Catriona – she called her Tree and it stuck. Her parents and Aunty Margot refuse to call her Tree, but most other people do.'

'But you call her Catriona?'

'It depends. When we had rows I wasn't allowed to call her Tree. Sometimes I call her Tree – more often it's Catriona, because I'm usually out of favour.'

June looked thoughtful. 'I liked Kim. What's Catriona like?'

'It's hard for me to say. We were close when we were children, but when we grew up there were problems and I wasn't allowed to go to Kingower for a while. There was a hell of a row. If you want to meet them all – '

June shook her head. 'I'd rather be with you. None of this is your fault.'

Fiona imagined June's anger and distress if she hated England. 'Listen, Juju. Much as I want us to go to England together, I don't want you to get there and decide you've made the wrong choice. I really think you should go to Kingower and have a look around. You can meet Aunty Margot, Uncle David and Catriona. You'd have a good life there with the horses. The cottages are small but pretty or you might be able to live in the homestead if you want. We can go together or with Mum and Dad.'

'The less I see of Aunty Virginia and Uncle Alex the better. I'll go to Kingower, but just with you.'

'Okay, I'll get Dad to phone Uncle David and tell him we're coming. Would you rather fly or drive?'

'How far is it?'

'About five hundred miles. If we drive it'll take two days. We'll stop at a motel overnight. I'll ask Dad if we can borrow his car.'

That night Fiona thought about what she would do if June wanted to live at Kingower instead of going to England with her. With June her life would be very different. They would live in the country and buy a riding school. Fiona could not envisage doing that alone. She would buy a flat in London and get a job with an airline – perhaps she could work at Heathrow Airport.

'Juju, did you ever see the letter Ruth wrote to me?' Fiona asked the next day.

June shook her head. 'I just heard about it. She sent a copy to Eleanor.'

'Would you like to read it?'

'I suppose so.'

Fiona went to a drawer and took out the letter. 'Promise you won't get angry and tear it up?'

'Okay. It's very long.'

Fiona gave her the letter and watched as she read it. At first her expression was apathetic, then she rolled her eyes and tutted.

'What?' asked Fiona.

'He only saw my ethereal sister Francesca. Laurence. Proud, impetuous, unpredictable, idealist Laurence. It wasn't just that he was handsome – '

'What's wrong with that?'

'Bit melodramatic, isn't it? Sounds like some trashy romantic novel.'

'She's describing our father, Juju, and Keith's. How would you describe Keith?'

June went on reading. She tutted again. 'He looked at Francesca like a man who is seeing heaven.' She shook her head. 'What a lot of slush.'

'Give it to me if you don't want to read it,' Fiona said. 'I gave you the letter so you could understand why things happened, not so you could make snide comments.'

'Okay,' said June. 'I'll stop my commentary.' On the second page she raised her eyebrows. On the third page she chewed her lip. From then on Fiona thought June wouldn't have been able to put the letter down if the house had caught fire. When she finished tears were streaming down her face. 'Poor Ruth,' she whispered. 'How old was she?'

'Twenty-six.'

'The same age as us.'

'Trashy, romantic novel?' Fiona queried.

'No.' June wiped her eyes. 'Sorry I said that. What would have happened if Laurence had known Francesca was dead before he saw Ruth?'

'I don't know,' said Fiona. 'I'd never thought about it.'

'Maybe we wouldn't have been born.' She folded up the letter and gave it back to Fiona. 'Not that it would have mattered much.'

Chapter 3

Douglas bought food in Whittlesea, the nearest town to Kingower, and drove up to the cottages. Stefan was sitting on the veranda stroking an unresponsive dog. He got out of the car and went up to them.

'Hello, Toby. I'm your new owner.'

Stefan stood up. 'Tree thinks we're going to have to put him to sleep. Margot's trying to get him to live with her, but he whimpers to be let out and comes back here when she opens her front door. She feeds and brushes him twice a day and takes him for walks, but he's so unhappy.'

'What was he like when Kim went on holidays?'

'Miserable – not this bad – he did eat, but he fretted. He was always overcome with joy when she came back. This time we were hoping he'd forget – we all made a huge fuss of him, but it's as if he knows – I don't know how.'

'He can sense your grief. It's not just one heartbroken person it's the whole family.' Douglas knelt down and stroked the dog. 'Don't give up on him yet. He might be better with some company.'

'We've tried to give him company.'

Douglas heard the annoyance in Stefan's voice. 'I know. It's just that he wants to be here – once I'm living here he might feel less deserted. Did Kim let him live inside?'

'Yes. His basket was in the lounge, but when it was cold he slept on her bed.'

Douglas stood up and patted his thighs. 'Want to come in, Toby?'

Stefan helped him get his cases out of the boot. Toby followed them inside.

'The cottage comes with a cleaner, but if you'd rather do it yourself – '

'How much?'

'Nothing. She's on the Kingower staff. She used to clean for Kim and she cleans up at the homestead and also does the surgery. She's got the key, but if you don't want her she'll give it back.'

Having a cleaner appealed to Douglas. He intended to get as involved in Kingower as he could, and the freedom from housework would give him more time. As he unpacked his suitcases after Stefan left he felt daunted. He remembered Kim's funeral in the packed church, and the palpable grief. He not only had to prove himself to the people of the town, but to a dog as well.

'Toby, you and I are going to be mates,' Douglas said firmly when he had finished unpacking. 'I'm your new owner and the first thing I want you to do is eat. I don't give up easily. I know you want to be with Kim, but you can't and I'm not going to let you join her on the other side.' He looked at the dog's mournful eyes. 'Well, not if I can help it.'

Although Toby didn't respond he was looking at Douglas, which was a good sign. He brought the dog bowls inside, washed them and put them on the kitchen floor. He took a tin of dog food out of the cupboard and opened it. 'Ugh. Revolting stuff, I wouldn't want to eat it either. Shall I make you something tasty? How about we eat the same thing?' He wrapped the tin in newspaper and threw it in the bin. 'We've got a bit of a dilemma. I'm a vegetarian. I will buy meat for you, but let's try you on a non-meat diet first. You might like it. What shall we have? I was going to make some potato and cheese patties with carrots and peas.'

He filled one of the bowls with milk diluted with water and was heartened when Toby drank it. When the potatoes were cooked he mashed them, mixed them with milk and butter and put a spoonful in Toby's other bowl. Not wanting Toby to sense his anxiety he went outside. When he came back the bowl was empty.

Douglas squatted beside him and stroked his ears. 'Tree's going to be happy when I tell her. Shall we try another spoonful?'

He had just finished washing up when there was a knock on

the door. It was Margot, Catriona's aunt.

'I just wanted to make sure you had everything you need.'

'Mrs Clarkson, thanks for coming over. Everything's okay. Would you like to come in?'

'I haven't since . . .'

Toby went up to Margot and licked her hand.

She smiled and stepped inside.

Douglas went to bed early. He left the curtains open and gazed at the myriad of stars until he fell asleep. When he woke it was to the sound of birdsong instead of traffic. He had four days before he started work and he wanted to get used to his surroundings. He left Toby asleep in his basket in the lounge while he showered and shaved. By the time he'd got dressed Toby was awake.

'Ready for breakfast, Toby?'

He put some cereal in Toby's bowl and poured milk over it. Toby ate it. When he finished he looked up at Douglas.

'Want some more? Good boy.'

Wanting to be certain that Toby was permanently recovering his appetite, Douglas didn't tell Catriona until he started work.

She looked at him in astonishment. 'You got Toby to eat? You're incredible. How did you do that?'

He pulled on his white coat. 'It's not me really. He's where he wants to be. Kim's not there, but he can still smell her scent and he's consoled by it. And although I'm not Kim he's got company. Lucky he seems to like me.'

$$\Omega \quad \Omega \quad \Omega$$

Stefan felt like an outsider. Catriona had invited Douglas and two of the veterinary nurses to dinner. Once she would have consulted him about it, but last week she told him who was coming and when. She decided what they were eating, instead of planning the menu with him. While Catriona was in the kitchen, Stefan had set the table with the tablecloth and serviettes Fiona had given them for a wedding present. Only a few moths ago his thoughts would have turned to her. Now all he could think about was Catriona, and hope that they would recapture the intensity and warmth of their relationship before he had become infatuated with Fiona. He feared that the only reason she did not divorce him was because she was pregnant.

During the first course of iced cucumber soup all the talk was about the surgery. One of the nurses attempted to draw him into the conversation, which, he thought dismally, was more than Catriona was doing. Douglas, who had been friends with Catriona since they were at university together, worried him. He was single, a better rider than Stefan and had a good personality. They worked together everyday and Stefan wondered if that would help or hinder anything other than friendship developing. Douglas had already established himself with the family and helped Catriona and her father with the Kingower horse treks. Because Catriona was so tall herself, height in a man was important to her. Douglas was as tall as Stefan and, although not handsome, his features were even. His thick hair was the same honey blonde as Catriona's, but as straight as hers was frizzy. He had settled down to country life far better than Stefan had.

'How long have you been in Australia, Doug?' he asked, trying to include himself in the conversation.

Douglas buttered his bread roll. 'My parents emigrated from Scotland in the fifties when I was seven.'

'You've picked up the Australian accent,' said Catriona. 'But you've still got a Scottish lilt.'

'Does it sound weird?' he asked.

'No, it's attractive,' said Catriona.

Stefan wished she hadn't said that.

'It's great that you've kept your maiden name, Tree,' said one of the nurses as Catriona brought in the aubergine and herb casserole.

'Professionally only,' she said. 'In private my surname's Jovanovics.'

To Stefan's annoyance Douglas said, 'Women changing their names when they get married is archaic.'

Although he knew he would be outnumbered he had to disagree. 'Why?'

'A woman's no longer a man's property when they get married,' said Douglas.

Catriona looked pleased.

'It's traditional,' Stefan argued. Even before he saw Catriona's scornful expression he knew what a pathetic argument it was. He was constantly impressing on his history students the how social changes had stopped children being be doomed to suffer painful deaths as a result of being chimney sweeps.

'A stupid tradition,' said one of the nurses. 'Burning witches was traditional once, so was chopping people's heads off.'

'So what would you propose?' Stefan asked trying to sound affable.

'Women can keep their own names,' Douglas said.

'Or,' said one of the nurses with a mischievous grin, 'Men could change their name to the woman's.'

'And what about their children?' Stefan asked, turning to Catriona. 'Hyphenating our two names would be a mouthful for any child.' He laughed. 'Jovanovics-Lancaster. And if that became the custom everyone would end up with dozens of hyphenated surnames.'

'Easy,' said Douglas. 'Boys have the man's name. Girls have the woman's name.'

'Awful idea,' Stefan said derisively. 'Brothers and sisters from the same family having different surnames. What about when they go to school?'

'They can speak,' said Douglas. 'They can tell people.'

Stefan shook his head. 'Crazy.'

'I think it's an excellent solution,' said Catriona.

The two nurses agreed.

Stefan knew he should concede, but he was reluctant to let Douglas win. 'And what if you only have girls or boys? Or only want one child?'

No one had an answer. Feeling he had made his point he let the matter drop.

'Have you got any names for the baby?' asked Douglas.

'Kim if it's a girl and David if it's a boy,' said Stefan, hoping his willingness to agree with Catriona's wishes would help to close the chasm between them.

Chapter 4

As Fiona drove the Jaguar through the gates of Kingower June looked at the rhododendrons that lined the driveway. Part of the reason she had agreed to come was curiosity about where her real mother had grown up. Reading the letter Ruth had written when she knew she was dying had made her more real, rather than a shadowy figure whose confession had wrecked June and Keith's plans to marry. Images of a frightened pregnant girl and the distraught man, who had just been told his wife was dead, crowded her mind. She wished she had taken more notice of Ruth when she had come to Eumeralla with Alex, but Ruth, bewildered by Eleanor's hostility towards her, had only made the one visit.

In contrast to the ramshackle house on Eumeralla the Kingower homestead was built of brick, simply designed and elegant, with a wide veranda surrounded by black cast-iron lacework. Fiona had told her it had ten bedrooms.

David was waiting for them.

'Hello, Uncle David,' Fiona said cautiously. 'This is June.'

He gave Fiona a brief kiss on the cheek and held out his hand to June. 'Thank you for your letter about Kim. We haven't got around to replying to everyone yet. How's Tom?'

'Broken up.'

'We all liked him. I would have been happy if he and Kim . . . anyway, I'm sorry about your . . . problems,' he said as he opened the door and led them inside.

'Thank you,' said June.

'Catriona and Stefan will be joining us for dinner and so will Margot.'

'How's Tree?' asked Fiona.

'She's well. Not even tired. No morning sickness. We've got a new vet – Douglas Farquhar. You may have met him – he used to come on the treks.'

Fiona shook her head. 'The name's not familiar.'

'He's just moved into Kim's cottage. He and Catriona were at university together. He came to Kim's funeral.' He opened the door to a bedroom with twin beds. 'I'll leave you to unpack. We'll have drinks before dinner – come into the lounge when you're ready.'

'Thanks, Uncle David.'

'You're uncomfortable with each other,' June whispered when he left.

Fiona nodded. 'We always have been.'

'Is he the one who tried to teach you to ride?'

'Yes.'

June went to the window. 'It's gorgeous, but . . . '

'But what?'

'It feels – I can't describe it – the atmosphere's wrong.'

'They're still suffering the shock of Kim's death. It'll take a long time for them to recover.'

Stefan wished he could get out of going to Kingower for dinner. It was not that he was worried about his reaction to Fiona, he was worried about how Catriona would interpret it. Whatever he did would be wrong. If he was cool towards Fiona, Catriona might think he was acting. If he greeted her warmly she would think he was still in love with her.

Best to be natural – as natural as I can be in an unnatural situation, he thought.

To his surprise Catriona seemed unconcerned. She came home from the veterinary surgery, had a shower and began to get dressed. As yet, her pregnancy was barely noticeable.

'Tree, this is all wrong. If June lives on Kingower what about Kim's prophecy?'

Catriona took her dark green linen trousers and a cream silk blouse out of the wardrobe. 'Fiona had nothing to do with Kim's death.'

'But what else is in store?'

'Nothing.'

'Kim's premonition was that May was going to destroy this family.'

'No, Stefan. Her exact words were 'tear this family apart'. Well her death did that.'

'As Fiona herself said, they were called May and June because one was born before midnight in May and the other was born after midnight in June. And no one knows who is who,' he argued.

'You scoffed before. What's changed your mind?'

He went to the wardrobe and looked at the row of ties. 'I believe you and Kim didn't know that Fiona's original name was May. Fiona was with Kim when she was killed . . . '

'Kim was killed because the horse she was riding was vicious.' She pulled on her trousers. 'Why are you suddenly so against Fiona?'

'I'm trying to protect you and your family.' He selected a navy tie. 'In September you and I will be parents – our baby will be a member of the Lancaster family. I don't want any danger to threaten it.'

'Its surname name will be Jovanovics.'

'But its bloodline will also be Lancaster.'

'June probably won't want to live here.'

'What makes you think that? She's got a whole new family here. She knew and liked Kim – '

She took the gold sea-horse pendant Stefan had given her out of the jewellery box. 'She might rather go to England with Fiona.'

'Is Fiona definitely going to England? What if she changes her mind? What if she wants to live on Kingower?'

'Thanks to you, Stefan, she knows about Kim's premonition. She told Kim that she's going to England. She also said that she didn't want to harm this family.'

'But that was before she knew she was a Lancaster. Now she knows that Ruth was her real mother she might change her mind.'

'And she might not.' She twisted her hair into a knot. 'Let's see what she decides before you start panicking.'

Her inference that he was being melodramatic hurt him. Serves me right, he thought. I've hurt her enough.

When they arrived at the Kingower homestead they went into the lounge. Stefan was pleased to see that Margot was already there. The more people the less awkward it would be. He greeted Fiona and June and made what he knew was an inane remark about how alike they were. If they had both been smartly dressed he would not have been able to tell which was Fiona, but June wore faded trousers and an equally faded check shirt with frayed cuffs, while Fiona wore a navy dress with a silver necklace and pearl earrings. June wore no jewellery. As soon as he could Stefan began a conversation with Margot.

Douglas Farquhar's arrival with Toby alleviated the strained atmosphere. June's eyes lit up when she saw the dog. She stroked him and to everyone's surprise he licked her hand and wagged his tail.

'For a while we thought he was going to have to be put down,' said Catriona.

'Why? What was wrong with him?' asked June.

'He was Kim's dog. He'd hardly eat he missed her so much, but Doug worked a miracle.'

'Ah.' June put her arm around him. 'Poor, poor boy.'

'He doesn't wag his tail very often,' said Douglas. 'He likes you.'

'How did you get him to eat?' asked Fiona.

'Well, apart from fretting for Kim, he didn't have any company and I think having someone living in the cottage helps. Dog food is revolting so I gave him what I ate – he seems to like vegetarian food, otherwise I would have had to ditch my ethics and buy meat for him.'

'How long have you been a vegetarian?' asked June.

Douglas grimaced. 'Part of our training involved visiting abattoirs – that was the end of my meat-eating days.'

Stefan studied Douglas's expression to see if he was captivated by the beauty of Fiona and June, but he acted normally and paid more attention to Toby than he did to anyone else.

June was astounded by the interactions at Kingower. Having met and liked Kim who had fitted in so well on Eumeralla, she had been unprepared for the formal, stuffy atmosphere at Kingower. She was unsure that Fiona's assessment, that they were still suffering from the shock of Kim's death, was correct.

'Everyone's like strangers with each other,' she said to Fiona the next morning when Fiona was showing her the stables. 'Catriona and Stefan are distant, even with each other. And I thought he was rude – he hardly looked at you. It was if he was deliberately ignoring you. Of all of them Aunty Margot seemed the most normal – I know she's the wicked stepmother – '

'Not so wicked – in fact not wicked at all.'

'I thought you hated her.'

Fiona nodded. 'After Kim's death Aunty Margot and I had a long talk. I understand things now. Mum, Laurence and Johnny were obnoxious to her when she became their stepmother. She overheard them say how ugly she was. And they were vile when she had a miscarriage. As Eleanor said it's not as if she'd broken up their family – our grandfather had been a widower for three years.'

June looked around the immaculate stable block in awe. 'It's in better condition than the house on Eumeralla.'

Fiona, hoping June wasn't warming to the idea of living here, said, 'I'll show you the cottage that you'd be living in. It used to be Catriona's. Douglas lives in the adjoining one.'

'These riding weekends – what happens? Where does every one stay?'

'Some of the riders live nearby. The ones who come from Melbourne stay in the homestead. On the riding weekends they hire a cook to help with the meals. It's all well organized.'

'It must make heaps of money.'

'Most of the money comes from the stud side of things and the riding school. And Aunty Margot poured our grandfather's money into Kingower. If you come to England with me, we could buy something like this.' As the cottages came into view, Fiona said, 'Some of the staff used to live in the cottages. During the second world war the gardener was killed and his wife moved to

Melbourne. At the end of the war the cook and her husband were given a grant of land, and so was the odd job man and his wife who did the cleaning, laundry and washing up in the homestead. There were two other cottages – they were tiny and when Aunty Margot moved here after our grandfather died, they were knocked together into one house. These two cottages were modernized for Catriona and Kim – they've lived in them since they graduated from university.'

Fiona opened the door to Catriona's old cottage. 'It's small, but it'd be all yours.'

'It's pretty,' said June.

By the end of the second day at Kingower June had made her decision. Although the thought of being on a plane for thirty-six hours filled her with dread, she would rather be with Fiona than with the Lancasters' even if they were related to her.

'Fiona, I can't live here. They're all so tense, cold and unfriendly,' she said as they walked to the paddock.

'Douglas is nice.'

'Yes, he's okay, but I'll come to England with you. Does Uncle David always sound as if he's planned what he's going to say in advance?'

Fiona smiled wryly. 'Only when he speaks to me.'

'His wife hardly talks. Why do you call her Aunty David?'

'She's so passive she used to irritate Mum. She's dominated by Uncle David, and one day Mum called her Mrs David – as an insult, but she took it as a compliment and it stuck.'

'You know what? I'd rather be with Aunty Virginia and Uncle Alex than here.'

Fiona grinned. 'I never thought you'd say that.'

'Neither did I. I'm still angry with them. How come Tom liked this place so much?'

'It was different then.'

'It must have been. It's beautiful – maybe I could live here, but only if you did too. We could both live in Catriona's old cottage. Come on, Fiona, what happened, why can't you live here?'

Fiona opened the gate to the paddock and went over to one of the horses.

June shook her arm. 'Tell me!'

'Okay. Kim, Tree and I were inseparable when we were children. I loved coming here and they looked forward to seeing me. Then when we got older – their boyfriends . . . they were like tomcats. They tried to flirt with me. Kim and Tree accused me of encouraging them. We fought, but made up. Some of the things they said still haunt me, even though they're not true.'

'What did they say?'

'That I was born in the gutter and that's where I should have stayed.'

'But – '

'And that the Lancaster family were too good for me.'

'Why did they say you were born in the gutter?'

'Mum told me that my real mother was an alcoholic.'

June was confused. 'Didn't she think Eleanor was our real mother?'

'Yes.'

'So what – '

'When she told me I was adopted and that she was really my aunt not my mother, I said I wanted to go and live with my real mother. She was so hurt that she lied.'

'Lies and more lies. Does anyone in our family tell the truth?'

Fiona shrugged. 'We shouldn't judge – we haven't been in the same situations. Imagine having a child you loved and having her tell you she wanted to be elsewhere.'

'If you wanted to be elsewhere that was her fault not yours. Anyway what happened that was so bad you can't live here?'

'Kim was engaged and I was going to be one of her bridesmaids. When I came up one weekend her fiancé had sprained his ankle so couldn't ride. When they all went off on the ride he tried to rape me.'

'God!'

'Aunty Margot's horse saw a snake and bolted and she fell off. She wasn't injured – just battered and shaken up and bruised.

Lucky for me that they came back early. They saw us and thought we were in a passionate embrace. They wouldn't believe that he was trying to rape me and he denied it and said I was the one who started kissing him. I suppose it did look bad – I was gasping and panting. I didn't scream because I didn't think anyone was near enough to hear me, otherwise I would have. Aunty Ruth and Mum believed me and that caused a big rift – '

'But what's this got to do with why you can't live here?'

'Kim was psychic. Last year she had two premonitions. One was that Ruth was going to die. She even got the timing right. The other one was that May was going to tear the family apart. At that time they didn't know, and neither did I, that my name was originally May.'

'Ah, I see. It's England then.'

Chapter 5

Fiona was pleased that June was less hostile to Virginia and Alex when they got back to Vaucluse. She wasn't friendly, but she was polite. She also looked secretive. The reason became clear three days later, when June reverted to anger and silence.

Virginia, obviously confident that the thaw was permanent, had called her Juju when they were washing the dishes.

'Don't call me that!' June snapped. 'Only my friends and people I like can call me Juju.'

Virginia looked startled.

Fiona, confused by the change said, 'For crying out loud, what's the matter with you now?'

'My period was late – I thought I was pregnant.'

'Thank goodness, you weren't,' said Virginia.

'What would you have done if I had been?' June flung the tea towel on the floor. 'Dragged me to the nearest hospital and forced me to have an abortion?'

'More to the point, what would you have done?' Virginia challenged.

'Married Keith. You would have all had to let us marry.'

'June,' said Virginia steadily. 'Stop blaming the past and everyone in it for your unhappiness. It's happened and can't be changed. Concentrate on your future. You can find love and happiness again, but – '

'It's all right for you,' June said bitterly. 'You've always had it easy.'

'Yes of course I have. There's never been any sorrow in my life.' Virginia's voice hardened. 'Coming home from school when I was twelve to be told that my mother had died two hours before was just a minor inconvenience. Nursing soldiers with terrible injuries in Singapore was easy. Escaping from Singapore when the Japanese invaded and hearing later that two of my nursing friends had been tortured and murdered – yes that was lots of fun. And watching my brother rush into a burning house to rescue a mother and her children and being held back by the crowd so I couldn't follow him and then seeing the roof collapse . . . ' Virginia's voice broke.

Fiona went to Virginia and put her hand on her arm. 'Mum.'

'Aunty Virginia, I'm sorry.'

But Virginia pulled away from Fiona and left the kitchen.

'I think the sooner we leave for England the better,' said Fiona coldly. She picked up the tea towel and threw it in a basket for washing. 'It will take a few weeks to get your passport, and I'd advise you to at least try and be civil – is that too much to ask?'

June shook her head. 'I'm sorry.'

'Don't apologize to me.'

Virginia stayed in her bedroom with the door shut for half an hour. When June heard her go into the kitchen she gathered the nerve to approach her. She stood in the doorway and watched Virginia, who had her back to her, peeling potatoes.

Expecting to be ignored she managed to say, 'Aunty Virginia.'

'Yes, June?' she said, without turning around.

'I'm sorry.'

'Your apology is accepted.'

'Can I do anything to help?'

'Yes. Would you like to string the beans?'

In spite of June's contrition, dinner that night was subdued. Alex who had been at work and knew nothing about June's outburst, was the only person able to act normally.

'Now that Ruth's house has got a buyer what do you want to do with the furniture and the rest of it?' he asked.

'What about asking Gabby and Keith if they'd like some of it?' said Virginia. 'Eumeralla could certainly do with better furniture. Is that okay with you, Fiona?'

'Yes.'

'Good. Yes. I'll write to them.'

Ω   Ω   Ω

After receiving Alex's letter Gabriella and Keith hired a van and drove to Melbourne. Alex met them outside Ruth's house in Hawthorn.

'Imagine their faces when we come back with all this,' said Gabriella looking at the furniture. It was plain, in the Shaker style, and would suit Eumeralla.

Keith opened the china cabinet. 'Are you sure you and Aunty Virginia don't want this?'

'No, we've got everything we need. Take it to Eumeralla.'

Gabriella picked up a plate with a rich burgundy and blue pattern and a gold rim. Even though her parents had only been able to afford the cheapest crockery, she knew quality when she saw it. She turned the plate over. 'Royal Albert,' she said. 'Uncle Alex, this would never be used at Eumeralla – it's too delicate and valuable. We'll just take the stuff in the kitchen.'

'Okay. I'll ask Catriona if she wants it,' said Alex.

Not wanting the Kingower Lancasters to get anything Gabriella said, 'Why don't we get it crated up and sent to Fiona and Juju? Ruth was their real mother – I know Fiona's inherited all her money, but I'd like to think that she and Juju have got some of her possessions . . . something she bought because she liked it. And the silver cutlery set too – it would never be used at Eumeralla either. The stainless steel set in the kitchen will be fine.'

Alex nodded. 'I know what you mean, but we don't know where Fiona and June will be living.'

'Could you take it back to Sydney with you and send it to Fiona when they've bought somewhere?'

'Yes. I'll do that. Good idea.'

Keith looked at the thick velvet curtains, the tiffany light fittings and the velvet upholstery. 'This must have cost a fortune. How come she was so rich?'

Alex smiled. 'Poseidon.'

'She had shares in Poseidon?' said Gabriella.

'Yes. Her stockbroker invested some of her money in Poseidon when the shares were almost worthless. He sold them when the price peaked in February 1970. I think it went to almost three hundred dollars a share. She said nothing about them to me or anyone else. We only found out that she'd had five thousand shares after she died.'

'A very canny stockbroker,' said Gabriella. 'Is that when she bought this house?'

'Yes, but when our father died he left her five hundred pounds. She used it to buy a small flat. By the time she sold it to buy this house it had quadrupled in value.'

'It's funny,' Gabriella said.

'What is?' asked Keith.

'We knew nothing about our father. Till just over a year ago we didn't even know he'd been married before. We thought Mum was the only woman he loved – but there were three.'

'I wouldn't call that funny,' said Keith.

'Not laughing funny – strange.'

'And I don't think he loved Ruth,' said Alex. 'Not in that way.'

'He must have felt something – after all he spent the night with her,' said Gabriella.

'He was distraught and so drunk and he thought she was Francesca,' said Alex. 'Now, choose what you want and let's get it all into the van. I'll ring some blokes I know to help us.'

Chapter 6

March 1973

England

Fiona saw June's expressions switch from despair to anger as they shuffled along with the crowds to the immigration desks at Heathrow. Unlike Fiona, who was used to planes and airports, June had only flown twice and they had been domestic flights. Their flight from Melbourne to London had been bad enough. June had refused to read, complained about the tasteless food and when she did sleep she woke with an aching neck. Fiona had hoped that once they were off the plane, June's mood would improve, but it got worse.

'I can't do this,' she muttered, as they stood in the queue for passport control.

'You have to,' said Fiona, trying to sound calm.

'I want to go home.'

'You can't, Juju. You've got to do this for Keith.' She watched June chew her lip. 'Look, I know this is depressing, but things will be better tomorrow.'

June grunted.

Finally they were through passport control, had collected their luggage and were waiting for a taxi.

'This is hell,' whispered June as she stared at the grey concrete surroundings and equally grey sky.

'We'll be in the country tomorrow.'

June shivered. 'Is this supposed to be spring?'

Feeling responsible for the weather, Fiona nodded.

June's reaction to the soulless hotel room near the airport was predictable.

'Come on, Juju. It's only for one night. Go and have a shower. Then we'll get some sleep.'

June sat on the edge of the bed. 'I want to go home.'

Knowing that June wouldn't know how to book a flight home or how to get to the airport, Fiona said, 'Go home then. We'll give up the idea of living in the country with horses and running a riding school. You go back to Australia and I'll stay in London and get a job with an airline.'

'Fiona, I didn't mean – '

'Make Keith even more miserable than he is now. If you go back to Eumeralla he'll have to leave – he's got nowhere else to go. Now go and have a shower. I'm unhappy too and you're making things worse. We should be helping each other. At least try and be a bit optimistic.'

A few minutes after going into the bathroom June came out in a rage. 'What's wrong with the water?'

'Oh, I forgot to tell you – it's hard water.'

'The soap turns to scum! Everything's wrong with this hideous place. I wish I'd stayed on Kingower.'

The following morning they collected the hire car and put their luggage in the boot. Fed up with June's sullenness Fiona stopped trying to cheer her up, and didn't respond to her moans about the tasteless breakfast.

'Where are we going?' asked June as Fiona put the key in the ignition.

'Why ask when you don't care?'

'Are you angry with me?'

'Yes.' Fiona wasn't angry, but gauged that her stony face was having a more positive effect on June than her coaxing.

'I'm not used to being unhappy.'

'Then you're lucky. You're not the only person suffering because of this. We've all lost something. Your father – '

'He's not my father.'

'I know, but he loved you as if he was. And he's lost you. That's why he's suffering.'

'I suppose I'm being selfish.'

'Not selfish . . . more self-indulgent and pessimistic.'

'So where are we going?'

Fiona put the car into gear. 'North up to Yorkshire. We're going to spend a month exploring different places. I love them all so you can choose which one you like best.'

'What if I don't like any of them?'

'Then I'll choose and you'll have to put up with it. We'll go to Yorkshire, the Lake District and Scotland, then head south to Wales, Devon and Cornwall.'

Until they got out of London the traffic terrified June, who had never seen so many cars.

'Juju, please keep quiet. I can't concentrate with you gasping and squealing every few seconds. Shut your eyes. I'll tell you when to open them.'

As soon as they reached the countryside June cheered up. The sight of the old houses captivated her, as did the greenness of the grass, the blossoms and the daffodils that were just coming into bud. She enjoyed the Ploughman's lunch in an old pub with low beams and a thatched roof, and for the first time in a month Fiona felt that everything was going to work out.

Three weeks later they were in Wales, when Fiona went into the building society and found that Alex had transferred all the money from Ruth's estate. In spite of June's protests, Fiona split the money evenly between them. 'She was your mother too. It's what she would have wanted.'

'If she'd wanted me to have it she would have put it in her will.'

'She probably knew what I would do. Stop arguing – anyone would think I was taking money from you instead of giving it to you.'

'I'm wealthy – I can't get used to it. Are you sure this is right? They haven't put an extra nought on by mistake?'

Fiona understood June's reaction. The value of Ruth's estate had amazed her too.

'It's true what they say about money not buying happiness,'

June said as she stared at her building society book. 'I've never had so much money, but I've never been so unhappy.'

Depending on where she was, June's mood fluctuated. In the country she was more cheerful and optimistic. She hated all the cities except York. She liked most of the smaller towns and the villages. Birmingham had filled her with horror. If it hadn't been for the torrential rain when they were in Yorkshire and Cumbria Fiona thought she would have chosen to settle there, but she said it was too wet and cold. As it had rained almost constantly since they left London Fiona despaired of June wanting to live anywhere in Britain.

When they reached Cornwall at the beginning of April the sun was shining. Daffodils in full bloom decorated the gardens and verges, and a faint haze of blue from the opening bluebells, carpeted the woodlands. Yellow forsythia and pink and white blossoms contrasted with the cloudless sky. Fiona booked them into a bed and breakfast near Liskeard. The next day they explored the surrounding countryside.

They were standing in front of Lanhydrock House, which was near Bodmin, when June said, 'Here. I want to live here.'

'We're not that rich and anyway it's not for sale – it belongs to the National Trust.'

June laughed. 'Not that house – in Cornwall – I want to live in Cornwall.'

Hoping she wouldn't change her mind when it rained, Fiona said, 'Good. We'll go to an estate agent tomorrow. Now let's go shopping. We'll go to Truro.'

'What for?'

'New clothes.'

'You don't need any new clothes.'

'I don't, but you do.'

'I hate shopping.'

'And I hate going around with a sister who looks as if she's found her clothes on a rubbish tip. If you go into an estate agency in those rags we'll get thrown out.'

'There're not rags.'

'Not quite, but almost,' said Fiona fingering the frayed cuff of June's shirt and poking her finger through the hole in her jumper.

In the morning after breakfast they walked into Liskeard and went into the first estate agency they saw.

The young woman sitting at one of the desks looked condescending when Fiona told her what they wanted. 'You want to a buy a what?'

'A farm,' repeated Fiona. 'With horses. We want to run a riding school and trekking holidays and breed horses.'

'You mean an equestrian centre.' Her voice had a accent that Fiona thought was Polish. The nameplate on her desk identified her as Urzula Luk.

Glad that June was wearing the new clothes they had bought yesterday Fiona stared back at Urzula's supercilious face. 'Yes. Have you got any?'

'Oh course.' She tapped her perfectly manicured nails on the desk. 'And how are you going to pay?'

'With money.'

Urzula rolled her eyes. 'We need proof of your financial state. We do not take people to view properties like that without checking on their finances. Come back with proof that you can afford such a place. They are very expensive, you know. I will need to see your passports too.'

'Why?' asked Fiona.

Urzula Luk looked as if she was taking to a simpleton. 'Proof of identity,' she said slowly enunciating every word as if she thought they might have difficulty understanding English.

'I thought you had our building society books and passports in your handbag,' said June when they were outside.

'I have,' said Fiona. 'But that girl was rude – '

'They're probably all like that. My new clothes aren't helping much, are they?'

'She would have changed her attitude if she'd seen our books,' said Fiona with a satisfied smile.

They crossed the road and stood for a few moments in front of another agency.

June pointed to a photo of fields with grazing horses. 'Look!'

Fiona quickly scanned the details. 'Oh, yes,' she said.

Peter Yelland liked to speculate what people who came into the agency wanted, before they asked. He immediately thought that the two girls needed directions to somewhere else. Lost tourists, he decided, judging from their platinum blonde hair, dark eyebrows and lashes and turquoise eyes that they were from Norway. Then he realized they were identical twins. One had a boyish haircut and wore a Cornish tartan kilt with black boots, a white blouse and a black linen jacket. Her amber and silver earrings matched the colour of the tartan. The other twin wore black trousers and a red jumper over a white shirt. Her hair was cut in a bob.

He smiled. 'Good morning. How can I help you?'

'We're interested in the property you've got advertised in the window,' said the one in the kilt. 'The equestrian farm place.'

Her Australian accent and request surprised him.

'We do have money,' she snapped, opening her handbag and dropping two building society books on his desk. 'Well, look at them. And here's our passports too. Just so you know we haven't stolen the books.'

Prepared for yet another surprise he picked up one of the books and opened it. Keeping his expression neutral, in spite of his astonishment, he did the same with the other one. The names in the books were June Clarkson and Fiona Lancaster. The passports were the same.

'Satisfied?'

He handed the books back to her. 'No.'

'What do you mean – no?'

'The amount of money you have is satisfactory, but your attitude isn't.' He walked to the door and opened it. 'I suggest you find another agency.'

The girl in the red jumper look anguished. 'Fiona . . .'

'We've been in another agency. She was rude to us.'

Urzula, he thought. 'Was I rude to you?'

'No.'

'Then please don't treat me as if I was.'

'Sorry,' said Fiona. 'But you looked as if you didn't believe – '

'Your accent surprised me – I thought you were Norwegian. Would you like to sit down and I'll tell you about the property you're interested in.'

June looked relieved. 'Thank you.'

He told them about the property and asked them to fill in forms so he could contact them. He was confused when in spite of their different surnames they both went by the title of Miss.

Although he wanted to know why identical twins had different surnames he knew his question would have been considered nosey. He speculated how they had made their money. Perhaps they were models. They were certainly beautiful enough.

Chapter 7

Queensland, Australia

April

Gabriella was beginning to regret her decision to come to live on Eumeralla. Living and working with four anguished men who rarely spoke, either to her or each other, was disheartening. At first Neil had tried to cheer them up. He was sure his mother would not last long in Brisbane and would come back to Eumeralla. But their depression had infected him and now he was as taciturn as they were. She wondered if it was too soon to give up and go back to teaching. In spite of the time they spent together Tom had not shown any interest in her other than friendship.

Not wanting to desert Keith she thought about the alternatives. 'Maybe I could stay living here, but teach in Dalby or even at the school in Cecil Plains,' she said aloud as she began to dry the dishes. 'Or I could just hang on here for a year and not renew the tenancy on my house and move back then. Am I being impatient? Should I give it more time? It's only been two months.'

The living conditions at Eumeralla had improved since she moved in. All the rickety furniture had been replaced with the furniture from Ruth's house. Gabriella insisted that they use the rent money from letting her house in Dalby to install a new inside toilet. The old one that was eighty yards from the house and stank made her feel nauseous every time she used it.

'Cooee! Anyone home?'

She hurried out of the kitchen onto the back veranda and saw a woman and two little boys standing at the bottom of the steps. A black horse and two ponies were tethered to a tree.

'Sorry it's taken us so long to visit, but we've been busy.'

Gabriella was confused. 'Hi, I'm Gabby. I haven't been here long.'

'Right. You don't have a clue who I am then?'

Gabriella shook her head.

'Irene Townsend. My husband Bruce and I are the new owners of Acacia – the property opposite.'

'Of course. I've heard all about you. Can you stay and have a cup of tea?'

'Love to.'

The boys bounded up the steps and Irene followed.

Gabriella pulled out the chairs. 'Lemonade okay for the boys? I made it this morning.'

The boys nodded.

'So, how are things here?' Irene asked when her sons had finished their lemonade and were playing in the garden.

Gabriela imagined Irene's expression if she told the truth and said, Terrible. Greg's wife left him, Tom's girlfriend was killed in a riding accident, and my brother Keith fell in love with his sister, not knowing she was his sister. Neil is still stunned by the revelations and is missing his mum and the girl he thought was his sister. Even the dogs are dejected.

She settled for saying, 'Things are tough, but I hope they'll get better.'

Irene looked concerned. 'Not in financial trouble, I hope.'

'No, money's probably better than it's been for a long time. How's Acacia?'

'Still lots to do. We've demolished the new homestead – what a monstrosity it was. We've just finished doing up the old one. It's gorgeous.'

'I'm glad you like it. My dad used to live there.' She saw Irene's embarrassment and laughed. 'Years ago. Not the horrible owners before you. The Clarksons.'

'Truly? Phew. I thought you were being sarcastic. Why did your father sell the place?'

'He didn't. There was a family feud and my dad and his brother were disinherited in favour of their stepmother who got everything. She sold Acacia and went to live on her brother's horse stud in Victoria. After the war it was in financial trouble – she poured all the money she got from selling Acacia into Kingower. It caused a lot of anguish.'

'I bet. The reason I called is to invite you all to a house warming party in June.' She handed Gabriella an envelope. 'Here's the invitation. We hope to have all the work finished by then.'

Gabriella smiled and opened it. 'Thanks. We'll be there.'

'How many of you?'

'Five. Me and four blokes.'

Irene looked baffled. 'Just after we bought Acacia, we dropped in here to introduce ourselves. There were twin girls too and their mum – Eleanor?'

Gabriella smiled as she tried to think of how to briefly explain what had happened. 'Yes. Eleanor lives in Brisbane now. Fiona and June went to England.'

'Right. For a holiday?'

'For ever. It's terribly complicated . . . I'll explain it all one day.'

'Sorry, I didn't mean to be – '

'It's okay. I would explain, but you'd be here for hours. So it's just me and my brother Keith, and Greg and his sons Tom and Neil.'

'Poor you. Got you tied to the kitchen then?'

'No. We've got rotas. I get my turn outside too. And the best cook is Neil.'

Irene looked at Gabriella's wedding ring. 'Is he the one you're married to?'

'I'm a widow. My husband died of leukaemia a few years ago.'

Irene looked horrified. 'God, how awful. You poor girl.'

Gabriella nodded. 'We'd been only been married just over a year. He was twenty. Can we bring anything to the party?'

'No. Just yourselves.'

'Um, I hope you don't think this is cheeky of me, and please say no if you'd rather, but my aunty, who lives in Sydney, used to live on Acacia. I know she'd love to see it again so I was . . . '

Irene smiled. 'Yes, invite her too.'

'And her husband?'

'Sure – I'm looking forward to meeting them.'

When Irene and her sons left, Gabriella speculated about her. She looked about thirty and even if she hadn't been the owner of Acacia that she was wealthy was obvious from the clothes she and the boys wore, the ponies and the Arab horse, and their expensive saddles. The diamond in her engagement ring must have been at least three carats.

Chapter 8

Eleanor hadn't expected to feel lonely. The evenings and weekends were the worst. At first she had savoured the peace of having a place all to herself. The flat had a television and radio, but the novelty had worn off and now she hated being alone. Her first few weeks in Brisbane had been stimulating. Hazel took her to the hairdressers where for the first time in her life she had her hair professionally cut, coloured and styled. Her furnished flat was modern, clean and had good carpets and new appliances. Hazel helped her buy make up and clothes suitable for wearing to the office, but tights made her legs itch in the heat, and the fashionable shoes made her feet ache. For the first time in her life she shaved her legs and under her arms. She could no longer tumble out of bed, have a shower and pull on cotton trousers or jeans and sandals, she had to wear dresses or skirts and blouses. Although her new appearance pleased her, she hated the discomfort of the clothes she had to wear. The journey to work on a crowed bus was torture.

Thinking she would make friends with the people at work, the unwelcoming cliques disappointed her. There were only two women her own age in her department and both disapproved of her because she was separated from her husband. Initially apprehensive because she had never worked in an office before, she had picked up the clerical work easily and now she was finding it boring.

The behaviour of many of the younger men appalled her. Behind the facade of their suits that they wore with ties, crisp shirts and polished shoes, they were crude, and unkind to any girl in the office who was plain, but they leered at the pretty ones. She was glad that she was too old for them to bother about. Their superficial outlook on life made her value Greg who, she realized, was far more of a gentleman than they were. The only time he ever wore a tie was when he went to weddings or funerals.

When Greg had told her that their daughter Hazel would be too busy with boyfriends and her own social life to see much of her, he had been right. Eleanor only saw her once a week, and she suspected that Hazel only wanted to see her so she could ask questions about Keith. Their meeting after work in a cafe this afternoon had been typical. Had Eleanor seen Keith? No? Had she heard from him? Did she think she should visit? Was he getting over June?

Eleanor's negative response to all the questions had exasperated Hazel.

'You must go to Eumeralla soon and find out, Mum.'

'He wasn't attracted to you before, so why will he be attracted now?'

'He was in love with June. Now she's gone . . .'

'A man like Keith doesn't get over things that quickly. The Clarksons are steadfast types. He doesn't fall in and out of love like you do.'

'But I'm your daughter. Johnny was Keith's uncle and he married you. It was Johnny, wasn't it?'

'Yes.'

'So the genetic history must be there. He'll fancy me if I give him a chance.'

Eleanor shook her head. 'You talk nonsense.'

When she arrived home that night there was a letter in her letter box.

> *Dear Mum,*
> *Would you like to come to lunch one Sunday? We've got a new toilet – an inside one.*
> *We miss you. Dad does too. So do the dogs.*
> *Tom and Neil*

Fighting the urge to pick up the phone and tell them she'd come back to Eumeralla for good, she found her writing pad and filled her fountain pen.

Dear Tom and Neil,
I'm spitting with fury that as soon as I leave you get a new toilet. I expect this is Gabriella's doing. Interesting that her wishes are so much more important than mine ever were. How many years did I ask for a new toilet and how many times was I told it was too expensive?
Yes, I will come to lunch. I can't this Sunday, but I'm free the Sunday after.
See you then.

Mum

She was always free at the weekends, but she wasn't going to let them know that. Before she sealed the envelope she rang Hazel, thinking it would be good to have an ally. Hazel was ecstatic about the chance to see Keith again. She added a PS to the letter to let them know Hazel would be coming too.

Greg read the letter in dismay. Not only was Eleanor still angry with him, she'd left his name off the salutation and the address on the envelope. 'I can't do anything right.' He saw Gabriella smile. 'What are you looking so pleased about? I was hoping – '

'You can still hope, Greg. I reckon Eleanor's unhappy.'

'Unhappy? What makes you think that?'

'I'd say she's angry, not unhappy,' said Tom.

Gabriella gave the letter back to Tom. 'If she was happy she wouldn't be angry.'

Keith, Tom, Neil and Greg looked at her doubtfully.

'What do you reckon she's doing this Sunday?' Greg said.

'Probably going out with one of her new city friends,' Tom said scathingly.

The thought that it might be a man depressed Greg. 'Could be a man,' he said.

Tom looked dubious. 'A man? She's too old for all that.'

Greg shook his head in exasperation. 'The last time she came here she had new clothes. She looked good – ten years younger.

All the grey in her hair had gone. A widower or a divorcee could have taken an interest in her.'

Chapter 9

Cornwall, England

April

Peter Yelland was not the sort of man Urzula had intended to fall in love with. His ambitions were limited to having a steady job, getting married and having a family and being happy. He loved picnics and eating in small cosy restaurants, bistros and wine bars. He wanted to buy an old house and do it up. His ultimate car was a Land Rover. He was content to live for the rest of his life in Cornwall. The thing he enjoyed most about being an estate agent was helping people find their ideal property.

Urzula wanted to be rich. She wanted to holiday in luxury hotels and eat in famous restaurants. Her ultimate car was a Rolls-Royce or Bentley. Failing those she'd settle for a Jaguar. She wanted to live, if not in London, then somewhere more urban. When she had children she wanted them to attend boarding school and mix with the wealthy and influential.

World affairs absorbed her. If it didn't affect Cornwall or England Peter wasn't interested. While the IRA bombings outraged him, as far as he was concerned the Vietnam war was nothing to with England. She loved opera and classical music. His tastes were limited to Elvis, the Beatles and the Rolling Stones. The only things she and Peter had in common were the theatre, especially plays by Shakespeare, Shaw and Oscar Wilde, the cinema and skiing. They had met in Austria on a two week skiing holiday. Peter had been with his sister and two cousins. She had been living in London in a seedy bed-sit where she had to share a bathroom and kitchen with the ten other tenants.

Although she loved London she hated her living conditions.

Peter's descriptions of Cornwall had seduced her into leaving her job at an employment agency and moving to Liskeard to be near him. She got a job in a rival estate agency and found it much easier than an employment agency.

'If people like a property they will buy it. The house cannot refuse to let the people buy it. In an employment agency you have to sell the job to the applicant and the applicant to the job. The applicant might love the job and want it, but the personnel department might not like the applicant. I found it so frustrating,' she told Peter.

She worked longer hours than she had in London, but earned more money and could afford to rent a small flat with one bedroom. The cost of living was far cheaper and she could walk to work. But she missed London and the close proximity of the opera houses, theatres, art galleries and museums.

She hated the fact that he shared a rented house with his sister and two of their cousins, and tried to persuade him to move into a flat by himself. In her opinion he was too close to his family. His parents and their siblings and children went on holidays together every October and alternate Easters and Christmases. They hired a house in the wilds where they went on long, gruelling walks. She had only joined them once when they had stayed in a manor house that had ten bedrooms in the Lake District. She had hated it and resolved never to go with them again. When she tried to persuade Peter to stop going on family holidays they had had a serious argument. That she seldom visited her parents, who still lived in Poland, puzzled him.

Because it was her birthday he was taking her out to dinner. Relieved that it would be just the two of them, she dressed in an orange satin dress, which was short enough to show off her slim legs, but long enough not to look tarty, a heavy gold necklace, bracelet and earrings and black high-heeled shoes. She had been to the hairdressers at lunchtime to have her roots retouched and was pleased with the result. Peter didn't know she was not a natural blonde. She arranged her shoulder length hair into a sophisticated knot. She put her cigarettes in her handbag. Peter hated smoking and tried to persuade her to give it up.

He arrived at her flat and gave her a gift wrapped rectangular present. Hiding her disappointment that it was a bottle of perfume, albeit an expensive bottle of perfume, she thanked him with a kiss. She wished he would buy her jewellery or something more long lasting and significant than perfume. In the hallway she put on her black fur coat.

She had chosen the restaurant, and she noticed his apprehension when he saw the prices on the menu. He looked disapproving when she lit a cigarette.

'It is my birthday,' she said with a smile. 'Surely you do not mind me smoking on my birthday?'

'The more you smoke the less birthdays you'll have,' he said.

'I took a couple to see Trelawney yesterday,' she said when they had ordered. She noticed he had chosen the cheapest things on the menu. 'They did not like it. Mr Bolitho should get a new kitchen – a modern one.'

Peter shook his head. 'The house is Victorian. A modern kitchen would look out of place. And if he does install a new kitchen people mightn't like it. At least this way the new owners can keep it if they like it or change it if they don't.'

'But it is so shabby. It might look better if he painted it.'

'I'm taking people to see it tomorrow – two Australian girls.'

'No, Peter. They came into our agency. They are frauds.'

'Frauds? Why do you think they're frauds?'

'They were very young. Dreadful Australian accents.'

He raised his eyebrows. 'How does that make them frauds?'

'It is obvious. They were tourists who just wanted to look at wealthy places for nothing.'

'Why was it obvious?'

She looked at him indulgently. 'Peter darling, you are so naïve.'

Urzula had expected him to look annoyed, but his expression was droll. 'You think so?'

'Yes. You were taken in by them. Identical twins?'

'Yes.'

'And I thought I had frightened them off playing their silly games. You idiot. They are time wasters. One looked half witted – '

'Dazed,' he said. 'Not half witted.'

'There is something suspicious about them.'

'Not suspicious,' he argued. 'Strange certainly.'

'How strange?'

'Both go by the title of Miss, but have different surnames.'

'Maybe one is divorced. Maybe they both are.'

'Then wouldn't they go back to their maiden name?'

'Maybe they do not like their maiden name. I hate mine.' She smiled and leant forward so he could see her cleavage. 'I would be very happy to change it to something else.'

'Different dates of birth too.'

'How can twins have different dates of birth?' she asked disheartened that he hadn't responded. Not so long ago he would have put his hand on her knee or made a risqué remark.

'One was born on the thirty-first of May and the other on the first of June.'

'Before and after midnight. I see. So why are you letting them see Trelawney? What bank will give them such a high mortgage?'

He grinned. 'No bank. They'll pay cash and have money left over.'

She felt uneasy. 'Did you ask for proof?'

'No.'

Her feeling that she had made a serious error of judgement vanished until he continued, 'They gave me their building society books and passports before I could ask. They were prickly as hedgehogs – well one was. Apparently another estate agent had been rude to them – you, I would guess.'

'I was not rude.'

'No? Maybe it was someone else then,' he said without conviction.

'How is it that they have so much money?'

'I don't know.'

'They must have got it fraudulently.'

'Why have you got such a malicious mind, Urzula? Maybe they've got rich parents. Maybe they won it. Anyway, if they like

Trelawney enough to want to buy it the sale will go through quickly because there's no chain.'

As they were eating their pudding she realized that he had talked about the twins throughout dinner.

'I was thinking it would be good to go to Italy for a holiday this year,' she said, desperate to change the subject. 'How do you feel about Florence?'

He frowned. 'No. You'll want drag me around art galleries and churches.'

'There are lovely places outside Florence if you would rather go to the countryside. Or would you like to go to one of the Greek Islands? Or the south of France?'

'I don't know,' he said disinterestedly.

'If you want to stay in England, we can. Or we can wait until winter and go skiing in France or Austria.'

'I'll think about it,' he said vaguely.

The waitress came to their table. 'Did you enjoy your dinner?' she asked.

'Very much,' Peter said firmly.

In spite of his glare, Urzula said, 'You English need to learn a lot about cooking.' She saw Peter looking furious so she smiled and said, 'It was edible.'

When he took her home and didn't come inside as he usually did, she felt despondent. Their nights together usually culminated in bed. Now she feared she was losing him, her doubts about his suitability as a husband faded and she could only focus on his good points. He was steady, reliable and faithful. He believed in women having the freedom and opportunity to have whatever career they wanted. He didn't look down on her because she was foreign. He thought the fact she could speak Polish, Russian, German, French and Italian as well as English, was amazing. He didn't bully her, like her previous boyfriend.

And he was handsome with unusual colouring. His auburn hair was wavy and thick, and judging from his father's hair he would never go bald. His skin was olive and he tanned easily. His eyes were slate grey with dark brows and lashes. He was close to six feet tall with long legs and broad shoulders. His teeth were perfect.

She suspected that the twins were the cause of his waning interest in her. As she got ready for bed she castigated herself. Not only had she turned away two rich girls who would have brought in a hefty commission, it was because of her that Peter had met them. She lay in bed and tried to think how she could renew his passion for her or deflect his interest away from them. At the weekend his parents were having a dinner party to which she was invited. She resolved to curb her condemnation of their parochial ways and be as charming as she could.

Chapter 10

Fiona hadn't written in her journal for months. Unwilling to leave them with Virginia in case she read them and got upset, she had left them all at Eumeralla with Keith and Gabriella. She and June had spent the day exploring Liskeard. It was when they were passing a newsagents that she felt the urge to buy a book and start a journal about her new life. After they had eaten dinner in a small cosy pub, they went back to the bed and breakfast. June sat in bed reading *The Loving Spirit* by Daphne du Maurier. Fiona found her fountain pen and opened the book.

Liskeard, Cornwall, England
April 1973

Tomorrow Juju and I are going to look at a farm – or as that girl in the first estate agent we went to, sneeringly informed us – an equestrian centre. There is an indoor riding school, which is a necessity here because of all the rain and cold weather. If the photos and descriptions are anything to go by, it will be perfect. As it is an established school we won't have to advertise for pupils. The price includes all the horses, the stables, three cottages and a Victorian farmhouse with six double bedrooms. There is even an orangery, so if we buy it, we can grow our own citrus fruit.
I'm trying not to get too excited, but I pray this will be the beginning of something great for Juju and me.
It seems inconceivable that this time last year I thought I was an only child, couldn't ride a horse, had never heard of Eumeralla and didn't know I had a twin sister.
But I've lost a lot too. My beloved Aunt Ruth who was in reality my mother. My cousin Kim, for whose death I know I am partly responsible.

What have I gained? As well as a twin sister I've got a half-sister and brother. Eventually when Juju and Keith fall in love with someone else, we can visit Eumeralla. And I can ride. Not as well as Juju or Catriona, but thanks to Tom I'll be able to teach children and adults – even nervous ones, because I'll never forget the riding lesson Uncle David gave me. It put me off for years, and if it hadn't been for Tom I would never have got on a horse again.

She didn't feel the satisfaction she normally felt after writing in her journal, and realized it was because she was writing for herself. Selfish ramblings, she mused. My time would be better spent writing letters to Mum and Dad. She put the book to one side and opened her writing pad.

When Peter pulled up outside the bed and breakfast hotel Fiona and June were standing on the steps waiting for him. He jumped out of his car and opened the back doors for them. His conversation with Urzula last night had left him with a shred of doubt. Just because they were wealthy, did not mean that they wanted to buy anything. They might be here on holiday and want to sample the English way of life. If this was the case, he argued to himself, why were they staying at a modest bed and breakfast place?

Apart from thanking him for calling for them, neither of them spoke on the way to Trelawney. Because Mark Bolitho, the owner, was leaving the place through necessity not choice, he advised him to go out when he was showing people around. It was upsetting hearing someone deride your taste or make a catalogue of the things they would change or didn't like, or put in an insulting offer. He drove over the cattle grid and down the drive.

'Stop,' cried June.

Thinking she was feeling sick, he stopped. She opened the door, leapt out of the car and ran over to the paddock.

Fiona caught his eye in the rear-view mirror and smiled. 'She likes horses.'

He watched June climb over the fence and stroke the horse nearest to her.

A dog ran up to the car, barking. Fiona got out and patted him. Urzula hated dogs and thought they were smelly, messy creatures who should never be allowed inside a house. She said the only reason she would ever have one would be to guard the house and that it would live outside in a kennel.

Peter switched off the engine and got out of the car.

Fiona crouched down and stroked the dog's ears. 'What's your name?'

'Barker,' said Peter.

'Do you bark a lot?'

Peter patted him. 'He hardly stops except when he's eating and sleeping.'

Fiona stood up and headed towards the paddock. Peter followed.

June turned to them. Her rapture was so different from the dazed expression he had first seen.

'It's terrific,' she said. 'All the trees and the green grass. Can we buy it?'

Fiona grinned. 'Hang on. We haven't seen the house yet, or the stables – '

'I don't care what the house is like.'

'Juju, don't be daft. The weather's colder here – it gets freezing in winter, so we'll be spending a lot more time inside than you're used to.' She looked at Peter. 'Why are they selling? How can anyone bear to leave this?'

'His wife died two years ago. He's in his sixties and hasn't got any children.'

June climbed back over the fence. 'Poor man.'

The house wasn't visible from the paddock, and Peter imagined their reaction when they saw it. Fiona had looked carefully at all the details in the office, but June had only been interested in the outside. He left the car near the paddock gauging that their first view of the house would have more impact on foot than inside a car. When the house came into view they stood still and gazed at it. Built of Cornish stone with a slate roof and Victorian windows that had been freshly painted in white gloss, it was surrounded by lawns and bushes. Daffodils adorned the grass.

'It's even better than the photos,' said Fiona.

Inside, their enthusiasm increased. June was more interested in the views from the windows than anything, but Fiona raved about the proportion of the rooms and stood in the old kitchen gazing around in rapture. 'It's enormous,' she said, looking at the slate floor and Welsh dressers and the table in the centre with six chairs.

'It's not a built-in kitchen,' Peter explained, remembering that the last people he had shown around had commented on how old fashioned it was and how it would cost a fortune to replace. 'So it can be easily modernized.'

'Modernized?' said Fiona with a frown. 'Why would anyone want to do that? It's beautiful as it is.'

'I think it's the original kitchen that was here when the house was built in eighteen-fifty. The bathroom's newer of course, but it was put in when the present owner inherited it in the forties, just after the war.'

'Selling this must be breaking his heart,' said June.

Peter nodded. 'It is.'

'Where's he going to go?' asked Fiona.

'He doesn't know yet.'

When he had finished showing them all the rooms, he said, 'Would you like to look at the cottages and the stables?'

'Yes,' they said together.

'One of the cottages is occupied by a couple who do the gardening, cooking and cleaning for the owner. Would you be prepared to keep them on?'

June giggled. 'I sure would – no more dreary housework. Fiona?'

'So would I.'

They were as delighted about the other two cottages and stables as they had been about everything else.

Then he saw Fiona looking doubtful. He dared to ask what was wrong.

'It's all so different here – '

'A horse is the same here as in Australia,' said June.

'Yes, but things will have to be done differently. The horses have to be kept warm rather than cool. It's freezing in the winter. And neither of us have got any experience of teaching anyone how to ride.'

'We can't back out,' June protested. 'I love it here – it's where I want to live.'

'I'm not saying I want to back out. It's just that I've had an idea.'

Mark Bolitho had been born at Trelawney and the thought of it going to strangers grieved him. In spite of the gardener and his wife helping him in every way they could, he hated living alone. His only relative apart from his sister was her daughter Yvonne, who had no interest in horses and was a physiotherapist. Trelawney had been on the market for six months. On two occasions it had almost been sold, but the chains were long and had broken.

He had been home for half an hour when Peter Yelland rang from the agency and asked if he could come over. Guessing someone had put in an offer, Mark put the kettle on, filled his pipe with tobacco, lit it and waited. Barker rushed about excitedly when he heard the car.

Peter strolled into the kitchen, accepted a cup of tea and sat down. 'Do you want the good news or the – '

'They are interested in it, but want to buy it for half the price,' Mark said dismally.

Peter shook his head. 'There's no bad news, just good news, very good news and great news.'

'It's so long since I had any good news, tell me in an order you want.'

'They'll pay the asking price. That's the good news. They're cash buyers so won't need a mortgage. That's the very good news. The great news is . . . well I hope you'll think it's great news. They want to know if you'd be willing to move into one of the cottages and be their manager – you can choose which cottage.'

Mark was silent for so long Peter thought he hated the idea.

Finally he shook his head. 'That's not great news – it's unbelievably brilliant news. Do you tell them about Rose and Jack?'

Peter nodded. 'They're willing to keep them on with the same pay and conditions. When would you like to meet them?'

Mark had assumed that Trelawney's prospective buyers were a middle aged couple who were selling their house in London for an enormous profit so they could retire early, live in the country and be mortgage free. When Peter introduced him to Fiona and June, the most exquisite girls he had ever seen, he was unable to hide his astonishment. His apprehension that there was a catch faded the better he got to know them. They were eager to learn and listened carefully to what he told them. His offer to leave his furniture in the house for them was rejected.

'But it's yours,' said Fiona. 'It belonged to your grandparents – '

'It's too big for the cottage and it would look out of place – it was bought for here and this is where it belongs. My wife and I chose the furniture in the cottage and I like it. If I moved this furniture into the cottage there'd be no room for me. But if you don't like it – '

'I do – it's the sort of thing I'd buy,' Fiona assured him.

So the furniture stayed in the house with Fiona and June.

'We must pay you for it,' said Fiona.

He shook his head. 'The sofa and armchairs are scruffy – you'll need to get them reupholstered.'

'But even so it wouldn't be fair,' June argued. 'We paid for the house not the contents.'

Mark smiled. 'I thought I'd have to leave here. Thanks to you I'm staying. I dreaded saying goodbye to the horses. Thanks to you I don't have to. I want you to have the furniture – it's a present from a grateful old man. Now let me show you everything in the house.'

'Was this your office?' asked June when he took them into one of the smaller rooms on the ground floor with a desk and bookcases full of ledgers.

'Yes.'

'I think it should still be your office,' said June. 'This is where you should work.'

Fiona agreed. 'You must keep the keys to the house – we'll get another set cut.'

Mark worried that his happiness was misguided. Something had to go wrong. Before the survey he worried that there would be something so wrong and expensive to fix that it would force Fiona and June to pull out.

'But the two other surveys didn't find anything wrong,' said Peter.

Mark's gloom could not be lifted. 'I know, but they might have missed something. What if something's happened since then?'

Because he and his wife had furnished and maintained the cottages to a high standard he knew he would be comfortable. Instead of living in the house he would see it from his front windows. He was happier than he had been since his wife's death. The survey report was excellent. But his disquiet remained.

'It's because you're worried about being happy, Uncle Mark,' said Yvonne when he confided in her.

'That makes me a daft old man – who worries about being happy? Why worry about being happy?'

'You were happy just before Aunty died, weren't you? You were going to have a party to celebrate your ruby anniversary – you were both looking forward to it . . . then she died. It was so unexpected. You must feel wary about being happy . . . that something dreadful will happen.'

Mark realized that she was right. He talked himself out of his negative feelings and concentrated on taking pleasure in the way the riding school was going and the new ideas Fiona and June were suggesting. Rather than stay in the bed and breakfast for six weeks they moved into the cottage that would be Mark's home when the sale was complete. They spent their time becoming familiar with the property and getting to know the horses and the pupils in the riding school. He would concentrate on the gymkhana pupils, Fiona would teach the beginners and June would teach the more experienced riders.

'Everything is working out perfectly,' he told himself firmly.

Chapter 11

Queensland, Australia

To Eleanor's annoyance Hazel decided not to go to Eumeralla.

'It's a strategic manoeuvre, Mum. Keith will be expecting me and when I don't turn up he'll wonder why.'

'He probably won't even notice, or if he does notice he won't care,' snapped Eleanor. 'He might even be relieved.'

Hazel looked hurt and Eleanor tried to soften the impact of her words. 'Whenever you saw him at Eumeralla you almost threw yourself at him and I could see he found it embarrassing. He's not the type that likes flirting. Juju never flirted with him. When you do see him again be natural.'

'Flirting is natural,' retorted Hazel.

Feeling uneasy about facing her sons and Greg alone she got into her car. During the drive she rehearsed what she was going to say. She changed her mind so often that by the time she reached the gates she gave up.

Even from the outside, Eleanor could see how much Eumeralla had changed. The house had been painted white, the corrugated iron roof green and the railings on the veranda were black. The fence enclosing the garden had been freshly painted and the gate didn't squeak. She went up the steps. The table with the wobbly leg and the mismatched uncomfortable chairs on the veranda where they all ate in good weather, were gone. In their place was a teak kitchen table and six chairs with comfortable looking cushions.

She went into the lounge. Instead of the sofa and armchairs with faded and torn upholstery and protruding springs was a suite covered in dark green velvet. At the other end of the room was a rosewood table and six chairs. The old dining table had been pitted with scratches and all the chairs had wobbly legs. The walls had been painted cream and a rug covered the worn lino. Feeling like an intruder she stood in the middle of the room wondering if she would look at the bedrooms.

'Mum,' said Tom from the doorway.

'Tom.' She wanted to hug him, but he looked so awkward they could have been strangers. 'How are you?'

'All right.' He shrugged. 'What about you?'

She mirrored his shrug. 'All right.'

'Enjoying Brisbane?'

'Yes,' she lied. 'Lots of changes here. Is the furniture Gabby's?'

He shook his head. 'She's let her house out fully furnished. It was Ruth's. Fiona said we could have whatever we wanted. Keith and Gabby went down to Melbourne and got it. They hired a van and drove it back.'

'What did you do with the old stuff?'

'Chopped most of it up for firewood.'

'Something I'd wanted to do for years.'

During the silence that followed Eleanor felt desperate. 'Where's everyone else?'

'Gabby's in the garden picking apples. She's going to make apple sauce to go with the pork.'

'That sounds nice. I like pork.'

Tom looked exasperated by her mindless comment, but said nothing. To cover the silence she asked, 'Where's Neil and your father?'

'Neil's back at our house – he was under the shower when I left. Dad didn't think you wanted to see him so he's not here.'

Her disappointment was so acute she couldn't hide it.

Tom looked surprised. 'What's wrong?'

'I would have liked to see him.'

'Why? So you can brag about your new life?'

'No.'

'Keith and Neil will be here soon.' He looked out the window and Eleanor saw his look of relief. 'Here they come now.'

'Where are the dogs?'

'Dad took them with him.'

When Neil arrived he was curt. Keith was polite, but constrained. Lunch was dismal. No one spoke until she commented on Ruth's crockery and cutlery and the new glasses.

Gabriella was the only one who responded. 'Uncle Alex is going to get Ruth's silver, crystal and china sent to Fiona and June. She sure had extreme tastes – '

'What do you mean?' Eleanor asked, desperate to keep the conversation going.

'The stuff he's sending Fiona and June is very elaborate – while these things are plain as can be. Very nice though – I didn't mean that as a criticism.'

Trying to think of something to say Eleanor looked at the white plates and simple cutlery and nodded.

No one else seemed to know what to say to her. At the end of the lunch she felt their tension ease, when she said that she was going home. Their goodbyes were clumsy and Neil was the only one who came to the car with her.

'Can't wait to get back to the big smoke,' he said.

'I'm sorry,' said Eleanor.

'Yeah, I bet you are.' He looked scathingly at her new shirt and the necklace Hazel had bought her. 'Earning lots of money to spend on frivolities?'

He had always been more caustic than Tom.

'It's small wonder you can't keep a girlfriend if you speak to them like that,' she said.

'It's no wonder I don't want to get married – you haven't been a great example of motherhood or being a wife. I don't want to end up like poor Dad.'

She disregarded his bitterness. 'Tell your father I wished I'd seen him.'

He looked surprised. 'Are you still going to give Eumeralla to Tom and – '

'Is that why you invited me to lunch?'

'Partly,' he admitted.

'I'm sorry to disappoint you.'

He looked worried. 'You've changed your mind?'

'Yes.'

'Why?'

'Eumeralla is mine and what I do with it is my business.'

'But you told Dad that you'd give it to Tom and Keith and me.'

'Yes, I did.'

'Mum, please don't sell it. I know Hazel's the only one of us you ever cared about – '

'Where do you get your strange notions from? I – '

'It was obvious. You made it obvious. You were always eager for Hazel's visits. You – '

'She was the only one of you who ever listened to me. You didn't care what I wanted and neither did your father. You were all against me. I didn't want much – just an indoor flushing toilet and none of you would let me have it. But as soon as Gabby came you – '

'She paid for the toilet.'

'And what about when Fiona was here? I wanted a toilet and what did she spend her money on? Getting a house moved here for you and Tom. A toilet would have cost a lot less. Nothing I wanted or said was of any importance to any of you.'

'Rubbish. And if you sell Eumeralla it's proof you never loved or cared about any of us either.'

'Of course I loved you and Tom. I still do and I'm sorry my actions have hurt you.'

'You never loved Dad.'

No, I didn't she thought. Or at least I didn't think I did. I miss him. It took not seeing him to make me realize what he meant to me. I was so used to his devotion and having him around.

'And if you sell this place it's not going to easy. You'll have to pay off Keith, and what about the house Tom, Keith and I live in? Officially it belongs to Eumeralla, but Fiona paid for it to be shifted here – so I suppose it belongs to her. How are you going to get around that?'

'It belongs to you and Tom,' said Eleanor. 'It was her gift to you.'

'What are we going to do? It's the only life Tom, Dad and I

know.'

Eleanor, aggravated by Neil's assumption that she would be so cruel and thoughtless, got into the car and slammed the door before he could say anything else.

When she got back to Brisbane she went into her flat wishing she had never left Eumeralla, and wondering if she had done too much damage to return. For the first time it occurred to her that in deserting her family at such a time of crisis had been selfish. Kim was one of the few girls Tom had been serious about, and the only one who fitted in well at Eumeralla. Eleanor had been certain that they would have married and would have loved having Kim as a daughter-in-law. Tom had been traumatized over Kim's death and it had left its mark on him. He was no longer relaxed and jovial. Then Ruth's letter had forced June to leave Eumeralla, the only home she had ever known. Eleanor's deserting her husband and sons had been the final blow and now she regretted that she had resisted their pleadings to stay.

'But at least I know what I've lost and if Greg wants me back I'll never hanker for Brisbane again,' she said to herself as she made a cup of coffee in the empty flat. Once she had revelled in its modernity. Now she found it claustrophobic. She longed for the clean air at Eumeralla, the silence and the far reaching views. When the person in the flat above her began to play loud music her longing increased.

Chapter 12

Cornwall

'Peter, I am going to Poland to visit my parents,' Urzula told him as he was driving to his parents' cottage. She was hoping that he would be dismayed, but he said nothing. 'I am also going to Russia – some of my mother's family live near Leningrad and I can visit the Hermitage – I have always wanted to do that.'

She was too afraid of the answer to ask him if he would miss her. 'Would you like to come with me?' she asked instead.

His horrified expression would have amused her if she hadn't desperately wanted him to say yes. 'No, thanks. I've never had any desire to go to a communist country. But I can drive you to the station so you can catch the train to Paddington.' The eagerness in his voice was unmistakable.

The cottage owned by Peter's parents was small. She hated their Alsatian dog, which was allowed all over the house even in the kitchen. Peter's mother had been incredulous when Urzula said it should be kept outside. With eight people at the dinner table it was uncomfortable. Urzula had not worn her fur coat, because Yvonne, Peter's cousin, was a vegetarian who hated fur on anything other than animals. Normally she would have not worried about antagonizing her, but wanted to be on her best behaviour. Peter had told her she didn't have to come to the family dinner, which was to celebrate his father's birthday, and she knew this was an indication that his interest in her was waning.

Urzula had prepared herself for the conversation to be about local issues and family matters, so she had read the local paper so she could add her own opinions and comments. To her distress the main topic of conversation was Fiona and June, who would soon own Trelawney. The family discussed the mysteries associated with them.

How was it they had such a lot of money? Urzula wished she could say she thought they had stolen it.

Why had they come to England?

To evade the law, Urzula thought.

Why did they have different names?

Because they are criminals, she wished she could shout.

'I've heard they're incredibly beautiful,' said Peter's sister Lynette.

Although her expression was guileless, Urzula knew it was a malicious stab at her. She wanted to say something cutting, but she didn't want to cause an argument and give Peter a reason to end their relationship.

In an attempt to steer the conversation away from the twins she turned to Charles, Peter's cousin. 'How is your work at the hospital?'

'Busy, but rewarding. Tragic sometimes.'

'Are you going to specialize?'

'I don't know yet.'

'What sort of thing would you do?'

'Certainly not surgery. And I don't like the thought of ear, nose and throat. I might do general practice. Psychiatry interests me.'

'Dealing with mad people?'

'Not mad,' he corrected her. 'People who have had traumas that they find hard or impossible to come to terms with.'

'They are weak,' she argued. 'Many people have problems and they do not rush to see a doctor.'

'Urzula, there are still people suffering intensely because of things they experienced during the war.'

She saw Peter shake his head. She disregarded him and gestured dismissively. 'The war has been over for nearly thirty years. My uncle was killed and his family did not go to a psychiatrist.'

'Urzula,' Charles persevered, 'I know a German woman whose parents were arrested because they were Jewish when she was six years old. Her neighbours hid her. She was smuggled out of Germany and arrived in England. She hasn't a clue what happened to her parents – they might have been murdered in a concentration camp or they might still be alive. She has severe problems with – '

'But I thought the Red Cross – '

'The Red Cross could not find everyone. How could anyone get over something like that? Would you have been able to?'

'Yes. I am strong.'

She saw Lynette looking at her with scorn and decided to change the subject. 'Do you do any private work?'

'No, and I'm not going to either. I believe in the NHS.'

'You would make a lot more money if you did private work.'

He looked at her coldly. 'I didn't become a doctor to make lots of money.'

Lynette laughed. 'Urzula, your face.'

'Well, yes, Lynette. Having grown up under a communist regime, I think socialism is too close to communism.'

'Yet you use the NHS?' said Charles.

'Well, of course – I can't afford to go to a private – '

'Exactly,' he said contemptuously.

'Urzula's going to Poland to visit her parents,' Peter told them.

She knew he had said that to ease the atmosphere, but they all looked so pleased she knew they were hoping she would stay there.

'How long are you going for?' Peter's father asked.

'Probably two weeks. I am going to Russia too. I have always wanted to visit the Hermitage.' Their blank expressions revealed they had no idea what it was. She smiled to hide her disapproval of their pitiful lack of knowledge. 'The paintings are magnificent.'

Their lack of interest was plain.

'When are the twins moving into Trelawney?' asked Charles, bringing the conversation back to something Urzula was sure he knew displeased her.

Anxious to get out of the dining room she offered to help Peter's mother with the washing up. She looked amazed. She thanked her, but declined.

Urzula was relieved when the night was over. 'That was a good evening,' she said to Peter on the way home.

He was silent for a while then he said, 'I'm glad you enjoyed it.'

'I know your sister does not like me. I would like to be friends with her. What have I done to make her dislike me?'

'You complain about England and the English.'

'I am just pointing out things that are wrong.'

'But you hate Poland.'

'Poland would be a wonderful country if it was not for the communists.'

'You upset Yvonne when you mock her for being a vegetarian.'

'It is not healthy, but I will stop making fun of her. I did not wear my fur coat tonight because I do not want to upset her.'

He dropped her at her flat and said he was too tired to come in.

'When are you going to Poland?' he asked.

'As soon as I can get a visa to Russia.'

The electricity bill arrived and she could just afford to pay it. She could not pay anything off her credit card bill, which was gathering a lot of interest. The bank refused to give her another overdraft.

When Peter had first met Urzula on a skiing holiday she had charmed him. She had been skating, and he had been entranced by her seemingly effortless skill. Afterwards he had congratulated her.

'Can you skate?' she asked.

He laughed. 'I can go forwards and that's all.'

'More than I can do,' said Lynette.

'And me,' said Yvonne. 'I'm very good at falling over.'

'And I won't even venture onto the ice – it looks far too dangerous,' said Charles.

'Would you like me to teach you?' Her question was to all of them.

He had thought her generous. Now he realized it had been her way of gaining his attention, and he marvelled at her ability to act patiently for so long. Patience and kindness, he had since discovered, were against her true nature. At the end of the holiday

Lynette and Yvonne could skate forward confidently and he could do a figure of eight and had almost mastered the skill of going backwards. Charles, having no desire to learn, declined her offer.

'She's lovely, said Lynette. 'So clever and sporty – she goes on the black runs.'

When Urzula moved to Liskeard they were delighted. But things went sour very quickly as her true nature asserted itself. The first conflict was with Yvonne, who was a vegetarian and was distressed that animals were killed for their fur.

'I don't know if you realize, Urzula, how cruel the fur trade is,' she said when Urzula wore her fur coat and hat. When Urzula looked at her blankly she continued, 'Animals are trapped and can take days to die in agony. I know many people think they are killed humanely, but that's not true.'

'I never thought about it, but I do not care. I love fur.'

Taken aback by her callous attitude Yvonne said nothing more, but her liking for Urzula ebbed. When Urzula continued to wear her fur coats and mocked Yvonne's ethics Yvonne began to loathe her.

Tensions multiplied when Urzula became possessive. She wanted Peter all to herself, and was blatantly resentful when they were all together. He had hoped her possessiveness was fleeting, because they had not been together long. Assuming someone who was so athletic would enjoy a walking holiday they were confounded when she said she was bored and hated it.

'But you love skiing and skating,' said Lynette.

'They are glamorous. Stomping around in the mud is not.'

Peter made excuses for her, but when her other faults of contempt, rudeness and arrogance surfaced her abilities ceased to enchant him. He hoped she would get fed up with Cornwall and return to London. He felt he was caught in a trap when she told him she loved him. He hated hurting people, but knew he had to end their relationship.

Urzula tried to keep the desperation out of her voice. 'Peter, I am a bit short of money,' she said as they were driving back to Liskeard from a house auction in Plymouth. Her client had bid way over the list price and she knew she would get a good commission, but her debts were increasing so rapidly that her pleasure in her triumph was overridden by worry.

'Why?' he asked.

The truthful answer was because she had bought a lot of new clothes. She had gone to London and spent all day shopping. 'Unexpected bills,' she said.

'Is there such a thing as unexpected bills?'

'Yes.'

'I've never had one. What was it for?'

'Nothing much. Could you lend me some just till I get paid?'

'No.'

'Look it was a bill I forgot about – they have sent me a final demand.'

'The answer is still no.'

'Why?'

'You're too extravagant, Urzula,' he said as they drove into Liskeard. 'You should get rid of your credit card and pay for things in cash – that way you'll know how much money you've got.'

Forgetting her resolution to be nice, she snapped. 'Do not lecture me, Peter.'

'Why not? You asked me to lend you money. I'm entitled to lecture you. You'd have more money if you stopped smoking.'

'Please lend me something. It is only till I get paid.'

'No.'

'I will not be able to go and visit my parents then.'

'Save up or ask them for money.'

She cursed herself for not lying and telling him her purse had been stolen or she had lost it. 'You can afford it, Peter. You must have got a big bonus for selling Trelawney.'

'Which you could have got if you hadn't been rude and jumped to conclusions.'

The truth made her angry with herself and even more angry with him. 'You are so mean.'

He pulled up outside her block of flats. 'I took you to a very expensive restaurant for your birthday.'

'Peter, please. I am desperate.'

'If you can't afford something – go without.' He got out of the car.

Hoping she could entice him inside to bed she put her arm around him. He pulled away.

'What is wrong?'

'I don't like being asked for money. I don't like being called mean.' He walked her to her door then started to walk back to his car.

She ran after him and grabbed his arm. 'What are we going to do at the weekend?'

'Urzula, we're finished.'

She tried to keep the panic out of her voice. 'Why? Peter, we love each other. What is wrong? I am sorry I called you mean. I am upset.'

'We're wrong – for each other. You must realize that. And I don't love you.'

'I love you.'

'I'm sorry. It's unfortunate but – '

'Why now, Peter?'

He sighed. 'There's no point in – '

'It is those twins, isn't it?' she shouted. 'That is why you want to end it with me!'

'It's you. I don't look forward to seeing you any more. In fact, I dread seeing you. You're spiteful, you're a snob, you're rude – '

'Honest – that is what I am, Peter.'

'Rude. And you can't stand my family and they can't stand you.'

She burst into tears. Peter got into his car.

'You will regret this, Peter,' she muttered as she watched him drive away. 'And so will those twins.'

Chapter 13

May

The pupils at the riding school liked Fiona and June. Instead of having to turn pupils away Mark found they could take on more, and profits increased. Although neither girl had taught riding before, after shadowing him they learnt quickly and were good teachers, taking each rider at their own pace. Fiona was especially good with anyone who was nervous.

June had told him about the bartering scheme they had at Eumeralla and when he asked all his neighbours they were enthusiastic. Now Trelawney gave three others properties fruit and vegetables in return for honey, eggs and dairy produce. The child of one of their neighbours, who had a pig farm, had free riding lessons in exchange for pork and bacon.

'I'd planned to have a leaving party,' he told Fiona and June. 'But I'd like to have a welcome party for you instead.'

Wanting them to meet as many new people as possible Mark invited the children and parents of everyone who came to the riding school, all his neighbours and friends and all the staff in the estate agencies to the party to welcome Trelawney's new owners.

As she stood by the window of her bedroom in Trelawney, June was astonished by the feeling of happiness that swept over her. She had expected to suffer misery for years. Fiona had been right when she'd promised her the day she had to leave Eumeralla that she would find other things to love. From her bedroom window she could see grass so green it didn't look real, and the bluebells looked like a mist of blue under the trees. Pink and white petals from the fruit trees carpeted the lawn. The camellia, azalea and magnolia bushes were laden with flowers, and she could see a section of paddock.

Her bedroom at Eumeralla had had a lino floor, a flimsy wardrobe and a chest of drawers. Her new bedroom had a double brass bed, and the wardrobe, chest of drawers, bedside tables and dressing table were walnut.

The riding school was well attended and the pupils were keen. The neighbours were welcoming. The horses were good natured, the saddles were top quality, the vet bills were affordable and life was far easier than it had been on Eumeralla. Although Rose Hayne had been willing to do all the household chores June and Fiona insisted on doing the washing up in the evening and the cooking.

'I don't want to loose my grip on reality,' Fiona had said.

June loved spending her days outside with the horses or helping Jack Hayne in the garden. Fiona was more domesticated, and did most of the cooking and food shopping. Freedom from housework gave her more time to be outside. People were always calling and they had already been invited to three parties. The house a mile away had a tennis court and although she couldn't play, the farmer's two sons, who were a similar age to her and Fiona, were eager to teach her. It made her realize how isolated Eumeralla was.

Because of her previous disinterest in clothes she was surprised to find that the new clothes Fiona had chosen for her gave her pleasure. The good quality shirts, jumpers and trousers fitted well and were far more comfortable than her shrunken jumpers and frayed shirts and ill fitting jeans. Fiona had even persuaded her to buy a kilt.

'I'm not wearing tights,' she protested.

'You won't have to. Look, it comes to the middle of your calf. We'll buy you a petticoat and a pair of knee high boots – the material's so heavy the skirt won't blow up in the wind and show your knickers.'

June gave in because she wanted to finish shopping and go home. She had no intention of wearing the kilt and thought Fiona would eventually give up and wear it herself. But she had to admit that the kilt in purple and green hunting tartan was comfortable, warm and looked good with all the jumpers and jackets Fiona had made her buy to go with it.

Her feelings toward Alex and Virginia had mellowed enough for her to write to them and sign herself as Juju. She received a reply that went some way to easing her guilt about her churlish behaviour in Sydney.

Dear Juju,

Thank you for your lovely letter. Your anger was understandable. In the space of a week you not only had shattering revelations to come to terms with, you had to give up the man you loved and leave Eumeralla and your family. I never meant any harm and I am sorry for all the turmoil I caused.
Eleanor and I loved Johnny, and she gave me Fiona because, in her words, 'She and June are all that's left of him and we can share that.' Till I read the letter Ruth wrote to Fiona I thought Eleanor was your mother. And neither of us had a clue that Laurence was your father not Johnny.
Gabriella rang yesterday. The new owners of Acacia are having a house warming party in June, and Alex and I have been invited. I will take lots of photos and send them to you.

Love,
Aunty Virginia and Uncle Alex.

Ω   Ω   Ω

The child looked terrified.

Fiona smiled at her. 'It's okay. You won't have to do anything you don't want to do.'

'She had a bad experience at the first riding school she went to,' said her mother. 'Their attitude was like throwing a child in the water and expecting them to swim.'

'I can relate to that. My first riding lesson was a disaster,' said

Fiona. She held out her hand to the little girl. 'Would you like to meet the horses and ponies – you don't have to get on them – just say hello and get to know them. Look I've got some carrots – they love carrots.' She turned to the mother. 'You can come if you like or you can go up to the house and have a cup of tea.'

'Is it all right if I come with you?'

'Of course. Your mummy want to meet the horses too.'

The child took her hand and they walked to the paddock. First they all stayed on the other side of the fence and Fiona showed the little girl how to feed the horses. When her terror subsided, and Fiona judged her confident enough, they went into the paddock and walked among the horses and ponies.

'This is Winnie. He's a lovely pony and he likes children. You can stroke him if you like. Feel his soft ears.'

The little girl and her mother spent the first lesson being introduced to the horses and feeding them.

'I can't thank you enough,' said her mother at the end of the lesson.

Fiona smiled. 'We'll make a rider out of her. Next week she might like to learn how to mount and dismount, but if she doesn't feel ready, I'll wait until she does. I'll show her all the tack and what their functions are.'

The woman paid Mark, and the little girl skipped happily beside her as they returned to their car.

'You reputation's growing and so are our profits, Fiona,' said Mark. 'You've got a knack with the nervy ones.'

'I was a nervy one myself once.'

'You'd never know it.'

Chapter 14

Sydney

Virginia felt useless. A gardener came once a week to mow the lawns and pull up the weeds, and their cleaning lady came three times a week. All Virginia had to do was cook, which she enjoyed, wash up, which she hated, and do the ironing, which she didn't mind. When Alex found a house he was interested in buying and doing up he always took her to have a look and give her opinion and she furnished it to give it atmosphere for prospective buyers. She volunteered for the local branch of the RSPCA, but that only occupied one day a week. She had friends, but they did not fill her emotional void. She found that most of her time was spent looking forward to going to see Gabriella and Keith and receiving letters and postcards from Fiona. Her letters to Fiona were mainly about her work at the RSPCA and description of the houses Alex was renovating. Fiona's were full of their new life, the people they met and descriptions of Cornwall and its history. She felt that her letters were dull in comparison.

To her surprise she realized that she wanted to talk to Margot. Since Kim's death relations between them had improved to such an extent that visits to Kingower were no longer an ordeal. Once she had only gone for Alex's sake. Now they went more frequently because she wanted to see Margot. Even at seventy-three Margot was fully occupied with the administrative side of Kingower. She took the bookings for the riding school and horse treks and did the accounts and tax.

She picked up the phone and dialled her number. She hadn't intended to confide in her, but when Margot asked her how she was, she told her exactly how she felt. Knowing that Margot would have been justified in being sarcastic, she trailed off uncertainly. 'Sorry, Margot, I'm being silly.'

'No. You need a project.'

'I could do more voluntary work – '

'What did you do with the journals?'

'What journals?'

'The ones I gave you after your father died.'

'Oh, them.'

'You didn't throw them away did you?'

'No – they're in a trunk somewhere. Why?'

'Did you read them?'

'Not in any detail. I skimmed through them.'

'I read them – your father gave them to me. They're a fascinating portrayal of what life was like in those days. And very few people who stole as much as your ancestors did got away with it. They were bold and . . . different.'

Unsure if it was admiration she heard in Margot's voice she asked, 'Do you think they were right?'

'Right?'

'To do what they did.'

'Read them, Virginia and then we'll discuss it. Did you know they weren't married?'

'No. I had no idea.'

'As I said – they were different. Did you know that Clarkson wasn't their real name?'

'Yes. They had to change their name in case they were tracked down – as you say they got away with lots of jewellery.'

'The man's real name wasn't James it was Nathaniel. When you've read them I'd suggest that you type them out and send a copy to Fiona and June and perhaps give the originals to Keith and Gabriella. It all started in England and Fiona and June might be interested in visiting – '

'Fiona did visit one of their London houses last time she was in England. She only saw it from the outside, of course, and she sent me a photo. I don't think she's been to the others. Margot, you're right. That's a wonderful idea. I'll find them and do just that.'

It had been over twenty years since Virginia had seen the journals and she looked in three trunks before she found them. They had leather covers and were heavy. The yellowing pages were thick. Although the first book was dated 1829 the writing was clear. On the front cover was the title. *For the descendants of James and Ellen Clarkson*. She opened it. The first page had one paragraph.

> *We did what we did for Sarah. We are what we are because of Sarah. It was because of her that we knew the hypocrisy could not go on. Things had to change, and we were going to change them. This is our story and the story of the life we made for ourselves on Acacia and Eumeralla. I lied. Ellen stole. Sarah told the truth.*

Until then Virginia hadn't realized that the association between the owners of Eumeralla and Acacia had gone back so far. She turned the page. She knew the basic story, but not the details. She carried the journals into the study and uncovered her typewriter.

```
I remember the day I went to collect Sarah Brown
and Ellen Ingram from the orphanage. It was 1829.
They were eleven years old. Two frightened girls
clinging to each other's hands. Ellen had
straight blonde hair and eyes the colour of
grass. Her dark eyelashes and brows made her
milky skin look even whiter. Sarah's dark hair
was curly and her eyes were brown. I had left the
orphanage seven years earlier and I had been sad
to leave too. I would have been even more unhappy
had I known more about the owners of Aylington
Hall.
   We were informed of our destiny of servitude
from an early age, but we were all taught to
read, write and do arithmetic. The boys learnt
carpentry, gardening, how to ride, light fires,
look after horses and saddlery and drive
carriages. The girls learnt needlework, cooking,
laundry and cleaning. When they were older they
helped look after the babies.
   I had started working at Aylington Hall as a
stable lad. We cleaned out the stables, kept them
tidy, and put the horse droppings in a
```

wheelbarrow for the gardeners. When I became a coach driver I looked after the horses that drove my coach and washed and polished it.

'Good morning, Nathaniel,' said Mrs Clarkson when I jumped down from the driving seat. She was as kind as she looked, but very strict. She told Sarah and Ellen that they were going to work at Aylington Hall for very important people – a lord and lady. They did not look any happier.

'Can't we stay here and work?' begged Sarah.

She shook her head.

'We will work hard – '

Mrs Clarkson shook her head. 'You are very lucky to get this work. They only take the best. Others have to work in mills, which is dangerous. Isn't that right, Nathaniel?'

'Yes. And the food is good.' I felt ungrateful saying that, but it was the only thing they would have to look forward to.

'Come now, girls. Don't keep Nathaniel waiting.' She looked at me. 'Their reports are in their bags.' She tried to smile, but her eyes were full of tears and her voice was husky.

Rather than put them in the carriage I let them ride on the top with me. It was a warm day and the sun was shining. I wished I could tell them they'd be happy in their new home, but I knew they would be miserable for the first few years. Like all of us from Mrs Clarkson's orphanage, they were well spoken, tidy and clean. I knew if they worked hard and behaved themselves they would soon be promoted from the scullery.

'They put you in the hardest jobs first,' I explained. 'The scullery is the worst. Two girls spend all day washing dishes, scrubbing pans and drying them or washing and peeling vegetables. But if you do that job well, keep quiet, cheerful and polite you get put somewhere easier and better. You'll be told that if you slack or do something wrong you'll go back to the scullery. It's their way of keeping you disciplined.'

I glanced sideways to see their reaction to my words. Ellen on my left wiped away her tears.

Sarah looked sullen and I knew she would not settle in as well as Ellen.

'Smile, Sarah,' I said. 'If you look sulky you'll stay on the hardest jobs longer.'

She lifted her lips into something more like a snarl than a smile.

'If you want to make things hard for yourself that's up to you – but you won't be happy.'

They had different surnames so I knew they weren't sisters, but I asked them if they were, just to get them talking.

They told me they were friends and had been born on the same day. I tried to cheer them up by telling them they would be in the same dormitory. I didn't say they would be sharing with eight others. The only thing I could tell them that was good was that the food was much better than the orphanage food, which had been meagre. Porridge in colder months and bread and butter in the summer with a mug of milk for breakfast, a stew or cold meats and salad for lunch and bread and butter and milk for dinner. But we had been allowed as much fruit from the orchard as we wanted.

'Aylington Hall has got herds of beef cattle and a dairy herd, orchards and vegetable gardens, chickens, pigs, sheep, geese and a river full of fish. They shoot pheasants and deer. You'll have meat everyday except on Friday when we have fish, and bacon and eggs for breakfast. Whatever the family have for dinner and lunch we do too. One hundred and forty people work there – sixty outside in the gardens and orchards, ten in the laundry and there are ten men to look after the horses and drive the carriages and keep them clean and repaired.'

Ellen looked awed, but said nothing. Sarah looked more interested. 'I wish I was a boy,' she said. 'I'd much rather be in the gardens than inside scrubbing pots.'

'Are your reports good?' I asked.

'Yes,' said Ellen.

'We don't know, we haven't read them,' Sarah

argued.

'But they will be good,' Ellen said. 'Mrs Clarkson told us.'

'I know you're not supposed to look, but I looked at mine,' I told them. Mrs Clarkson was obviously very fond of them, so I knew their reports would be good. 'Open them and have a look – I won't tell anyone.' I slowed the carriage down so they could read them.

The only subjects that Ellen didn't get marked excellent were arithmetic and needlework and she got a very good for those. Sarah got an excellent for everything except cooking and she got a good for that. Their conduct reports were glowing.

'You'll soon be promoted,' I told them.

I wrangled with myself whether to warn them about the Earl. Three years ago, I was walking back from the paddock when I saw him forcing himself on one of the young maids. I hadn't recognized him because he was on the ground on top of her. At first I thought I was interrupting a lovers' tryst so I ducked behind a tree and began to creep away. It was then that I heard her cry out. I cautiously peered out from my hiding place and saw that his hand was over her mouth. It was only then that I knew what I was witnessing.

I was about to intervene when he said, 'Keep quiet, slut,' and I realized that he was an aristocrat. When he had finished he pushed her away as if she disgusted him.'Don't tell anyone or you'll get the sack and end up in the workhouse,' he told the sobbing girl.

'I'll tell Her Ladyship.'

As he hauled her to her feet and grabbed her hair I saw he was the Earl. 'And I'll get you hung for stealing.'

'I never stole,' she gasped.

'But I'll say you did. I'll put something under your bed or among your possessions where it will be found. They'll believe me – they won't believe you.' He gave her a violent shove and she tumbled to the ground.

Although I wanted to punch him I kept out of sight. At the orphanage we were punished when we were naughty, but we had to do something very bad before we were whipped. I had only been whipped once. The day after the whipping Mrs Clarkson, the owner of the orphanage, took me into her office.

'Your punishment yesterday was regretful, but necessary, Nathaniel,' she said sternly. 'When you leave here and go into the outside world the punishments are far more severe, depending on your crime. You could be hung. It is a slow and agonizing way to die. Hangings take place in public. People laugh and jeer. Conditions in prisons are so bad that perhaps it would be better to hang – depending on the length of your sentence. You could be transported to Australia. The voyage is long and the convict ships are crowded and riddled with disease. Many people die of disease or starvation before they reach Australia. I hope this has taught you the folly of your actions.'

I assured her that it had.

The memory of the whipping and Mrs Clarkson's lecture had stopped me from attacking the Earl. I didn't want to be hung or transported to Australia.

When he strode away, I helped the distraught girl rearrange her clothing, and I took her to the stream so she could wash. I realized how badly he had hurt her when I saw the blood on her petticoat. When she became pregnant she was first humiliated in the servants' hall with an announcement of her immorality and then sacked. I wanted her to denounce the Earl. I wanted to denounce him myself, but I was too much of a coward. The thought of what had happened to her plagued me. That night as I lay in bed I regretted my inaction. I might have got away with killing him. The girl would have kept quiet. If I could have been hung for punching him, he, who committed a far worse crime, deserved to be dead. Sarah and Ellen were both very pretty and I dreaded that the same fate would befall them.

'I just have to warn you about something.' I hesitated. How could I defend myself if they repeated my warning to the housekeeper? Although they had been babies when I was still at the orphanage, I didn't really know either of them. But I still reproached myself when I thought of what I had witnessed. I had done nothing. I reasoned that if I had punched the Earl I would probably have been hung or transported to Australia.

'What do you want to warn us about?' Ellen asked.

'Keep away from the Earl.'

'Why?' asked Sarah.

Suddenly I thought what I could say in my defence if one of them, either in innocence or malice, repeated what I had said.

'Things have to be done right. If he sees you doing things wrong you'll end up sacked and in the workhouse. He's very particular. So keep out of his way. Don't let him see you. When you go outside try not to be alone.' I hoped my warning was enough.

An hour later I delivered them to the servants' door and the housekeeper took charge of them. The next time I saw them was in the servants' hall when we were having dinner. They were dressed in the scullery maids' uniform of a black dress, a white cap and apron. The plain garb denoted their low status. Kitchen maids had ruffles on their aprons - the higher their position the more ruffles they had. Housemaids' uniforms were trimmed with lace. The head cook and her assistants wore blue and white striped dresses and had lace on their caps. In spite of the delicious and plentiful food Sarah and Ellen looked even more wretched.

I understood why. At the orphanage they had been the big girls who had excelled in their lessons and helped with the younger children. Now they were the lowest and least important in the strict hierarchy of the Aylington Hall servants.

>   Why they were considered the least important
> was puzzling to Ellen. 'What would the family do
> if no one was here to wash the pots and pans?'
> she said to me.
>   'There'll always be people around to do all the
> dirty work,' I replied.

When Margot had given her the journals, Virginia had been too involved in bringing up Fiona to do more than skim them. It was also shame that her ancestors had been criminals that had made her put them in a trunk. She had thought that Margot had given them to her so she could gloat that the Lancasters, who had made their fortune on the goldfields, were better than the Clarksons, who were robbers, and had been cunning enough to escape justice. Now she realized that Margot had been genuinely interested in the history of her husband's ancestors.

She surmised that Nathaniel had changed his Christian name because it was unusual, while Ellen had kept hers because it was more common. She wondered if they had chosen Clarkson as their surname after the woman at the orphanage. Considering that they had stolen so much jewellery it was amazing that they had got away with it.

She was so engrossed she was still typing when Alex arrived home from work.

Chapter 15

Whittlesea, Victoria, Australia

May

Stefan put his arms around his sobbing wife. 'Darling,' he whispered. Unable to think of anything comforting to say, he stroked her arms and hair.

The nurse came in and gave her an injection. 'It'll make her sleep and calm her down.' She looked sympathetically at Stefan. 'Go home. You look as if you need some sleep yourself. I'm terribly sorry, especially with this happening so soon after Kim's death, but as the consultant said, you're both young and miscarriages don't happen for no reason.' She put her hand on his shoulder. 'I bet this time next year you'll be walking out of here with a lovely healthy baby in your arms.'

Stefan went straight to bed. Tomorrow he would break the news to Catriona's parents and her Aunt Margot. He lay in bed for an hour upset and worried. Catriona's pregnancy had been the one spark of light after Kim's death. He had treated Catriona so badly he feared she would want to divorce him now she had lost the baby. His infatuation for Fiona had wrecked the first four months of their marriage. When Kim had been killed in January his terror that the victim had been Catriona, had made him realize that he did not love Fiona, he had been mesmerized by her beauty and haunted demeanour.

During the first few months of their marriage most of their conversations had been stilted or ended in a quarrel. They should have been able to talk about her work at the surgery and his work at the school, but Stefan's mind had been occupied with Fiona and he frequently thwarted Catriona's attempts to have a conversation.

Stefan knew David had never forgiven him for making Catriona unhappy and probably never would. Catriona had never told her parents or Margot what was wrong, but her desolation had been evident, and that Stefan was the cause, was obvious.

In the morning he drove to Kingower to see Catriona's parents. Her mother cried. David was stoical but concerned about Catriona's health. They all walked to Margot's cottage to tell her. Stefan drove them to the hospital, stopping in the town to buy flowers and chocolates.

Catriona was pale, but composed. To Stefan's shame, he struggled to find anything to say. He kissed her, squeezed her hand and called her darling. Her mother burst into tears. Although he felt sorry for her, Stefan was irritated. Not for the first time he wondered how such an ineffectual woman had given birth to strong, independent and courageous daughters like Kim and Catriona. After hugging his daughter David took his wife outside. The nurse came in with a vase for the flowers and put them near the window. 'All these lovely flowers,' she said as she left.

Stefan saw a large bouquet by Catriona's bed. He wondered if it was from Douglas. He saw a card, but not wanting to look as if he was prying, he stopped himself from picking it up.

Margot sat on the bed. Before Kim's death in January, Margot had looked ten years younger than her seventy-two years. Now she looked her age.

'What did the consultant say?' she asked.

'That we can try again, but to give it twelve weeks. There's no reason why I can't carry a baby to full term and have a successful delivery.'

'What about you and Stefan going on a holiday?'

'Maybe,' Catriona said noncommittally.

'When are they discharging you?'

'Tomorrow.'

'I'll see you then.' Margot kissed her and stood up.

'Bye, Aunty Margot. Thanks for coming.'

'How are you feeling, Stefan?' she asked when the door closed behind Margot.

'Me? Darling, don't worry about me. It's – '

'You've lost the baby too. Not just me.'

'Yes, but you're the one suffering physically as well as emotionally.' He kissed her hand. 'I love you, Tree. You do know that, don't you?'

She nodded. 'Thanks for the flowers. They're beautiful.'

He hoped she would say she loved him too, but she didn't.

When he arrived home he tried to think how he and Catriona could put the past behind them and make a new start. Fiona was in England, so Catriona would not feel threatened by her presence. A holiday would be just what they needed if she would agree. Soon the schools would break up for two weeks' holiday and he and Catriona could go away. He would let her choose where. He was in the front garden trimming the edges of the lawn when he saw David's Bentley turn into the driveway. With a feeling of dread he stood up.

David handed him a letter. 'From Fiona. Addressed to both of you. She sent it to Kingower – she must have forgotten your address.'

'Thanks, David, come inside.' As they went down the hall he tore open the flap and took out the letter and three photos. One showed a beautiful house. The other one was of Fiona and June standing in a paddock with some horses. The other was a photo of the stables. He handed the photos to David and read the letter aloud.

Dear Tree and Stefan,
How are the three of you? Hope all is going well with the pregnancy. I think of you often. Am looking forward to seeing photos of the baby when it arrives.
June and I are the proud owners of a riding school. Enclosed are some photos.
There is a vegetable garden, apple, plum and pear trees and gooseberry bushes, raspberries canes and strawberry plants and

lots of greenhouses.

I'm longing to hear all your news, so please write when you've got time.

With Love to all three of you,

Fiona

'I can't let Tree see this,' said Stefan.

'Why not? It's not going to remind her she's lost the baby – it'll be on her mind constantly. And if she finds out you've kept a letter from Fiona secret, she'll be suspicious – as she's got reason to be. Don't look like that, Stefan. Do you think I'm a fool? I saw the way you looked at Fiona on your wedding day. You made how you felt about her plain. And you and Catriona both looked wretched when you got back from your honeymoon.'

'It was my fault.'

'Of course it was. It certainly wasn't Catriona's.'

It wasn't Fiona's either, thought Stefan. 'I hope you believe that nothing happened with Fiona. And I didn't love her. I was infatuated. I'm not any more. I never think about her. It's Tree I love.'

David look sceptical. 'And how does Catriona feel about you?'

'I'm not sure,' Stefan admitted. 'I've got to give her time to trust me again.'

'What if she wants to divorce you?'

'I pray she doesn't, but I wouldn't blame her if she did. Look, David, I know I've been a rotten husband and son-in-law. Do you want her to divorce me?'

'It's her decision, but I'd support her if she did, even though I don't believe in divorce.'

'What about her mother?'

'What about her?'

'What does she think?'

'She doesn't think. Things just are. They happen around her. She's simple.'

David's dismissal of his wife shocked Stefan. 'Why did you marry her?'

'She was suitable.'

'Suitable? How calculating. Was she suitable because she agreed with everything you said – never had opinions of her own? You may not think much of me, but at least I've got feelings. I love Tree. I've made mistakes, but I never meant to hurt anyone. People suffered because of what I did, but I'm sorry and ashamed and trying hard to make things right. Is your marriage still going because you have no feelings?'

'I don't mean she's soft in the head. I mean she likes the simple life.'

'Yes, with you telling her what to do and her doing it. Don't come here disapproving of me, David, you cold and calculating – '

'Of course I'm calculating. It's the only way to be. Your generation have got it all wrong with your free love and ignoring your parents' wishes. The last thing I wanted was a wife like Virginia with her strong opinions and argumentative ways.'

'She and Alex seem happy and – '

'Because he does what she wants.'

'Like your wife does what you want? No there's far more than that to their marriage.' He saw David looked weary. 'I'm sorry, David. Shall we have a drink?'

'No thanks. I'm going home.'

Chapter 16

When Catriona came home from hospital Stefan cooked her a special vegetarian meal, put a bottle of white burgundy in the ice bucket and made chocolate mousse for dessert. He set the table in the dining room with the silver cutlery Alex and Virginia had bought them for their wedding present. He picked flowers from the garden, lit candles and hoped Catriona would be lulled by the romantic atmosphere.

She wasn't. She ate the food, drank the wine and praised his cooking, but he could see her responses were mechanical.

'Where would you like to go on holiday?' he asked.

'They're busy at the surgery – I can't get away for a while.'

Now he knew how Catriona had felt when he had been so offhand with her. He tried again. 'What about moving? Making a new start. There's a house for sale on the other side of town – this house has got too many bad memories.'

'A new house isn't going to erase the memories. A new house isn't going to change our characters or the past.'

'It's not your character that needs changing, Tree. It's mine.'

She didn't respond.

He did the washing-up trying to work out the best way of winning her back. He cursed that their happiness had been more easily obliterated than their misery. While Catriona seemed to have forgotten the blissful times they had shared, she remembered their bitter quarrels and the agony of his emotional betrayal.

'Darling, are you sure you should go to work?' Stefan asked a week later.

'Yes, I feel fine.'

He kissed her. 'Don't overdo it. I'll see you tonight.'

'Yes,' she said.

He was so worried by Catriona's distant attitude he found it difficult to concentrate during his classes. He set the children their projects and let them get on with it.

When he arrived home he had two hours to fill before Catriona came back. As soon as she walked in the door he started talking about going away on a holiday. 'I got some brochures. Look. There are some – '

'Stefan, we need to talk.'

She went into the lounge and sat in an armchair. He sat opposite her.

'Our marriage isn't working, Stefan. I – '

'Darling, give it a chance. I know I was a bastard, but I thought we'd put that behind us.'

'I tried,' she said. 'And when Kim was killed you tried too, but it's still not working – not for me anyway. I'm going to move back to my cottage.'

'A trial separation?'

'No. Divorce.'

'Oh, God.'

'I'm sorry, Stefan. But now there's no baby . . . '

'Tree, when we went to Ballarat and had a picnic by the creek – you said you still loved me.'

'Yes. But I suspected I was pregnant and I wanted our baby to have a father. Divorced parents are not good for a child. And it would have been unfair to you. I wanted us to have lots of children. And I was still in shock about Kim. In the hospital I had to face the truth.'

'Tree, I love you.'

She shook her head. 'Your love wasn't strong enough to stop you from falling in love with Fiona. When things are back to normal, what's to stop you falling in love with some other beautiful girl?'

'I was never in love with her. I was infatuated. Nothing ever happened – I promise.'

'I believe you, but I think that was more to do with Fiona than you. When you went to Melbourne to see her, if she hadn't been aggressive and told you to get out – if she'd thrown herself into your arms and dragged you to bed – would you have made love to her?'

He didn't know whether to lie or tell the truth. Deciding she would not believe a lie he said, 'I'm ashamed to say I would, but I would have lost respect for her.'

Catriona looked scornful. 'Chauvinist.'

'I'm not – '

'You are. A girl gives you what you've been gasping for and you despise her for it. Except she didn't give you what you wanted and that increased your desire – and you put me through hell.'

'Kim told me that if you divorced me I would have lost the best wife I could ever have. She was right. I came to my senses too late.'

'What will you do, Stefan?'

'I don't know. I'll have to think.'

'Will you stay here?'

'And see you all the time? No. I couldn't bear it. I'll have to hang on till the school holidays – to do anything else would be rough on the school. I'll go back to Melbourne.'

'You can keep all the money from the sale of the house.'

'No. Half and half. I wrecked the marriage not you.' Before his emotions could get the better of him, he got up and went into the garden.

That night Catriona slept in the guest bedroom. At the weekend they went through their belongings, most of which were wedding presents, and discussed who would keep what. Stefan had hoped that the task would prove too emotional for her, but she was clinical and efficient. He was the one who found it upsetting. She began by handing him the diamond engagement ring he had bought her.

'Tree, please keep it.'

She shook her head. 'You're going to have a lot of expenses – moving back to Melbourne, finding somewhere else to live and another job. Sell it and – '

'No. You sell it and give the money to whatever charity you want.'

'Thanks, Stefan. I'll put it into Kim's memorial scholarship fund.' She put the ring on the mantelpiece. 'Do you think it's fair to let me keep any presents from my family and friends, and you keep the ones from your family and friends?' she asked briskly.

He nodded and noticed she was not wearing her wedding ring.

'Except,' she said, 'I don't like the furniture we chose.'

'But your family bought it for us.'

'I know. But I gave into your wishes for modern stuff. You can keep it.'

'Are you sure?'

She nodded. 'I've got all my old furniture at the cottage.'

'In that case, can I buy it from you? I know how much it cost,' he said remembering the day they had all gone shopping in Melbourne. They had tried to compromise, but had ended up buying Scandinavian style furniture in pale wood rather than the Victorian styles in mahogany and walnut that Catriona liked. Now he realized how selfish he had been.

'Tree, I'm not being offensive, but has your decision to leave me got anything to do with Doug?'

He had expected anger or an instant denial, but she looked thoughtful and finally shook her head. 'We like each other. I'm not leaving you for him, if that's what you think.'

Catriona knelt by the bookcase and began sorting their books into piles. 'What do you want to do with this?' she asked holding up their album of wedding photos.

'I don't know.'

'We'll chuck it out then.'

'No!'

'Why not?' She opened it somewhere in the middle and smiled bitterly. 'Even on this day you were too busy gawping at Fiona to look at me.' She turned the pages. 'Nowhere – not in one photo are you looking at me with love.' She pointed to one of them leaving the church. 'You look at if you're at a funeral.' She thrust it at him. 'You want it – you can keep it – in memory of the day you married one girl when you were in love with another.'

He took the album and looked through it. She was right. The day had been purgatory for him and it showed. He looked at photos on the first pages. There was one of Catriona and Kim, taken before the hairdresser had arrived to tease their hair and pull it into ridiculously elaborate styles and plaster it with hair spray. They were both in their dressing gowns. Kim was smiling and Catriona was laughing. He slid it out. 'Do you want to keep this one?'

She looked at it and nodded. 'And any others with Kim – just by herself – not with me.'

'What about the ones of you with your father? Why don't I take out all the ones without me in them?'

'Okay.' She went to the bookcase and took their wedding photo off the shelf. She opened the back and shook out the photo. 'I'll keep the frame, if that's okay.'

The photo drifted to the floor. He crouched down stared at it. It showed them standing on the lawn in front of the church. He remembered that he had been looking at Fiona taking in every detail of her. He realized how despicable his behaviour had been. It was his wedding day and all he had done was long for Fiona.

Margot invited Catriona to have dinner with her one evening. 'Darling, you look unhappy,' she said as she slid the cheese and spinach flan on their plates and added mashed potatoes and carrots. 'Are you sure you're making the right decision?'

Catriona shrugged. 'Who knows? My marriage has only lasted seven months – that makes me a failure – '

'It's not your fault.'

'Some of it is. I'm the one who's ending the marriage,' she said as she carried their plates to the table.

'With good reason.'

Catriona shook her head. 'Since Kim's accident he's been marvellous. He said he was only infatuated with Fiona. I believe him. He told me he loves me. I believe that too. It's not that I can't forgive him – I can. It's because I no longer love him. I don't hate him – it's worse than that – I feel nothing for him. When I come home at night I realize I haven't thought about him all day. I don't miss him or look forward to seeing him when I leave work. That makes me . . . what does it make me? Fickle? Shallow?'

'No. Your love for him is dead – he killed it. And no matter how marvellous or kind he's been recently once something is dead it can't be brought back to life.'

'His infatuation with Fiona brought out the worst in him. It brought out the worst in me too. In many ways it was my fault, mine and Kim's, that Stefan felt drawn to Fiona – '

'Don't be absurd. How was it your fault?'

'Before he'd even met her we told him she was a slut. He was expecting a tarty looking girl with long red fingernails, heavy make-up and sexy clothes – we set up an expectation – the reality was the opposite.'

Chapter 17

Two days later a van arrived to take Catriona's possessions back to the cottage on Kingower where she had lived before their marriage. After giving David a cheque for the furniture, Stefan stayed out of the way and only returned when the van and Catriona's car had gone. He began to write down all the things he had to do, but unable to concentrate, he gave up. He roamed restlessly around the house trying to find something to occupy him. In the spare room he saw Kim's diary on the floor and realized it must have fallen out of the box he had taken from her cottage.

He picked it up. 'Might as well make myself even more depressed,' he muttered as he opened it. He flicked through the pages. Some were just accounts of her day and the number of people who had come on the horse treks. Others were a list of things she had to do.

August
Uncle Alex is here. He looks unhappy. Aunty Margot thinks he's having problems with Virginia.

A few days later she had written:

Will we never be free of Fiona? She came to Kingower with Aunty Ruth – ostensibly to see Uncle Alex, but really all she wanted to do was cause trouble – and she did. Instead of telling us that she could ride she asked if she could come on the horse trek. Remembering her terror of horses Dad and I were sarcastic. She expertly led us into her trap. She's so good at stage managing incidents.
'I can sit on a saddle now,' she said.
'Was it on a horse?' I asked.
The next day she showed us that she could ride. We should have

guessed that living on a sheep station she would have had to get over her fear of horses. She was obnoxious to Dad and said that she could ride because she had a good teacher.
When she came second in the race I know I should have been sporting and congratulated her, but I was angry that she had beaten me. Stefan, the traitor, praised her. He can't stop looking at her. He tries not to, but he can't help it.

Yes, thought Stefan. I was a traitor and an idiot. He snapped the diary shut. I'll give it to Tree, he thought.

Although she wanted company Catriona decided to spend the first day and night in her cottage alone. She braced herself knowing that there would be no knock on the door heralding Kim's arrival. Her parents had suggested they all have dinner at the homestead together, but Catriona refused and told them the reason. Douglas asked if she would like to have dinner with him in his cottage and she turned him down and told him she had to face the first day and night alone.

He nodded. 'If it gets too much for you, just come in.'

The cleaner had cleaned her cottage and it smelled of furniture polish and fresh air. There was a vase of flowers and a card on the small dining table.

Welcome home, darling,
Aunty Margot

Willing herself not to cry, Catriona lit the fire, which made the room warmer and look more cheerful. She kept busy unpacking her clothes and putting them away and arranging her books on the shelves. She had given the china that Kim had given her and Stefan for their wedding present to her parents. 'It's too good for the cottage and I've got all my old stuff there,' she told them. She opened the box from Kim's cottage last. Her graduation photo was on top.

'Why, Kim? Why?' she whispered as she put it on the mantle piece.

When she and Stefan had married she had left all her furniture in the cottage, and that was where her Aunt Ruth had lived when she was diagnosed with incurable cancer. Fiona had visited her every weekend. Catriona almost expected to feel the essence of Fiona and Ruth when she entered the cottage, but she felt nothing except her own failure. She was tempted to go next door and accept Douglas's offer of dinner, but stopped herself.

'I'm not going to turn into one of those helpless, dependant women who cry all the time and need a man to comfort me,' she told herself as she blinked away her tears. But the memories of the evenings spent with Kim discussing their work over dinner or mugs of coca invaded her mind. Even though she had lived alone for years before she married Stefan, she had rarely prepared solitary meals. When they were both home she and Kim had shared their dinners, taking it in turns to cook, and they had eaten at the homestead with their parents a couple of times a week.

She opened a tin of vegetable soup and heated it. She followed it with beans on toast and an apple. She was washing up when she heard a whimper. She opened the door. 'Toby.' She let him in and hugged him. He greeted her joyfully. When Toby made it plain that he wanted to spend the night in her cottage she knocked on Douglas's door.

'Toby's with me. I didn't want you to worry.'

'Ah, that's where he went. Thanks. Everything okay?'

'Yes. See you in the morning.'

After listening to the news she went to bed and lay there staring at the stars and longing for the morning.

Am I happier today than I was yesterday? she thought. Will I ever be happy again? Do I miss Stefan? No. At least that's something. I've made one right decision.

She had been reluctant to admit it to herself, but when Fiona and June were at Kingower she had been interested in Douglas's reaction to them, and indifferent to Stefan's reaction. That Douglas had not, like so many men, seemed bewitched by Fiona's charisma pleased her.

Douglas had known where Toby was. Thinking that his presence would help Catriona he had left his door open and was pleased when Toby wandered to her door. Her separation from Stefan did not surprise him.

At university Catriona was the only girl in their year. She was friendly, didn't smoke, drank moderately and detested the drug scene. In spite of her wholesomeness he hadn't liked her at first. In his opinion she spent too much time socializing and not enough time studying. That she had wealthy parents was obvious. Her car was a Mercedes, her clothes, although simple, looked expensive and she always brought good wine to parties. When she gave a party herself the food was excellent. She threw herself into the social life of the university. She joined a tennis club, a debating society and a swimming club. In spite of her plainness she was popular with the male students. Convinced she was using university to find herself a husband, and would fail her first year exams he was confounded when she came top of their year.

Douglas had turned down two of her invitations to spend a weekend horse trekking at her father's property. Only his friends raving about what a fabulous time they had had, and his regret that he had misjudged her, made him accept the third invitation. By now he had realized that she was not frivolous, but was brilliant, which was why she didn't have to spend hours revising. He had to work hard and spent most of his free time studying.

His respect for her grew on his first visit to Kingower. He could ride, but she had a grace and ease in the saddle and a way with horses that he envied. Her sister Kim, who was in her final year at school, was as passionate about horses as Catriona was, and it was clear that they were very close. When Kim came to the university a year later, she and Catriona rented a furnished flat within walking distance of the university. It was not the usual student dump. They had separate bedrooms and the rooms had good carpets and curtains. Their aunts bought them crockery, cutlery and had given them money to buy bed linen. The place was always clean and tidy and was a favourite venue for student parties and gatherings.

He had been on the horse trek the first time Stefan came. His admiration for Catriona had been noticeable. At first Douglas thought they were well suited. When they got engaged they both looked joyful and content. They talked excitedly about their future and it impressed him that Stefan was prepared to give up his teaching position at an exclusive boys' school in Melbourne, move to Whittlesea and teach at the local school.

But even before their marriage Douglas had sensed that something was wrong. Stefan appeared distracted and Catriona's sense of fun had diminished. Kim's enthusiasm about the wedding and having Stefan as a brother-in-law dimmed and was replaced by disquiet. He suspected that Stefan's love for Catriona had been overshadowed by his infatuation for her cousin Fiona.

The first time he had seen Fiona was at one of the horse treks. Catriona and Kim's dislike had been unconcealed and he wondered about it. Neither of them were jealous types. When they stopped in the clearing for a barbecue lunch he noticed that Stefan was solemn and Catriona was watching him. Fiona had three men vying for her attention. Far from being gratified she had been detached. She had foiled their attempts to get her to sit with them and had gone and sat next to her father. Then he saw Stefan gazing at her, and Catriona's expression of distress.

At their wedding Douglas had noticed that Stefan had looked at Fiona far more often than he had looked at Catriona. He wondered if Fiona's indifference had been contrived. Although he appreciated the allure of beauty, he was more interested in someone's personality, conversation and hobbies. At Kim's funeral Fiona had been deathly pale. Her face had been grazed and her arm had been in a sling. On that occasion Catriona had all Stefan's attention. He hadn't even seemed to notice Fiona. It seemed that the fracture in their marriage was healing.

When he moved to Kingower he noticed that Catriona and Stefan's roles had been reversed. Stefan was the devoted husband. Catriona was unresponsive.

Chapter 18

Stefan felt paralysed by the empty feel of the house, even though all the furniture remained. Despite knowing she never would, he never lost hope that Catriona would decide she had made a mistake and return. He longed for the knock on the door that he would answer and find her standing there.

She had returned to the life she had known before their marriage. He wondered how difficult she would find it without Kim. Would she resent Douglas's presence in the cottage that had belonged to Kim? Or would she find it comforting having a neighbour so close? How did Douglas feel about Catriona? Would his close proximity both at work and at home be an advantage or disadvantage to any romantic relationship developing? Before Stefan had moved from Melbourne to Whittlesea he and Catriona had only spent weekends and holidays together.

While he would have to find a new teaching position and somewhere to live, Catriona would have the security of her family, her cottage and her job. Apart from no longer being with him, her life would go on as before, but without Kim. He dreaded telling his parents and sister. They loved Catriona. He knew they would ask endless questions that he would be unable to answer honestly.

He thought of all the things he could say. We found we couldn't live together. We argued all the time. It wasn't working. I hated living in a country town. Catriona refused to move to Melbourne.

If he told his parents and sister the truth they would be furious with him. His oldest friend, who had been the best man, was the only one who knew the truth. Relations between them had been strained since Stefan's wedding. Owen had despised Stefan for his infatuation with Fiona. His one visit to Stefan and Catriona's house had been uncomfortable. Stefan knew it was his fault that the atmosphere between him and Catriona had been icy.

Owen had left a day early. As he got into his car he had muttered, 'You're a fool, Stefan.'

He had come to Kim's funeral, but had only stayed one night.

He was tempted not to tell Owen anything, but they had been friends since their schooldays and he was unwilling to let their friendship drift. When he moved back to Melbourne he would be sure to run into him and he needed all the support he could get. Not that he'll be sympathetic, thought Stefan. But he wrote to him and was surprised by a phone call a few days later. Owen offered to help him find a flat and said he could stay with him till he did.

He made an appointment to see the headmaster and told him he was resigning. He went to an estate agent and put the house on the market. The amount it had increased in value since they had bought it gave him no joy, even though he would have enough to buy a flat in Melbourne. He bought newspapers and replied to adverts at three private boys' schools. At the weekends he went to Melbourne, stayed with Owen, and looked at flats.

'You look terrible, Stefan,' were Owen's first words when they saw each other.

'I know.' Stefan pulled his overnight bag off the back seat. 'Let's get it over with. Tell me I deserve it – I know I do. Tell me you think Tree's done the right thing – I know she has.'

'I didn't mean to sound condemning.'

'I deserve your condemnation.'

They went up to Owen's flat.

'You behaved badly and you've paid for it,' said Owen when he had made tea for them. 'I'm not going to keep going on about it and I'm sorry to see you like this. I'm surprised though. I – well I thought you and Tree might be okay – funerals are grim, but you seemed to be looking after her well and, unlike at your wedding, your eyes didn't keep straying to Fiona. Anyway, I might have a bit of good news for you. I think I've found you a flat – it's empty so it'll be a quick sale. It's in East Melbourne.'

The flat had two bedrooms and a balcony. It was perfect.

'Stefan, buying a flat's a good idea, but applying for jobs at private schools isn't.'

'Why not?'

'You're only going to meet other males.'

For the first time since Catriona's miscarriage Stefan was amused. 'I'm not even divorced yet. And I was teaching at a private school when I met Tree.'

'But you met her at the horse treks. Are you going to find another riding place?'

'I suppose so – I hadn't thought that far ahead.'

'There are lots of them around.'

'A long way from Whittlesea, I hope,' said Stefan.

The day after he got back to Whittlesea the estate agent told him the house had a buyer. The day before he moved out he was surprised by a visit from Margot. Stefan had always felt more rapport with her than with David.

'I've come to say goodbye, Stefan. And to say how sorry I am that things have turned out like this. I know you made Catriona unhappy and I know why, but in spite of that I'll miss you. I was hoping, that with the baby coming, things would work out between you.'

'So was I. But it's too late.'

'Yes. I thought Kim's accident . . . death, had brought you together.'

To his embarrassment he started to cry.

She put her hand on his arm. 'Come into the kitchen. I'll put the kettle on.'

'Sorry,' he mumbled.

'Don't be. I hate this nonsense about men not crying. It's unnatural.'

He followed her into the kitchen and sat down. 'I was only infatuated with Fiona – I didn't love her. I only realized the day of Kim's accident. Tree hadn't come home. I went into town and everything was shut. I drove to Kingower. The homestead was deserted. The kitchen looked as if . . . I thought you'd all been kidnapped . . . sounds melodramatic, but it was the only thing I could think of. The meat was covered in flies. I went outside and saw all the cars coming up the drive. I was relieved until David got out and I saw his face. Then you got out and I saw yours. I knew something terrible had happened. I thought it was Tree. I was so frightened I could hardly breathe. I didn't think about Fiona once – just Tree – my terror was for Tree.'

'I don't think we would have got through those days without you, Stefan. You were a rock. Did any of us ever thank you?'

'I didn't expect thanks. I didn't deserve it either.'

'Then I'll thank you now.'

He saw the parcel addressed to Catriona. He picked it up and gave it to Margot. 'It's Kim's diary – if you think Tree should have it could you give it to her?'

> *Darling Tree,*
> *I'm now teaching at Melbourne Boys Grammar in South Yarra. This is my address and phone number. If you need me I'll come to you. I love you.*
> *Stefan*

Catriona put his letter in a drawer. After a moment she took it out and was about to tear it up when she realized she would need his new address for the divorce proceedings. She wrote it down on a sheet of paper then screwed up his letter and threw it in the bin.

Chapter 19

Virginia disciplined herself to type out the journals at least four days a week.

I had a small room to myself over the stables. Considering I was the junior coachman the bed was comfortable. I had a chest and a wardrobe for my clothes, which were grand with gold braid on them. I was in charge of the stable lads. It was my ambition to be head coachman one day and drive the big coach with the coat of arms in gold on the door. I drove the smallest and least important coaches. I never picked up guests or family members from the station, but I did take hampers of produce to their houses in London when they were there, and I drove one of the coaches that took the luggage to and from London.

As I predicted, Sarah and Ellen were quickly promoted. They did a year as laundry maids, which they both said was better than working in the scullery bending over a sink scrubbing pots and pans, peeling vegetables and washing the floor. I used to see them sometimes wringing out sheets outside the laundry. Ellen had hold of one end, Sarah the other and they twisted them in different directions and then pegged them on the line.

We had half a day off a week. Once Ellen and Sarah were promoted they were not as exhausted as they had been in the scullery.

'We can move around,' said Ellen, 'Instead of being stuck at a sink all day.'

'And we do lots of different things,' said Sarah.

Because of their neat writing they were allowed to fill out the laundry registers, which gave them the chance to sit down. Sometimes we visited

Mrs Clarkson at the orphanage. Other afternoons when it was not raining we sat by the stream. I had found a secret place that I'm sure no one knew about. It was far upstream and thick with trees and ferns.

By 1831 Ellen and Sarah were junior housemaids. Their promotion meant sharing a dormitory with six maids instead of ten and having a thicker mattress and an extra blanket. A few weeks after they began their housemaids duty, Ellen reported that one of his Lordship's daughters was being forced to marry.

'It's terrible,' she told me when we were down at the stream. 'She said she refused and her parents beat her till she gave in. There have been awful rows. It's all to do with money – the man's rich.'

'Haven't they got enough money?'

'Apparently not – I only heard bits, but it seems they've got lots of debts and her marrying this man – I heard her crying and saying he was ugly – '

'She's nothing to look at herself,' I said.

'I know – he must be grotesque.'

I wondered if Ellen was exaggerating, but on the day of the wedding all the servants had to stand in a line in front of the house and welcome the bridal carriage when it returned from the church. The groom was shorter than his bride and his bulbous features made her look attractive. She made no effort to smile and her eyes were red.

'It makes me glad I'm not a member of this family,' said Ellen. 'I used to envy them, but not now.'

'He looks very old,' said Sarah. 'Maybe he'll die and she'll be a rich widow.'

It was during that time that I learned something interesting. Many of the wedding guests stayed at Aylington Hall and one day when I was grooming the horses the head coachman of one of the guests came up to me. He was probably about forty.

'Do you like it here?' he asked.

I didn't know what to say. Not wanting to sound disloyal I said, 'It's all I know.'

He smiled. 'It was all I knew once. I worked here many years ago. Rotten lot the Gordon-Seymours are.' He saw my look of alarm. 'Don't fret, lad. No one around to hear.'

Not knowing what to say, I went on brushing the horse.

'The aristocracy aren't all like this, you know.'

'Where are you from?' I asked.

'Newington House in Norfolk. I was in your position – just been promoted from a stable hand. They had a huge party here to celebrate the start of the hunting season. I got talking to some of the guests' servants. The head coachman told me there was a position coming up at Newington – there were more than one – they'd had an outbreak of scarlet fever. Ten servants and seven members of the family had died. He asked me if I wanted to work somewhere better – well when he told me about the family and the way they cared for their servants and the wages that were more than I got here, I said yes.'

I listened in astonishment. The money was a lot more than I earned here. But it was more that the servants were treated with respect that tempted me. I was about to say that I wanted to leave and join Newington when I thought about Ellen and Sarah.

'Are there any positions for housemaids? It's just that there are two girls here – we're friends – '

He shook his head. 'Not likely to be either – they're all young.'

I reluctantly turned his offer down, but he promised to send me word if any of the housemaids got married. Sometimes I think about how things would have been if I'd accepted his offer.

It was Sarah who showed the first signs of discontent. She and Ellen were now fourteen and had been housemaids for just over a year. 'It's wrong,' she said when we were sitting by the stream in the sun. 'It's not what the Bible says. We work hard and get nothing – '

'We get good food, somewhere to live and clothes to wear,' I argued.

'And so do they,' she retorted. 'But they don't do anything to earn it, do they? And they don't sleep in a dormitory – they've got big bedrooms with servants to help them dress and wash and empty their chamber pots. They never clean or polish or light their own fires or cook their own meals. We've been up slaving for hours when they're just getting out of bed. Yes, we've got clothes, but not silks and furs like they've got. They do nothing, why should they get everything?'

'Sarah,' I said. 'Talk like that will get you into trouble. You'll get sacked if someone hears you,' I warned her.

Ellen nodded vigorously.

Sarah looked around. 'There's no one near. Tell me honestly, Nathanial, do you think it's fair?'

'Well, no,' I said, lowering my voice. 'But that's the way things are. They are lucky. It is what we were born to.'

'Things are like that because people like us let them be like that – we don't do anything to change it. We bow and curtsey to people who are too lazy to do anything – '

'What can we do?' I asked.

Sarah looked at Ellen. 'And what do you think?'

'You're right, but there's nothing we can do to change it. We have to make the best of it.'

'How?'

'Work hard – '

'We already work hard – '

'Yes and we got promoted. Maybe we'll end up as a lady's maid or the housekeeper.'

'I want to be free,' Sarah insisted.

I had to stop this dangerous talk. 'Free to starve and die of cold in the winter, Sarah.' The memory of the maid who had been raped and sacked hit me. That the Earl had thrown a young woman out who was carrying his baby, still appalled me. Sarah was right. The people we worked for were worthless, but there was nothing we could do about it. I jumped up and we walked back to the house.

But nothing I had said had changed Sarah's mind. One Sunday after church she made the mistake of telling the vicar how she felt and asking him why it was. I say mistake, but it changed all our lives for the better, although it could have changed them for the worse and ended with our deaths on the gallows.

Sarah told me that the vicar was going to do something about it. He did. Two days later we were all told to assemble in the servants' hall before breakfast. We were told to stand to attention. Every servant was there – even the nanny and the governess and the lady's maids. The housekeeper told Sarah to come to the front.

'This,' she said pointing at Sarah, 'is a very ungrateful girl. She has complained about her betters. She called them lazy. Do you know what happens to such girls, Sarah Brown?'

Sarah was so white I though she was going to faint.

'Answer me!'

'No,' Sarah whispered.

'They are dismissed. You no longer work here. The Countess is very generous – she will allow you to keep your clothes. But you will receive no wages. Now go.'

Memories of the innocent girl who had been raped by the Earl hit me. Then I had done nothing. The thought of Sarah in the workhouse or working as a prostitute was excruciating. I had to think fast. I put up my hand. 'We don't want her hanging around here causing trouble and maybe stealing,' I said as harshly as I could. 'Shall I drive her to Chichester? Get her out of the way?'

'Thank you, Nathaniel,' the housekeeper said.

I went to the front and grabbed Sarah's arm. 'Come on, you,' I said as I pulled her outside.

I had just bundled her into the carriage and was about to shut the door when the cook rushed into the carriage house. 'Sarah, I'm sorry. She had to do it or she would have been punished. She had to do what she was told – we all have to.' She thrust a bundle at her. 'Here's some food – it's not much, but I had to make sure no one saw me take it.' She glared at me and ran back towards the kitchens.

As soon as we were out of sight of the house and grounds, I stopped the carriage, jumped down and opened the door. 'Come up here with me, Sarah.'

She looked at me with loathing. 'I don't want to be anywhere near you. I thought you were my friend.'

'I am your friend – '

'Yes, you showed it. You could have defended me.'

'What good would that have done? None. This way I can help you without anyone getting suspicious. Get up with me – we've got to make plans. I'm not going to dump you in Chichester. We've got to work something out – it's risky and I could get sacked too, so we've got to be careful.'

She climbed up with me and I let the horses amble.

'Do you want me to take you to Mrs Clarkson? She might – '

'No!'

'Why not?'

'I'm too ashamed. I've let her down.'

'But she might be able to give you a job or find somewhere else for you to work.'

'No.'

I thought about the alternatives, but could only think of one. 'It's risky, but I could smuggle you into my room over the stables – you'd have to be very quiet.'

'I'm sorry I doubted you,' she said.

I squeezed her hand. 'It's good I fooled you – that means everyone else will be fooled too. I have to keep this a secret from everyone – even

Ellen. You understand?'

She nodded.

Just in case someone was spying on me I drove to Chichester and then back again. Sarah got into the carriage and crouched on the floor as we neared Aylington Hall. I led the horses into the carriage house, unhitched them and told Sarah to stay in the carriage until I got back. I led the horses into the stables and filled their water troughs. Then I returned to the carriage house with a bucket of water and washed, dried and rubbed the paintwork till it shone. Then I pulled the doors of the carriage house shut and opened the carriage door. Sarah slid out and scrambled up the ladder to my room. I went into the servants' hall ready for dinner.

Ellen refused to speak to me, and I was pleased. It she was convinced of my betrayal then others would be too. And her attitude to me would make my hiding of Sarah less likely to be discovered. The servants' food was plentiful and it was easy for me to slip some food into a napkin and take it to Sarah. It was hard though. No one trusted me any more. No one smiled at me or said hello. If we had not had our allotted places in the servants' hall I'm sure no one would have sat next to me. Even the stable lads greeted me sullenly and reluctantly. If I hadn't been in charge of them they would have ignored me or been insolent.

I spent my half day off a week by myself. As the weeks passed and the days were hotter I grew more confident and suggested to Sarah that she slip out of my room just before dawn and I'd meet her by the stream in the afternoon. For three weeks we did. She washed her clothes and herself in the stream and hung her clothes on a tree to dry. I always brought food for her – usually bread, butter and cheese or meat, but at dawn she went to the orchards and picked up fruit from ground. Occasionally she found the courage to climb over the wall into the vegetable garden where she picked tomatoes, pulled up a few carrots, and tore the leaves off lettuces. She took them to the stream where she washed and ate them.

On the third week we heard someone coming. Sarah dropped the pear she had been eating, climbed up the nearest tree and disappeared into the branches just as Ellen came into view. She saw me, scowled and then picked up a handful of earth and flung it in my face. It went in my mouth, up my nose and into my eyes.

I stumbled to the stream, fell to my knees and stuck my head in the water. She jumped on my back and slapped my head. Suddenly she was off my back and Sarah was beside me.

'Nathaniel, are you hurt?'

'Oh, God,' I heard Ellen say. 'What – '

I lifted my head out of the water and coughed. Sarah and Ellen were hugging each other.

'He helped me,' Sarah whispered. 'He was only pretending – '

'Quick,' I urged them. 'Get up the tree in case someone comes.'

'I'm sorry,' Ellen said to me.

'Hush,' I said. 'Get up the tree.'

'We've got a good view up here,' Ellen said when they climbed up into the leafy branches. 'No one's coming. Please forgive me, Nathanial.'

'Of course,' I said. 'But you'll still have to act as if you hate me.'

'I love you,' she said.

Sarah giggled. I hoped Ellen was serious.

Now Ellen knew, things became easier. She still acted as if she hated me, but when no one was looking she would give me some of her food to take to Sarah. Sometimes I even managed to smuggle out a mug of milk. While the clothes and bedlinen for the family and their visitors was entered in a register in the laundry office, the servants' uniforms were not. Ellen managed to get Sarah a change of clothes, which they exchanged at the stream at our weekly meetings.

I knew we could not go on like this forever. In

spite of the food Ellen and I managed to smuggle out for her, Sarah was getting thin. Winter was coming and it would be too cold for her to go outside during the day. Our luck would end and we would be found out. I tried to work out how I could persuade Sarah to go to the orphanage and see if Mrs Clarkson could either give her a job there or write references for her to take to another house. Would her conscience allow her to lie and say she had employed Sarah?

   As I worked I thought about what sort of person I would be if, by some miracle, I owned a house like this with lots of servants. As implausible as it was I sometimes fantasized that far from being an orphan it was a mistake and my rightful and rich parents would come and claim me. I would be kind to my servants. I would give them one whole day a week off instead of half.

'I feel as if I'm reading a novel,' Virginia said to Alex when he had finished reading what she had typed. 'I have to keep reminding myself that this is real and that they're my ancestors.'

'Now I can see where you get your sparkiness from,' he said with a smile. 'I can imagine you beating the hell out of poor Nathaniel.'

'Sparkiness? More like a wildcat, I think. It's a wonder you liked me. I was insulting and caustic.'

'You were unique. David's wife is too sweet – she irritated me – even back then. She's insipid. You were just the opposite. Odd that as far back as that, Ellen looked like you and Sarah looked like Eleanor.'

Chapter 20

Aylington Hall – Sussex

May 1973

Beatrice Gordon-Seymour was deliberately late for the meeting that her stepmother Anne had arranged. She wandered into the room hoping her contemptuous manner would please her brother Quentin, but he didn't seem to notice. He was slumped in a chair and was obviously suffering from a hangover. His bald head glistened with perspiration and his clothes were so crumpled she guessed he had slept in them. There was stubble on his face and his eyes were bloodshot. As she sat next to him she could smell sour whisky on his breath and body odour, which the smell of cigar smoke did not diminish.

In contrast Sebastian, their half-brother, who was casually dressed in a white shirt and dark grey trousers, looked immaculate. His clothes were ironed, his thick black hair shone, his face was clean shaven and his green eyes were clear. He sat on the other side of the table, but she knew that he would smell of toothpaste, shampoo and soap. For many years she had thought that Quentin's opinion that Sebastian was not their half-brother was spite, born from resentment against their father because of his undisguised preference for Sebastian. But since Sebastian had grown up whenever he and his mother were together Beatrice could see that they were nothing alike. As Sebastian bore no resemblance, either in colouring or features, to the Gordon-Seymours Beatrice concluded that, unless he resembled some distant ancestor on Anne's side of the family, Quentin's accusation might be true.

The sight of her stepmother always made her envious. Her skin was creamy and unblemished, her red hair was glossy and fell in casual waves over her ears and her brown eyes were an unusual feature for a redhead. At fifty-five she looked younger than both her stepchildren.

Her father had yet to arrive. His lateness would irritate Anne, who liked everyone to be punctual.

'Meetings, meetings. I'm fed up with meetings,' she complained for Quentin's benefit. He didn't react and Beatrice regretted her enforced pretence of hostility to the stepmother she had once loved. She still did love her and hated not being able to show it. At one time she contemplated confiding in Anne, but Quentin was sly and would be bound to find out. 'It's Saturday – I want to go riding.' She picked up the agenda and minutes of the last meeting from the table and scowled. 'Is all this formality necessary? Anyone would think we were on Wall Street or in the Bank of England.'

'Yes,' said Anne. 'They are an important record of what was discussed and decided. If you don't want to take part, stay away and Sebastian and I will make all the decisions.'

'You'd like that, wouldn't you?' said Quentin.

Beatrice glanced at the agenda. 'Servants' quarters – what's all this about?'

Quentin sniggered. 'Are you moving up to the attics, Anne? Maybe we could find out which bed was your mother's and you could sleep in that.'

Anne did not react, and Beatrice admired her restraint. 'Where's your father, Beatrice?'

Beatrice pulled out a chair and sat down. 'He's your husband – you should know where he is.'

'If he doesn't come in a minute we'll start without him,' said Anne.

Quentin lit a cigar. Beatrice knowing he was doing it because Anne hated the smell of cigar smoke, watched her go to the window and open it, giving no hint of the annoyance she must have felt. Sometimes she wished Anne and Sebastian would lose their tempers. It was their vague amusement that infuriated

Quentin.

'Can we hurry up and get this over with. I've got things to do,' said Beatrice. 'First item – servants' quarters – what about them?'

Anne looked at her watch. 'Your father – '

'Start without him. He's probably forgotten.'

'Very well. I thought it would be an idea to clean up the servants' attics, arrange them as they would have been in Victorian times and have them on the visitors' route,' said Anne.

'Good,' said Quentin. 'That means the philistines will have less time to poke around in the rest of the house.'

'Passed,' said Beatrice. 'Next. The gardener's cottage. What about it?'

'I'm going to live there,' said Sebastian.

Quentin laughed. 'How fitting.'

'My apartment can be either opened up to the public to view or turned into a self-catering flat for guests. The dressing room can be turned into a kitchen and – '

Quentin scowled. 'Do we want plebs actually staying here in the house? It's bad enough having them in the cottages and wandering around the grounds.'

'My apartment is a long way from yours,' said Sebastian.

'But it's close to mine,' snapped Beatrice. 'No, open them up to visitors during the day – then we can be free of them.'

'Turning it into a self-catering flat would generate a considerable amount of money,' said Anne. 'Specially during the summer months.'

'No. And that's final,' said Beatrice.

'Wait,' said Quentin. 'How much money?'

Anne handed him her outline of estimated income and a tourist brochure of similar apartments.

He put his cigar in the ashtray. 'Well, the money looks good and we only have to put up with them during the summer months, Easter, Christmas and other holidays. You can move out of your rooms, Beatrice, and be further away from them – I appreciate your reluctance to be anywhere near them – '

'I want my own bathroom.'

'After this meeting we'll have a scout around. Don't fret. We'll sort it out for you, won't we, Anne?' he said pointedly.

'Yes. Sebastian's apartment will have to be refurbished. Based on the work done on the cottages, he's worked out an estimate.'

Beatrice nodded impatiently and looked at the agenda. 'Opening times. Sounds ominous.'

'We are going to have to open the house more than three days a week,' Anne began.

'Why?' Beatrice snapped.

'We need the money.'

Quentin picked up his cigar. 'You must be mishandling the finances, Anne.'

Beatrice raised her eyebrows. 'How careless. Your father can't have trained you very well or perhaps you weren't paying attention.'

'She was probably too busy daydreaming about how to seduce our father,' Quentin said with a sneer.

Sebastian opened a folder. 'My mother did not run up these bills.' He tossed them one by one across the table. 'Fortnum and Mason. Harrods. Peter Jones. Selfridges. John Lewis. None of the bills are hers.'

'Where are her bills?' asked Quentin.

'I haven't got any.'

'We wouldn't know if that's true or not.'

'Are you accusing me of being a liar, Beatrice? Because if you are –'

Quentin blew a cloud of cigar smoke in Anne's direction. 'Can we get on with the meeting, please?'

Beatrice slid all the bills back to Sebastian. 'Pay them out of the estate money.'

'Your private bills are not what the estate money is for,' Anne said. 'You know that.'

Sebastian picked them up and placed them in front of Beatrice. 'You and Quentin pay them out of your allowances. We have to cut down our expenditure.' He looked at Beatrice and Quentin. 'Or at least you two have to. The other thing we have to do is open the house every day and at weekends during the summer.'

Beatrice looked at him in horror. 'Well I hope you're going to take the tribes of frightful people around, because I'm certainly not.'

'If you're not going to put something into this we'll have to sell everything and leave. Would you rather we did that?'

'Don't be ridiculous!'

'He's not being – '

'You're being defeatist,' said Beatrice. 'If we sold the place where would you go? Aylington Hall does not belong to you – Quentin and our father will get the money from the sale, not you.'

Quentin sneered. 'He'll have to live in a tent somewhere – just make sure that it's no where on this land.'

'I earn good money at the bank, and I've got a healthy bank balance – I'll buy a cottage or a house somewhere.'

'I'm not exaggerating,' said Anne. 'We either open the house more often or we sell up – as we will be forced to do.'

Beatrice sighed. 'Oh no. Sebastian, get a loan from the bank – '

'No,' he said. 'The house has already got a huge mortgage – thanks to Quentin's gambling debts. As it's belonged to the family for hundreds of years it shouldn't have any mortgage at all.'

Anne took a sip of water. 'Beatrice, however distasteful you find it, you will have to take some of the tours. I can't do them all.'

'I don't see why I have to take any tours.'

'Well if you want to give the visitors the freedom to roam around the house unaccompanied – '

'We don't,' said Quentin. 'They might steal something.'

'Then Beatrice will have to take some of the tours.'

'We don't want visitors in the house at all,' said Quentin.

'Then do I have your permission to hand it over to the National Trust?'

'Don't be a fool.'

'Quentin, don't speak to my mother like that,' Sebastian said. 'You are the fool. You don't work, but you spend money, you gamble, you drink too much – if it wasn't for my mother this place would have had to be sold twenty years ago.'

'Don't keep harping on about it,' said Beatrice. 'Why can't you give up your job at the bank and you and your mother can do all the tours. Opening the house to the common herds was her crazy idea.'

'Her crazy idea has made it possible for us to keep the house. And I'm not giving up my job. You've got to contribute something, Beatrice. I work all week – you do nothing – '

'I do a lot. Who looks after the horses?'

'The grooms.'

'I exercise them – '

'You ride them and hunt. You don't do any of the hard or messy work. When was the last time you mucked out the stables?'

'I've got better things to do than taking a lot of ignorant tourists round the house and having them ask stupid questions – it's something you relish, Sebastian – it must be your grubby working class roots.'

He grinned. 'Bound to be.'

Quentin picked up his cigar. 'I can't comprehend why you're so proud of them.'

'I'm not proud of them. I'm not ashamed of them either. It's just something that is and I can't change it.'

Beatrice look at her watch. 'You're a traitor to your class.'

He winked at her. 'But not my conscience.'

'Apart from cutting down on expenses,' Anne said, 'I suggest that Beatrice and Quentin do their own cleaning, washing and ironing. Sebastian and I do ours – '

'You're used to it,' snapped Quentin. 'I've always had servants and I'm not giving them up. As Beatrice mentioned grubby working class roots – I'll emphasize it – your mother, Anne, was a maid here before our estate manager was fool enough to marry her.'

Sebastian stood up. 'As this meeting is proving unproductive I suggest we finish it,' he said dispassionately. 'But for the record I propose that if you want people to do your washing, ironing and cleaning because you're too lazy to do it yourselves, that you find the money to pay for it. It should not come out of the estate accounts. And also for the record – Quentin could take some tours if he wasn't always drunk or hung over.' He walked out the room before either of them could retort. Anne followed him.

Chapter 21

Anne and Sebastian went into the estate office. She dropped the folder on the desk. 'Things would be all right if Beatrice and Quentin stopped spending money and actually did some work around the place instead of organizing hunts, parties and hunt balls – ' She rubbed her head. 'It's ludicrous. We make enough money, but they just spend it. Your father's no better. Sometimes I feel like walking out of this place and leaving them to it. If it wasn't for you I would.'

'I feel like walking out too,' Sebastian said.

'I'm not serious.'

'I know, but I am.'

She pulled out a chair and sat at the desk. 'It's not really their fault. It's the way they were brought up. It's how their friends live. Quentin and Beatrice are the result of centuries of inbreeding – cousins marrying cousins, marrying cousins. Their parents were first cousins – it's small wonder they're as they are. They find it impossible to reason or work things out. They need someone else to do things for them because they're incapable of doing it themselves. The only thing either of them are any good at is riding.' She gestured to the folder. 'All these bills they've run up – I think they've genuinely forgotten what they've bought. Your father's the same. I told him about the meeting – I wrote it in his diary, but he's so vague he's forgotten.'

'I'm pleased they agreed about opening up the servants' quarters. Their reasoning was wrong, but at least they agreed. I can't understand Quentin – he's going to inherit this place one day so why – '

'Quentin didn't have a hope of being normal. Long before you were born – he was still at prep school – he told me he'd been raped by one of the teachers. I was only young myself and didn't really know what he was saying. He didn't use the word rape, but later I realized what he meant.'

'He must have developed a liking for it. It was all he knew. Can we go up to the servants' rooms and see what has to be done to make them presentable?'

Anne nodded. 'I suppose it's too much to hope that Beatrice and Quentin will help. Have you ever been up there?'

'Only once when I was a child. I was playing hide and seek with some friends and scared myself witless.'

'My father said they took all the old letters and ledgers up to the servants' attics at the end of the first world war. We can look through them. They might be boring, but if they're interesting perhaps we could have them on display.'

They climbed the servants' staircase to the attics. Written on the door facing them was, *Scullery and Kitchen maids*. The sun streamed though the dirty window on the landing and thick layers of dust covered the floor. The hinges creaked when Sebastian pushed open the door. There were ten beds, five on each side of the room.

Anne shivered. 'What a gloomy place.'

Sebastian sat on one of the thin mattresses. 'Poor little maids – after working hard, for God knows how many hours, they had to come to these hard beds.'

Anne opened the windows and the cobwebs hanging from the ceiling stirred in the breeze. 'I suppose they were so exhausted they fell asleep immediately. I wonder which bed was my mother's.'

'Did she tell you much about it?'

'She told me she started off in the scullery then ended up as a housemaid. Her father was one of the gardeners. She hated the Gordon-Seymours. She tried to persuade my father to leave and move to Chichester or London, but being an estate manager was all he knew. He took over from his father – he was born here so he was reluctant to move away. I suppose he was frightened of the unknown.'

Sebastian switched on the light. Boxes were piled at the far end of the room under the windows.

'Her records might be here. I hope they haven't been damaged by damp.'

Anne lifted one of the lids. 'They seem all right.' She looked around the room. 'We could make something of this. It'll need a good clean. We can make up the beds.'

'We'll get this place clean before we go through the boxes, otherwise we'll end up filthy.'

Sebastian went downstairs and came back with disinfectant, a broom, a bucket and a mop. He was followed by the cook who was carrying a vacuum cleaner. 'Lady Gordon-Seymour, you can't do this by yourself.'

'I'll be helping,' said Sebastian.

She looked worried. 'It's not right. Let me help you.'

Anne smiled. 'You can help us by making us some tea in an hour.'

'I'll bring it up.'

'No,' said Sebastian. 'If you can bear the thought of two dirty people in your kitchen, we'll come down.'

'I'll bake some scones.' Looking more cheerful she hurried out of the room.

They put all the boxes and ledgers on the beds and vacuumed and then washed the floor and cleaned the windows.

It took four hours to get the first attic room clean and free of cobwebs. They then concentrated on putting the files of letters, servants' records and ledgers in date order. Everything was clearly labelled, which made the task easier.

'Ah, look what I've found,' said Anne passing him a letter and its envelope. 'Careful – it's old.'

> *Vicar,*
> *God was on my side the day I was thrown out of work five years ago – the day you caused me to be thrown out. The hand of God saved me. I thank you for what you did. If you had not betrayed me I would still be in service. Instead I am a wealthy and respected lady in Australia.*
> *I have servants now and my husband and I treat them far better*

than we were treated when we were in service for those lazy and immoral Gordon-Seymours that you fawn over at Aylington Hall. I won't call them lord and lady for they are scum. Did you know that the Earl is a rapist? I suppose you did, but it suited you to do nothing about it. The girl was dismissed for being pregnant. It was his child, of course. What sort of a man puts the life of his own blood in peril? If he had any morals he would have made sure it and its mother were looked after.

Our servants don't have to curtsey or bow to us. They do a job for us. In return we pay them. We talk to them. We care about them. We are interested in their lives.

You are an obsequious snake. You are a hypocrite. You are not a man of God. You do the devil's work. Next time you thunder from your pulpit remember my words and be fearful about where you will go when you die. It will not be to heaven.

Sarah Osborne (formerly Brown)

Sebastian grinned. 'Good for you, Sarah.'

'That's exactly what I thought.'

He expelled his breath. 'What a stinging letter. She was clearly well educated – beautiful handwriting and wide vocabulary. How did she end up in service? From this letter I'd judge that she would have been more likely to be a governess. A rapist. Was she his victim? Though it might not be true. She was in Australia – she could have made up anything. Strange that they kept her letter – you'd think they would have destroyed it.'

'The other thing that's strange is that it's addressed to the vicar, so how did it end up here?' Anne wondered.

'The vicar was outraged and showed them?' he suggested. 'Maybe he thought they could sue her about the accusation of rape – she was a wealthy woman, although she, sensibly, hasn't put her address on the letter or the envelope.'

'Perhaps the vicar took the accusation seriously. Maybe he confronted the Earl. When was the theft?'

'I'm not sure. Why?'

'How did she go from being sacked to being wealthy and living in Australia? A sacked housemaid wouldn't be able to afford the fare to Australia.'

'Yes, that puzzled me too, but I didn't connect it with the jewellery theft. We could find out the date.'

'Let's have a look.'

Going by the date on the letter written by Sarah they opened one of the servants' registers. It recorded what they were paid and Sebastian and Anne were shocked to discover that for the first year, which was described as 'in training', they worked for nothing. When they did receive wages they were meagre. The records were detailed, with where each servant had come from, when they were promoted and when and why they left. A lot were sacked, and the reasons were written in red.

'Look at this one – dismissed for immorality,' said Anne. 'Pregnant. I wonder if that was the maid who was raped.' She turned the page. 'It might be – maybe not – here's another one – he could have attacked more than one maid.'

Sebastian pointed to another entry. 'Dismissed for being too slow. I suppose the poor devils ended up in the workhouse.'

She looked at another entry. 'Dismissed for disloyalty. Ah – that's Sarah Brown.'

'The same Sarah Brown? It's a common name.'

'The dates are right. Came from an orphanage . . . what do you think about having these on display for the visitors? Do you think they'd be interested?'

Sebastian nodded. 'Definitely. And the letter.'

She smiled. 'Quentin and Beatrice would never agree to that.'

'They don't have to know. When you do the tours show the visitors. When she does them put the letter away. Don't let her see it – she'll tear it up. Nothing must besmirch the reputation of the family.'

The servants' records absorbed Anne. During the week, when Sebastian was at work, she searched through them to find out what she could about the theft of the jewels. Nathaniel Saunders and Ellen Ingram had a red line drawn through their names with *thief* written beside them. She found a letter intended for the police, but apparently never sent, in which the Earl had called them bumbling fools. In a file marked *evidence* she found the note that Ellen had left.

> *I, Ellen Ingram, have stolen the jewels. I don't want anyone else to be blamed.*

'But the lady's maid was,' murmured Anne, who had seen the entry, *Dismissed for carelessness resulting in the theft of valuable jewels.* 'So much misery. This was an unhappy house – and it still is.'

There was a note from Nathaniel Saunders.

> *I have been offered, and have accepted, another job. The pay is much better and I realized that we have been badly underpaid for years. I am leaving immediately.*

Pinned to his note was a sheet of paper.

> *This was in his room above the coach house. I now have reason to suspect that he was involved in the jewellery theft. We have asked everyone we know and no other house has taken him on or offered him employment.*

She also found a letter from a Winifred Clarkson.

> *I find it impossible to believe that Ellen Ingram or Nathaniel Saunders would steal anything. I fear that Ellen has become the victim of foul play. I have heard stories about Aylington Hall that distress and disturb me, so that Nathaniel found more congenial employment elsewhere does not surprise me. He may not have gone into service. He might be working in a shop or as a clerk. Just because no one you know has employed him, does not mean he was lying.*
> *I shall not be placing any more of my orphans with you and will*

advise other institutions to find more suitable houses.

'I wonder how many of them really were orphans,' she said to Sebastian. 'I think it's more likely that most of them came from poverty stricken families who could not afford to keep them, or they were illegitimate.'

'Death rates were high in those days,' he said. 'It's possible that a man was killed in the mines or drowned at sea and his wife died in childbirth. Winifred Clarkson's orphanage must have been an excellent one judging by Sarah's letter.'

'Stories that distress me . . . I wonder . . .'

'You're thinking about the rape?'

'Yes. It was something serious enough for her to refuse to send any more orphans here. But why wasn't she specific?'

'They were aristocrats – she could have been sued and lost everything. Judges in those days would have been on the side of the rich. She wouldn't have had any chance of winning.'

Chapter 22

Eumeralla

June 1973

'Are you looking forward to going to Acacia?' Gabriella asked Keith as they arranged the chess pieces on the board.

'No point in looking forward to anything.'

'Oh, Keith.'

'Well there's not, is there? There used to be a girl where I worked – I always thought she was a miserable baggage – she once said that the only point of life was that there was no point. I used to think she was crazy – now I think she was right. Us Clarksons lose everything. I thought I'd found happiness when I moved here and Juju and I fell in love – and look what happened. You've had dreadful unhappiness. Dad's first wife died. He lost Acacia. Johnny died. Dad died. Mum died. It's just a whole catalogue of loss and misery. Fiona said the Clarkson family are cursed. I think she's right.'

Gabriella didn't know what to say. At least Keith's handling his unhappiness better than I did, she thought as she moved her pawn.

'It's us, isn't it?' he said as he picked up his knight.

'What's us?'

'Eumeralla used to be a happy place – shabby, but everyone was happy.'

Gabriella studied the board. 'Eleanor wasn't.'

'And whose fault was that? Johnny's – a Clarkson. He left her because he thought she couldn't have children. Well he was wrong about that, wasn't he? She had three children, but not with him. But everyone else was happy – now look at them.'

'It's not the Clarksons.'

'It is. It must be. Fiona introduced Kim to Tom. We came here on the trail of a family mystery and look what havoc we've caused. Ruth only wrote that letter because Juju and I were going to marry. If we hadn't come here everyone would still be happy.'

Preparations for the arrival of Virginia and Alex lifted some of the gloom as menus were planned and their bedroom was organized. Ruth's bedlinen, tablecloths and serviettes, that Greg had deemed too posh for everyday use, were unpacked. Keith collected Virginia and Alex from the airport two days before the housewarming party at Acacia.

The last time Virginia had seen the homestead at Acacia it had been empty. Now it was full of furniture and people. It looks loved again, she thought. Trees and shrubs had been planted on the site of the demolished homestead and Virginia was delighted that it was beginning to look more like the place of her childhood. Irene and Bruce were friendly and interested in what Acacia had been like before the previous owners had chopped down all the trees and turned it into a place more suited to the city, with the swimming pool, tennis courts and garages for their expensive cars.

'We're keeping the swimming pool – it's nice for the boys to be able to cool off when they get home from school,' Irene told them. 'We'll keep the tennis courts too – we can have tennis parties. Any time you want to play just pop over,' she said to Keith, Gabriella, Tom and Neil. 'Now, let me introduce you to people.'

An hour later Virginia saw Keith talking to an attractive girl. 'Who's the girl Keith's talking to?' she asked Gabriella.

'Bruce's youngest sister – I've forgotten her name.'

Two hours later they were still talking. When someone put on a Rolling Stones record and people started to dance, she watched Keith and the girl go outside onto the veranda.

'That girl you were talking to seems nice,' Gabriella said casually the day after the party when she and Keith were hanging out the washing. 'What's her name?' she continued when Keith looked embarrassed.

'Sophie.'

'Where does she live?'

'Dalby.'

'Where does she work?'

'At a doctor's surgery.'

'Nurse? Doctor?'

He took a pillowcase out of the basket. 'Receptionist.'

Gabriella laughed. 'I'm not interrogating you – I'm just interested. Tell me to shut up if you think I'm being too – '

'I know – it's just that . . . '

'What?'

'I feel I'm being . . . disloyal.'

'To Juju?'

He nodded. 'That probably sounds mad, but – '

'No, it's not a good way to feel, but I do sympathize. You loved each other and wanted to get married. Fate tore you apart, not something you or she did wrong. I don't think you feel that it's disloyal. I think it's more that you are still emotionally attached to her and being interested in someone else seems as if you're being unfaithful.'

He nodded. 'That's sort of how I feel.'

'You want Juju to find happiness and love with someone else don't you?' She pulled a sheet out of the basket. Keith held one end and they threw it over the line.

'Sure.'

'And I reckon she feels the same. Maybe one day when you've both found love you'll be able to meet again. You'll always love her and she'll always love you, but that doesn't mean you can't love someone else too. She was your first love. I hope she's not your last. If you were walking or hiking and the path you wanted to take ended in a dead end or at the edge of a cliff – you'd turn back and take another path. You wouldn't stay there and starve to death or jump over the cliff. Sophie looks nice. Her brother's nice and we'll all become friends now they've settled in.'

Keith grinned. 'So I should look on Sophie as an alternative path.'

'Definitely. Have you got her phone number?'

'And her address. Alternative paths. It's a sort of analogy . . . I wonder if Dad felt he was being untrue to Francesca's memory. What about you, Gabby? If you got interested in another bloke – would you feel – '

'I am interested in another bloke.'

'Who?'

'Tom.'

He looked astonished. 'Since when?'

'Last year.'

'Ah. You hide it well.'

'But he's still in love with Kim. I can't compete with her – she was brilliant and magic with animals – I'm nothing special.'

'It takes time, Gabby. I know you and Brett were married and it's different, but when Tom's love for Kim becomes a memory, I hope he turns to you.'

Chapter 23

Aylington Hall

June 1973

Knowing that Beatrice would not deign to come up to the attics Anne typed out the information about the jewellery theft and took it to her rooms. 'I've found some interesting facts you might want to include in your tour,' she said before Beatrice could tell her she was too busy to talk.

She stopped sorting out her clothes and studied the sheet of paper. 'Um, yes. Thank you. That should entertain the festering tourists.'

'Yes, that's what I thought. Sebastian and I have got the servants' attics in order – would you like to look at them and see what you think? You might have some ideas. Hopefully it will recreate the atmosphere.'

She had expected Beatrice to refuse, but to her surprise she agreed. 'Nothing much else to do on a foul day like this,' she said, gazing out the window at the torrential rain.

Usually Beatrice either snapped at Anne or disregarded her. Wanting to keep the neutral mood going, she said, 'Do you want to look now?'

Beatrice nodded and followed her.

'Have you ever been up here?' Anne asked as they reached the top of the stone staircase.

'No.' She went over to the window and looked out. 'We were never allowed. We had to keep away from the servants. When I was little I was friendly with one of the servant's children – I think it was the gamekeeper's daughter. When my mother found out she thrashed me.'

Anne had heard about that from her own mother who was appalled, not just by the snobbery and cruelty, but also because, apart from the servant's children, there were few children in the area that Beatrice could be friendly with when she came home for the holidays from boarding school.

'Worse – she wouldn't let me go outside for a week.'

Careful to keep any trace of condescension out of her voice Anne said, 'I'm sorry, Beatrice.'

'Why? It wasn't your fault.'

'I know, but that doesn't stop me from being sorry that you had a miserable childhood.'

'I wasn't always miserable. I loved boarding school. I could never understand why Quentin hated it. When the headmistress came into the class room and took me into her office and told me my mother was dead, I was pleased, but I had to pretend I was upset. When your mother died, I remember how sad you were – how much you cried – I wish I'd had a mother I could have loved.'

Anne opened the door to the first servant's room.

Beatrice looked around critically. 'Do you really think this is interesting enough to show people? It's awfully bare.'

Anne chose her words carefully. 'It's a direct contrast to the rest of the house. Two opposite ways of life that most people today have never experienced. Very few people live in houses like this, and very few people, if any, live in dormitories like this.'

'The dormitory at boarding school was like this – not as bleak. We had curtains and wardrobes.'

'It reminds me of the wards at Guys where I did my nursing training, except it's smaller.'

'I wish it all hadn't ended,' Beatrice said wistfully. 'I wish we still had plenty of money and lots of servants. I wish we could spend money and not have to worry.'

Anne didn't know what to say. To agree would be to lie. To disagree would make Beatrice hostile. She said nothing.

'It's all right for you, Anne,' she burst out. 'I have to work hard just to make myself look reasonable.'

Anne knew she was not fishing for compliments or expecting

Anne to deny her statement. 'You look good in your riding outfits,' she said honestly.

'Only because I look masculine and that's okay when I'm riding, but it's not okay when I'm at a ball or a party trying to look feminine. I look more male than I do female – that's why I've got to wear fur coats and expensive clothes. People look at me and don't know if I'm male or female. You look younger than I do. You have no idea how it feels to look in the mirror and see a face like mine. No chin, big nose, small eyes, flat cheekbones, dull hair . . . '

Anne knew it would be futile to talk about character and personality. She wanted to say something comforting, but couldn't think what.

'What can I expect,' Beatrice went on bitterly, 'my father's ugly, my mother wasn't much better.'

'You've been married – he found you attractive. You've had lots of boyfriends – '

Beatrice's laugh was harsh. 'Money – that's what the husband was after – money and prestige. As soon as he discovered there was lots of prestige and hardly any money he left. That's what the boyfriends are after too. If I lived in a suburban house no one would be interested in me. Stop looking at me like that, Anne.'

'Like what?'

'With pity!' she spun around and left the room.

Anne heard her footsteps clattering down the staircase. Despondent, but unsurprised, that their discussion had ended with Beatrice getting angry Anne ran after her. 'Beatrice!'

Beatrice went into her bedroom and slammed the door. Anne pushed it open.

She was sitting at her dressing table crying. 'Go away.'

'No. We were in the middle of a discussion and it's not over yet,' Anne said firmly. 'You want money – I'm trying, with no help from you or Quentin, to make money. And think about this. Your circle of friends is very narrow – opening the house to visitors might widen – '

'I have no intention of becoming friends with plebs who live in hideous semi-detached houses in the grim suburbs – I don't want them as my friends.'

'But you're happy to have boyfriends who are only interested in your money – not that you have much money, thanks to Quentin. If this venture fails Aylington Hall will have to be sold. If you don't believe me come and look at the books and I'll show you. And people who visit here may not all be from the suburbs – there might be some wealthy Americans, Canadians, Australians, or South Africans. One of the troubles with this family is that they have been too insular – they have never married out because they were snobby about Americans and anyone else who wasn't English. Most of the financial woes are because of Quentin and – '

'It's not his fault.'

'Then whose fault is it?'

'The revolting Labour Party and their vendetta against the aristocrats. They've made the lower classes think they're as good as we are.'

Although Anne wanted to remind her that the family had been forced to sell their house in London to pay off Quentin's gambling debts when the Conservatives were in power, she knew that to get into a argument about politics was pointless. Nothing she said, and no amount of evidence, would make Beatrice change her mind. 'Think about what I said, Beatrice. A rich American might be the answer to your prayers.'

Her stepchildren's antagonism grieved Anne. Once they had both loved her. No matter how badly Quentin treated her she could never hate him. Her memory of the little boy, who was only seven years younger than she was, was still sharp and distressing. She had found him sobbing in the stables when he was home on holidays from prep school one Easter.

'Are you missing your friends?' she had asked.

'I can't ride my pony.'

'Why not?'

She had listened in horror to his stories of brutal beatings, which she hadn't believed until he had pulled down his trousers and she had seen where the cane had cut into his buttocks a dozen times. He had let her comfort him, but begged her not to tell his father, because he would beat him again for having misbehaved at school.

'What did you do?' she asked expecting him to say he had stolen money or something equally serious.

'I talked in class.'

She told her parents, and her father said, 'If he escapes with no worse than being beaten, he'll be lucky.'

Anne hadn't understood then, but she did later. It was the reason she had been determined that Sebastian would be educated at the local state schools.

The Earl had refused. 'My son is not going to mix with just anyone.'

'He's not going to inherit Aylington Hall,' Anne argued. 'He's going to have to get a job.'

'No, Anne, and that's final.'

When Quentin was expelled from school for being found in bed with another boy, Anne's father condemned boarding schools as breeding grounds for homosexuality. 'The boy would have been normal if he'd gone to a normal school. Do you want Sebastian to turn out the same way?'

The Earl hesitated and Anne pushed the point. 'It looks as if Quentin is unlikely to marry – do you want an heir to carry on the family name and look after Aylington Hall or not?'

The Earl had reluctantly agreed to let Sebastian go to the local school.

When Anne had married their father Beatrice had been ten and Quentin sixteen. When Sebastian had been born eight months later Beatrice had adored him. She had also loved Anne. Her own mother had been too occupied hunting, riding and going to and giving parties to take much notice of her or Quentin apart from criticizing or punishing them. When she fell from a horse during a hunt no one, not even her husband, had mourned. Beatrice, starved of affection, had been thrilled to have Anne as her stepmother. She had sat on Anne's lap at every opportunity and was enthralled by the bedtime stories she read.

It was Quentin who had poisoned Beatrice's mind, and that, Anne knew had been his father's fault. He had made no secret of the fact that Sebastian was the favourite son. Disillusioned with Quentin he had hinted that Sebastian would be his heir. It was not until much later that Quentin discovered that the property was entailed and on his father's death had to go to the eldest son. Sebastian would only inherit it if Quentin died. Now forty-seven Quentin was still single. He never brought men to Aylington Hall, but Anne was convinced that he had male friends in London.

Beatrice had married at twenty and divorced three years later. Now she just had affairs. Anne suspected that the men were interested in the fact that she lived in a mansion and they thought she was rich.

Chapter 24

Eumeralla

June 1973

It was almost like the last time she had seen him. Like then he was digging the garden. He heard her car and looked up. Eleanor was so nervous she had forgotten everything she had planned to say. Last time she had come to tell him she was leaving. He stabbed his spade into the earth and began to walk away. She got out of the car and hurried through the gate.

'Greg.'
'What?'
'Hello.'
'Hello.'
'How are you?'
'Why are you here, Eleanor?'
'To see you.'
He looked wary. 'What about?'
'You weren't at lunch when I came.'
'I guessed you didn't want me there.'
'You were wrong.'
'Wrong? Neil told me you've changed your mind about handing Eumeralla over. Is that true?'
'Yes, but not – '
'What are you up to, Eleanor? Tom and Neil have had enough disruption without you selling Eumeralla.'

Intimidated by his coldness she blurted out, 'I want to come back.'

He looked astounded. 'Back? To here?'
'Yes.'

'Why?'

'I loathe Brisbane and you were right about Hazel. I rarely see her. And now you've got a proper toilet . . . '

Instead of looking pleased he frowned. 'Eumeralla belongs to you. I can't stop you coming back if you want to. We'll have to rearrange things.' He went back to the patch he'd been digging and picked up the spade.

'What sort of arrangements?'

'Gabby and I live here, she's got the boys old room, and Keith's moved in with Neil and Tom. Do you want our old bedroom or the other one?'

'Our old one.'

'Then I'll move into the other one.'

She wanted to touch him, but his expression was forbidding. 'Greg, when I said I want to come back to Eumeralla I mean I want to come back to . . . you too. But only if you want me.'

He was silent. She had thought he would at least smile, but his expression was thoughtful.

'Greg?'

'I'll have to think about it.' He resumed digging.

The only way she could stop herself from sounding as if she was pleading was to snap, 'Do you want me or not?'

'I don't know.'

'Thanks very much.'

'Eleanor, you're the one who left.'

'You were the one who forced me to leave.'

'Rot.'

'It was you who said your feelings for me were dead – you said you didn't need me.'

He stopped digging and leant on the spade. 'I was angry.'

'And I'm angry now.'

'Eleanor, one of the last things you told me was that you didn't love me and never had. You took the wedding ring Johnny gave you and left mine here. If Keith and Juju hadn't wanted to get married I would never have known that Ruth, not you, was her real mother.'

'How long do you want?'

'Want?'

'To think about it. To think about how you feel about me. To think about if you can bear to have me near you.'

'I don't know.'

'Then I'll give you one week.' She wrenched open the gate and stalked to her car. She heard him coming after her.

'Eleanor.'

'One week, Greg. I'll come back then.'

He grabbed hold of her arm. 'You can't just leave Eumeralla, talk about divorce and then came back and expect me to welcome you with no questions, can you? Brisbane's a disappointment. Hazel's a disappointment. Are you coming back because we've got what you've been going on about for years? If the toilet was still the same, would you want to come back? When did you decide? When you found out about the new toilet? When you saw all Ruth's posh furniture? Are you coming back to me and your sons or are you coming back because of the improvements?'

She pulled her arm out of his grasp, got into the car and drove away. Greg hadn't reacted as she had anticipated. When she'd said she was coming back she had expected him to be pleased.

'Serves me right,' she thought as she got out of the car and opened the gates.

At work that week the thought of enduring the boredom and loneliness till she retired tormented Eleanor. At least her days at Eumeralla had been productive. She thought about looking for another job, but suspected that only the location would be different. She would still be a pariah because she was separated from her husband. The men would still be vulgar. The work would still be monotonous.

Trying to work out what she would do if Greg didn't want her back, Eleanor parked the car under a tree. Although Eumeralla belonged to her she did not want to live there with a belligerent man. For months Gabby had been the only woman. Would she resent Eleanor's presence? What if Tom and Neil wouldn't forgive her? For years she had lied about June and Fiona. She had lied about loving Greg. Would they ever trust her again?

She was so nervous she was reluctant to get out of the car.

Maybe no one wants me back, she thought, remembering Neil's antagonism, Tom's disinclination to talk to her and Keith's awkwardness. But they've got to be pleased that I'm not going to sell Eumeralla. Has Greg told them, or doesn't he trust me not to change my mind? She closed her eyes. When she opened them she saw Greg walking towards the gate. Getting out of the car she tried to fathom his expression. He wasn't smiling, but he wasn't scowling. Was his neutrality a good or a bad sign?

He held the gate open for her. 'We have to talk about why you want to come back.'

'I told you.'

'You don't like Brisbane. Are you running back here because it's all you know? Because if you are I'll move into another room or you can have another room. You choose. Or I can go back to the hut – it's where I started off.'

'No. Do you think I'm so mean?'

'I haven't got a clue – once I thought I knew you, but . . . '

Trying to speak coherently she said, 'I'm one of those people who only discover what something means to them when they've not got it anymore – oh to hell with it – I miss you, Greg. Being away from you has made me realize I . . . love you. Not the same way I loved Johnny, it's more subtle – not as obvious that's why I didn't recognize it. I'm sorry for all the things I said and did.'

He stared at her in bemusement. For a frightening moment she thought he was going to tell her that he didn't love her, or that he didn't believe her. Then he smiled.

Relief flooded through her. 'Say something.'

'Would you like a cup of tea?'

She laughed. He took her hand and led her up the steps to the veranda.

'Where is everyone?'

'Out. I told them to stay away for a few hours.'

'Did they know I was coming?'

'Yes, I said we had things to discuss. I didn't tell them you wanted to come back in case you changed your mind. They're probably out there fretting that you're going to sell Eumeralla.' He put his arm around her. 'Welcome home, Eleanor. I've missed you.'

The table was set with cups and saucers, a plate of biscuits and a white tablecloth edged with lace that must have been Ruth's.

'Gabby made the biscuits.'

'Have you still got my wedding ring?' she asked when he had made the tea and brought it to the table.

He nodded. 'Do you want to put it on?'

'I sure do.'

'I'll get it.'

When he came back she pulled off the heavy eighteen carat gold ring Johnny had given her and put Greg's cheaper nine carat one on her finger.

'Thanks,' said Greg. 'That means a lot – it's . . . I don't know.'

'Symbolic?'

'Yeah.'

'We're going to do things differently – I've got to have a say.'

'That's fair. I know I was wrong to take over as much as I did. But now we've got a proper toilet and furniture, there's not much else, is there?'

'Yes. You and I are going on a holiday.'

'A holiday?'

'Yes, Greg. A holiday. We've never had a holiday and we're going to start. We never even had a honeymoon.'

He looked worried. 'We can't afford – '

'Yes, we can. I'll book the holiday. I'll make the arrangements. I'll pay.'

'But – '

'Apart from when we were children when did we ever have any fun?'

'Fun?'

'Yes – fun.'

'I've been happy – till last year and all this happened. I know

now that you weren't – I always suspected you weren't, but I hoped I was wrong.'

'Fun and happiness are different. We've always worked hard, but we've never done anything for fun.'

'No. We haven't had time or the money, I suppose. I don't think we've got time now – there's the – '

'We have. Gabby and the boys are capable of looking after everything while we're away. I'll pay for the holiday with the money I've saved from my job.'

'You've saved money? How? You've got a new car, new clothes, the rent – '

'The car looks new, but it's second hand. The rent was reasonable. There's a subsidized canteen at work and I eat there. Hazel helped me buy the new clothes and paid for most of them. Sometimes I earned more in a week than we made in a month on Eumeralla. Yes, I've got money saved.'

'No debts?'

She shook her head.

He looked impressed. 'Where were you thinking of going?'

'Have you ever seen the sea?'

'No.'

'Neither have I. Let's go to the sea.'

'What'll we do there?'

'Lie on the sand. Swim in the sea.'

'I can't swim.'

'Then just paddle in the water. Go for long walks. Relax. Get to know each other.'

'Know each other?' He smiled. 'Haven't we been married long enough – '

'There was always something going on. Juju and Fiona were babies when we got married. Then the others came quickly. We've never had time alone.'

'When are you coming back?'

'I have to give notice at work and let the agent know I'm leaving the flat. Two weeks – I'll be back then. Have Tom and Neil forgiven me?'

'I'm sure they will when they know you're not going to sell – '

'What if they don't want me back?'

He smiled. 'I reckon they will.'

'And Gabby and Keith?'

'Yeah, I reckon they will too.'

Hazel looked dismayed. 'You're going back to that dump? Mum, why? Have you gone crazy?'

'No.' Eleanor put her suitcase on the bed. 'I was crazy when I left it. I've regained my sanity. And Gabby's made a lot of improvements. Ruth's furniture makes a lot of difference. The whole place has been repainted inside and out. I doubt that even you would think it's a dump any more.'

'Well, at least your being there will give me a reason to visit and see Keith. Um . . . you're not going to need suits and skirts anymore, are you?'

'No, thank goodness. You can have them – you paid for most of them. But I like the blouses – '

'Keep them to remind yourself how civilized Brisbane is compared to Eumeralla. I suppose you'll go back to looking like a frump again.'

'No. I like the way I look now. I'm taking the make-up and the hair colouring kit.'

'Dad will moan about you using too much water – I can just hear him being cross because you waste time putting on your make-up.'

Eleanor folded up her shirts. 'I've found out a lot about myself and about you.'

'What about me?'

'That your father was right when he said you were superficial.'

'I'm not! I bought your new clothes for you, I helped you find this flat.'

'And I thanked you and I am grateful. It was generous of you. But I hardly ever see you – Greg was right about that.'

'I'm sorry, Mum, but I'm busy.'

'I know. Why are you so keen on Keith?'

'Because he's gorgeous. He's the best looking bloke I've ever met.'

'And apart from that?'

'I don't know him well enough to . . . '

'Exactly,' she said as she took her clothes out of the wardrobe.

'Come on, Mum. Looks are the things that attract or repel people.'

'Initially.'

'You were married to Keith's uncle – judging by the photos he was handsome too. Are you going to tell me that his looks didn't attract you?'

'Yes. We met when we were babies. I never considered his looks. We grew up together and I loved him.'

'And you knew Dad for ages – when you were both children – he loved you too, so how come you chose Johnny?'

'I'd always loved him and he felt the same. Although I was very fond of Keith's father Johnny was the one I loved. If it had been something to do with looks alone I would have loved both of them equally. So, no, Hazel, looks had very little, if anything to do with it.'

'Dad's not the best looking bloke on earth. I'm glad I look like you.'

'Your father's got more important qualities. Mixing with city types has made me realize that. And I think Keith's met someone he likes.'

'Have you met her?' Hazel asked in alarm.

'Yes.'

'What does she look like?'

'Looks again, Hazel? She's got bronze hair and olive skin – she looks a bit like Gabby.'

'Why do handsome men latch onto plain women?'

'Gabby's not plain.'

'Yes she is. Hard to believe they're brother and sister.'

'She looks like her mother.'

'See? How come someone as handsome as Keith's dad, married someone plain? What was his first wife like?'

'Francesca was a nurse – but you don't care about that aspect, do you? You want to know what she looked like. She was exquisite.'

'So is Juju. Keith loved her and now he's going around with someone plain. Don't you find that strange?'

'No. Francesca had more than just beauty – she was a good pianist, an excellent rider and had a delightful personality. Some men appreciate the qualities of kindness and humour. And the sooner you do the same the happier you'll be.'

Chapter 25

June 1973

Urzula arrived back from London with two outfits. She had spent too much money, but justified her recklessness by telling herself that she had to get Peter back. She had bought a lime green sundress that she would wear if the day was hot and a red linen trouser suit if it was cooler. She had also bought new make-up and perfume. She dreaded receiving her credit card bill, which had already accrued a lot of interest. The day of the party was warm with cloudless skies and a slight breeze. She wore her sundress. She arrived at Trelawney at the same time as her three colleagues who had all come in the same car.

The first time she had seen the house it had been a wet day in winter when it had first come on the market. Fiona and June had made a lot of improvements. The sofa and chairs had been reupholstered in royal-blue brocade, which matched the curtains. The walls had been stripped of wallpaper and painted Wedgwood blue. All the windows were open and the scent of pipe tobacco and the mustiness were gone, although the smell of paint lingered. The kitchen, which had looked shabby when Mark lived there, now looked fresh. The previously drab cream Welsh dressers had been repainted white and the walls were a soft yellow. The table and chairs were now forest green. Outside the kitchen door was a black cast iron table and six chairs. In the Victorian conservatory was a forest of plants. It was the sort of house Urzula wanted, but in London. She noticed that with the addition of burgundy velvet curtains the twins had made the conservatory a place they could use all year.

There were vases of flowers and photos on the mantelpieces, desks and tables. In the dining room the long table was covered with a green damask cloth and there were bowls of salad, platters of meat and smoked salmon, cheese and sandwiches. Urzula hadn't thought to bring a present and hoped no one noticed. Guests arrived with flowers, chocolates, wine and champagne. A white cyclamen and a fern were exclaimed over and put on a windowsill in the kitchen. She saw Peter give them champagne, chocolates and an African violet, which one of the twins put in the conservatory. When she saw Lynette, Yvonne and Charles she turned away, but not before she had seen Lynette scowl.

Fiona and June wore plain cotton dresses that looked as if they had come from Laura Ashley. They were the same style with square necklines and short puffed sleeves, but one was emerald green and the other was yellow. The twin dressed in green wore a pearl necklace and pearl earrings. Urzula tried to tell herself that her own dress, gold jewellery and high heels were sophisticated, but she couldn't help feeling that, compared to Fiona and June, she was overdressed. She didn't know which twin was which, until she heard Peter call the one in the emerald green dress Fiona. Feeling it was important to get their names right she thought, Fiona's hair is shorter and she wears pearls. June has got longer hair and does not wear jewellery.

She knew Peter was avoiding her. After an hour she went up to him. 'Hello, Peter,' she said. She tried to sound casual, but her voice sounded strident.

He nodded curtly and walked away.

After the salads, sandwiches, cheese and meats had been eaten, Fiona, June and Rose brought out cakes, bowls of fruit salad, a trifle and a pavlova decorated with strawberries.

Deciding it would be advantageous to be friendly Urzula went up to Fiona as she was putting out cake plates and forks and dessert spoons. 'It looks delicious,' she said with a smile.

Fiona's chilly expression faded. 'Thanks.'

She held out her hand. 'I'm Urzula – '

Fiona looked amused. 'Yes, I know. We went into your agency and you – '

'Yes, I remember. I apologize. It is just that a while back I got into trouble because I wasted a lot of time with someone who I thought was a potential buyer, but they just wanted to look at expensive places,' Urzula lied.

Fiona looked mollified.

Urzula couldn't bring herself to say she hoped they would be friends. Instead she said, 'Anyway, I'm Peter Yelland's girlfriend.'

She noted Fiona's surprised expression with satisfaction. Looking at the piano she asked, 'Do you play?'

'I had piano lessons when I was at school, but I was more interested in going to the beach than practising.'

'Do you mind if I play?'

'Please do. There's plenty of music in the stool and – '

'I do not need music.' She sat at the piano and opened the lid. I will show that ignorant Australian how cultured I am, she thought. She played a brief piece of Rachmaninov and then turned around expecting to see Fiona's admiration. The room was empty. She continued to play. People came in, helped themselves to food and either left or began talking instead of listening appreciatively. No one even clapped. Philistines, she thought. Incensed by their indifference she gave up and cut a slice of pavlova. I am not wasting my talent on them, she thought.

'Where did you buy everything?' she asked Fiona when she came in with more plates of food. 'Or did you hire caterers?'

'We made it ourselves.'

'Really? What a lot of trouble – '

'It was no trouble, Rose helped and I love cooking.'

'Oh.' She injected as much scorn into her voice as she could. 'How tedious. I rarely bother with cooking. There are too many interesting things to do.'

'Like being rude to people who come into your agency,' Fiona said clearly and loudly.

Urzula looked around in alarm, hoping her boss hadn't heard. She cursed herself for letting her true feelings show. Later in the afternoon she saw that June was in the garden surrounded by young men. Fiona was in the kitchen helping Rose clear away the dishes. The kitchen was full of young men, and she was dispirited to see that Peter was one of them. She went outside and joined the group June was with. Some of them were smoking so she took her cigarettes out of her bag. None of them offered to light it for her so she lit it herself. She tried to engage one of the men who was smoking in conversation, but he ignored her. He was gazing at June. They were all gazing at June.

Anyone would think they'd never seen a girl before, she thought.

'Would you like to come hunting, June?' one of them asked.

June looked perplexed. 'A treasure hunt?'

They laughed.

Urzula rolled her eyes. 'I think they mean a fox hunt, June.'

'A fox hunt?'

'Yes, such fun,' said the one who was smoking. 'Don't they have them in Australia?'

June shook her head. 'What happens?'

When they finished describing what a hunt entailed June's eyes were wide with horror. 'You kill them?'

'We don't – our dogs do.'

'But that's barbaric – cruel.'

'No it's necessary, June. Foxes are vermin.'

'One fox against dozens of dogs?' June's voice shook with anger. 'Being chased for hours by men on huge horses? If they need to be controlled why don't you shoot them?' June turned and strode across the garden into the house.

Urzula tittered at the men's astonishment. 'I don't think she will be going hunting with you.'

'Shame – she looks divine on a horse.'

'She looks divine off a horse too.'

'She'd look divine anywhere.'

'For her I could give up hunting.'

'It's not fair – I don't even hunt and she's lumped me with you lot,' protested one. He left the group and headed in June's direction.

Now June was gone Urzula hoped they would talk to her, but when they'd stopped regretting that June didn't hunt, they talked to each other about their plans for the holidays.

I might as well be invisible, she thought. 'Do any of you ski?' she asked.

Finally they paid attention to her. All but one of them skied, but they went to the most expensive resorts. One of them said that he went with Prince Charles who was his friend.

That is what I need, she thought. Someone with a royal connection. She tried not to look too keen. She saw that some of them were looking towards the house. Fiona was standing on the lawn.

'How lucky can we be? Two sensational looking girls.'

'I'd heard about them, but didn't believe how gorgeous they were till I saw them,' said the one who claimed friendship with Prince Charles.

Wishing she could scream at them, Urzula wandered off. They did not call her back.

Peter stayed behind after most of the guests had left, and helped clear and tidy up. When Fiona said she would make everyone tea and coffee he followed her into the kitchen. He hoped that he was imagining that her attitude towards him had become aloof.

'Fiona, would you like to come on a picnic?'

She filled the kettle. 'Who else will be there?'

'Just you and me.'

'What about your girlfriend?' she asked coolly.

'I haven't got a girlfriend.'

'Really?' She looked sceptical. 'Does Urzula know?'

'She's my ex-girlfriend.'

She put cups and saucers on the table. 'I don't think she realizes that.'

'She does. I've made it plain enough. We haven't been out together for weeks. Why do you think she's my girlfriend?'

'She told me,' she said as she filled two jugs with milk.

'She lied.'

Fiona smiled. 'Then yes, I will come on a picnic.' Her expression changed to alarm. 'Oh.'

'What?'
'Do you hunt?'
'God, no.'
'Good.'

> Dear Mum and Dad,
> The party was terrific. Juju made a great impression on the blokes, but unfortunately some of them hunt and when one of them asked her out she said she wouldn't go out with anyone who was cruel to animals. I hope they don't all hunt. I asked Mark if he had ever hunted and he said no, thank goodness. Like Juju and me he finds it repellent. I try to avoid matchmaking, but I can't help looking at blokes with Juju in mind. She's happier, but it will take her a while for her to feel like getting involved with anyone. The chaps who live a mile away tried to teach her to play tennis, but after one lesson she gave up, saying she couldn't see the point of hitting a ball over a net for hours. She'd rather be with the horses or working in the garden.
> It was funny. She said to them, 'If tennis wasn't a competition would you spend ages bashing a ball about?' They had to admit, and so did I, that they wouldn't.
> They were disappointed, but I sometimes play with them at weekends. In case you're wondering, they are very nice, but I don't feel attracted to either of them. However – I am getting interested in the estate agent who showed us round this house. He's been very helpful to Juju and me and advised us what sort of car to buy and drove us to the showrooms. At the weekends he's taken us on trips to the towns, villages and countryside. Tomorrow he's taking me on a picnic.

Virginia tried not to feel jealous as she read the rest of Fiona's letter. It was full of details about Rose and Jack the cleaner and gardener at Trelawney.

> Juju still hates shopping so Rose and I went to Truro to buy all the things I needed for the house – mainly new saucepans, sharp knives

and kitchen stuff. Because Aunty Ruth's china is so elaborate and rich I bought plainer crockery for everyday use. It's blue and white Delft and suits the kitchen.

Rose and Jack don't see much of their two sons. The eldest married an American and lives in New York. Their one visit was uncomfortable. They found New York noisy and crowded. Neither of them like their daughter-in-law and she made it clear she didn't like them either. Their other son is a stockbroker who lives in London and makes an obligatory visit once a year. Apparently both their sons feel that their parents' occupations are shameful. So Jack and Rose treat us like the daughters they never had.

Having them is a great help. When we have dinner parties Rose serves the food, waits on the table and washes up, which leaves Juju and me free to chat with our guests and not miss out on any of the conversation.

'Fiona's got a better relationship with Rose than she had with me,' she said to Alex when he came home that evening. 'I know I should be happy for all of them, but I can't help feeling jealous. I failed so badly as a mother.'

'You did your best – '

'It wasn't good enough. You're lucky not to be cursed with jealousy. I don't suppose you have any idea how it feels.'

'Yes I do.'

'Who are you jealous of?'

'The same as you.'

'Really? You hide it well. The dreadful thing is that if it hadn't been for me and my possessive nature we would have been a much happier family.'

'You don't know that.'

Virginia took the letter from him and put it back in the envelope. 'Yes I do. And so must you.'

Chapter 26

Peter took Fiona to the old swimming pool at Lanhydrock. It was an atmospheric and deserted spot, with the dappled sunlight glinting on the water. Lynette, elated by the blossoming relationship, had helped Peter buy and pack the food and wine.

He put the picnic basket down. 'What do you think?'

Fiona smiled. 'It's enchanting and . . . slightly eerie . . . not in a bad way. I can imagine carefree children running around and relishing their freedom. But it all went wrong, didn't it? They had all this and then the war came and they lost it – sons, their male servants and their horses. It's terribly sad – I think that's what I can feel – loss. Nine children and only one of them had a child.' Her smile was wry. 'And she was a girl, so she didn't count.'

He spread the rug on the grass. 'When I was at school we had to do a project about the good that came out of the war. I wrote about the social changes. Things would have changed eventually, but it probably would have taken another hundred years. Working conditions improved and women got the vote.'

Fiona knelt on the rug and helped him unpack the food. 'Yes,' she said. 'But if I had been a women in that era and had the choice of getting the vote or getting married – I'm sure I would have chosen marriage. If I had been married – and the choice was having my husband killed or getting the vote – I would have gone for no vote.'

Delighted that she was the marrying kind and not a man-hating feminist Peter found the corkscrew and opened the bottle of wine. 'Yes, I can understand that. Families are important.'

'Do you get on well with yours?'

'Very well.' He hesitated. 'Your . . . '

'What?'

He poured wine into her glass. 'It's none of my business, but I am curious.' She was silent so he went on. 'You and June both have the title Miss, so why have you got different surnames? If you don't want to tell me that's okay.'

'It's very confusing.'

He looked at his watch. 'We've got hours.'

'About eighteen months after my grandmother died, my grandfather, William Clarkson, met Margot Lancaster at a horse sale. She was fifteen years younger than him. She was the oldest of five children. My grandfather had three children, Laurence, Jonathan and Virginia. He had a sheep and wheat property called Acacia. Margot's father had a horse stud a thousand miles away called Kingower. They got married and Margot became Margot Clarkson. That's the simple bit. After that it gets tangled – very tangled.'

'That's okay.'

'Margot's brother Alex and his two sisters, Ruth and Francesca, came to visit Margot on Acacia. Laurence fell in love with and married Francesca. Alex and Virginia fell in love and they got married.'

'Right,' said Peter. 'Three Clarksons' married three Lancasters' and that made them not only stepchildren but also in-laws. So Laurence was Margot's stepson and her brother-in-law and Virginia was her stepdaughter and her sister-in-law. Have I got that right?'

'Yes.'

'What about Jonathan?'

'He married Eleanor – she's the owner of Eumeralla, the property opposite Acacia. But what no one knew until a few months ago was that Ruth was in love with Laurence. Francesca was asthmatic and her application to be an army nurse when war was declared, was rejected. Ruth was accepted, but Laurence and the rest of the family persuaded her to stay in Melbourne with Francesca. During the war she and Ruth shared a flat. Francesca had a fatal asthma attack at the end of the war when Laurence was on his way home. Communications were down. Virginia couldn't send him a telegram so she wrote to him. He didn't get the letter. He arrived at the flat expecting to see Francesca.'

'God, how tragic.'

Fiona nodded. 'Ruth had to tell him she was dead. She was so shocked that he didn't know, she just blurted it out. That night they got drunk. As Ruth put it, the inevitable happened. She wrote me a letter to be given to me after she died. I've read it so often I almost know it off by heart. She said that Laurence was so drunk he thought she was Francesca. Juju and I were conceived that night.'

Peter took her hand and kissed it.

'No one knew she was pregnant. For sixteen weeks she was so ill she had all day sickness and lost weight instead of putting it on.'

'What about Laurence?'

'He walked all the way from Melbourne to Queensland – that's about one thousand miles.'

'Bloody hell,' said Peter.

Fiona gulped and tried to stop her tears. 'He said he wanted to walk away all the pain. He never knew we were his.'

He put his hand on her arm and squeezed it. 'You don't have to tell me any more if you find it too upsetting.'

She wiped her eyes. 'I'm okay. When Ruth stopped being sick she went to Eumeralla. She was going to stay there till the baby was born and give it to Eleanor and Jonathan – they'd been trying to have a baby for ages. When she arrived Eleanor was alone – Jonathan had left her the day her period started. He went to Brisbane. The timing for passing the baby off as his was wrong, but we were born eight weeks early. Johnny came back when he heard about us, but Eleanor was engaged to Greg – he used to work on Acacia and they'd been friends since they were children. Not long afterwards Jonathan was killed in a fire. Infertility seems to be a Clarkson problem – because Virginia couldn't have children either. Greg said it was because they were too anxious. When Juju and I were about twenty months old Eleanor and Greg gave me to Virginia and Alex – they lived in Sydney. They adopted me.'

'Ah, so that's why you've got different surnames.'

Fiona nodded. 'It was kept secret till my cousins Keith and Gabby were clearing out their mother's house after she died. They found letters and photos that puzzled them. They had no idea that their uncle Jonathan had ever been married. They went to Eumeralla and saw Juju and thought she was me and that's how I found out I had a twin.'

'How traumatic and . . . complicated.' Peter put his arm round her and kissed her cheek.

She turned her mouth to his and wound her arms round his neck. 'To be continued,' she whispered.

When Peter arrived home he found Charles sitting at the kitchen table, drinking coffee and reading a book on psychiatry.

'You look happy. How was the picnic?'

Peter put the basket on the table and opened it. 'Great. Fancy some leftovers?'

Charles looked inside and took out half a French loaf, some smoked salmon, butter, a tomato and a wedge of cheese. 'Thanks.' He pointed to the percolator. 'There's more coffee if you want it. It hasn't been made long.'

Peter put the ice packs in the freezer, poured himself a mug of coffee and sat opposite Charles.

Charles shut his book. 'Did you find out the answers to the mystery – or mysteries?'

Peter nodded. 'I'm feeling a bit shell-shocked. If you decide on psychiatry you could write a paper about them.'

'Identical twins fascinate people. June and Fiona look . . . haunted is the best word to describe it, I think.' He buttered the bread and piled it with smoked salmon. 'Because they have different surnames I'd guess they were separated at birth.'

'Not quite at birth. They were almost two.' He rubbed his head. 'It's complex – hard to get it all in order. They were reunited when they were twenty-five. Both had very different lives. Fiona grew up in Sydney and went to an exclusive private school. Her adoptive mother, who was actually her aunt, was possessive and Fiona went to Melbourne to get away from her. When June found her she was working for an airline. June lived and worked on the family sheep and wheat property in the Queensland outback.

Fiona moved to Eumeralla – '

'Eumeralla?'

'The family property and it was where she was born. She was happy for six months. Then two things happened. She was almost bitten by some sort of snake – a taipan – I think she said.'

'If she had been bitten, she would have either died or been left with very grave heath problems,' said Charles. 'Then what happened?'

'She fell in love with Tom. At that time they thought they were half siblings. So she left Eumeralla and went back to Melbourne and lived with her Aunt Ruth. Then Ruth was diagnosed with terminal cancer. Before she died Fiona's cousin Kim was killed in a riding accident – Fiona was with her. Kim was going out with Tom – the chap Fiona was in love with. This bit's uncertain – she told me that she went on the ride with them in spite of Ruth's begging her not to. Fiona's convinced that Kim chose to ride a very difficult horse because she had never got over thinking of Fiona as a rival.'

'What sort of a rival?'

'Where men are concerned.'

'Right. I should have guessed.'

'Fiona believes that if she hadn't gone on the ride Kim wouldn't have ridden this horse.'

'What makes her think that?'

'She thinks Kim wanted to show Tom that she was better rider than Fiona, which she was. She wanted to impress him. Anyway Kim was killed when her horse attacked another horse and then bolted. Fiona blames herself.'

'When did that happen?'

'Beginning of January this year. Then Ruth died and left a letter for Fiona confessing that she was her mother, not her aunt. By this time Juju and Keith were going to get married, but they couldn't because they weren't cousins, they were half brother and sister. That's why they came over here.'

'Poor girls,' said Charles. 'What a story.'

Chapter 27

August

Catriona and Douglas had just finished operating on a sheep dog when the receptionist hurried into the room. 'There's been an accident – a lorry carrying cattle hit a tree and overturned – lots of injured cattle. The police are here – they'll give you an escort to the scene.'

The other vet was at a farm tending to a sick cow, so Douglas and Catriona had to deal with the carnage alone. It was dark by the time they arrived back at the cottages. They were both covered in blood, urine and faeces.

'When I said being a vet here would be more challenging, I didn't mean this,' said Catriona in a shaky voice. 'I've never had to deal with anything so horrendous – I hope I never do again.'

He touch her arm. 'You're trembling – I've got some brandy – '

Tears spilled down her cheeks. 'I'll need a shower first.'

'So do I. Have your shower and then . . . shall I bring the brandy in to you or do you – '

She took a deep breath. 'I'll come to your cottage.'

'Sure?'

'Yes. Do you mind if I'm in my dressing gown?'

'No. I'll be in mine. You know the only thing that kept me going back there was that they were going to the slaughterhouse anyway.'

She nodded. 'That's what I kept thinking too.'

'Tree?'

'What?'

He moved close to her, leant over and kissed her lips.

'Doug,' she whispered, thinking how bizarre it was that they both stank.

'I've wanted to do that for ages.' He smiled. 'But can we continue this when we've cleaned ourselves up?'

In her cottage Catriona stripped off all her clothes and put them in a bucket, which she filled with hot water and disinfectant. She scrubbed under her nails with a nail brush before she got under the shower. She soaped herself thoroughly and washed her hair three times. When she was sure she was clean she dried herself and got into her pyjamas and white towelling dressing gown. She cleaned her teeth and rinsed her mouth with mouthwash. She considered splashing herself with perfume, but after the shocking events of the day she rejected the thought as frivolous.

Douglas had left his door open. Toby ran to her and Douglas came out of the kitchen wearing a navy dressing-gown over blue pyjamas. He held her hand and led her inside. Because all Kim's furniture was still there she hadn't expected it to look so different. The fire was burning and he had rearranged the furniture. He had put the sofa in front of the fire. A bottle of brandy and two glasses were on the coffee table.

'I don't know if you feel like any food?' he asked.

'Just the thought makes me feel sick,' she said.

He sat beside her and poured out the brandy. 'Me too.'

She could smell his after-shave and she wished she had worn perfume. He took a sip of brandy and put his glass down. His arm gently went round her shoulders and he kissed her. She would never have thought that the first time she went into Kim's cottage she would make love to its new occupant. She never thought that she would feel happy. Afterwards he kissed her hand. The day that had been so agonizing had ended well. She fell asleep with her head on his shoulder. When she woke she was in his bed.

'How did I get here?' she murmured.

'I carried you. I can carry you back to your own cottage if you want.'

She snuggled closer and ran her hand through his hair. 'No.'

When she next woke the sun was shining through the gap in the curtains and Toby was on the bed. She could hear Douglas in the kitchen. She got out of bed, opened the curtains, pulled on her dressing gown and went into the kitchen. 'Good morning.'

He turned around and grinned. 'How are you feeling?'

'Surprisingly happy. But I feel a bit guilty.'

'I hope it's because of the cattle and not – '

'Yes. Strange how something so horrific leads to something beautiful.'

He put his arms around her. 'I would have kissed you eventually, Tree. Are you hungry?'

'Starving.'

'Cereal, eggs and tomatoes on toast, coffee?'

'Perfect.'

'How do you like your eggs? Scrambled or poached?'

'Scrambled, please. Have you got any porridge?'

He chuckled. 'I'm Scottish – of course I've got porridge.'

'Just what I need. Last night I never thought I'd feel hungry again.' She pulled out a chair and sat down, thinking how natural everything felt.

It was when Douglas was making the porridge that, for the first time since Kim's death, Catriona felt her presence. It was something she had yearned for and had concluded that it would never happen. Kim was gone. Whatever her psychic powers on earth they had not materialized to comfort Catriona when she was suffering. Joy overwhelmed her. It was as if Kim was in the kitchen with her telling her that everything would be well.

Her pragmatism told her that it was because something good had happened at last and she felt that Douglas could be part of her future. Then Toby ran into the kitchen looking ecstatic and she knew that he had also felt Kim's presence. It's not just me, she thought. Her eyes flooded with tears. Thank you, Kim.

Catriona's fears that she and Douglas might find it difficult to work together now their relationship had changed, were unfounded. When they went to dinner at the homestead a week later holding hands her parents seemed pleased and Margot looked delighted.

When Margot had given her Kim's diary she had been too

distraught to open it. She had put in a drawer, doubting that she would ever have the fortitude to read it. Since she had sensed Kim's presence she felt differently. She knew Kim had a diary, but thought, that like herself, she had used it to record appointments and social engagements. She took it out of the drawer and opened it at a random page.

> *Is the wedding on or off? Who knows? I hope it's off, but I daren't say anything to Tree. Stefan's been different since he met Fiona. I thought he was better than that, but no. Fiona has beguiled him like all the other boyfriends we've had. Years ago Aunty Virginia said our boyfriends were tomcats. Funny that they only behave like tomcats when they meet Fiona.*
> *Tree's different too. She's giving into Stefan and not being herself. She's being calculating. She won't answer the phone when he rings – she gets me to do it and then I've got to sound cagey and say she's not in and I don't know where she is or when she'll be back. She wants him to think she's got another bloke or is having a good time without him. If I wasn't so concerned I'd think it was funny. Stefan sounds so worried. What an idiot he is – and what an idiot she is to bother about someone who's so superficial he's interested in Fiona just because she's beautiful.*

'Yes, I was an idiot,' murmured Catriona as she turned the page.

> *Hell. Her tricks worked. Stefan arrived at her cottage with champagne and flowers. The wedding's on again, but she's given in to Stefan's wishes for a smaller wedding and I'm the only bridesmaid now. And we've had to cut the guest list. He said he's worried about all the expense. Stupid. Stupid. We nearly had an argument about it, but it's her wedding not mine. I never thought she would be submissive – and I never thought Stefan would want her to be. I'll never be submissive – never ever!*

Tom would have been ideal for you, Kim, she thought.

Chapter 28

Peter thought carefully about what to buy Fiona for Christmas. He considered jewellery, but she already had pearls and many beautiful pieces in silver, white gold or marcasite.

'What can I give her that is lasting and will give her pleasure for years,' he murmured to himself.

June had been easy. Months ago when they all went out for a walk with his family he noticed that she was always borrowing Fiona's camera and had decided to buy her one.

'A silver photo frame?' he said to himself. 'A book is too impersonal. She's got all the furniture and china she needs. I can't afford a horse.'

When the idea came to him he asked his sister what she thought.

'Brilliant,' said Lynette.

June dreaded Christmas. It reminded her that she should be spending it on Eumeralla with Keith who would have been her husband. In November when it got dark early she craved the warm balmy days in Queensland. Now instead of wearing a sleeveless shirt and a pair of shorts she had to wear layers of clothing, thick jumpers, woolen socks and a scarf. It took her three times as long to get dressed. Fiona who had spent two Christmas holidays in Austria skiing assured her that Christmas in the cold was more fun than in the heat. June was sceptical. It amazed her that plans were made so far in advance.

Peter and his family had intended to hire a big country house for a week over Christmas. Two years ago they had gone to Wales, but as early as September, to June's astonishment, Fiona had invited all of them to celebrate at Trelawney.

'But there are eight of us,' Peter told her. 'Yvonne's boyfriend is going to his parents in Ireland.'

'Great. Mark's coming and so are Rose and Jack so that makes thirteen – lucky I'm not superstitious.'

Christmas at Eumeralla had only lasted two days – one of the few days of the year when no one in the family did any work. They never had a tree or decorations, but they had special meals and exchanged gifts. It was always hot so they feasted on seafood. In November Fiona started talking about trees and she and Rose went shopping for decorations and lights. The tree was bought at the beginning of December, and June had to admit that it was fun helping decorate it, and that it looked magical when the coloured lights were switched on. She had forced herself to go into Liskeard to buy presents. She bought a leather wallet for Peter, and a cashmere scarf, gloves and handbag for Fiona.

She thought that was the end of her shopping, but Fiona insisted that June accompany her to Truro to help her buy presents for Rose, Jack and Mark. They had lunch in a pub, but just as she was looking forward to going home, Fiona said she was going to buy Peter's present and wanted June's opinion. She bought him a black leather briefcase and had his initials embossed on it in gold.

'Do you think he'll like that, Juju?'

'Yes. Is that all? Can we go home now?'

Fiona laughed. 'When I dreamed of having a sister I imagined we'd have a good time going shopping together. Yes, we can go home now.'

It was at a carol service in Lanhydrock church on Christmas Eve that June found herself gripped by the spirit of Christmas. Fiona had made her buy a scarlet cashmere coat, black leather boots, which reached her knee, and thick socks to wear under them. A black scarf and hat completed the outfit. June, who had never worn a hat before, blushed when Charles told her she looked like a film star. She saw Fiona looking speculative and knew she was wondering if something would develop between them, but June guessed that Charles was a dedicated doctor and when he married it would be to someone in the medical profession.

On Christmas morning she put on the kilt. That'll surprise Fiona, she thought. When she went downstairs to start breakfast, she saw that Jack had been in earlier to light the fires, which were blazing in the drawing room and dining room. She opened the curtains and gazed at the frosty lawn and mist, which shrouded the bushes and trees. She switched on the Christmas tree lights. Presents wrapped in coloured paper were piled underneath. Rose and Fiona had decorated the mantelpieces with vases of cuttings from fir trees, intertwined with ivy and holly and tied with red ribbons. She was intrigued by Peter's present for Fiona, which was a large flat envelope wrapped in red paper and tied with a green ribbon.

Fiona's right, she thought as she went into the kitchen to make the porridge. Christmas in the cold is more fun.

Peter was already in love with Fiona, but when he witnessed her attitude to Rose and Jack when they all gathered for Christmas lunch, his love and respect deepened.

She allowed Rose to help, but would not let her to wait on them. 'No, Rose, you're our guest. Sit down,' she said when Rose told her she would clear away the plates from the first course.

Many people found Yvonne's being a vegetarian inconvenient, but Fiona welcomed the opportunity to do something different. She asked everyone if they would rather have an alternative to Christmas pudding and his father, who found it too heavy, told her he would go without dessert.

'No, you won't,' she said.

'Please don't go to any trouble,' he said.

'It's no trouble – it's part of the fun,' Fiona assured him.

The alternative pudding was an orange that Fiona and peeled, covered in dark chocolate and dusted with icing sugar. His father said it looked too good to eat. The whole meal, although elaborate and delicious with three courses, was served without fuss or drama.

As he had hoped Fiona was thrilled with her lifetime National Trust membership.

Urzula spent Christmas alone. She was pleased when the holiday was over and she could get back to work. Her colleagues were all chatting about what they had done and the presents they had received. Unwilling to let them know she had spent it alone she was going to tell them that she had spent it with friends in London, but no one asked her.

Chapter 29

January 1974

When Urzula heard that Peter and Fiona were engaged she cried all night. During the week she managed to conceal her distress from her colleagues. It was only then that she realized how much they disliked her. They seemed to take satisfaction in talking about Fiona and extolling her cooking and her beauty.

If I hear one more person say how lucky Peter is I will throw something, she thought.

Much as she wanted to condemn Fiona and call her boring she said nothing, knowing that they would tell her she was jealous and point out that Fiona could not only ride a horse, she was a riding teacher and could play tennis.

On Sunday morning she showered and dressed then drove to Trelawney. She parked her car at the gates and walked down the drive to the house. The front door was ajar. She cautiously pushed it open and went inside. It was bitterly cold outside, but the house was warm. A large vase of red and yellow chrysanthemums, which she assumed had come from one of the greenhouses, stood on the hall table. There were two photos on either side. One of a man in army uniform and the other of a young woman in nursing uniform. Their parents, she thought.

She could smell coffee as she crept down the tiled hallway to the kitchen. Fiona was squeezing oranges and humming. She was wearing a pink towelling dressing gown over a long white nightdress trimmed with lace. Her tousled hair and lack of make-up should have made Urzula feel superior, but instead she felt overdressed in her flame red satin blouse, fur coat and tight black leather trousers.

Fiona picked up a coffee percolator.

'Fiona.'

She looked startled. 'What are you doing here? How did you get in?'

'The door was open.'

'There is a knocker – it's polite to use it, instead of barging in. What do you want?'

'I must warn you.'

Fiona looked dubious. 'What about?'

'Peter is after your money.'

Fiona put the coffee percolator down. 'Get out, Urzula. Take your spite and jealousy with you.'

'When he marries you, he will be rich. You have got everything – a new car – he will not even have to buy furniture. Have you seen his parent's house?'

'Yes. What's that – '

'Do you think it is small? They are retired and all they have is a small house.'

'It's bigger than your mind.' Fiona poured the orange juice into a glass and cut another orange in half.

'His father was only a train driver.'

'A necessary and important occupation,' said Fiona without looking at her.

'Hardly intellectually demanding, though.'

'Skill and concentration are required. Otherwise the train would crash. If I was fool enough to believe your lies and broke our engagement do you think he'd resume his relationship with you? Is that why you're doing this?'

'It is you I am thinking of, Fiona.'

'Rubbish. You're just – '

'What has he told you about me?'

'Nothing much. You're not important enough to – '

'Peter likes money – the only way he is going to get it is to marry it. He could not believe his luck when he saw how much money you and your sister had.' She saw doubt flare in Fiona's eyes and pressed her advantage. 'Yes, he told me all about it. He told me lots of things about you. How you and your sister have got different surnames. Did he buy your engagement ring or did you have to buy it yourself?'

'He bought it – not that it's anything to do with you.'

'Think hard, Fiona, what does an uncultured Australian have in common with Peter? He loves literature and Shakespeare – '

'And so do I,' Fiona snapped. 'For God's sake hence and trouble us not, you bottled spider – *Richard the Third* – not an exact quote, but you'll understand it I hope. Now get out.'

'Peter wants your money – why else would he want to marry you?'

'Because she's beautiful, classy and elegant,' said Peter from behind her.

Urzula spun round. He was standing in the doorway wearing a dark green dressing gown. Her face flamed with embarrassment, jealousy and anger. She had often begged him to stay the night with her and he had always refused. If she had known he was here she would have gone away. She wondered where he had put his car. Until now she hadn't noticed the tray with the two mugs on it. If she had she would have guessed that Peter was here and that Fiona, rather than making breakfast for herself and June, was going to take the orange juice and coffee up to their bed.

'Something you will never be, no matter how hard you try or how much money you spend at the hairdressers or on make-up and clothes,' he continued. 'And more importantly, she's got a lovely nature, which you lack. And she's far more interesting than you are and she's got manners. You're rude and arrogant and you look like a peasant, which is what I suspect you are. Now do as Fiona asks and get out of her house.'

June came into the kitchen, looking worried. 'What's on earth's going on?'

'An unwelcome intruder,' said Fiona. 'It's just leaving.'

When Urzula left Fiona poured the coffee into mugs and carried the tray upstairs. Peter was getting dressed and his overnight bag was on the bed.

'Peter, what are you doing?'

'Going home.'

'Why?'

'You heard what Urzula said.'

She put the tray on the chest of drawers. 'You can't think I believe her?'

'It's been said. It can't be unsaid.'

'Just because it's been said doesn't mean I believe it. Just because it's been said, doesn't make it true.'

'But it'll come between us.' He shoved the rest of his clothes in his bag.

'It won't. Don't you want to see me again?'

'Oh yes. But I can't. Not now.'

'Then she's done what she set out to do.' Fiona bit her lip. 'She's won, and you're letting her win.'

'Lies are corrupting. Her lies will corrupt our relationship.'

'Only if you let them.'

'It's gone too deep. What she said is plausible. You've got lots of money – I haven't.' He picked up his bag. 'Good bye, Fiona. Be happy.'

'How can I be happy without you?' she shouted as he left the room. She ran downstairs after him.

June came into the kitchen ten minutes later and found Fiona slumped at the table with her head in her arms.

'Fiona! What's the matter? What's happened?'

Fiona looked at her. 'Why does everything always go wrong?' she said furiously. 'What is the point of living, if it's just to be miserable?'

'Where's Peter?'

'Gone.'

'Not with – '

'No.' She told June what had happened.

Lynette was sitting at the kitchen table reading the *Sunday Times* when Peter arrived home. She saw his face. 'Oh crikey, have you and Fiona had an argument?'

'No.' He told her what Urzula had said.

She was incredulous. 'And Fiona believed her?'

'No.' He described Fiona's reaction.

'I understand how you feel, but if Fiona – '

'These things leave a mark. Somewhere deep inside Fiona must be a speck of doubt – it'll grow whenever we disagree about anything or have an argument.'

'How many arguments have you had so far?'

'None,' he admitted. 'But we've only been engaged for a week.'

She tried to persuade him to see things differently. When he refused she enlisted the help of their cousins Charles and Yvonne. They were still in bed, but came downstairs when Lynette told them what had happened. They added their arguments to Lynette's, but Peter was adamant.

'I own nothing – '

'You've got a car,' said Lynette.

'A second-hand one. As well as a six bedroom house, Fiona's got a brand new Land Rover – '

'That you helped her buy,' Yvonne pointed out.

'No, she and June paid for it.'

'Stop being so obtuse. I mean you advised her what to buy and drove her to the showroom.'

'So what? She owns horses, acres of land, stables and cottages.'

'That she owns with her sister,' Charles said.

'It's still a lot more than I've got.'

'You bought her engagement ring – '

'Yes, but apart from her possessions she's got money earning interest in the building society. Not surprising Urzula thinks I'm after her money.'

'I give up,' said Lynette. 'If you're determined to be – '

The doorbell rang. It was Mark.

'There are two very upset girls at Trelawney, Peter,' he said when he came into the kitchen.

'And one very unhappy and stubborn man here,' Lynette told him. 'Maybe you can talk some sense into my bone-headed brother, because we certainly can't.'

'Uncle Mark, do you want a cup of coffee?'

'Yes, please, Yvonne.' Mark sat at the kitchen table opposite

Peter. 'Trelawney's got a history of men marrying money. Not marrying *for* money, you understand, but marrying money. There's a big difference.'

To Lynette's relief Peter was looking attentive.

'My father was a groom at Lanhydrock House. He tried to enlist when the horses were commandeered, but he was too young and His Lordship wouldn't hear of it. It was 19 16 when he became old enough and he joined up straight away. Amazingly he survived with only a broken leg when he fell off his horse – which is how he meet my mother. She was a volunteer nurse – a VAD. They fell in love. Her family were wealthy aristocrats. Before the war her parents would never have allowed them to marry and would have disinherited her if she had insisted. But at the end of the war there were so few men, let alone those who were whole in body and mind, and she was the only child they had left. Their two sons were killed – one at the start and the other when it was nearly over. It was, they thought, the only way they were going to get grandchildren.

'As he had been in service at Lanhydrock House he knew how to behave. He loved horses and was good with them, which was another thing in his favour. Her parents bought them Trelawney as a wedding present. He had no intention of living off his wife and her family, so he started the riding school and horse stud. Now if – when – you and Fiona get married, what are your intentions? I mean, would you still work?'

'Of course.'

'So you wouldn't laze about all day and live off her?'

'No.'

'Then there's no problem. I don't expect you to make up your mind now – nasty lies have been told and you have to sort it out in your own mind. Will you think about what I said?'

'I don't know . . . every time we disagree about something it will be there in the background plaguing us.'

'Plaguing you,' said Lynette.

'There are things you can do,' said Mark.

'What sort of things?'

'When you get married you can refuse to have your name included on the deeds, if she offers – and she's the sort that would offer. Then you'll be earning money so you pay all the bills and for food and holidays. And the house needs a new bathroom – you can pay for that and any improvements. What do you think? It's more to prove it to yourself than to Fiona.'

To Lynette's relief, Peter nodded. 'I'll think about it.'

On Monday Urzula was on the phone when she heard the door open. She didn't look up.

'Good afternoon, Fiona, can I help you?' she heard her colleague say.

'No thank you. I want to speak to Urzula Luk.'

When Urzula finished the call she put the receiver down, hoping Fiona wasn't going to make a scene.

Fiona glared at her.

'Yes, can I help you?' she asked. 'Well?' she said when Fiona continued to glare at her. 'How is Peter?'

Fiona reached over and picked up the mug of coffee on Urzula's desk and threw the contents at her. Urzula screamed. Fiona slammed the mug on the desk, picked up the ashtray and tipped the cigarette butts and ash over Urzula's head, hurled the remainder in Urzula's face, and walked out.

Urzula saw to her fury that her colleague was laughing.

'What did you do to upset her?' he asked.

She spat ash out of her mouth. 'Ring the police!'

'You're not burnt. That mug's been on your desk for thirty minutes or more. What did you do to upset her?'

She tried to rub the ash out of her eyes, but only succeeded in blurring her vision. 'Ring the police! I have been assaulted. I cannot see properly.'

'Serves you right for smoking so much. Go home and change your blouse and wash your hair.'

She blinked furiously trying to get the ash out of her eyes. 'I'm taking a couple to see a house.'

'I'll take them. They'll run off with fright if they see you looking like that.'

She picked a cigarette butt out of her hair and threw it in the bin. 'And you'll get the commission if they buy it.'

He grinned. 'Naturally.'

As she changed her clothes and washed her hair she thought that had it been her who had thrown coffee and cigarette butts over Fiona, her colleague would have not hesitated to call the police.

Beautiful women have power, especially blonde beautiful women, she thought bitterly.

Lynette had just got home from work when the doorbell rang. 'Fiona! I'm so – come in.'

'I've come to give Peter back his ring.'

Lynette grabbed her arm and pulled her inside. 'Peter!' she yelled.

'What?'

'Come down here.'

He stood at the top of the stairs. 'Fiona.'

'Peter.'

'I heard what you did to Urzula today.'

'I'm not sorry.'

He laughed. 'Neither am I.'

'What did you do?' demanded Lynette.

Fiona held out her hand. 'I've come to return your ring.'

'Peter's been doing some thinking, haven't you?' Lynette said firmly.

'Yes, but I hadn't reached a decision yet. But I don't want the ring back.'

'No, you don't want the ring because you want Fiona.' She pushed open the door to the lounge. 'Go in there. I won't listen.'

Half an hour later she was in the kitchen when Peter and Fiona came in holding hands.

'Thanks goodness! You talked some sense into him.'

'Do you want me to move?' June asked as she and Fiona were

washing the dishes after dinner.

'What are you talking about? Why would I want you to move?'

'Now you and Peter are getting married – '

'Right. Yes, I've been worrying about it for weeks – this house is so small I don't know how we're going to fit another person in it. No, you daft galah, I don't want you to move.'

'What about Peter – I thought you'd want the house to yourselves – '

'Juju, this house is yours too.'

'It doesn't feel like mine.'

Fiona looked contrite. 'I'm sorry, Juju. Have I made you feel like that?'

'No – it's just that, well – you knew Ruth – I didn't. I only met her once and that was very briefly – it's her money and no matter how hard I try I can't think of it as mine.'

'It is yours, so stop talking as if you're a lodger. I was going to tell you – Peter said we should turn the smallest bedroom into a bathroom for you – so you can be private.' Fiona laughed. 'He was worried that you might feel he was invading your privacy.'

Ω   Ω   Ω

Gabriella finished reading Fiona's letter and smiled. 'Tom! Fiona's getting married.'

He dried his hands and took the letter. 'She's asked you to be her bridesmaid. Bit far to go, isn't it?'

'Well, I'd stay more than one night.'

'How long would you stay?'

'A month, I suppose. Can't go all that way for a week or two. Aunty Virginia and Uncle Alex are going.'

That night at dinner Keith said that if she wanted to go to the wedding he would drive her to the airport.

She had difficulty concealing her joy when Tom said, 'No, I will.'

Chapter 30

January 1974

Peter would have come to love me if Fiona had not been here, Urzula thought. Working with her colleagues was becoming intolerable. As they talked about Fiona's engagement ring and the engagement party they had attended, she tried to work out how to ease her heartache. She went into a travel agent and got some brochures for a skiing holiday. She chose a different company from the one she and Peter had travelled with. She looked for a hotel that catered for all price ranges. If she stayed in one that had rich patrons she had a good chance of meeting a wealthy man. On the top floor of one hotel there were rooms for what they called 'enterprising singles'. The only room she could afford slept four and the bathroom was down the hallway. She booked it, hoping that next year she would return with a rich man and stay in one of the en-suite rooms with a balcony on the first floor.

Winter suited her more than summer. She could look glamorous in her fur coats and hats. She excelled at skiing and that, she knew, was a good way to gain a man's esteem. The most difficult slopes were also a good place to meet men. She considered moving out of Liskeard, but decided to wait and see what happened in Austria. If she was lucky she would meet a wealthy man who lived in London. However hard she tried to avoid seeing Peter she was always bumping into him, which increased the pain of his rejection.

When she arrived at Heathrow she was pleased to see there were plenty of men among the group. Then she saw Fiona and Peter. She managed to stay out of their way and they didn't see her until they were having dinner at their hotel. They were seated at a table for two. When she and Peter had gone skiing he had never wanted to go alone. 'It's more fun if we're with other people,' he had told her. That he was alone with Fiona hurt and angered her.

Urzula wanted to sit with her back to them, but she had taken so long to get ready the only free seats at the table, which she was to share with seven others, were facing them. Absorbed in each other they didn't see her at first. They smiled at each other. They held hands when they weren't eating. Fiona's hair was longer and she wore a yellow polo necked jumper and a silver locket. The diamonds surrounding the oval emerald in her engagement ring, flashed in the light. Urzula was wracked with jealousy. Fiona saw her first. She looked agitated. Peter looked in her direction and glowered. She felt her hopes for a successful holiday disintegrating. She was so upset she forgot to speak in German to the waiter.

She was on her way back to her room when Peter saw her. Instead of avoiding her as he did whenever he saw her in Liskeard, he marched up to her.

'What are you doing here, Urzula?'

'I am on a skiing holiday, just like you are. Do not flatter yourself that I am here because I want to see you. I do not. I was annoyed to see you at the airport. I booked with this tour company because it is different from the one we went on when we were together. I have a new boyfriend – I am not interested in you.'

'Oh, good. I hope you'll be happy,' he said.

'I am happy,' she said. 'Much happier than I was with you. He is a better lover than you were or could ever be – more of a man.'

Instead of looking insulted Peter looked relieved. 'Good,' he said.

Angered by his indifference she said, 'Marry that pathetic little housewife type, and when she bores you to death – think about the life you could have had with me.'

The look he gave her was a mixture of pity and disbelief. Repressing the urge to slap his face she turned away.

On the slopes the following day she earned the admiration of several men when she hurtled effortlessly down the most difficult runs. Peter was an intermediate skier so she knew there was no chance of seeing him during the day. She was euphoric that she was the only woman on the black runs. If Fiona had been there she would have wanted to go home. She hoped that she was fumbling around on the nursery slopes.

At lunchtime she and four of the men, one of whom was a German working in Cambridge, went into one of the restaurants at the top of the mountain. They competed with one another for her attention and argued about who would have the privilege of paying for her lunch. In the afternoon they went back to the slopes for another gruelling couple of hours. Two of them were staying in the same hotel as she was. The other two, who were brothers, were in a smaller place nearby. They all agreed to meet in the disco in the basement of Urzula's hotel after dinner.

Her pleasure was marred when they were walking back to the hotel and she looked up and saw Peter and Fiona sitting on the balcony outside their bedroom. Her hope that Peter would look down and see her with two men came to nothing. He and Fiona were deep in conversation.

One of her companions followed her gaze. 'She's beautiful, isn't she?'

The other man, more tactful, said, 'If you like blondes.' But his rapt expression belied his nonchalance.

She went upstairs, hoping that the bathroom would be free. Gathering her sponge bag and towel she hurried down the corridor. She quickly showered and dressed and, wanting to sit with her back to Peter and Fiona's table, went down to the dining room pleased to see only one other girl was at their table. Peter and Fiona's table was empty.

'Didn't see you on the slopes, Urzula,' said one of the men when they had all arrived for dinner.

'I was there,' she said. 'On the black runs.' She was gratified by their amazement.

Now she couldn't see Peter and Fiona she felt more confident. She further impressed the others by speaking German to the waiters.

One of the girls at her table looked at her in awe. 'You can speak German and Polish and English?'

'And Italian, French, Russian and Spanish,' Urzula said, trying not to sound as if she was bragging. 'I can't read Spanish, only speak it.'

In the disco after dinner she was surrounded by males. Fiona and Peter were there too, which diluted some of her pleasure, but she was elated that Peter would see how popular she was with the men. As she gyrated sexily to the music of Abba and the Beatles she hoped Peter would remember how fantastic she was in bed.

Avoiding Fiona and Peter during the evenings was difficult. Although their room was on the first floor, she frequently met them on the stairs as she was going up to her cheap room on the top floor. Fiona had two ski suits. One was emerald green and the other royal blue. She always wore different coloured jumpers, and now more than ever, Urzula envied her wealth and her looks.

Urzula's only consolation was that the men competed with each other for her attention. She rejected their sexual advances hoping it would make them more keen. It did. Because they paid for her she was able to go on a moonlight sleigh ride, tobogganing and an excursion to Salzburg. When the occasion was right she always wore one of her fur coats and hats, which as well as adding glamour to her appearance, gave her a reason to react with a seductive smile when the men stroked the fur.

Wanting to build friendships over dinner and at the disco she delayed going to the outdoor ice-skating rink. She was pleased when everyone came with her, when she finally suggested it. As she was putting on the skates she'd hired she saw Fiona and Peter on the ice. Fiona was wobbling and giggling, and Peter was trying to hold her steady. Urzula stepped onto the floodlit ice. Lost in the beauty of Tchaikovsky's music she was so intent on moving with the rhythm she didn't notice the man gliding toward her until he took her in his arms and effortlessly led her in a waltz.

They had been skating together for five minutes when she saw they were the only two people left on the ice. Everyone else was standing at the edge watching. She was pleased to see that Fiona and Peter were among the audience. The man lifted her in the air and spun around. The audience clapped. When he put her down she glided away from him and then returned, executing the most difficult steps, which earned them more applause. Fiona didn't matter any more.

I am the centre of attention, not her, she thought.

The man bowed to her and the crowd and left the ice. He blew her a kiss from the edge, and the onlookers cheered. Urzula stood alone revelling in the attention, then she curtseyed and skated off the rink.

'Is there anything you can't do?' asked one of her male companions when she joined them.

'I'm sure we could find something, if we looked hard enough,' said one of the girls without malice.

'I can't sing,' she confessed.

Every night after dinner she skated with the mystery man, who refused to tell her his name. All she knew about him was that he was German. He was about forty and had a scarred face. She wondered what had happened. She wasn't attracted to him, but loved skating with him. She was gaining fame in the resort and people would greet her warmly in the hotel.

'I am better than Fiona,' she told herself. 'I can skate, ski, play the piano and I know all about opera and art. Compared to me she is boring. She can only speak English.'

At the end of two weeks she had the names and addresses and phone numbers of four men. They separated at Heathrow with promises to write, ring and invitations to visit each other.

After two weeks her phone had not rung and no letters had arrived. When she wrote letters there were no replies. When she rang one number a woman answered the phone.

'Who is that, please?' said Urzula.

'Well, who is that?' came the snappy reply.

Urzula hung up. Her first thought that the woman was his wife was replaced by the thought that it could have been his mother. 'But I do not want a man who lives with his mother,' she muttered. Two numbers rang unanswered whatever time or day she phoned. When she tried another number there was a message that the number was unavailable.

Chapter 31

Stefan was unable to settle in Melbourne. His flat was in an excellent location and he could walk into the city, and when it wasn't raining or too hot he walked to school. But although Owen had found another good riding stable in the wild beach area of Portsea, Stefan dreaded the weekends. He was unfulfilled and discontented. As he rode along the beach and the sand dunes he wished Catriona was beside him. He found himself unable to get to know girls well enough to start a relationship. He was morose and sometimes brusque. He was lonely. Owen was the only friend he had left.

His parents and sister, unable to accept that his marriage was over, kept ringing him and the first question they asked was always, 'Have you heard from Catriona?' His sister was convinced that once Catriona had recovered fully from her miscarriage they would get together again. His parents kept asking what went wrong and were never satisfied with his vague replies about incompatibility. He knew that if he told them the truth they would be angry and horrified.

'Why don't you get right away for a while?' Owen said when they were at a party Stefan hadn't wanted to attend, but Owen had persuaded him.

'Where? I'm still me. The memory of how I've wrecked my life and hurt Tree will be with me wherever I go.'

'The trouble with Melbourne is that it's where you lived and worked when you met Tree and started going out with her – happy memories and all that. If you go somewhere else – somewhere new – you'll have new experiences, you'll have to get used to a new way of life and different ways of doing things.'

'I could go to Africa and get eaten by a lion or bitten by a black mamba. That'd solve all my worries.'

'Or you could go to America, England or what – '

'England? That's where Fiona lives now.'

'So? It's unlikely you'll ever bump into her – anyway doesn't she live in Cornwall?'

'Yes.'

'I was thinking of London – a big city with all that history. You can rent out your flat here, so you've got something to come back to. You need a break, Stefan. I reckon you should go away for at least a year – you could get temporary teaching jobs when you're not travelling around, but if you get enough for your flat you mightn't need a job.'

The next day Stefan thought seriously about what Owen had said. He went to an estate agent who viewed the flat. He was pleased by the amount of rent he could charge.

He arrived in London in the middle of January 1974 and stayed in the London Walkabout Club, which was full of young Australians and New Zealanders. He was pleased to discover that Owen had been right. London was an exciting city, and the museums, history and old buildings enthralled him. He formed friendships with others in the hotel. After two weeks they all found a flat together in Kensington. The rent was high and the flat was at the top of four flights of stairs, and had obviously been where the servants slept when the house had been prosperous. Together they went to concerts, plays and the cinema in the evenings and explored the tourist sights, museums and parks during the day. He felt happier and more relaxed. He no longer brooded over what he had done wrong, but was determined never to make the same mistakes. He and three other Australians booked a skiing holiday to Austria at the beginning of February and an under thirties five week tour of Northern Europe and Russia in August.

When they got back from skiing they hired a car and drove around Britain. When they reached Devon in the middle of March two of the others had an argument and the atmosphere was tense and got worse, so he spent a lot of time alone. In Cornwall he was tempted to ring Fiona, but decided against it. If Catriona found out, she might misinterpret his intentions and any hope that they could be reconciled would vanish. He imagined Fiona's innocent letter to Catriona telling her that he had come to visit.

It was when they were staying at a bed and breakfast in Fowey that he went into a pub to have lunch and saw Fiona again. He had ordered his food at the bar, and was carrying his lager to a table. He was so engrossed in trying to work out how to ease the conflict between his fellow travellers that he was unaware of anyone else till he heard his name and looked back.

She stood up and smiled. 'It is Stefan, isn't it?'

'Yes, Fiona.' He knew it was Fiona because she wore pearl earrings and a silver locket even though she was casually dressed in jeans, a white polo necked sweater and a tweed jacket in smoky blue.

'Would you like to join us?' she asked.

It would have been churlish to refuse, so he thanked her and put his drink on the table.

He was confounded that he felt nothing for her. He had fallen in love with a haunted and angry girl. Now that she was serene and relaxed he felt nothing, although he still found her beauty mesmerizing.

What's wrong with me? he thought.

She told him she was sorry to hear that he and Catriona had separated.

He wanted to tell Fiona that it was her fault and that he wished he had never met her. Why did you have to turn up at Kingower? he thought. You weren't invited – you just told them you were coming. If it hadn't been for you, Tree and I would have been happy. We'd still be married.

The unfairness of his thoughts struck him as he remembered Fiona's fury when he had arrived unannounced at her flat on the pretext of trying to make peace between her and Catriona and Kim.

'Fowey's a lovely town,' he said trying to erase the memories.

She grinned. 'It's pronounced Foy.'

He had assumed that June was with her, so he was surprised when a man came to their table carrying a glass of wine and a cup of coffee.

'Stefan, this is Peter – my fiancé.'

He noticed her emerald and diamond engagement ring, and the reason for her happiness became clear.

Peter was asking him about his travels and he pulled his mind back to the present. He told them his plans for a trip to Northern Europe and Russia. When Peter said he and Fiona had been skiing they exchanged stories about the snow and how different it was from the Australian slopes. When he told them of the arguments between his two travelling companions Fiona invited him to stay at Trelawney. If he had still harboured a passion for Fiona he would have refused, but wanting to be away from the rows and tensions he accepted.

Catriona can think what she likes, he thought.

He was pleased that Peter did not seem to regard him as a rival. They waited in the pub while he went back to the bed and breakfast, told the others he was leaving, packed his suitcase and paid his share of the bill.

The photos of Trelawney that Fiona had sent him and Catriona had not done it justice. Although he'd only intended to stay three nights he ended up staying two weeks. His room was simply furnished, and Fiona apologised for the bare walls. 'We haven't got round to getting pictures for this room yet.'

He didn't tell her that he preferred bare walls and a room free of ornaments, plants and flowers. 'It's perfect,' he said, fingering the brown velvet curtains.

The furniture was mahogany, and the bed was comfortable with soft cotton sheets. The luxury made him realize how rough he had been living since he arrived in Europe and thought it strange how quickly he had got used to lumpy or sagging mattresses, poky rooms, which sometimes smelt of damp, and cheap nylon sheets. Rose Hayne fussed over him and did all his washing and ironing.

'I hope you don't mind Rose looking after you,' said Fiona. 'I know how much you value your independence.'

He smiled. 'I'm enjoying it. I've never been looked after. My mother taught my sister and me to look after ourselves from a very early age. I started ironing my own clothes when I was six. She was very strict about us keeping our bedrooms clean and tidy.'

To his consternation he began to understand why some men wanted housewives, and he reluctantly found himself appreciating the attraction of arriving home from work to a clean and tidy house with dinner in the oven. He and Catriona had shared the housework, but because of her irregular, and longer, hours at the surgery he had done the cooking, ironing and cleaning more often than she had. When she became pregnant they intended to have a cleaner when the baby was born. He reconsidered his opinion that girls who wanted to be housewives were dull.

My marriage to a clever and independent girl was a failure, he thought. But it wasn't because of her, or what she did, it was because of me.

Fiona relished driving him to different places and acting as his tour guide. He hadn't meant to get onto personal topics, but one afternoon when they were having lunch at The Rashleigh Inn on Polkerris Beach two glasses of wine had relaxed him enough to say, 'You're different to the angry girl I first met. So different you could be someone else.'

She nodded. 'I know.'

'What changed you?'

'Juju finding me. Discovering that my real mother wasn't an alcoholic. Living on Eumeralla. Learning to ride. Kim's death. Finding out that Ruth was my real mother and that I was a Lancaster – before that I felt like an outsider in an exclusive clan – my presence only tolerated because my adoptive father was one of them. When Juju had to leave Eumeralla she was angry – petulant, rude and obnoxious. That's what I used to be like.'

'She's happy now – or she seems to be.'

'She is. As long as she's got horses and the land, she's happy.'

In the evenings Fiona cooked delicious dinners, and often Mark, Rose and Jack joined them. Peter stayed at Trelawney at the weekends, arriving on Friday evening and leaving Monday morning. His family were frequent visitors. On Lynette's birthday, which fell on a Saturday, Fiona had a dinner party for her. Unlike some wealthy people Stefan had known Fiona did not embarrass Lynette with expensive presents, but she gave her a silk scarf and turned the day into an occasion, which began with morning tea. Lynette played the guitar and Fiona made her a guitar shaped cake.

'Only the guitar strings are inedible,' she said as she put it on the dining table. 'They're spaghetti.'

'It's gorgeous,' exclaimed Lynette.

Yvonne stared at it in amazement. 'It looks so real. You could make cakes professionally.'

Fiona shook her head. 'If I did it for a living it wouldn't be fun any more.'

She and Rose had prepared smoked salmon sandwiches and scones. The table was laid with Ruth's china, which Stefan thought was hideous. It was the sort of elaborate china that Catriona had once admired. He had told her that if she bought anything like it he'd never eat at home. The only thing he approved of was the white tablecloth. Even with ten people at the table it was not crowded.

Lynette and Yvonne were, Fiona told him, between boyfriends. Both girls were attractive with dark hair, hazel eyes and ivory skin. There was such a strong family resemblance they could have been sisters not cousins. It irked him that he was unable to think about either of them in romantic terms and he wondered if Fiona hoped that something promising would happen.

There were fourteen at dinner that evening. Fiona, with Rose's assistance, had made carrot soup, chicken casserole in cream and white wine sauce, a vegetable casserole for Yvonne and the most delicious bread and butter pudding Stefan had ever tasted. The compliments were sincere and well deserved. Mint chocolate truffles, that Fiona had made, were served with coffee. The conversation was lively and interesting. Charles told amusing or sad stories about his work at the hospital, Yvonne explained the importance of physiotherapy, Lynette talked about her secretarial work at the solicitors and Fiona and June chatted about the horses and the riding pupils.

Fiona included everyone in the discussions with remarks like, 'Oh, Jack said something similar a few days ago, didn't you Jack?'

Wanting to thank her for her generosity he went into a wine merchants and asked for a dozen bottles of champagne to be delivered after he left.

As he was leaving to return to London Fiona invited him to her wedding. 'If you're still in England,' she said. It's in May.'

'Is Tree coming?'

'I doubt it – I've invited her, of course, but it's a long way to come. And it's not as if she likes me very much.'

'Then thank you, Fiona. I'd love to come.'

She gave him an invitation and drove him to Liskeard station. On the train back to London he contemplated never returning to Australia. If I can get a teaching job here I'll stay. I'm free from the shackles of the past. Free from the obsession of a girl who could never, and would never, be mine. If only it was as easy to be free from my emotional bond to Tree.

Chapter 32

Kingower

Catriona had just given the horse an injection of antibiotics when Margot walked into the stables.

'How is he?'

Catriona threw a clean blanket over him. 'Getting better. His temperature's gone down – it's still high, but he's brighter than he was this morning.'

'Good. Virginia rang earlier. I'm going to Fiona's wedding,' Margot said.

Catriona looked at her in surprise. 'But she's getting married in England.'

'I don't intend to walk there – I'll catch a plane. I've never been out of Australia and I haven't even got a passport.'

'Neither have I.'

'Well, I was hoping that you would come with me.'

'Oh.' Catriona washed the thermometer and stood it in a jug of sterilizing solution. 'I hadn't given it a thought. I was going to send her a card, of course, and thought we could all send money so she could buy something she wanted. Are you going with Uncle Alex and Aunty Virginia?'

'Yes. We could all travel together. What do you think?'

'I don't know. How long are you going for?'

'Alex and Virginia are going for six months – they'll go to Europe too and make a big trip out of it.'

'I'll miss you.'

'I won't stay that long – six weeks I thought. You're due some annual leave aren't you?'

'Yes, but not six weeks – I suppose I could take three weeks.'

'It might help you sort out how you feel about Douglas.'

'I know how I feel about him.' Catriona put the syringe in the sterilizer. 'Or I think I do. That's the problem. I'm a divorcee. Stefan still loves me – or says he does. He didn't want the divorce. I don't know if I dare commit myself to marriage again. And the fact that I don't love Stefan any more makes me wonder about myself and what sort of person I am.'

Margot stroked the horse's ears. 'That's why I think a holiday in England would do you the world of good. Away from all the memories. It's what you need.'

'I'm surprised you want to go to her wedding – is it because you now know she's Ruth's daughter and therefore your real niece?'

'Partly. Although I should have guessed the truth a long time ago.'

'How?'

'As Ruth said in her final letter – Fiona looked very much like Francesca.'

'Did she – look like Francesca, I mean?'

'Yes. Although she also looked like the Clarksons, so I suppose that's why we all missed her close resemblance to Francesca. And when Ruth vanished I did suspect she was pregnant at first.'

'Did you?'

'Yes. Why else would she vanish?'

'Didn't you all think she was having a breakdown?'

'Yes. It was one of the reasons she could have vanished.'

'But you were so certain that Fiona wasn't a Lancaster – why? If you thought Ruth was pregnant . . . '

'The time was wrong. She was sixteen weeks when she went away and she didn't look pregnant. The twins were born eight weeks early, so I thought I was wrong – or that she'd had a miscarriage. If I had known before she went away the future would have been so different.'

Catriona went to the sink and began to wash her hands. 'How?'

'William and I wanted children, but I'd only had miscarriages. We would have adopted Ruth's babies.'

'Really? Would you have told them the truth?'

'I don't know. I was forty-six when they were born so it was possible they could have been mine. But I don't know if Ruth would have wanted them to know who their real mother was – she went to a lot of trouble to hide it. If Keith and June hadn't wanted to marry none of us would have ever known.'

Catriona dragged the nailbrush through the bar of soap and scrubbed under her nails. 'Wouldn't you even have suspected it when she left Fiona everything?'

'I don't know. It was the way it happened after the birth. Eleanor had letters from Ruth that she'd written in Melbourne. They forged the Melbourne postmark on a letter, which Ruth wrote and addressed to me. They put it in Acacia's letter box after dark. The letter said that Ruth was arriving at Brisbane station and could I meet her. She went to the extent of driving to the station before Brisbane and getting on there in case I arrived before the train came and saw her. And, as Eleanor and Ruth had planned, I was distracted in any case – just before I left to drive to Brisbane Eleanor turned up at Acacia with the twins, so I was delayed and almost forgot about Ruth. It was a brilliant deception and no one suspected anything.

'But all that aside – Fiona and I had a long talk the night before Kim's funeral – before I knew she was Ruth's daughter. And recently I've been dredging my memory to the day we found her and Kim's fiancé on the sofa. I think I misread the situation. Her expression when David, Kim and I came into the room was relief – not guilt. I think she was telling the truth. He was trying to force himself on her.'

'I never liked him,' Catriona said thoughtfully as she dried her hands. 'I was glad when Kim broke their engagement – sorry about the reason, of course, and that she was so distressed. I think it suited Kim and me to blame Fiona not him.'

'Ruth believed her. Ruth's unconditional love for Fiona should have been another indicator of their real relationship. Does it upset you that I want to go to her wedding?'

'No. It just surprised me. I think Fiona will be surprised too. You and Virginia seem to be getting on much better. She's changed. She's almost . . . likeable.'

'Virginia is, and always has been, splendid in a crisis. That's why she was such an outstanding nurse. Giving it up was such a waste.'

Catriona was puzzled. Margot was strongly opposed to mothers working when they should be dedicating themselves to looking after their children. 'But didn't she give it up when she and Alex adopted Fiona? You're forever saying – '

'No. She gave up nursing before she adopted Fiona. It was Alex's fault. He wanted her to be at home when he got back from work. He wanted a clean and tidy house and dinner ready shortly after he got home from work. He said he went out and earned the money and he wasn't going to start doing housework when he got home.'

'And Aunty Virginia agreed? I can't imagine her letting anyone tell her what to do.'

Margot smiled. 'He was clever. They were trying to have a baby with no success. He convinced her that she would get pregnant if she relaxed more and didn't go to work. The doctor agreed with him.'

'That was sneaky – I've never thought of him as being deceitful.'

'No, he really believed it – he wasn't lying.'

Catriona sprayed the sink with disinfectant. 'It didn't work though. She never got pregnant.'

'No. And she was bored and frustrated. Of course as soon as they adopted Fiona things changed. She was fulfilled, but she worried too much. Someone like Virginia should have had lots of children – one child was too precious and she was forever worrying that something terrible would happen to her.'

Catriona nodded. 'I used to dread it when she came down with Fiona. It was fine when Fiona came by herself, but even when we were children I can remember Aunty Virginia fussing and panicking about every little thing. It's hard to imagine her being any good as a nurse.'

'After I'd sold Acacia and moved here, she and Alex came to visit. She hardly spoke to me and it was all very uncomfortable.

Then I became very ill. I had pneumonia. Virginia nursed me for four weeks – devotedly. I couldn't believe it. She was kind and gentle. I'd never seen that side of her before. Alex had to go back to work in Sydney and she stayed on to look after me. When I was better and she was going home, I held her hand and thanked her. She snatched her hand away and said that she was only doing her duty as a nurse. I felt as if she'd punched me. The next time she and Alex came here she was as frosty as ever. She never passed up the opportunity to snipe at me. Any improvements here and she would mention Acacia's money. 'I see you are making good use of Laurence and Jonathan's money,' she would say.'

'Didn't anyone tell her to shut up?'

'No. She seemed to have power over all of us. We should have confronted her, but we never did. She was too formidable.' Margot sighed. 'But that all seems to be forgiven now. So what do you think about coming to England with me?'

'I'll have to check at work. I'll do it tomorrow and let you know. I know Fiona sent us an invitation, but I don't think she expected us to come.'

As Catriona walked back to her cottage she recalled the dozens of postcards and letters Fiona had sent to her and Kim from Europe years ago. Neither of them had replied, or thanked her when she arrived back in Australia. When she had tried to talk about her trips at family gatherings they had cut her off or changed the subject.

'I owe Fiona an apology,' she said to herself.

Chapter 33

Nathaniel's journal was full of details about the workings of the coaches, how he cleaned the saddles and harnesses and what he had to do when a wheel fell off or broke. Virginia decided to leave out the technicalities and concentrate on their lives.

I had just made up my mind to visit Mrs Clarkson by myself and tell her what had happened to Sarah. My plan was to ask her if she could recommend Sarah for a position somewhere and say she had been working at the orphanage. Before I could do anything a housemaid in one of the London houses fell down the stairs and broke her leg. Ellen was chosen to replace her when the family travelled to London. The prospect of going to London excited her.

As I would be busy driving the coach to and from London with luggage and produce from the gardens this left Sarah alone. Because the regime was more relaxed when the family were away the broken routines meant that Sarah was in more danger of being discovered. The lady's maids, governess, nanny, nursery maids, housekeeper, the butler, some of the laundry maids and all the footmen went to the London house. The gardeners all stayed at Aylington Hall. The cook, the assistant housekeeper and the head footman were in charge. The coach drivers came and went as required.

After a sleepless night spent worrying, I hit upon the idea of taking Sarah with me in the coach. Two days before the family travelled to London I had to transport all the luggage so it would be ready for them when they arrived. When the leather cases were put in the coach Sarah hid among them. We left at dawn. Just before we reached the house, which was near Buckingham Palace, she left the coach. After the luggage had been unloaded and carried into the house, I drove to the mews, which was half a mile away. My room above the stable was far smaller than at Aylington Hall. Sarah followed me on foot. No one saw her enter the mews and get into the coach, where she spent the night. I fed and watered the horses, and we left for Sussex after breakfast. I had put a rasher of bacon and some bread spread with butter into my pocket for her. The cook in the London house had packed my lunch of bread, cheese, a can of milk and a slice of apple pie, which I shared with Sarah. I had to return the next day with produce from the garden, butter, cheese and cream from the dairy and eggs packed in straw to prevent them from breaking.

The family stayed in London for one month. I only saw Ellen if she happened to be around when I went into the kitchen, which was located in the basement. Keeping up the charade of hating me, she scowled whenever she saw me. We met on our half day off in Hyde Park. One day Ellen arrived breathless. She threw herself down on the grass. 'The key to the safe,' she said dramatically.

'What about it?' I asked when she said nothing else.

She looked around to make sure we were alone. 'I know where it is.'

'The safe in London?' asked Sarah.

'Yes. It's in a little pocket sewn into the inside of the curtain. I saw her ladyship's maid take it out and unlock the safe. I've had an idea.'

'What?' I asked, even though I suspected what it was.

'If I take something Sarah can sell it and buy or rent somewhere to live.' Her eyes glittering with excitement she turned to Sarah. 'You could even set yourself up in business – a shop or something – it depends on what I take.'

'And what if you're caught?' I asked angrily.

'She's got so much jewellery she probably won't miss it – I'll take something she doesn't wear very often.'

Sarah was gazing at Ellen as if spellbound. 'What about taking enough for all us . . . not just for me?' she said slowly.

It was too bold and dangerous for me to consider. 'We can't,' I said firmly.

'It's the only way we can escape from here,' said Sarah.

'We'll get away from here all right and from this earth. We'll be hung.'

'No,' said Ellen. 'Only if we're caught.'

'And we will be,' I warned.

'Not if we're careful and plan properly. I'll do the stealing. If I'm caught - I won't tell - '

'If we do it, Ellen,' I said. 'I'm in with you, but - '

'So am I,' said Sarah.

'Nathaniel, what do you think? Really think,' Ellen persisted. 'If we get away with it would your conscience trouble you?'

'We can't do it.'

'But would your conscience trouble you?'

I thought about the Earl and the rape. 'No. But it's too risky. We'll have to think of something else.'

'What?' Ellen demanded.

Unsure how Sarah would react to my plan to see Mrs Clarkson, I said, 'Could you take a sheet of notepaper from one of the rooms or the estate office?'

'What good is that?'

'I could write a reference for Sarah and she can get work somewhere else. Or - '

'No!' said Sarah. 'I'm not going to be a servant all my life - I want something better, I deserve something better - we all deserve something - '

'It won't work, Nathaniel,' Ellen said. 'Everyone knows everyone else around here - '

'In London?' But as soon as I'd said that I realized that most aristocrats, whether they lived in London, Wales or Scotland, knew each other. And if Sarah did not want to be a servant any more my going to Mrs Clarkson was useless.

'We have to think hard and plan,' said Sarah. 'What else can we do if we want to leave here and not be servants?'

I didn't know. But the more I thought about it the more appealing the plan became - if we could get away with it. I pushed aside visions of us all hanging on the gallows and put my mind to thinking how we could get away with it and how our life would be afterwards. After Ellen and I returned to the house Sarah went to Mayfair and checked the location of the jewellery shops.

The following day I had to go to Aylington Hall and Sarah came with me, full of plans.

'If we split the jewellery between the three of us,' she said, 'we can each go to different shops to sell it.'

I justified the planned theft by reminding myself that in denying Sarah the wages she was owed when they sacked her they had stolen from her. But I still thought the risk was too great and the punishment too dire. No judge would be interested in that as a defence.

'Do you want to be a servant all your life?' demanded Sarah.

Until Ellen had started talking about the possibilities, I had been, not content exactly, but I had accepted my lot. Now I realized that things had changed and so had my ideas. 'No, but I don't want to hang either. I want a safer way to get out. We have to plan and think. Do you want to hang?'

'No. There must be a way. If we go a long way from here - Australia - '

'That's where we'll go if we get caught - if we're lucky and they don't hang us.'

Back in London I thought hard. Sarah found out when the ships sailed to Australia and where they sailed from.

'Can't we all just go to Australia as free settlers?' I suggested.

Sarah enquired about the fare, and I, who earned more money than they did, couldn't afford it. It would take years before I had enough.

'Can't we do this next time they come to London?' I asked, hoping that by that time they would have abandoned the idea.

'No,' said Ellen. 'I might never get to London next time. The maid might be better by then, or they might want someone else to go.'

'It's this time or never,' said Sarah.

I prayed it was never, but Ellen and Sarah were swept up with visions of our new future. They needed me. They could not do it alone. We worked out that Ellen would have to take the jewels one night when the Gordon-Seymours were out at a party or at the opera. That gave us only a few hours the next day to sell the jewels and catch a train to the port. Once the ship left the dock we would be safe. Ellen and I would book under the names of Mr and Mrs James Clarkson. Sarah wouldn't need to change her surname because it was Brown, and as far as anyone else knew she was in Chichester and had nothing to do with the jewellery theft.

At first Sarah and I had to do nothing. It was Ellen who took all the risks. Because they had worked in the laundry and the laundry office Sarah and Ellen knew the arrangements at Aylington Hall. Each member of the family had their own hamper in their dressing room where they put the clothes for washing. The maids carried the hamper to the laundry office where each item was entered in a register. Each family member had their own register too. We discussed what type of person we had to masquerade as.

'We can't be servants,' said Ellen. 'Because we know they couldn't afford the fare. And we can't be aristocrats.'

'Why not?' Sarah asked. 'We sound like them. Mrs Clarkson taught us to speak properly – '

'Because why would aristocrats want to go to Australia?'

'Nathaniel can be the youngest son of an aristocrat,' said Sarah. 'Lots of brothers, so he's not important and he's not going to inherit anything. You can be his wife, Ellen. Or maybe he refused to marry who his family wanted him to and he was cast out.'

'What will you be?' I asked. 'My sister?'

'No. Ellen's maid. That way she won't have to take too many clothes from the family.'

'No,' I said. 'Not a maid – that's what you want to escape from and – '

'But if they miss their clothes there will be an outcry. If a servant's clothes go missing – it won't matter so much.'

'A widow then – your widowed sister,' said Sarah.

Ellen nodded. 'You can dress in black. I'll take a bit of black lace from one of the hampers or the sewing room so you can make your dress more elaborate, and if you're heavily veiled no one will see your face.'

'Will they even miss their clothes?' I asked.

Ellen shook her head. 'They've got so many. It's not until the clothes reach the laundry that they are entered in a register. If I take them out of the hamper in the bedrooms I can – '

'Be careful,' I said.

'Don't worry. I'm allowed to be in the bedrooms and it's my job to help carry the hampers to the laundry room.' She smiled. 'And it's also one of my duties to take garments to the sewing room to be mended, so even if someone does see me with a pile of clothes they won't be suspicious.'

'Where are you going to hide them?' asked Sarah.

'In the luggage room. The suitcases are empty now. The night I take the jewels I'll take the clothes too.'

Over three days Ellen stole four dresses, bonnets and gloves belonging to the Countess and her three oldest daughters. It would, I hoped, be weeks before the items were missed.

My mind whirled with thoughts of what could go wrong and how we could lessen the risk. 'I think it will be less suspicious if I stay at the house after Ellen takes the jewels.'

'Why? You're not going to back out, are you?'

Sarah asked.

'No,' I snapped. 'You should know me better than that. Why do you always think ill of me?'

'Sorry. But why do you want to stay on?'

'Because they'll be looking for both of us. If you and Sarah go to separate jewellers with just one or at most two pieces of jewellery – '

'Ellen and I have worked out what we're going to do and say,' said Sarah impatiently. 'Our husbands have fallen on hard times or they gamble or we're widows. We'll tell a different story of woe in each shop. I think we should stay away from the shops in Mayfair and go further – '

'Yes, good plan,' I said. 'How many shops do you think you can do in a day?'

'Depends on how much negotiating we have to do. It might look suspicious if we accept the first price they offer,' said Ellen. 'But we can't stay too long. We've got four days before the ship leaves Portsmouth. That gives us three days to sell the jewels. We'll travel separately to Portsmouth – we can't afford to be seen together.'

There was a letter I felt compelled to write.

Dear Mrs Clarkson,

I feel it is my moral duty to tell you that Earl Gordon-Seymour is a rapist. Years ago I saw him attacking one of the maids. When she became pregnant she was dismissed. I pray she went back to you and did not end up in the workhouse. I would have told you before, but knew that I might have ended up in jail or put in the workhouse if it was discovered that I was the accuser. Now I am leaving their employment I can speak out.

Fearful of being interrupted, I had to keep the letter brief.

At the London house I felt sick with trepidation the night of the planned theft. I saw the carriage taking the Earl and his wife to the Opera House in Covent Garden and I knew that they were going to a party afterwards. I regretted leaving the horses. If we had been staying in England I would have taken them and the carriage with me. The next morning my stomach was churning when I went down to the kitchens for breakfast. Thanks to my reputation of disloyalty, I had no friends and the other servants only spoke to me if it was necessary.

The housekeeper looked disapprovingly at the empty place. 'Ellen is late.' She turned to one of the maids who slept in the same dormitory. 'Do you know where she is?'

The girl looked confused. 'No. I thought she was down here. Her bed was empty when I woke.'

'Was she in the dormitory last night?'

The other maids in the dormitory nodded.

'Has anyone seen Ellen this morning?' asked the butler.

No one had.

I tutted.

'Nathaniel?' the housekeeper asked coldly.

I put as much moral indignation into my tone as I could. 'I saw her yesterday in the park with a man – a gentleman. He looked wealthy. If she does not return by tonight, I think we can conclude that she has gone off with him.'

'Did he look the type who would do her harm?' she asked anxiously.

'No. She will be all right. More than all right.' I shook my head in disgust. 'Girls like her always are.'

I pretended I didn't notice the glares. I managed to eat my breakfast. I managed to do my work as if everything was normal. All day I expected to hear an uproar about the missing jewels, but there was nothing. Everything seemed normal. The Earl and Countess entertained at home that evening and there was still no mention of a robbery. My fear was replaced by confusion. Had the hiding place for the key been changed? If Ellen had lost her nerve and not taken the jewels, where was she? I had no idea what to do. If I went to Portsmouth and they were not there I would have to return and explain my absence.

Lies swirled around in my mind. I had gone for a walk and been robbed and knocked unconscious? But as I would be wearing livery why would anyone try to rob me? I had gone for a walk and become so ill I collapsed? I gave up in despair. I would rather be answering questions about the robbery than having this uncertainty.

I decided to go to Portsmouth to meet Ellen and Sarah as arranged. Alternatives shot in and out of my brain, but the only thing that made any sense was that they had found an easier and less risky target. Or had they themselves been set upon and robbed? I arrived at Portsmouth not knowing if they would be there. I didn't see them at first.

A young woman I hardly recognized came up to me and held out her hands. 'James, I'm so glad you made it. We were getting worried. Come on, it's time to board.'

I had never seen Ellen in anything other than her uniform. The elegant, pale blue silk outfit, kid gloves, which hid her work roughened hands, and a bonnet covering most of her distinctive blonde hair, transformed her appearance.

'Ellen,' I whispered in relief. 'Did you take the jewels?'

'Of course. And sold them – most of them. We're rich.'

There was another girl beside her dressed in black. Her face was heavily veiled. It took me a few seconds to realize it was Sarah.

Chapter 34

The voyage was terrible. We hit storms and spent most of the time in the cabin feeling or being sick. On five occasions I was convinced the ship was going to sink. Although it was hell I reflected later that it worked in our favour. We rarely saw the other passengers or the crew. Even as we approached Sydney the sea was rough. Weak and exhausted we disembarked. Ellen and Sarah were thin and pale and I guessed I was too. No one we knew would have recognized us. Immediately we were on dry land we felt better. A porter took our luggage to a nearby hotel.

It was only the following day after we had eaten and had a good sleep that I discovered how rich we were. Sarah and Ellen had kept some of the more unusual pieces of jewellery. There was a pearl and diamond tiara and a diamond, ruby and emerald brooch. The flowers were made of rubies and diamonds and the leaves and stems were emeralds.

'We thought they would be too easy to recognize,' said Sarah. She went through her case and pulled out a pair of gold cuff links. 'And as these have got the family crest on them we kept them for you. And this,' she said, indicating the sapphire and diamond ring on Ellen's finger, 'is Ellen's engagement ring. You'll have to buy her a wedding ring to go with it,' she finished with a conspiratorial smile. 'So, Nathaniel when – '

'James – my name is James,' I whispered.

'Sorry, James. Are you pleased we did it?'

'Very.'

'You didn't hate them as much as I did.'

'He had no reason to,' said Ellen.

'Yes, I did, and I think I hated them even more than you did.' It was then that I told them that I'd witnessed the Earl raping one of the maids.

'I wish I'd killed him.'

'I wish you had too,' said Sarah. 'But you might have been caught and hung.'

'It haunts me – I wonder what happened to the maid.'

'Probably the workhouse,' Ellen said grimly. 'If the baby survived it might have ended up with Mrs Clarkson.'

This rekindled childhood memories of screams. The first time I'd heard them, I was terrified. But one of Mrs Clarkson's staff had explained that a girl was giving birth. Sometimes the screams were followed, much later, by the cry of a baby. Sometimes there was silence and a vicar would arrive. Sometimes there was a tiny coffin. More often there was a bigger one as well.

And it occurred to me that had the maid's baby survived it might have been placed in service at Aylington Hall when it was old enough.

We spent a week in the hotel making plans. We discovered that we could have up to seventy convict workers. We decided to get away from Sydney, which was fast growing into a flourishing town. We all bought new clothes in a shop called David Jones, which was almost as grand as any shop in London. I purchased two carriages and eight horses, a compass and maps.

I chose the convicts carefully and interviewed them first. I checked the convict log books and rejected anyone who had been convicted of murder or any sort of violence. Initially I wanted twenty. I selected them by their occupation before their conviction, and the way I felt about them. The incongruity of my selection process did not escape me. I had stolen jewels worth a fortune, but wanted honest convicts – men and woman who had either been innocent of any crime and wrongly convicted or those who had stolen out of desperation.

Among the men I liked the look of were a blacksmith and a builder, both of whom claimed to have been wrongly accused. I believed them. If I had got away with robbery, it was reasonable to assume that many people must have been wrongly convicted. The others, a baker, two mill workers, a coal miner and a tin miner, four labourers, another blacksmith, a footman, a gamekeeper, five maids and a governess all admitted their guilt for the thefts of items worth under one pound. I tested their honesty by giving them money to buy tents, sheets and blankets, pots and pans and provisions for the journey to Queensland. They all came back with their purchases, and gave me the change.

Two horses pulled each carriage and we changed them over every fifty miles. We took our time and we earned the respect and loyalty of our convicts. When we stopped for a rest in the afternoon of the first day I addressed them.

'This is a new country. My wife, my sister and I came here willingly. You did not. But we are all in the same place. After seven years you will be free and you will be given a grant of land. During your time with us, you will be treated fairly. We all want the chance to build a new life away from the injustices in England. I hope that we will all work well together.'

We always chose a place near a stream or river where we washed, collected fresh water and let the horses drink. Ellen, Sarah and I helped erect the tents when we stopped for the night. As Ellen and I were supposed to be married we shared a tent. On the first day's drive Sarah had built up such a good relationship with three of the women convicts that they all slept in the same tent. We all ate the same food. We made sure the horses were not overworked.

We talked to the convicts and listened to their stories. John Osborne, the builder from London, had been lodging with a man and his wife who owned a pub next door. He did not drink and resisted their efforts to get him to patronize their pub. He also spurned the wife's efforts to seduce him.

'They set me up,' he said. 'One day some aprons

and caps and handkerchiefs went missing. They called the police who searched the house and found them under my mattress. When I protested my innocence and asked what they thought I would gain from stealing aprons they said I would sell them. The accusation was so wild I was shocked when they arrested me. I was even more shocked when I was found guilty.'

When I thought what we had got away with I felt like giving him a packet of money and telling him to escape, but I liked him and I needed his skills as a builder. I told him I believed him and would do all I could to make his life with us as easy as possible.

Bored by the many details about the number of sheep and where and how they were purchased, the amount of wheat, prices and details of plantings and wheat varieties Virginia left them out. 'It's their lives that are important,' she thought.

The day work started on building the homestead I asked Ellen to marry me. 'I know everyone except Sarah thinks we're married, but – '

'No,' she said.

'But it's a sin not to.'

'Is it? In whose eyes? The church? I despise the church with their well-fed vicars who live in big vicarages preaching at us, fawning to lords and ladies and telling us to be grateful for our lot. We will have a ceremony – but just you and me.' She took off the wedding ring she had been wearing since I had bought it in Sydney, gave it to me and pulled me over to the oak tree we had planted when we first bought the land. It was still small, but in twenty years it would shade the front of our homestead.

'Sarah, should be with us,' I said.

'Later. This is just between you and me.' She looked at the sky. 'And whoever or whatever is up there. What shall we say?'

I took her hand and kissed it. 'I love Ellen and will always love her. I will work hard for her and make her happy.'

Ellen looked at me. 'I vow to love Nathaniel till the day I die. Please bless us with children - healthy children who we will love and teach. We will be kind to them and not force them to marry anyone they don't want. We will be kind to our servants and our convict workers.'

'And, God,' I finished. 'It might be wrong of me to ask this, but we stole a lot of valuable jewellery, and so far we have escaped, please let us stay free for the rest of our lives. We will put the money into the land and make it beautiful.'

The sun was setting and the sky was red and gold as I slid the ring back on her finger.

'What shall we call our place?' she asked.

I saw a tree with yellow fluffy flowers. 'Acacia.'

One of our first priorities was to cultivate a vegetable garden and get an orchard planted. We worked all day digging and marking the layout, making it similar to the vegetable garden and orchards at Aylington Hall. The soil is rich and fertile and it wasn't long after we planted the seeds that the soil was dotted with green shoots. There is a stream with plenty of fish. That, along with eggs from the chickens we bought, will be our main source of food until we get pigs, cows and sheep.

Yesterday Sarah and John Osborne got married, **Nathaniel had written in 1834.** She wore the pearl and diamond tiara, which looked better on her than it did on the forlorn Gordon-Seymour girl who was forced to marry a fat, ugly old man. Ellen helped her make her dress and she looked beautiful with her dark hair going well with the white dress and the pearls. As a wedding present we gave them five thousand acres of our land, which they have named Eumeralla.

1835

Ellen is expecting a baby. I worry about her and she tells me not to. Sarah is also expecting her first child.

1836

Joy! Ellen has had a son. She insists that we call him Nathaniel. Thank God they are both well.

Sarah has had a son. There is only three weeks between our boys and we hope they will become good friends.

1842

A terrible day. Sarah and John's oldest son came galloping to Acacia. John was bitten by a snake. We gathered as many of the men as we could and rushed to Eumeralla, but by the time we arrived John was dead. What a tragedy for Sarah. She and her five children are distraught. Ellen and I will do all we can to help them. We are making the funeral arrangements and have sent five of our convicts to Eumeralla to help Sarah.

'I always wondered why the homestead at Eumeralla was not as beautiful as the one at Acacia,' Virginia said to Alex. 'But John Osborne had died before he could build a new one.'

The last entry was in 1881

I'm an old man now – I've just had my seventieth birthday. All these years later it still amazes me that we succeeded. Luck or God was on our side. Ellen is sixty-three and so is Sarah. She has seven grandchildren. Ellen and I have been blessed with five sons and six daughters and we are grandparents to five boys and eight girls.

```
Acacia is in safe hands.
```

'It was in safe hands for generations and then – no,' Virginia said to herself. 'I mustn't think like that again. It's in safe hands now, just not the Clarkson's safe hands.'

When Virginia finished typing the diaries she photocopied them and put them in binders. She sent a copy to Fiona and another to Gabriella and Keith at Eumeralla. When she and Alex visited Kingower one weekend she gave a copy to Margot.

'Did anything strike you about them?' Virginia asked her.
'In what way?'
'About the robbery. Something strange?'
'No, but I read them years ago.'
'One thing puzzles me. How did they get away with it? Did you ever wonder?'
'No. I just accepted that they did. What is it that puzzles you?'
'The timing – they had so little time to escape. Such a huge robbery – I would have thought there would have been an enormous manhunt.'
'There were no phones in those days. Someone would have had to go to the police station to report the crime – I don't know how long that would have taken. If I remember correctly the three of them divided the jewels between them and took them to different jewellers to sell them. Is that right?'
'No, just Ellen and Sarah. They dressed in her ladyship's daughter's clothes and they were well spoken, but jewellers were the first places the police would go, I imagine.'
'It depends how many jewellery shops there were in the area. And how quickly the jewels were sold. Was the London house in Mayfair?'
'Yes. They had two. I think the other one was in Victoria near Buckingham Palace. The ship to Australia sailed four days after the theft. Surely that's plenty of time for the police to question the jewellers and set up a manhunt. They must have suspected that they'd leave the country – why weren't the ports teeming with

police?'

'Well, it's no use speculating. They got away with it and that's all that matters.' Margot smiled. 'And I've got a stunning ruby and diamond brooch and a pearl necklace, the tiara is worn by family brides and you've got a pearl necklace. I'm going to give away all my jewellery – '

'Why?'

'I'm getting old and my generation of female Lancasters haven't got a record of longevity. I'm the only one to have reached old age. Since Kim's death I'm not as energetic as I used to be. Getting up in the mornings is more difficult and I look forward to going to bed at night. I thought the other day that if I was told I was going to die soon I'd be happy. Anyway – I'll give the pearls to Catriona and I want you to have the brooch.'

'Thank you, Margot. I know I don't deserve it. I was horrible to you and I'm sorry.'

'You were only a child – '

'I was fourteen – I should have been more mature about it. And as Eleanor was always reminding me – my father was a widower. It wasn't as if my father had divorced my mother so he could marry you.'

'I was so sure that you'd all love me, or at least like me. I wasn't used to being hated. Your father should have known how you'd all react – you were his children after all. He should have alerted me – I would have been more prepared. I was excited about meeting you all and being your stepmother. I never thought about replacing your mother, but I did want to mother you all and look after you.'

Remorse battered Virginia. She had turned what should have been a happy time for Margot into an unhappy one. That Margot had heard her cruel words about being ugly would have been painful.

'Fiona told me you'd had a long talk. She told me about the things you'd overheard. It made me ashamed. You did nothing to deserve the way Laurence and Johnny and I treated you. Eleanor was right – we should have listened to her.'

Part 2

Repercussions

Chapter 35

April 1974

'I want to know what happened to the Gordon-Seymour family,' said Fiona when she finished reading Nathaniel's journal. 'All those curses raining down on them – if they were horrible employers, how would they have fared when social reform took hold? Is there any way we could find out?'

'Easy,' said Peter. 'You've got their name and the name of the house in Sussex.'

'But where in Sussex? We haven't got an exact address, just that it's near Chichester.'

'There are four things that could have happened. The house could have been demolished or fallen down. If that's the case it might have lots of houses on it.' He grinned. 'It might be a council estate.'

Fiona laughed.

'It might be a National Trust property – if that's the case we can visit it,' he continued. 'Fancy a few days away in Sussex?'

Fiona put her arm around him. 'What about a week? What else might have happened to it and them?'

'It could be a hotel. You're not going to like this, but the house could still belong to the family and the family might be flourishing.'

'Is that likely?'

'It depends how rich they were and how well they managed their wealth. And their heirs might have been different – kinder.'

'How could they survive? They weren't royal or dukes or anything. The two wars killed off lots of men. Women from the poorer classes found they could go into nursing or work in factories and not have to bow and curtsey. From what Nathaniel's written they sound atrocious, and their servants might not have felt loyal to them. The owners of Lanhydrock had to give up their property and they were good people – they were progressive – they even called their servants staff instead of servants.'

'If you had the choice would you rather work in a sweatshop in a big city with smog and polluted air and go home to a slum every night or would you rather live in the country with fresh air, wholesome food, clothes provided and somewhere to live? Okay they weren't paid much, but I know what I'd rather.'

'I would have rather been a nurse – but I agree with you about the factories. How badly would the loss of the jewels have affected them?'

He shook his head. 'If they were stinking filthy rich, and it sounds as if they were, they probably would have just bought some more. If they couldn't they might have had some paste ones made up.'

'Found it,' said Peter three weeks later. 'It's still owned by the Gordon-Seymour family – '

'Oh hell,' said Fiona.

'Hang on. From what I can see on the new and old maps a lot of the land has been sold. The house is open three days a week. Some of the rooms in the house have been turned into holiday apartments. And three cottages on the estate are holiday lets. The largest one sleeps six. How about asking Juju, Lynette, Yvonne and her boyfriend to join us?'

'Some good news at last,' Anne told Sebastian. She opened the booking diary. 'The cottages are all booked up for the next eight weeks. Six people have booked the butler's cottage for a week. A group of friends, I think.'

'I hope they don't make a terrible mess like the last lot,' said Sebastian. 'That sort of thing gives Beatrice and Quentin ammunition. Where are they coming from?'

She looked at the booking form. 'Cornwall.'

There were twelve people in the group waiting to be given a

guided tour around the house. A tall woman, who looked about forty, arrived with a click of high heels on the polished parquet floor.

'I'm Lady Beatrice Gordon-Seymour. My family have lived in this house for over three hundred years. The tour of the house will take about an hour. Please keep together and don't touch anything.' Her smile was frosty and Fiona wondered why she bothered. 'I will be happy to answer any questions you may have. Follow me.'

You won't be happy about answering the questions I'm going to ask, Fiona thought.

Peter winked at Fiona. 'Charming,' he mouthed.

'Lady nothing,' she murmured in his ear. 'Bossy Beatrice more like it.'

As they were shown around the ground floor, which included the kitchen and larders, Fiona imagined Ellen and Sarah at the sink scrubbing the pots and pans and peeling and washing the vegetables all day. The drawing room had antelope heads on the walls and tiger skin rugs on the floor.

'Did the family shoot these themselves?' asked a man.

'Yes,' said Lady Beatrice proudly. 'They went on hunting expeditions to India, Africa and Canada.'

'Disgusting,' murmured an American woman. 'Poor animals.'

Looking affronted Lady Beatrice turned away.

Upstairs Fiona thought about Ellen and Sarah removing chamber pots from the bedrooms and emptying them in the sluice room. She could almost see them in their housemaids' uniform changing the sheets, making the beds and polishing and dusting. She wondered what would have become of them if Sarah had not been sacked and Nathaniel and Ellen had not rebelled in the only way they could envisage.

When she saw the portrait of the woman at the top of one of the staircases she nudged June, who look up at it and grinned.

'This,' Lady Beatrice said, 'is one of my ancestors – my great – I can never remember how many greats – grandmother.'

She looks like a man in drag, thought Fiona. 'It's a beautiful tiara,' she said innocently.

Beatrice looked pained. 'I was just coming to that. The tiara was stolen. So were many other valuable pieces of jewellery.'

'Oh dear,' said June. 'When were you burgled?'

'We weren't burgled. It was a disgusting betrayal of trust.'

Fiona gasped. 'Your friend stole them?'

Lady Beatrice looked down her nose. 'No. Some servants stole them over one hundred years ago. Everything that my ancestor was wearing in that portrait was stolen. The diamond bracelet, the ruby and diamond brooch, the ring and the diamond necklace.'

'Were they caught?' Fiona could not resist asking.

'No. They were too clever. One was a coachman, the other was a housemaid. Somehow they found where the key to the safe was kept – we think the lady's maid was careless and the housemaid saw where the key to the safe was hidden.'

'How come they weren't caught?' said Fiona.

'It took a week for the theft to be discovered because they left the boxes and just stole the jewellery. They closed the empty boxes and put them at the back of the safe and the ones with jewels still in them they put at the front. Many of the boxes were black or dark blue velvet, so the lady's maid didn't notice anything was wrong at first. It's only when the Countess wanted to wear a specific brooch that she opened one of the boxes at the back, found it was empty and realized they had been robbed.'

So that's why they got away with it, thought Fiona. I wish I could tell this disdainful hag what really happened and why. She imagined her reaction if she told her that although Nathaniel had been part of the plot it was Ellen alone who had stolen the jewels.

'The lady's maid was sacked, of course.'

'Why?' asked Peter.

'She should have been more careful. It's because of her carelessness that the housemaid knew where the key was hidden.'

'Not necessarily,' said Fiona. 'The housemaid could have looked for the key and found it herself.'

Beatrice looked annoyed.

'How do you know who stole the jewels?' someone asked.

'She left a note.'

'Did they take the most valuable things?' asked June.

'Steal – not take,' Beatrice corrected her sternly. 'And all her jewellery was priceless. She had fifty brooches – they stole twenty of them.'

'That's a lot of jewellery,' said a woman with an American accent. 'How could one woman wear all that?'

Fiona grinned encouragingly at her.

'She didn't wear it all at once,' snapped Beatrice.

'I should hope not,' said a man who sounded like a Cockney. 'Would of been awful heavy. If she fell over she wouldn't be able to get up.'

The group chuckled.

'I suppose they just went out and bought more,' said Yvonne.

'No. The family was going through a bit of a bad patch. His Lordship was drinking too much and gambling. This robbery made him worse.'

And he was also raping young maids, thought Fiona.

'Were any of the jewels recovered?' asked Peter.

'No. I suppose they were broken up and sold separately. They'd be unrecognisable.'

No, thought Fiona. That tiara's in Australia and my sister's bringing it over for me to wear on my wedding day in four weeks time.

'It was an appalling act of treachery – they were trusted servants,' Beatrice declared passionately. 'I wish they had been caught and hung.'

Fiona couldn't resist it. 'But maybe they felt they were more deserving – if the man of the house gambled and drank – '

Beatrice's expression was so outraged Fiona almost laughed. 'The servants were well treated – '

'Well, I don't know about that,' said the American woman. 'They worked long – '

'It's how things were in those days,' Beatrice said coldly.

Yvonne shook her head. 'Doesn't make it right.'

Beatrice gave her an imperious look. 'While many people

starved on the streets the servants had somewhere to live, a job, they had food and their clothes – what more could they want?'

'More than half a day off a week,' said Fiona.

'More money,' said the American woman.

'A shorter working day,' said Lynette. 'I wouldn't want to finish work at midnight and then have to get up at five in the morning.'

Beatrice looked at her watch. 'Can we get on with the tour? I'm not here to discuss social issues from a hundred years ago.'

Peter squeezed Fiona's hand. 'Doesn't look as if the character of the family's improved much,' he whispered.

Fiona was pleased. If Beatrice had been pleasant she would have felt guilty.

Chapter 36

Sebastian was driving past the paddock on his way home from work when he saw a blonde girl stroking some of the horses. At first he thought she was a friend of Beatrice's, but she looked as if she was alone. He got out of his car and walked over to the paddock.

'Hello,' he called.

The girl turned around. 'Hi,' she said.

Momentarily speechless he stared at her, captivated by her beauty. 'You're Australian.' He held out his hand. 'I'm Sebastian.'

'June,' she said shaking his hand firmly. 'How long are you staying here?'

'I live here.' He gestured to Gardener's Cottage. 'There.'

'Do you know the Gordon-Seymour family?'

He nodded.

'What are they like?'

'Obnoxious.'

To his surprise she said, 'Good.'

'Can you ride?' he asked.

'Yes. Do you know if it's all right to ride one of the horses?'

Beatrice never allowed anyone she didn't know to ride the horses. 'Yes,' he said. 'Do you mind if I join you?'

She smiled. 'I'd love you to.'

Regretting that their ride was almost over Sebastian rode back to the stables with June. 'How long are you here?' he asked.

'Just the week.'

He lifted off one of the saddles. 'Where in Australia do you live?'

'I used to live in Queensland.'

'Where do you live now?'

'Cornwall.'

'Whereabouts is that?'

She looked at the sky and then pointed westwards. 'That way.'

'You mean – Cornwall in England?'

'Yes.'

He smiled. 'Can I see you again?'

'Are you doing anything tonight?'

'No.'

'Would you like to come to our cottage for dinner? You can meet my sister and her fiancé.'

Anne knocked on the door of Butler's cottage. It was opened by a stunning blonde girl. 'Hello, I'm the estate manager. I'm just checking to make sure everything is all right or if there's anything you need.' She never introduced herself to the guests as Lady Gordon-Seymour because she thought it would intimidate people.

The girl smiled and said, 'Hi, it's perfect. We love it.'

Her Australian accent startled Anne.

The girl looked concerned. 'Are you okay?'

Anne nodded. 'You're Australian.'

'Yes.'

'I haven't heard that accent for years – not since the war.' Feeling foolish she continued. 'I was a nurse in the Air Force and I was friendly with an Australian.'

The girl looked interested. 'Have you ever been there?'

'Unfortunately not. What part are you from?'

'I've lived in Queensland, Sydney and Melbourne – would you like to come in?'

The girl's friendliness contrasted so dramatically with Beatrice's superiority Anne was charmed. 'If I'm not interrupting you – '

'You're not.'

'Thank you.' She held out her hand. 'I'm Anne.'

'Fiona.'

Sebastian, I wish you were with me, she thought. I'm being so silly. I mustn't give in to such romantic notions. He'll find his own girl – but . . .

Fiona took Anne into the kitchen. 'This is Peter – we're getting married next month.'

Anne smiled and hid her dismay. To her amazement another girl, identical to Fiona, wandered into the kitchen. 'I've just met a gorgeous man – I've invited him to dinner and – ' She saw Anne and stopped.

'And this is June – my twin. Sit down. Would you like a drink – water, fruit juice, wine?'

'If you're having wine – I'll join you.' Although she hoped that Sebastian was the man June had met, she didn't say anything.

'And who is this gorgeous man?' asked Peter.

'I don't know his surname – but he lives in one of the cottages. We've got the same philosophy – he hates competitive sport. He can't see the point in bashing a ball over a net all day and he said that cricket is so boring that one day at school he almost fell asleep when he was fielding. He said people should work together instead of playing games where they have to beat someone else. He calls rugby 'thugby' and says that whips should be banned in horse racing. He likes chess though – says it stimulates the brain and is strategic.'

'Is his name Sebastian?' asked Anne.

'Yes – do you know him?'

Feeling elated, Anne smiled. 'He's my son.'

'Whacko,' said Fiona.

The word brought the memories flooding back. Afraid that she might burst into tears, she finished her wine and stood up.

'Do you want to stay for dinner too?' Peter asked.

She would have loved to accept, but she thought it better for Sebastian to not have her around.

Dear Sebastian,

The promised postcard from Cornwall. Fiona's parents, aunt and cousin, have arrived for the wedding and we are taking them all over the place. Anytime you feel like a holiday let me know. You can stay in the house with us or in the cottage if you'd rather. Hope all is well with your job and horses. We are busy with preparations

for the wedding, but all is going well. Best wishes to your mother.
June

Sebastian was mystified by the reference to Fiona's parents. Thinking he had somehow got their names muddled he showed his mother the card.

'Yes,' Anne said. 'I'm sure she said her name was Fiona. The other two girls were Lynette and Yvonne.'

'But they're identical twins, so why didn't June write *our* parents, aunt and cousin?'

Chapter 37

May 1974

The mantelpiece in the lounge was full of wedding cards, so Fiona took the new pile into the dining room to open them. She arranged them on the mantelpiece between the two lamps and the vase of flowers. She tore open the last envelope and took out the card. It wasn't a wedding card it was a sympathy card. Thinking it had been delivered to the wrong address, she checked the envelope, but it was addressed to her.

'Hell,' she murmured, thinking someone had put the cards in the wrong envelopes. 'Someone's going to be expecting a sympathy card and they'll get a wedding card instead.'

She opened the card.

> *Fiona,*
> *You will need all the sympathy you can get. The only thing Peter wants from you is your money. It is not too late to cancel the wedding.*
> *Urzula*

June, Lynette and Gabriella entered the room in their bridesmaids' dresses.

Gabriella swirled around. 'How do we look?'

Fiona stared at them.

'What's wrong?' asked Lynette.

'Nothing.'

Lynette saw the card in her hand. She reached over and took it.

Urzula had been off work for three days with flu. Her throat felt as if it was imbedded with glass splinters, her head ached and her chest hurt from constant coughing. She got out of bed and went into the kitchen. When she lifted the lid of the bin the stench hit her. She remembered that the rubbish was being collected today. Hoping she wasn't too late she opened the door. When she saw Lynette she tried to close it, but Lynette kicked it open and marched into her flat.

'How dare you come in here, Lynette. I did not invite you in –'

'You went into Fiona's house uninvited to spew out your lies – if you can trespass on others then we can trespass on you.' She batted Urzula's face with the card she had sent Fiona, hard enough for it to sting. 'Now listen to me, you ugly Polish peasant – '

'I am not a peasant. My father is a lecturer at the university and my mother is a dentist.'

'So you say. You look like a peasant.'

Lynette had caught her at her worst. She hadn't had a shower and her hair needed washing.

'You are the peasant, Lynette, not me. How many languages can you speak?'

'English – the only one I need. Are you familiar with the words slander and libel?'

Urzula tried to speak, but Lynette went on, 'Because you can be sued – and if there is any more of this rubbish you will be. Get it?'

'You have always hated me because I am a foreigner.'

'Yes, you're right – I do hate you, but it's nothing to do with you being foreign. It's because you're rude and think you're superior.'

'I am superior. Now leave my flat.'

'I will leave as soon as I can – it stinks.' She wrinkled her nose. 'And you stink too. You might be able to speak lots of languages, but you're dirty – '

Urzula pushed her. 'Leave my flat.'

'You should go to a psychiatrist, Urzula. You're insane.'

'Go away.'

'You're insane with jealousy. Fiona's got everything you want – beauty, money and Peter. And she's a natural blonde not like you. By the way, your mousy roots are showing. Ugly, dirty, stinking, peasant,' she said slowly spitting out every word. She left the flat and slammed the door.

Urzula went to the mirror. 'I am not ugly,' she whispered. 'I am ill. Fiona would look just as bad as I do if she had flu.' She stared at her reflection. Tears ran down her face. 'You will be sorry, Lynette. No one insults me and escapes my wrath. Fiona will be sorry too for running to you and telling tales like a child. Does she think you are her mother?'

When Urzula arrived at Lanhydrock one Saturday two weeks before Peter and Fiona's wedding to familiarize herself with the area surrounding the church, she was pleased to see a wedding car arrive. Now, instead of guessing, she would know where the bride would get out and her route to the church. It was a sunny day and the Bentley stopped a distance from a gate. The bride and her father got out and were joined by the bridesmaids. The photographer took some photos and they all went through the gate, down the narrow pathway bordered by trees and shrubs, and into the church.

Visitors to the house and gardens stood and watched. In one way this suited Urzula, as it meant she could stand behind the onlookers and remain unseen till she ran forward a threw the jug of coffee over Fiona. But unless the element of surprise was so great, she could be grabbed and unable to break free. When the bride was out of sight and people drifted away, she explored the area surrounding the church. For her plan to work she had to remain unseen till Fiona arrived. She would have to watch from a distance. She couldn't risk being seen by Peter or anyone she knew.

She went through the gate and followed the path to the church. Perhaps she could hide in the bushes and step out in front of Fiona.

'I will have to work out my escape route too,' she murmured.

She had almost planned her strategy when the church bells rang. She went home. It was time to make her concoction. She put the kettle on and put six heaped table spoons of instant coffee into a jug. When the kettle boiled she poured it in the jug and stirred in milk and sugar.

'Not only are you going to look a mess with your ruined dress, you are going to stink, Fiona. This will ferment nicely for two weeks.' She covered it with a plate and put it on her balcony. 'Smelly, sticky and stained – that is what you will be. You throw coffee over me, I reciprocate. And I hope some goes over your bridesmaids too – especially Lynette.'

She thought about the consequences. Fiona could not walk down the aisle in a dress dripping with coffee and smelling of rancid milk. 'If there are other weddings that day they will have to postpone the wedding – postpone the wedding!' The new idea hit her. There would be no immediate risk of her being arrested. By the time an arrest was imminent she would be in London and no one would know her address.

Chapter 38

May 1974

Fiona had said that she didn't want any wedding presents, but Catriona and Margot wanted to mark the occasion with something permanent.

'What about a tree?' suggested Margot.

Mark had driven them to a nursery and they had chosen an oak sapling. From an ironmonger they ordered a plaque to be stuck in the ground beside it with the inscription :

> To Commemorate the Marriage of
> Fiona Lancaster and Peter Yelland.
> May 1974

Fiona said it was a perfect present, and Mark and Alex helped her plant it immediately.

Later in the day Catriona found Fiona alone in her bedroom. All the drawers in the chest were open and there was a pile of underclothes on the bed.

She knocked lightly on the door. 'Have you got a free moment?'

'Yes, Tree. I'm just making room for Peter's clothes when he moves in.'

Catriona knew the walnut bedroom suite had been left by Mark Bolitho, but the room suited Fiona, who had softened the masculinity of the furniture by having pale blue walls and floral curtains with crimson roses and green leaves on a navy background. She thought how Stefan, with his abhorrence of floral patterns, pastel colours and antiques would have detested this room. She wondered if he had seen it when he was staying here. The windows were wide open and the smell of the newly mown grass mingled with Fiona's perfume. A photo of Ruth in nurse's uniform stood on the mantelpiece, along with a vase of red roses and a lamp.

Everyone else was downstairs and Catriona hoped they would not be interrupted. 'I wanted to say thank you for inviting us and putting us up. Things have been . . . difficult between us and I was surprised to be invited.'

'Oh, Tree, I'm so glad you came. Dare I think that we're friends at last and that you've forgiven me?'

'I haven't forgiven you.' She saw Fiona's downcast expression. 'Because,' she went on hurriedly, 'there isn't anything to forgive – and there never was, was there? Kim's fiancé – he was attacking you. You didn't lie, did you?'

Fiona shook her head. 'I don't know how far he would have gone – he might have come to his senses and stopped. I promise I didn't encourage him.'

'I believe you. It's you who have to forgive me, Fiona. Can you?'

'Oh, Tree, of course I can. Thank you.'

Catriona found herself wishing that Fiona and June lived in Australia.

'Are you all right, Catriona?' asked Margot the morning of Fiona's wedding. 'You're not worried about meeting Stefan are you?'

'No, I'm fine, Aunty Margot.'

'I'm surprised he's still coming. Fiona told him you'd be here.'

Catriona nodded. 'I'm surprised too. I thought he'd back out when Fiona told him. Don't worry about me. Seeing Stefan again – when Fiona told me I just didn't care. It was as if she was talking about some casual acquaintance. We probably won't see much of him anyway.'

'You will at the reception – I'm not sure what table Fiona's put him on, but she said it wasn't ours. There's going to be a disco afterwards . . . he doesn't know many people so it'll only be natural for him to approach us.'

'Don't worry about me, Aunty Margot.'

But the familiar feeling of jealousy was gnawing at her. On her own wedding day, she had suspected that Stefan was more interested in Fiona than he was in her. Peter looked deeply in love with Fiona and she looked deeply in love with him. Any thoughts she had that he might have been marrying Fiona because she was wealthy were dispelled as soon as she saw them together. His family seemed to adore Fiona as much as Stefan's family had adored Catriona.

I'm divorced, she thought. Living where I've lived most of my life. I used to feel superior to Fiona in everything but looks. Now the only things I've got that she hasn't are brains and a career – and where have they got me? It hasn't made me happy. Fiona's got a sister – two sisters if I count Gabriella, and I haven't. Fiona can ride – not as well as I can, but who cares? Doug thinks he loves me, but he'll find someone else. Barring disaster Fiona and Peter are going to have a terrific life together – the sort of life Stefan and I should have had.

Fiona's found love. I've become so cynical and bitter I don't know if I ever want to commit myself to marriage again. Doug says he loves me, but Stefan said the same. Ha! I've got two men wanting me and telling me they love me, but how long would it take for things to go sour? Am I going to end up lonely like Aunty Ruth?

Catriona had expected Virginia to at least cause some conflict, but everything was calm, everyone got on well, and yesterday Rose and Virginia had an companionable time picking the flowers and making them into bouquets and headdresses. She heard Virginia praising Rose and telling her that she should have been a florist. The family dinner two nights ago had been a triumph of excellent food and stimulating company and conversation. Fiona had planned the menu, which had a vegetarian option for Catriona and Peter's cousin Yvonne. While Fiona, with help from Virginia and Rose, had prepared the dinner, Catriona, Margot and June had set the table with Ruth's silver cutlery and crystal glasses, in Trelawney's beautiful dining room. Ruth's china had been the sort of thing Catriona would have preferred, but she had given in to Stefan's dislike of elaborate designs and Kim had bought them plain white china with a silver rim.

I gave in to Stefan too much and too often, she thought.

'Tree, Aunty Margot! Breakfast's ready,' called Fiona from the foot of the stairs.

After breakfast Catriona got dressed and then helped the bridesmaids and Fiona. They had all done their own hair. Unlike Catriona's stiff hair on her wedding day their hair was free of hairspray and teasing, and shone in the sunlight that streamed through the window. She thought how lovely and natural they all looked.

'You're not wearing those,' June announced with glee when Fiona picked up her pearl earrings. 'Because you're wearing these instead. From Peter – he asked me to give them to you.' June handed her a velvet box.

Inside was a pair of emerald and diamond earrings.

'They match your engagement ring,' Catriona said hiding her envy with a smile. 'You look lovely, Fiona.'

'Thanks, Tree.' Fiona took her hand and squeezed it.

Gabriella did up the clasp on Fiona's pearl necklace. Lynette helped her put on the diamond and pearl tiara and arranged her veil.

Catriona had been to dozens of weddings, but they had all been similar and unmemorable. Only Fiona would be imaginative enough to have the bridesmaids' dresses in different colours, she thought. Only Fiona would have colourful bouquets made from the flowers in her garden. Only Fiona would get married in a small and ancient church with atmosphere. Her wedding photos with Lanhydrock House in the background would be spectacular. The only unusual thing about Catriona's wedding had been the horseshoe shaped cake, which Fiona had copied.

Chapter 39

On the morning of the wedding, Urzula woke to brilliant sunshine. She imagined how pleased Fiona would be when she looked out the window, and how her pleasure would make Urzula's actions more painful. Everything was ready. Her cases were packed and she'd put them in the boot of her new car the night before. The furniture had come with the flat and the only things she owned, apart from her clothes, were a few pieces of cutlery and crockery and bedlinen.

Confident that Peter, or anyone else she knew, would not notice her sitting in her new car, Urzula got to the church early so she could watch everyone arrive. Her trepidation grew when Peter and Charles, his best man, drove into the parking area, but they parked a safe distance away. In a morning suit with a white carnation in his button hole he looked handsome and cheerful.

She looked at her watch. 'You will be far from happy soon – just the opposite,' she whispered.

They left the car park and went through the gate into the grounds of the church. When people she knew arrived she sat very still. No one noticed her. When a woman who looked like Fiona and June got out of a car accompanied by Mark Bolitho, Urzula's heartbeat increased. Fiona's mother, she thought. Mark opened the back doors and two other women, who were tall and thin joined them. The older woman looked as if she was in her seventies and the younger one in her mid twenties. In spite of the difference in their ages they were very alike.

Ten minutes later two black Rolls-Royces, with white ribbons fluttering over the bonnet, drove over the cattle grid into the car park. Three bridesmaids got out of the first car. Urzula was surprised to see that their long silk dresses were the same simple style but different colours. Lynette's was blossom pink, June's was pale blue and a girl Urzula had never seen before wore pale yellow. They all wore floral headdresses. The second car stopped and the driver got out and opened the back door.

Urzula caught her breath and bit her lip in a jealous rage. Fiona was devastatingly beautiful. Holding her diaphanous veil in place was a tiara. She wondered if the pearls and diamonds were real. A single strand of pearls encircled her long neck. The photographer took photos of Fiona and her father and visitors to the house came into the car park to watch. When the bridal party went through the gate, Urzula waited five minutes before getting out of the car. She was so nervous her legs were shaking.

The onlookers were drifting away. She opened the gate and walked slowly up the gravel pathway. She almost fell over with alarm when she heard footsteps hurrying behind her, but fortunately she didn't know the late arrivals. She stepped aside to let them pass. The wedding march stopped just as she reached the door. In the porch were arrangements of white, pink and yellow carnations with blue hyacinths and fern, which matched the flowers in their bouquets.

She waited for her breathing to steady. When the first hymn ended she walked into the church and stood in the central aisle. Talking a deep breath she said loudly, 'Peter Yelland is already married!'

For a few seconds there was silence. Then Peter spun round. 'Liar.'

'You are already married. There is proof. I have seen it.'

The congregation started murmuring.

'Can the wedding party and the accuser, please come with me,' said the vicar. He spoke briefly to the organist who began playing, *Jesu, Joy of Man's Desiring*.

In the vestry Peter's face was white. Fiona was looking stunned and her father was looking furious. If they had been alone she thought Lynette would have hit her.

'She's a liar,' said Peter. 'I am not married and never have been.'

'One moment,' said the vicar. He looked at Urzula. 'Do you have proof?'

'The proof is in the records at Somerset House in London.'

'Did you get a copy of the certificate?'

'No. I did not think to.'

'She didn't get a copy, because none exists,' said Peter.

'Yes it does. In February 1969 Peter James Yelland married Janet Elizabeth Jones at the Chelsea registry office.'

'I've never heard of her!'

'Why have you waited so long to make this accusation?' the vicar asked. 'The bans were read – '

'It is something Peter told me – '

'This is – '

The vicar held up his hand. 'Mr Yelland, please. Let her speak.'

'Peter told me when he had had too much too drink one night. We had been going out for a while . . . I mentioned something about us getting married and he told me that he was already married to someone else. He had been drunk and didn't know her very well – '

'This is utter lies,' Lynette exploded. 'Peter doesn't get that drunk – and he hardly ever goes to London!'

The vicar looked at Peter. 'Were you in London in – ' He turned to Urzula, 'what year did you say?'

'1969. February.'

'I can't remember – '

'The Beatles – you saw them playing on the roof,' she prompted.

Peter looked trapped. 'Yes,' he said. 'I remember now.'

Fiona sank onto a chair. Her father put his hand on her shoulder.

'But I didn't marry anyone. I was there with friends. We heard the Beatles do their last performance on the roof. But I never married anyone. I've never heard of this girl. Urzula knew I was there because I told her I'd heard the Beatles on the roof. We hadn't planned it – it just happened. We were wandering around exploring London.'

'Peter told me he had been drunk and they had got married. They were together for a week and then she disappeared. He said they had an argument. He came back to Cornwall knowing he had made a bad mistake. He tried to find her so they could get divorced, but he did not know where she was – he went to the address she had put on the certificate, but she did not live there any more. He only told me because he was drunk. At first I thought he was lying because he did not want to marry me – '

'Who would?' said Lynette. 'They'd have to be – '

The vicar silenced her with a stern look, then said to Urzula, 'Continue.'

'When I heard he was going to marry Fiona I had forgotten about what he said until a few days ago. Then I thought I had better make sure he was not about to commit bigamy, so I went to Somerset House and there it was – the certificate of marriage.' Urzula could see from the vicar's expression that he knew she was lying.

'There are certain procedures that have to be followed,' he said. 'One can't simply walk into a registry office and get married. Did Peter say how long he had known this girl?'

Urzula hadn't thought of that. She lowered her head pretending to think. 'They were at school together . . . I think that is what he said.'

'I wasn't,' said Peter.

'You said earlier that they hadn't known each other very well,' said the vicar. 'Now you're saying that they were at school together.'

'I got the impression that, although they were at school together, they did not know each other well. I do not know if they were in the same class. They were not friends. They bumped into each other in London . . . and got to know each other better – much better.'

'You said you were in London with friends,' said the vicar to Peter. 'Are any of them here today?'

'No,' said Peter. 'One lives in America. The other one was going to come, but – '

'He did not want to witness the wedding that he knew would be bigamy,' said Urzula.

'His father died suddenly,' Peter finished, emphasizing every word.

'Even if they were here they would not have been with you all the time when you were in London, would they, Peter?' she said, worried that the vicar would dismiss her accusations.

'The wedding can't go ahead until the records have been checked,' said the vicar.

Peter turned to Fiona, knelt beside her chair and held her arms. Looking her straight in the eyes he said, 'Darling, I swear to you that she's lying. I hope you believe me.'

To Urzula's vexation Fiona, instead of looking doubtful or angry, stood up, threw back her veil and nodded. 'Yes,' she said firmly. 'I do.'

'Now,' said the vicar to Urzula. 'I need your name and address. You've made a serious accusation – '

Urzula told the vicar her address and he wrote it down. 'Peter can verify the address. He has spent many nights there with me.'

'That's enough,' said the vicar looking at her with distaste. 'Is this her address?' he asked Peter.

'Yes.'

'Are you aware, Miss Luk, that an accusation that stops a marriage service and is proved to be false, is a criminal offence?' asked the vicar.

'I had not thought about it, but it makes no difference. When you check the records you will know that I am telling the truth.'

'Then an announcement will have to be made to the congregation.'

Catriona had never thought she would admire Fiona. When the vicar made his announcement the congregation sat in silence.

Then Fiona turned and faced them. Her voice was amazingly steady. 'Peter and I will marry as soon as these allegations have been proved false. But the reception at Trelawney will be as arranged. The marquee is up and the food has been prepared, and it would be a crime to waste it. Even the photographs will go ahead and we'll all try and look as if none of this has happened.

Urzula Luk has ruined our wedding day, but not our lives or our future.'

Margot walked up to Fiona and kissed her. 'Bravo, Fiona,' she said. 'Bravo.'

Urzula was so anxious to get away before the guests came out of the church she slipped on the gravel path, tearing her tights and grazing her knee and palms. When she scrambled to her feet Lynette was standing in front of her. She struck Urzula across the face with her bouquet, and grabbing the front of her dress pushed her so hard she fell over again. When she was able to stand up Lynette had gone. Her knees and palms stung and were bleeding. She limped to her car and drove to Trelawney. The marquee that was lined with swathes of white silk was on the lawn. Urzula went inside. The tables were set with white cloths and there were vases of flowers which matched the bouquets, on each one. Urzula picked up a menu card.

Starter
Smoked Salmon
Cheese and tomato tartlet
Main
Beef Wellington
Harvest vegetables in Hollandaise sauce
Pudding
Pavlova
Strawberries and cream

What a waste, she thought. The head table was festooned with pink, blue, yellow and white ribbons and a three tier wedding cake stood on another table. Gathering saliva in her mouth Urzula went over to it intending to spit on it.

'Can I help you?'

Urzula swallowed and turned around.

A woman wearing a black dress and a white apron and cap was staring at her in alarm. 'Heavens, they haven't finished already, have they?'

'No,' said Urzula. 'I got lost on the way to the church – then I had an accident.'

The woman looked at Urzula's knees. 'Oh, dear, poor you. Sit down and I'll see if I can find some thing to bathe them with. Some look quite deep.'

'Thank you,' said Urzula. She watched the woman go towards the house. As soon as she went inside, Urzula hurried back to her car. She drove out of Trelawney and took the road to London.

During the photos outside the church and in the grounds of Lanhydrock House Catriona found herself standing next to Stefan. He smiled at her, and to be polite she smiled back. At the reception he was sitting at a different table and had his back to her, but during the disco he came over and asked her to dance. Suspecting that he had deliberately waited for an emotional number she accepted. *Send in the Clowns* was not only poignant it was fitting to their situation.

'How's Doug?' he asked.

'Good.'

'Are you . . . '

'Yes.'

'Then I won't tell you I love you.' He squeezed her hand. 'Be happy, Tree.' When the song ended he led her back to her table and left shortly afterwards.

I knew Fiona's wedding would be memorable, but not this dramatic, she thought when all the guests, and Peter's family, had gone home. They were in the drawing room. Fiona was still in her wedding dress, but had taken off her veil and tiara. Rose was in the kitchen making coca.

'If you are married to someone else I'll punch you on the nose,' said Alex calmly.

'Alex!' protested Virginia. 'We don't – '

'And even if she was lying,' he continued, 'how on earth was your judgement so bad as to become involved with someone who is malevolent enough – '

'Alex, please,' said Margot. 'Let's wait until the registers have been searched.'

'It's not as if we were engaged,' said Peter. 'At first she seemed lovely – generous and intelligent.'

'It's not Peter's fault, Dad,' said Fiona.

'Well whose fault is it?'

'Urzula's,' said Margot.

'I hate seeing Fiona hurt.'

'I'm not hurt.'

'You will be if he's married to someone else,' Alex retorted.

Rose came in with the mugs of cocoa.

'Thanks, Rose,' said Fiona taking the tray from her. 'It's not as if Peter was going out with an ignoramus – she could speak seven languages and was a fantastic skater – '

'Why are you defending her?' Alex asked.

'I'm not defending her, I'm defending Peter's choice of girlfriend. You're the one who questioned his judgement.'

'Who ended the relationship, Peter, you or Urzula?' Alex asked.

'I did.'

'Why?'

'I'd begun to see her true nature – '

'Which was?'

'Rude, arrogant – she wasn't like that at first. Our break up coincided with me meeting Fiona.'

'It sounds as if she can't cope with being rejected,' said Virginia. 'I think we should all go be bed soon – it's been a dreadful day – '

'Not really,' said Fiona. 'No one died or got murdered or injured.'

'Fiona, you're phenomenal,' said Catriona sincerely. If someone had told her what would happen she would have expected Fiona to explode with fury or burst into floods of tears, but she was calmer than everyone else. Lynette had been furious and had ended up crying. Gabriella had been so shocked she had hardly spoken all day. Peter's parents had been dazed.

The guests had tried to do as Fiona had asked and enjoy the

reception. Although she had requested that no one give them presents, the marquee had been crowded with gifts, most of which were shrubs or rose bushes. Their neighbours had clubbed together and bought them a foal.

Would I have been able behave with such dignity and grace if this had happened to me? she wondered. What would I have done if Stefan hadn't turned up at the church?

'Yes, there have been worse days,' agreed Margot quietly.

'Our future plans are to get married as soon as the registers have been checked,' said Fiona. 'I don't know how long it will take. The good thing is that we'd put off our honeymoon so we could spend more time with you, before you go back to Australia. But, Dad, please apologize to Peter.'

'I will – when the registers have been checked.'

When the registers had been checked Fiona and Peter got married on a weekday with only the family members as witnesses. Fiona decided not to wear her wedding dress and wore a linen suit in emerald green and a small hat. Alex and Virginia left the next day on a trip to Europe. When Fiona and Peter went on their honeymoon to Yorkshire two days later Mark worried about Urzula. Was she insane enough to cause even more harm? He confided in Lynette, Charles and Yvonne.

'What else can she do?' Charles asked.

Mark shook his head. 'Difficult to say – harm the horses, set fire to the stables – she's not an animal lover. She might even set fire to their house.'

'But she'd be the obvious suspect,' said Yvonne.

'If no one saw her – no witnesses . . . '

'She wouldn't risk being seen in Liskeard,' Lynette said. 'Not after she walked out of her job and raided the petty cash. I heard that she left her flat in a filthy mess, the cheque for her rent bounced and she didn't pay the electricity bill. With any luck the creature's gone back to Poland.'

Chapter 40

When Urzula arrived in London she stayed in a cheap bed and breakfast and looked for somewhere to live the following day. The only place she could afford was worse that the one she had lived in before she had moved to Cornwall. The bedsit was tiny and she shared a kitchen and a bathroom that stank of mildew. The owner lived in a flat in the basement and he collected their rents. As he demanded cash payments it was the opinion of the tenants that he did not pay tax. Urzula would have reported him, but guessed that he would put up their rents to cover the tax he would have to pay.

She knew she couldn't get a job as an estate agent without a reference, so she looked for other positions. Knowing she would be unable to afford to go to the hairdressers she dyed her hair to match her natural colour of brown. She looked at the mirror. 'Drab, ordinary brown,' she muttered. 'But at least no one will recognize me.'

She did not inform the credit card company of her new address and was pleased to have escaped paying them what she owed. To prevent being traced she decided not to use them again and cut them up. She found a job in a small grocery shop, which she hated. The hours were long, the owner was surly and the money was half of what she had been earning as an estate agent. The only thing she liked about it was that she was paid weekly in cash. The three weeks she had been there felt like three years. Any well paid position needed a reference. She had never wanted to contact Peter again, but she was desperate.

Before his marriage Peter had always looked forward to the end of the day and the weekends. Now he longed for them. Living with Fiona had increased his love for her. There were no irritations or conflict. He had known couples who were madly in love, but when they got married they became aggravated with each other and their love waned. Peter, who had lived in harmony with his sister and two cousins, found it difficult to understand.

Life in the rented house, although fun, had been chaotic. He had usually skipped breakfast and made do with tea or instant coffee when he arrived at work, and bought sandwiches or a pasty from the nearby bakery for lunch. He always had clean shirts, but often forgot to iron them. The house was untidy and when they had a party or visitors they had a frenzied cleaning spree beforehand.

Life at Trelawney was organized. The house was always clean and smelt of furniture polish and fresh air. He never ran out of clean clothes. Rose ironed his shirts and put his folded underwear and socks in the chest of drawers. On weekdays Fiona got up before he did, and prepared breakfast. June always woke early to see to the horses and Fiona would call her when breakfast was ready. When Peter came into the kitchen there was a smell of toast and coffee. She took as much trouble over breakfast as she did with other meals, and set the table with jars of honey, marmalade and jam and glasses of fruit juice. There was a variety of cereals, or she cooked bacon and eggs when he wanted them. She made sandwiches for his lunch with bread she had baked herself.

When they visited National Trust properties she bought recipe books from different periods and had fun experimenting. She bought a food processor and made her own soups. They ate in the kitchen during the week and the dining room at weekends and holidays. In the darker months there were candles on the table. In the warmer months vases of flowers replaced the candles. She enjoyed giving, and going to, dinner parties. She got on well with his family and she, Lynette and Yvonne had become friends. June, subtly, made sure they had plenty of time alone.

His colleagues and friends envied him. 'She's not only beautiful and rich she can cook,' said one.

His freedom from financial worries added to their envy. To his amusement they kept pestering him about June. Did they think she'd be interested in any of them? Did she have a boyfriend?

Could he invite them to dinner? Peter had arranged a dinner party, but to their dismay, none of them had aroused her interest. 'That's because you were all competing for her attention,' he told them. 'You behaved like slavering dogs. She was embarrassed.'

After he went to work Rose would arrive to wash the dishes and do the cleaning. Fiona, who insisted on having fresh meat or fish, went to the butcher or fishmonger in Liskeard and then spent part of the day outside with June and Jack, gardening, tending to the horses or teaching at the riding school. In the late afternoon she picked the vegetables for dinner and went into the house to start cooking. Peter's arrival home was always met with affection and a cup of tea. So he was shocked when he arrived home one evening and found her fuming.

'Will we never be free of this bloody woman?' she stormed, thrusting a letter at him. 'It's addressed to you, but I opened it, because I recognized her writing.'

> *Dear Peter,*
> *As you will know I have left Liskeard and am living in London. I cannot get a job as an estate agent without getting a reference. I will leave you alone and cause no more trouble if you agree to give me a good reference. I will say that I was working at your agency and that you were my manager.*
> *If you refuse you will hear from me again. This is just a warning. You know what I can do and the lengths to which I will go.*
> *Urzula*

'This is what I feared,' said Mark when they showed him the letter. 'I didn't think you'd heard the end of her.'

To Peter's surprise when he got home on Friday evening, Fiona and June were no longer upset or worried. Mark was with them and still looked concerned. After making Peter a cup of tea Fiona gave him a letter she had drafted.

> *Urzula,*
> *Due to her father's ill health, Fiona and I have moved to Australia.*

After much soul searching June came too. Naturally we will not tell you our address.
Why don't you go back to Poland? If all Polish people are as cunning and nasty as you, then you should get on very well. You might find some peasant desperate enough to marry you.
Peter

'But how – '

'Hang on, Peter, this can work. We address the letter to Urzula, put it in an airmail envelope and send it to Eumeralla. I'd send it to my parents if they weren't in Europe. Keith or Gabby can post the letter in Dalby, so it'll have a Queensland post mark.'

Peter laughed. 'Where did you get that brilliant idea from?'

She looked droll. 'It runs in the family.'

Mark looked doubtful. 'She mightn't believe you. She might come here to check if you've told the truth. And even if she does believe you – Fiona, I'm sorry, but I think she's mad. Your letter's very insulting.'

'But true,' said Peter.

'Yes, but it might make her even more deranged than she already is.'

'The things she's done to us so far have been risk free to her,' said Peter. 'What else do you think she might do?'

'She knows where all your family live. She might target Lynette or your parents because she knows how much they mean to you.'

'And she hates Lynette,' said Peter slowly.

'But Lynette, Charles and Yvonne have moved to a smaller house,' said Fiona.

'But my parents haven't, and she knows their address.'

'Oh, Christ,' said Fiona. 'But they have got a dog.'

'We can say that they've gone to Australia too,' Peter said.

Mark shook his head. 'But if she decides to check to see if you've told the truth – it'll be easy for her come down here at night and wander around.'

'Actually all she's got to do,' said Fiona, 'is ring up the agency from London and ask for you. If you answer she'll recognize your voice. What are we going to do?'

Mark was silent for a minute. Then his expression brightened. 'I've just thought of something.'

'What?' they asked in unison.

'I've got to go somewhere. I'll be back later tonight. I'll call in first thing tomorrow morning.'

The next morning Peter and Fiona were making breakfast, when Mark and June came into the kitchen. They were both holding puppies.

'Your guard dogs,' said Mark. 'I bought the whole litter – two for you, one for me and one for Rose and Jack.'

Fiona stroked the head of the puppy June was holding. 'They're very sweet, but they don't look as if they could guard a mouse.'

Mark put one of the puppies on the floor and it scampered around sniffing. 'Rottweilers – best guard dogs in the world. Easy to train too. You could leave your doors and windows open all night and be secure.'

'What does Barker think of them?' asked Peter.

'He's mothering them. They all slept together in his basket last night.'

'What are we going to call them?' said Fiona.

'I usually let them choose their own names – Barker barked incessantly and the name came naturally.'

Fiona looked down at Peter's feet where one of the puppies was chewing his shoelaces. 'We could call that one Chewer.'

June giggled. 'No – it sounds too much like sewer.'

'How long will that letter it take to get to Australia?' Mark asked.

'About a week,' said Fiona.

'Then another week for your reply to get to Urzula. Then she's got to work out what to do – if anything.'

'And if she does nothing, then we've got two pets,' said Peter picking up the puppy from the floor. 'Do you think I should moderate the letter – make it less abusive?'

'The more insulting it is, the more she'll believe we've gone to Australia,' said Fiona. 'If it sounds cautious she might suspect we're lying.'

'I've just remembered what the vicar told her,' Peter said. 'She's committed a criminal offence. I'll let the police know. We've got no address, but we have got a box number. And this is a threatening letter – I'll show them.'

Chapter 41

Urzula had given up hope that Peter would reply. There had been letters from her parents, but nothing else. When she went to the post office and opened her box she recognized Peter's writing on the airmail envelope with an Australian stamp.

'Miss Luk,' said one of the postal workers. 'There's a parcel here for you – it's too big to fit in your box. Hang on, I'll get it for you.'

She opened Peter's letter and read it while she waited. In despair she screwed it up and dropped it on the floor.

The man came back five minutes later looking flustered. 'Sorry it's taken so long – someone's put the wrong shelf number on the docket. Would you like to sit down while we find it for you? Come out the back,' he said holding up the leaf of the counter for her to go through.

She was about to follow him when she saw the other workers staring at her. Suddenly wary she said, 'It is all right. I will come back in ten minutes – I have got some other things to do.' She gave him a brilliant smile and walked away as nonchalantly as she could. She went into the supermarket opposite and watched the post office from the window. She didn't have long to wait before a police car pulled up. She left the supermarket by the rear doors and ran across the car park. By the time she reached the house where her bedsit was she was breathless. She found the door open and the hallway crowded with luggage. She was so anxious to get inside she tripped over the strap of a handbag.

'Sorry! Are you hurt?'

Urzula was helped to her feet by a girl who looked about twenty.

Before she could speak the girl said, 'I've just come back from a trip – '

A young man came running down the stairs. 'Quick, before old misery guts in the basement sees you,' he said softly. He picked up two of her cases and went up the stairs.

The girl picked up the other one and her handbag and hurried after him. On the landing she whispered, 'I'm not supposed to be here, I'm between trips.'

'I see,' said Urzula, who didn't see.

'Would you like a cup of tea?'

Normally she would have refused, but she was in desperate need of company so she accepted. The small room the girl was sharing with the young man had one bed and two inflatable mattresses and sleeping bags on the floor.

'Illegal lodgers,' he said with a grin. 'But it's only for a few days at a time. Rents are exorbitant in London – for the money I pay for this room I could have a flat with two bedrooms in Brisbane.'

Over a cup of tea Urzula learned that the girl was from New Zealand and was travelling around Europe for a year before going home.

'You can speak seven languages?' asked the girl in amazement. 'How come you're living in this dump? You should be earning a fortune.'

'I have not been here long. I am finding my way – '

The girl looked triumphant. 'Become a courier!'

'A courier?'

'Yes. There's a vacancy with European Adventure Tours – that's who I've just been on holiday with,' the girl said excitedly. 'The courier's mother had a heart attack and he's gone back to Australia. Hang on – I'll see if I can find their address. It's somewhere in Bayswater Road.' She searched through her handbag. 'Here it is.' She handed Urzula a card. 'It's fab. I've just been on the five week Russian one – they go to Poland and Scandinavia, Denmark, Finland and Norway. It's better than the camping trips – but it's far from glamorous.'

Until she saw the European Adventure Tours brochure Urzula was pessimistic. The company advertised itself as a cheap but more comfortable way for young people to experience Europe than camping.

The accommodation is basic, but you don't have the hassle of putting up tents, she read. *Instead, there are separate rooms for the males and females, which accommodate up to ten each, and small double rooms for married couples. Instead of having to leave the building there are showers in the block, as well as a kitchen for the sole use of the resident tour company.*

At her interview she could see that she had impressed the three tour managers and was relived to be offered the job. It would solve a lot of her problems. She would be paid, have free food and lodgings and be able to use her languages. Perks included free admission to the opera and ballet, art galleries and museums. She knew that the police would not only be after her for her false declaration, but she had sold her car to a man who had no idea that it had not been paid off. The estate agent in Liskeard would have reported the theft of petty cash and the landlord of her flat might have reported her non-payment of rent and utility bills.

'The travellers are mostly Australian, but on the last Russian trip there were five New Zealanders and two South Africans,' she was told.

'South African? I did not think they were allowed into communist countries.'

'You're right. They travel on different passports – don't worry it's legal. Many South Africans have British, Irish or American parents, so they can get passports from those countries. We want our couriers to have a trial run before we throw them into the job – it also gives them a chance to see if they like it and are suited to it. Because of your languages we think you would be perfect for the Russian trips, which are also the most difficult, as I'm sure you'll appreciate. The border controls into and out of the USSR are rigorous and as you speak Russian this will help speed up the process. Are you working at the moment?'

'No,' she lied. 'I have not been in London very long. I was staying with a friend in the country.'

'Do you have a Polish passport?'

'Yes.'

'I don't suppose you have a visa for the USSR?'

'Yes, I do. I was going to visit my mother's brother who lives just over the border, but he was in some trouble with the regime and they thought it was better if I did not come,' she said, glad that she could tell part of the truth. The only reason she had been willing to go to Russia was not to see her family, but to visit the Hermitage.

'Excellent. The tour we would like you to have a trial on leaves in three days – would that be time enough for you to prepare?'

Urzula beamed. 'It will.'

Chapter 42

June 1974

Catriona had been expecting her father to meet her at the airport when she arrived back from England, but Douglas was there. Her first alarmed thought that something was wrong was dispelled by his smile when he saw her. He hugged her and told her he missed her and took her to a restaurant for lunch instead of driving straight back to Kingower. It was early and they were the only two customers. After they ordered he looked at her seriously.

'Tree, we have to talk about our relationship.'

Her spirits plummeted. He wants to end it, she thought. When he said he missed me he meant at work not for myself. She sat in silence. He looked ill at ease. I'm not going to help him say it.

'I have a confession to make.'

He's found another girlfriend. That didn't take long, she thought. Or maybe he wants to go back to Melbourne.

'Years ago, I wanted to ask you out,' he said. 'When we were at uni. I was a bit shy then and kept putting it off – I thought I had plenty of time.'

'Because I was plain?' she asked her voice tinged with irritation.

'No! You're not plain – I never thought of you as plain. Anyway, I didn't get around to asking you and then you and Stefan started going out. I was cross with myself, but then told myself that you wouldn't have wanted to go out with me and Stefan had saved me from making a fool of myself.'

Not sure what he was trying to say, Catriona nodded.

'Will you marry me, Tree?' he asked softly. 'You don't have to give me your answer now. Think about it.'

Her doubts dwindled, as did her thoughts about reminding him that she had failed in one marriage and was he sure he trusted her constancy. 'I don't need to think about it.' She smiled. 'Yes, let's get married.'

Over the next few weeks they made plans for a small wedding. She wanted an engagement ring as different as possible from the solitaire diamond one Stefan had bought her.

'What about this one,' said Douglas pointing to a central oval ruby flanked by two smaller ones and the trio surrounded by diamonds. 'It's classical.'

She slipped it on her finger.

The jeweller nodded. 'You have beautiful hands – it suits you.'

She smiled. 'Yes. This one.'

Catriona thought that they would have to get married in a registry office because she was divorced, but she and Douglas wanted a blessing in the local church.

'Why just a blessing?' asked the vicar.

As he knew the family well and had married her and Stefan and conducted Kim's funeral Catriona was puzzled. 'I'm divorced. I didn't think I could get married in a church.'

'It's at the discretion of the vicar, and I'd be happy to marry you in this church.'

Catriona's parents' suggestion that she and Douglas move into the homestead and they move into one of the cottages, was rejected.

'But this house is far too big for the two of us,' said David.

'There's only two of us,' said Douglas.

Margot smiled. 'At the moment.'

'Well, yes,' said Catriona.

'Have you talked about what you want to do when you get married?' asked David. 'The cottages are perfect for one, but a bit crowded for two. A double bed would take up most of the room.'

'What do you want to do, Tree?' Douglas asked. 'We could buy a house in the town – that way we'll be able to walk to work. I feel bad about not contributing anything – if we bought a house together – '

'You are contributing – you help with the weekend horse rides and – '

'I meant financially.'

'I know you did – but there's more than one way of contributing.'

'There certainly is,' agreed Margot. 'We have three options. You move into the homestead, which you don't want to do and I understand that. We can knock your cottages into one – Alex can draw up the plans and oversee the work. The other option is – my house is too big for just one. I could move into the homestead – I spend a lot of my time here anyway. You and Douglas move into my house and we can use the cottages for the riders from Melbourne who want to stay at weekends.'

'Don't make a decision now,' said David. 'Think about it.'

'What do you think, Tree?' Douglas asked her when they were making dinner in her cottage that evening.

'I'm not sure.' She laid slices of buttered bread in the bottom of a casserole dish. 'There are good things about all the choices. Which one do you favour?'

'Buying a house together in the town. I should support you when we get married.'

'Rubbish – any more talk like that and I'll call everything off.'

He stopped whisking the eggs and milk, and put his arms around her. 'Stop being so fierce. I'm not expecting you to give up work – except when you get pregnant.'

She kissed him. 'Good. Sorry I got fierce.'

He picked up the whisk. 'Do you have any objection to buying a house in the town?'

'No . . . but Mum and Dad are getting on. Dad's sixty-five and Aunty Margot's seventy-four.' She sliced a tomato with a sharp knife. 'When I lived in the town Kim was still here. My choice would be moving into Aunty Margot's.' She arranged the tomato and slices of cheese on top of the bread and butter.

'She's been independent for so long, would she feel stifled in the homestead – I know it's got ten bedrooms but . . . ?'

'She might do. My mother irritates her – she's incapable of making a decision about anything – even what to have for dinner.'

'She might be happy for Margot to take over,' he said as he poured the beaten eggs and milk into the casserole dish.

'Yes, she probably would.'

'What about suggesting that Margot move into the homestead before we get married to see how she feels about it,' suggested Douglas.

Catriona mashed the potatoes. 'Yes. That way she can change her mind and not worry about causing inconvenience.'

'Or . . . I've just thought of another alternative. Your Uncle Alex could draw up plans for a section of the homestead to be converted into a flat for us – nothing huge. Just one bedroom, lounge, kitchen and bathroom.'

Catriona pulled a face. 'This is going to sound horrible, but living so close to my mother would drive me crazy.'

He laughed. 'It'd probably drive me crazy too. I've never said anything before . . . she's so nice – '

'Too nice,' said Catriona. 'She hardly ever says anything, just nods like a mechanical toy when my father speaks. He could say something outrageous and she'd agree with him. When Kim and I wanted to be vets Dad was against it – he thought we should get married and have lots of children, preferably boys, for Kingower. It was Aunty Ruth who was our champion – she and Dad had a huge argument – '

'What about Margot?'

'She's a lot older so I can understand why she agreed with Dad – she didn't come out and say it, but she didn't defend us either. It's the only time I've ever felt angry with her, but it's a generational thing. Ruth understood us because she'd wanted to be a doctor, but her father wouldn't let her study medicine so she had to settle for nursing instead. She was very bitter about it. Dad blamed her when we came home from uni with different ideals from his.'

'What sort of ideals?'

'Conscription, the Vietnam war and politics. He agreed with conscription and the war, and was a liberal, so he was incensed when we came home and challenged him about his beliefs.

Although Aunty Ruth disagreed with us she said we had a right to our own opinions. Dad said it was her fault that we were being brainwashed.'

Douglas laughed.

'Is it all right if I keep my own surname – personally as well as professionally?'

'Absolutely. You know how I feel about that.'

'What about our children's surnames?'

'The boys can have mine and the girls can have yours.'

She hugged him. 'I hope we have one of each.'

He kissed her. 'I hope we have lots of each. When can we get married?'

'How about as soon as possible?'

Catriona enjoyed her small wedding to Douglas far more than she had enjoyed her wedding to Stefan. She wore a suit, did her own hair and had no bridesmaids. Only family and close friends were present. Their ten day honeymoon in a simple hotel in Sherbrooke Forest was far happier than her disastrous two week honeymoon with Stefan in a luxury hotel on the Great Barrier Reef.

When they arrived home there was a letter from Stefan.

> *Dear Tree,*
> *I'm living in London. I've sold my flat in Melbourne and have bought a flat in Windsor not far from the castle. I'm teaching at the local school and am enjoying it, but it's only temporary.*
> *Fiona told me about your marriage to Doug. Congratulations and my best wishes for your happiness.*
> *Stefan*

Ω   Ω   Ω

'I've missed Gabby,' said Tom, as he and Keith were bathing Toddles on the lawn.

Keith nodded. 'Even with Eleanor back Gabby not being here

makes a lot of extra work.'

'I didn't mean it like that – I meant – you know.'

Keith kept his expression neutral. 'No. Toddles, keep still. I know you hate it, but the more you wriggle the longer it'll take.'

'The thing is I've come to realize that I want to – do something with her.'

'Bake a cake?'

'No, you dag,' said Tom flicking water at him.

Keith grinned. 'You've have to spell it out for me.'

Tom wiped the soap suds away from the dog's eyes. 'She means more to me than just a friend. Thing is with her being a widow – I don't want to rush things – frighten her off. How is she about . . . well, starting up with someone else – me?'

Keith poured clean water over Toddles. 'Ask her.'

'Come on, mate, be helpful.'

'When did you start feeling like this?'

'As soon as I knew she was going to England. It just hit me. Now I worry that she won't come back – that she'll like England so much she'll stay there. She raved about the place in her letter – how green it is, all the lovely old buildings and the history. Life seems to be a lot of fun over there – more fun than she had here.' He released his hold on Toddles and she sprang out of the tin bath.

Before she could shake herself all over them Keith wrapped her in a towel and began to rub her dry. 'She is coming back – go and meet her at the airport.'

'But what if she wants to go back to England?' said Tom as he tipped the bath water over the lawn.

'And what if she doesn't? Wait till she gets back. You never know what'll happen if you let her know how you feel.'

Gabriella was overjoyed when she saw Tom waiting in the arrivals hall.

He swept her into his arms and hugged her tightly. 'Gabby, I've missed you so much.'

'Have you, Tom?' She looked into his eyes. 'Have you really?' she whispered.

'Sure have.' He kissed her lips and her joy merged with amusement that their first kiss was in such a public place.

'I was right, wasn't I?' said Keith as he led the horse out of the paddock.

Tom grinned and swung himself into the saddle. 'Sure were, mate. Things are good – about time too. Never seen my mum as happy as she is now. You and Sophie are getting on. Gabby and me are getting on too.'

Keith shut the gate and mounted his horse. 'I hope things go on being good.'

'Me too,' said Tom steering his horse towards a group of sheep. 'Life has a vile way of turning on you. We can't do anything to stop the bad things, we just have to adjust when they do hit us.'

'We can do things to make catastrophes less likely – '

'How?'

'Be cautious – careful. Don't do dangerous things.'

Tom nodded. 'Kim did something dangerous – I didn't want her to ride that horse – never knew why she did.'

'Maybe she felt infallible – as I suppose she had good reason to feel.'

'But Gabby's husband dying – there's nothing anyone could do about that,' Tom said. 'And you and June – neither of you knew – no one knew except Ruth.'

'But my Uncle Johnny,' said Keith, 'he shouldn't have rushed into that burning house again. He'd rescued one child – he must have known the roof was about to fall in.'

'Maybe he heard them crying or screaming – hard to ignore – but as you say, he took an enormous risk that killed him. And my ancestor – he was an unlucky bloke, according to those journals – transported for a crime he didn't commit – then got bitten by a snake – wonder if he could have prevented that.'

'Probably not. He was English – they didn't know much about snakes.'

Chapter 43

Urzula arrived back from the Russian tour in the middle of July. Determined to make a good impression she had suppressed her intolerance and offered help to the courier whose only language was English. The courier, driver and cook had brought cassettes of the Beatles, Rolling Stones, Abba, Elvis and the Seekers to play on the coach, and Urzula vowed that when she was the courier she would try and instil some culture into her travellers. She hid her contempt of the mostly Australian tourists who knew little about art, nothing about opera or ballet and the only classical music familiar to them were the tunes made popular by advertisements. She secretly agreed with the Soviet Intourist guide when he called them Australian capitalist pigs. To her amazement they had all burst out laughing.

After the trial run she had a meeting at the office. The courier, cook and driver had all praised her. As well as being offered tours for the summer and autumn she was offered the post of courier for the winter skiing trips in Austria, which ran from December to February.

'It's unfair to expect you to do all the Russian tours, so we'll give you one ten week Southern European one. It'll give you a bit of variety and although they are long, they are less of a hassle. How does that sound?'

'Perfect,' said Urzula.

The company owned a house in Notting Hill where the drivers, cooks and couriers could stay between tours. She shared a room, which she didn't mind, because the occupants were always changing. The furniture was basic and the bathrooms and showers were clean. There was one other female courier in the company and she spoke French and Italian and did the southern European tours. Urzula had two weeks leave before her first solo trip to Russia and Scandinavia began. During the day she visited museums and art galleries and at night she went to the theatre, concerts, opera and cinema.

She studied the list of travellers, pleased to see that there were plenty of men and no married couples. They were mostly Australian with some New Zealanders and two South African men, one of whom was travelling on an Dutch passport. The other had an Irish passport. The company liked the couriers to familiarize themselves with the people they would be spending five weeks with, before they met them. Attached to the list of travellers were their passport photos. The man she most liked the look of was Stefan Jovanovics who was a teacher. His name was a plus even though he had an Australian passport. She hoped he would be cultured and like classical music and art.

For the first time since she had arrived in England she was financially secure. She bought new clothes, mostly jeans, casual trousers and T-shirts and some more formal outfits for the opera and ballet.

At the beginning of August she packed her case and searched through all her opera, ballet and classical music cassettes. In Moscow they were going to the opera *Eugene Onegin* and the ballet *Swan Lake*. She had the complete recordings but, thinking that the Australians would be more receptive to excerpts, she bought cassettes of the highlights.

Stefan didn't realize who she was until she spoke. As the coach set off from London to drive to Dover she picked up the microphone.

'Good afternoon. I am Urzula Luk, your courier.'

He stared at her. He hadn't seen much of her in the church, but her name was on everyone's lips after the cancelled wedding. She introduced the driver and the cook and told them how long the ferry crossing would take. He tried to recall the event in the church. He had been sitting somewhere in the middle and, like other members of the congregation, he had turned around to look at her, but others had partly obscured his view.

Surely she was blonde, he thought. Perhaps I'm wrong. How common is the name Luk? It might be like Smith in Poland. She might not be Polish – she could be Russian. He knew that the girl at the church was Polish because he had heard Peter's sister ranting against 'that Polish peasant.'

Over the next few days he hoped he was wrong. She was an excellent courier and her fluency with languages was impressive. She was passionate and knowledgeable about opera, classical music and art and her stories about the composers and artists were absorbing, witty and educational. She would have been a great teacher, he thought.

Girls whose only interest was finding a husband and having a family bored him. He liked independent girls with careers and ambition. He convinced himself that the Urzula who had wrecked Fiona's wedding and this Urzula could not possibly be the same person. This Urzula would not have been an estate agent in Cornwall. She was too urban and cultured to bury herself in a country town with no theatre or major art gallery. But the voice is the same, he thought. But then I only heard her speak briefly. She's so good at this job she must have been doing it for years – at the time of Fiona's wedding she was probably somewhere in Europe.

Urzula was aware that Stefan kept looking at her, but she pretended not to notice. He likes me, she thought. She hoped her detached manner towards him would make him more keen. On the fourth day of the tour she saw him standing alone in front of a painting in the Van Gogh gallery in Amsterdam.

'Hello, Stefan, are you interested in art?'

'Just generally. I look at a painting and know whether I like it or not, but I don't analyse why. Your talk about Van Gogh was interesting – it's changed the way I view his art. I'm seeing things I wouldn't have noticed before.'

'If you were rich would you buy paintings?' she asked.

'No. I prefer bare walls. I hate ornaments – the less things in a room the better. How long have you been a courier?'

'This is only my second tour – the first I have done solo.' She was taken aback by his expression. 'What is wrong?'

'Nothing. When . . . I mean – what part of Russia are you from?'

She smiled. 'I am Polish – my father is a lecturer at the university – '

To her bewilderment he walked away. A few hours later she saw him later sitting alone outside a cafe.

'Good afternoon,' she said. 'May I join you?'

He shrugged. 'I'm minding the table – the others are inside getting more coffee so there won't be much room when they come back.'

'Shall we bring the other table over?'

He shrugged again. Perplexed by his attitude she dragged the nearest table so that it joined his. He made no effort to help her and she was about to dismiss him as an uncouth idiot or a misogynist when five others emerged from the cafe. He stood up and helped the three girls unload their trays and pulled out their chairs for them. As Stefan smiled and joined in the conversation about the paintings they had seen Urzula realized that his indifferent attitude was for her alone. Not wanting to be humiliated in front of the others she didn't speak to him again, but chatted to the others and answered their questions. She was able to impress them with her knowledge about art in general and Van Gogh in particular.

Stefan felt discouraged and torn. Short of asking Urzula if she had ever lived in Cornwall, which she would no doubt deny, he deliberated over what else he could do. I'll write to Fiona and Peter, he thought. Until they answer I'll avoid Urzula.

Chapter 44

The two dogs rushed to greet Peter when he got out of the car. Mark had been right about their names coming naturally. One always came into the kitchen when the kettle was being put on, so they called her Polly, and Kettle seemed an obvious name for the male. Mark had the other female, and as Barker followed her everywhere they called her Leader. Until he was trained Jack and Rose's dog persistently dug holes in the garden so his name was Digger.

He patted them. 'Have you been looking after everything? Did any nasty people come?'

Fiona was standing at the front door. 'No nasty people, but we've had the most extraordinary letter from Stefan Jovanovics,' she said after she kissed him. 'He's on a tour of Russia and Scandinavia and guess who the courier is?'

He put his briefcase down and loosened his tie. 'Not Urzula?'

'Yes, but he wasn't sure if it was the same Urzula, so he's asking us – speaks seven languages, loves art and opera, says her father's a lecturer at a university – '

'That's her,' said Peter.

'She's not blonde any more. He's given us the date they are due to arrive back in England and the address of the head office so we can inform the police if we want.'

He grinned. 'We do want.' He scanned the letter. 'We'd better let him know that it's her. He's given us all his mail addresses and the dates – the next one's in Russia – the one after that's in Poland. We'll send the letters to both – just in case there are delays.'

Fiona nodded. 'It sounds as if he's hoping it wasn't – he's admitted he likes her. Shame.'

'It makes me feel less foolish.'

'How?'

'What your father said.'

'He was upset. And I never thought you were foolish. I went out with a boy once who was charming at first, but he became increasingly nasty – it happens and you weren't married to her or anything.'

'I think we should ask Mark to address the envelope – she'll recognize my writing.'

'Yes. I've been on these trips so I know how things work. The courier collects the mail and distributes it so we should also post it out of Cornwall and put a fake name and address on the back. Lynette's going to London in a few days – she'll post it for us.'

Urzula collected all the mail at the site offices. Stefan received letters mostly from Australia, but he also received some from England. After receiving the letters in Leningrad his attitude toward her changed from indifference to hostility. They were on a river trip in Leningrad when Urzula found herself alone with Stefan. She had a headache and was sitting on the deck outside when Stefan walked over to the rail. She stood up and joined him.

'What did you think of the Hermitage?' she asked.

He looked at her coldly.

'Stefan, have I done something to offend you?'

He didn't reply. He turned his gaze back to the view.

'You do not like me, do you?'

'No.'

'Is it because I am Polish?'

'No. I have many faults, but hating someone because of their nationality is not one of them. I'll tell you why on our last day – when the ferry is heading back to England and the White Cliffs of Dover are visible.' He walked away.

Apart from Stefan's peculiar behaviour Urzula had enjoyed the trip and she was happier and more fulfilled than she had ever been. She met new people all the time and if she liked someone she could keep in touch with them and if she didn't they would vanish from her life when the tour ended. The ever changing people she met would increase her chances of finding a suitable husband. Added to her sense of achievement was the fact that she had succeeded in turning some of her group into fans of opera, ballet and classical music. Wisely she also played the pop music that the driver and cook had brought with them. Her close contact with Australians had softened her attitude towards them. Most of them were generous and friendly. There were some she disliked, but that was to be expected. She even found herself getting used to their accents and they no longer grated on her. The contrast between them and the two arrogant South Africans was vast.

She was looking forward to a week's rest in London. The accommodation was free and all she had to pay for was her food. Her future was secure. The pain of Peter's rejection was fading and she went for days without thinking about him. Everyone except Stefan had filled in the customer satisfaction forms she had handed out. She knew she should not read them, but she had read them last night in her cabin. They had all praised her. The cook and driver were also praised, but the most enthusiastic accolades were for her.

She had just finished breakfast on the ferry when she saw Stefan approaching her.

'Urzula, I promised I would tell you why I don't like you. Can we go out on deck?'

'Well?' she said, looking at the White Cliffs of Dover.

'I was a guest at Fiona and Peter's wedding.'

Although staggered she tried to look bemused. 'Who? What – '

'Don't pretend, Urzula. Your red face gives you away.'

She felt her face burn even more. 'I really have no – what makes you think I had – '

'You're an outstanding courier,' he said softly. 'It mostly due to you that I've enjoyed this trip so much and I've learnt a lot.'

'Good. Thank you. But what has a wedding got to do with me?'

'Causing a wedding to be stopped with a false accusation that the groom is already married is a crime.'

In spite of her burning face she felt cold. She gripped the rail. She thought about what she would do if the police were waiting for her at Dover.

'We all do dreadful things, Urzula, and that's why I'm going to give you a chance. Why did you do it?'

Tears filled her eyes, more from relief that he was giving her a chance than anything else. 'I loved him.'

'No, you didn't. If you had you would have let him go,' Stefan said. 'Have you never broken off a relationship with a boyfriend?'

She nodded.

'Did they seek revenge?'

'No,' she whispered.

'You not only stopped a wedding with a false accusation, but you publicly slandered Peter by saying he was about to commit bigamy. You've got lots of talents – you're the only person I've ever known who can speak seven languages. I think there's a lot of good in you. Go back to Poland – your father's a lecturer at the university – '

She wiped her eyes. 'I detest Poland. The communists are evil. I am not going back.'

'If you don't I'll tell Adventure Tours that you're wanted by the police. I'll tell them what you've done. Even though you're a brilliant courier I suppose you'll get the sack.'

'Please, Stefan do not do this to me – '

'You've done it to yourself. Every act, good or bad, has a consequence. If you get away with this you won't learn anything. The lesson you must learn from this is not to tell lies or harbour grudges. Instead of wasting your time plotting against Peter you could have found a new boyfriend. Fiona and Peter are married – I can't think what you thought you'd achieve. Go back to Poland. Tell Adventure Tours that your father is ill – or your mother. Otherwise . . . '

'Otherwise what?' she asked fearfully.

'In one week I'll go to the head office and ask for you. If I'm not told that you've gone back to Poland, I'll tell them. You'll get the sack and I'll also inform the police. It's up to you. You can save face, or face a ruined reputation and the police. But they may already know.'

She shivered. 'How?'

'I wrote to Fiona and Peter. I doubt that they will do nothing. They don't know where you live, but they know the date this tour is returning to England . . . the police might even be waiting for you at the port.' He began to walk away.

'Do you love her?'

He turned around. 'Who?'

'Fiona.'

'No. I love someone else.'

'Who?'

He seemed surprised by her persistence. 'Someone brilliant and talented.'

Hope flared in her. 'Me?'

His smile was cynical. 'You have got an enormous ego – that's something else you have to learn to modify. No, Urzula, not you. I treated her badly and lost her – that was my lesson.'

'I can not imagine you treating any woman badly.'

He shook his head. 'Trying to flatter me won't work, Urzula. You're on your own.'

When he went inside she looked at her watch. She had an hour to calm herself before they disembarked at Dover. She knew that if the police were not interested in her false allegation at Peter's wedding they would want to question her about the car she had sold, on which she had only made two payments.

She tried to look composed as she left the ferry. It is not as if I am a murderer or a spy or an IRA terrorist, she thought in an effort to ease her thundering heart. By the time she reached passport control her hands had stopped shaking and she was able to smile charmingly at the immigration officer. Thankful that she was not arrested she got onto the coach. Back in London there were hugs and farewells and a reunion was arranged for a week later. Terrified that the police would be waiting for her she delayed her return to the house until it was dark. She had dinner in a cafe and tried to work out a plan.

I will tell them at head office that Stefan kept pestering me on the trip and could they tell him, if he asks, that I have gone back to

Poland because my father is ill, she decided.

The next day she went to the office. The receptionist greeted her coldly and she knew that something was wrong. Stefan was right. Peter had written to them.

'We received this letter while you were away. It seems that you are wanted by the police, Miss Luk.'

'That is a lie – '

'No. We checked.'

'But he did tell me he was married and I – '

'It's not just your false allegation, Miss Luk. You purchased a car, made two payments on it, then sold it without telling the hire purchase company. You made no further payments. You stole the petty cash from the estate agency when you left without giving notice. There are unpaid utility bills at your flat in Cornwall and there was rent owing. There is also a lot of money outstanding on your credit cards. And you write threatening letters. A member of staff will come to the house tomorrow morning and escort you off the premises and take your key. Make sure you are packed and ready to leave.'

She was so frightened that she almost missed the significance of the envelope. If she hadn't recognized Peter's writing she would not have connected what he had told her in his letter with the plain envelope with the British stamp. If he and Fiona were living in Australia the letter would have been in an airmail envelope and have an Australian stamp.

When she left the office she went to a travel agent and booked her flight to Poland. She got one that left the following evening, by telling them her father was very ill. Terrified that the employee of European Adventure Tours would arrive with the police she left the house at dawn and caught a bus to the airport.

I will come back, she thought as the plane gathered speed down the runway. Maybe in two years when they have forgotten about me. The police will not be interested in me after so long – they have murderers and robbers to catch. I will get a job as a courier with another company.

She recalled every word of the insulting letter he had written.

You will pay for this, Peter. When I come back to England you will be sorry. You made me suffer. If it had not been for you I would have made a new life for myself. I was doing well. You have destroyed everything for me. I will do the same to you.

Chapter 45

September

When Anne came back from the hospital after visiting her husband, she called a meeting with Quentin, Beatrice and Sebastian.

'The news is bad,' she began. 'I spoke to the consultant . . . your father has cancer.'

Neither Quentin or Beatrice looked upset. She had already told Sebastian.

'How long has he got?' asked Quentin.

Anne knew what he really wanted to know was how long before he inherited Aylington Hall. 'They don't know,' she said. 'Until then I am your father's power of attorney.'

'What's that?' Beatrice asked.

'It means I have full financial control – '

Quentin looked furious. 'Who said?'

'Your father.'

Beatrice sighed. 'Stop spending money, get rid of the grooms, the cleaners and the cook, open the house for more days, stop having fun, work hard, et cetera.'

'Exactly. I'm pleased you agree.'

'I don't. I was being sarcastic. How about you making a few sacrifices?'

'I was coming to that. I'm going to move into the cottage with Sebastian. That will make room for the grand apartment to be turned into a self-catering flat and – '

'What about when our father comes home?' Beatrice interrupted.

'I'm sorry, Beatrice, but your father won't be coming home.'

Quentin looked pleased. 'So he's not got long then?'

Anne ignored him. 'I'll contact the travel agent and ask him to add another apartment to the brochure for next year's season. It'll have to be refurbished and as the last company did such an excellent job – '

'You're leaving the furniture,' said Quentin.

'Of course. Gold gilt furniture and silk brocade upholstery would look ridiculous in a cottage, and the four poster bed wouldn't fit through the door.'

Quentin puffed on his cigar. 'When he dies I will be the owner of Aylington Hall and your management will cease. I will put an end to all your schemes.'

Sebastian smiled. 'Oh my mother and I won't want to come back to our apartments.'

'I was about to say – except that one. You can stay in the cottage. If you wish to leave, I won't object and neither I'm sure will Beatrice.'

Beatrice looked apologetic. 'We'll still need Anne to be our estate manager. And Sebastian's work at the bank is useful – we'll need a loan to get the apartments done up.'

'Maybe. I'll think about it. But we will close the house to visitors – I'm fed up with hearing their common accents.'

Anne stood up. 'Then I predict that under your ownership this place will be bankrupt in two years – probably less. Perhaps we should ask the National Trust if they want it now.'

'Shut up, you.'

Sebastian glared at him. 'Don't speak to my mother like that.'

'I'll speak to her how I like. She's just a working-class tart who married our father for his money and – '

Sebastian stood up. 'If that's how you want it – fine. We'll leave here and you can let the place fall down.'

'Beatrice and I won't be giving you any money – I'm the heir.'

'We don't need money from you. And I can't stand this mausoleum of a place. I'm much happier in the cottage.'

'We shouldn't quarrel, Quentin,' said Beatrice. 'Our father's dying. We need Anne and Sebastian.'

Anne knew that Beatrice was worried about the future of Aylington Hall if she and Sebastian left. It was not because she liked either of them but, unlike Quentin, she knew when things had gone too far.

The day after her father's funeral Beatrice confronted her stepmother who was in the estate office going through the books. Anne looked up when Beatrice entered and then seeing her expression looked back at the column of figures.

'Give me the jewellery my father gave you, please.'

'No.'

'I knew you'd be obstinate – so let me put it this way. Give me the jewellery or I'll call the police.' She pointed at her stepmother's hand. 'Get those rings off.'

'They're mine. Your father gave them to me. *My* engagement ring. *My* eternity ring. *My* wedding ring.' She fingered the pearls around her neck. '*My* pearls and *my* earrings.'

'They are family heirlooms – they belong to me. I'll prove it.'

Anne sat back in her chair. She had been expecting Beatrice and Quentin to demand the jewellery back, but the swiftness and lack of subtlety had taken her by surprise.

'Do you understand me, Anne? You're a widow now – this place belongs to Quentin and he wants the family jewels back.'

Anne put some figures in the calculator. 'Take me to court then.'

'We will. You can be sure of that.'

'Go away – I'm trying to sort out the financial mess you and your brother have got us into. If this doesn't get sorted out you'll have more to worry about than a few pieces of jewellery. Instead of trying to get me to hand over what belongs to me, I suggest that you and Quentin do something to help. Quentin could give up drinking, gambling and smoking those stinking cigars – '

Beatrice stabbed her fingers on Anne's desk. 'Now my father is dead those jewels belong to me. It's our belief that Sebastian was not our father's son – he doesn't look like him and he doesn't look like you. So whose bastard is he?'

'Drop dead, Beatrice,' Sebastian said from the doorway.

Beatrice turned around. 'Quentin and I have discussed this.'

'Good. I hope I'm not related to you – you're both detestable.'

Beatrice folded her arms. 'We also want you to pay rent for the cottage. Don't see why you should live there for nothing.'

'Then why is Quentin not with you?' Anne asked. 'Why does he send you to make the demands?'

'He's probably too drunk to stand up,' said Sebastian.

Anne nodded. 'As I said, take me to court. I will not pay rent for the cottage, because – '

'Well just wait for the eviction notice.'

'Your father knew you and Quentin would make life as hard and unpleasant as possible for me after he died. That's why he's given me the deeds and put the cottage in my name. So there will be no eviction notice.'

'I don't believe you.'

Anne shrugged. 'Then go to the solicitor and check.'

Sebastian pointed toward the door. 'Scram, Beatrice. If you want us to pay rent for the cottage you'll have to pay my mother for her services. Otherwise she will leave all the accounts and filling in forms to you. You're both so useless you'll end up in court for tax evasion and debt.'

Beatrice stalked out of the room and slammed the door.

Sebastian sat in the chair opposite his mother. 'Are you okay?'

She nodded. 'Did you mean what you said about not wanting to be related to Beatrice and – '

'Yes. Is it true?'

Anne stood up. 'Let's go for a walk.'

They stopped at the cottage first. Anne went upstairs to her bedroom. She took a photograph album from the bookcase and removed a photo which she had hidden under another photo. She put it in the pocket of her jacket and went back outside. They walked into the forest and sat on a log by the stream.

'You don't have to tell me if you don't want to,' said Sebastian softly.

Anne pulled the photo out of her pocket and gave it to him.

'Ah. My father. He looks like me.'

'Yes. You not only look like him you behave like him. You've got his humour and good nature. I loved him very much. We were going to get married.'

'What happened?'

'Can't you guess?'

'He was already married? His wife refused to divorce him?'

'It was 1944. He was in the Air Force.'

'Oh, Christ. He was killed?'

Anne nodded. 'He was a reconnaissance pilot. He got the DFC.'

'What's that?'

'Distinguished Flying Cross. Posthumous.'

'What was his name?'

'Harry Johnson.'

'How did you meet? Where?'

'I went to London when I left school and did my nursing training at Guy's Hospital. I was desperate to get away from this place because Lord Gordon-Seymour was always leering at me and pestering me to sleep with him. Once he tried to kiss me, but I kicked him where it hurt and then lived in terror that my father would be sacked and my parents would lose the cottage and be homeless. But, luckily for me, he wasn't the vengeful type. I think it made him even more amorous. He and his wife abhorred each other. It was a marriage their parents forced on them. Some of those marriages can work, but she was obnoxious. When war broke out I became a nurse in the air force.

'Harry had a rough landing in a storm and sprained his wrist and fractured a few ribs. That's how we met. I remember the exact day in 1942. He joked about his injuries and said they could have been worse. He was so . . . relaxed and polite, but not stuffy. In the two years we were together he never lost his temper. He reasoned with people when they got angry about something. He had a way of calming things down.

'He went into reconnaissance because he didn't want to be responsible for killing anyone. Indirectly he was of course, and he knew that, but it was more remote. He wouldn't drop the bombs on towns and cities. He wouldn't see the face of the German fighter pilot the gunners on his plane would shoot. That's where you get your hatred of hunting and shooting from. Are you upset?'

'Heavens no. I'm pleased. Very pleased. My real father was a good man. I'm not related to Quentin or Beatrice.' He laughed. 'Why would I be upset?' He studied the photo. 'You can bring it out of hiding now – put it in a frame. If I'm upset about anything it's the thought of what could have been. Where did he live?'

'He was Australian.'

'Really?'

'His father was English, his mother was born in Australia – her grandparents were English.'

'So I would have grown up in Australia?'

'Yes. In Adelaide.'

'We would have been happy.'

'Very happy.'

'I'm sorry you had to go through all that. Did he know you were pregnant?'

'No. If he had we would have got married straight away. It happened the night before he left for the last time. Normally we were careful, but that night we weren't – I don't know why. If we had been married I would have been a widow instead of an unmarried mother. I wouldn't have had to marry – '

'What would your parents have said?'

'I'm sure they would have been angry. They wouldn't have disowned me, but they would have been upset.'

'So when you found out you were pregnant you came back here?'

'No. I was here, on leave, when I realized. I was so regular and the baby – you – made your presence felt immediately. Her Ladyship had been dead for over a year – she fell off her horse during a fox-hunt. He was hardly a grieving widower – he began pursuing me as soon as I arrived home. He asked me to marry him and I said yes. I know I cheated – '

'There was nothing else you could have done – '

'Yes there was. I could have gone back to London, had the baby and had it adopted. But the thought of giving away something that was Harry's . . . I couldn't do it. You were born eight months after we got married. I don't know if he ever suspected you weren't his son. He never acted as if he did.'

'Thank you for telling me. Now I know . . . I think we should get away from here. This is nothing to do with me – not in my blood. Quentin's going to be rabid with rage when he finds out you own the cottage. Let's sell it and move – '

'But where to?'

'Cornwall?'

Anne smiled. 'I thought you'd say that.'

Chapter 46

October

Fiona's reputation as a teacher who was good with nervous riders was growing. Some of the children were simply nervous types. Others had parents who made them anxious. In those cases Fiona persuaded the parents to go away and pick the child up at the end of the hour. If they didn't want to leave Mark would engage them in conversation, show them around the place and make them tea or coffee in the tack room. Initially things could be awkward with the more dominating parents, but they were soon so pleased by their child's progress they did as Fiona asked.

As soon as she heard the man's bullying voice she knew that the child would be nervous. She heard him before she even saw him. He bellowed at his wife and son to hurry up.

Fiona looked at Mark in consternation and hurried out of the tack room. 'Good afternoon,' she said, deliberately looking at the woman, whose expression was as petrified as her son's.

'Len Burdette. My son's got a riding lesson,' he said pushing the boy forward.

She looked at the little boy and smiled. 'Hello, you must be Paul.'

The child nodded and Fiona hoped he wasn't going to cry.

'Are you this teacher we've heard so much about?'

'I'm Fiona,' she said, wishing she could say, I'm not deaf so please lower you voice.

He grinned at her. 'Well I hope you can do something with this useless lump – scared stiff of horses. Scared of most things to tell the truth.'

And of you, she thought.

Mark came outside and held out his hand to the man. 'Would you like to come inside?'

To Fiona's relief they went inside and she took the boy's hand and led him to the paddock. Unsurprisingly the boy immediately relaxed.

'How old are you?' she asked.

'Five.'

She took him over to the Shetland ponies and told him their names.

She was pleased when he said, 'Can I ride one now?'

'Of course you can – but only if you really want to.'

'My father will be angry if I don't.'

Fiona debated whether to tell him his father didn't have to know and that she would lie to him, but thought that encouraging a child to lie was unethical. Instead she said, 'You can do anything you like when you feel ready. You don't have to do anything you don't want to.'

'He wants me to be a show jumper.'

'Do you want to be a show jumper?'

'I don't know. He wanted to be a show jumper, but he had an accident and hurt his back.'

She helped him up on the pony and showed him how to hold the reins. 'Are you comfortable?'

He nodded. 'I haven't been on a little horse like this.'

No wonder he was frightened, she thought. 'I'll lead you around the paddock.'

By the end of the lesson the boy had steered the horse himself with Fiona walking alongside them. His father bombarded him with questions when they returned to the tack room.

'Did you trot?'

The boy looked pleadingly at Fiona.

'Yes, he did,' she lied.

'The horse was big.'

His mother hugged him.

'Don't smother him!' snapped her husband.

I wish someone would smother you, Fiona thought.

'The only thing wrong with that child is his father,' said Fiona to Mark when they had left.

'Did he really go on a big horse?'

'One of the Shetlands – his father's the sort that you lie to . . . self preservation.'

'His wife's a nervous wreck,' said Mark. 'Didn't say a word for the whole hour.'

The following week the man came alone with his son.

'Where's your wife?' asked Mark.

'Told her to stay at home – she fusses and worries too much. Right, Paul, let's see you ride.'

'We prefer parents not to watch,' said Fiona seeing the child's expression of terror. 'Children are – '

'I'm paying for these lessons, so I want to watch – keep up with how he's progressing.'

'I understand,' said Fiona firmly. 'It's just that children are so desperate to do well in front of their parents and that causes things to go wrong.'

Mark smiled. 'Yes, I know whenever my parents were watching me ride I always fell off – they soon got to know that – ' he laughed. 'Stay here with me while Fiona gives Paul his lesson – I'll show you around. Would you like a cup of tea first?'

Fiona took Paul's hand and led him outside, before his father could object.

'That man is evil,' said Mark later. 'I don't think you should ever be alone with him.'

'That bad?' said Fiona in alarm.

'Yes. I didn't like the way he looked at you. I'll make sure I'm always here when he brings Paul for his lessons. And if he ever suggests I give Paul a riding lesson and you stay here – I'll refuse.'

'You think he's that dangerous?'

'Yes. Understandably you avoided looking at him, but I took note.'

Five days later June was putting down fresh straw in the stables when she saw a shadow. She turned round expecting it to be Mark, but it was a man she'd never seen before. As he came closer she could smell his overpowering aftershave.

'Fiona, I want to talk to you about my son. Are you alone?'

'Yes, but I'm not – '

He grabbed her. 'I know you're married and so am I but – '

June tried to pull herself free.

He pushed her further into the stall. 'I can't stop thinking about you.'

She took a deep breath intending to scream, but he clamped his hand over her mouth and pushed her jumper up. When his hands went to the waistband of her jodhpurs she tried to knee him in the groin.

'Silly girl – I knew you'd try that – I was ready for you.' He put his foot behind hers and gave her a shove. She fell backwards onto the straw. Before she could scream his hand covered her mouth again.

Realizing struggling was futile she stopped.

'That's better,' he whispered. 'No point in fighting it – you'll only get hurt. Just relax and enjoy it.'

She shut her eyes. Controlling her terror she went limp, and rolled her head to one side as if she had fainted. As soon as he removed his hand she screamed. He slapped her face twice and clamped his hand over her mouth so hard she tasted blood. She heard him unzipping his trousers with his other hand. He was tugging down her jodhpurs when she heard the growl. Polly sprang and gripped his arm in her teeth. With a howl of pain he tried to shake himself free. He clenched his free fist and tried to punch the dog, but June deflected the blow by pushing him away.

She struggled to her feet, just as Mark rushed into the stables. 'You!' he said furiously. 'Did he – '

'Nearly!' June gasped as she pulled up her jodhpurs. 'I'm all right.'

Kettle and Leader ran in followed by Fiona.

'Juju! What – '

'I'm okay – thanks to Polly.'

Mark whistled and Digger ran into the stables. 'Stay right there, Burdette. I'm going to ring the police.'

Clearly bewildered by the arrival of Fiona, Burdette tried to pull up his underpants and trousers.

'No!' snapped Fiona. 'As revolting as the sight is,' she shuddered, 'it's evidence of your intentions. At one order from me all these dogs will attack and rip you to pieces, so stay very still. Juju, your lip's bleeding – no don't wipe it – the police will need to see it. Sit down.'

June sank onto a bail of straw. Polly went to her and licked her hand. 'Thanks, Polly,' she murmured stroking her head. 'What a good and clever girl you are.'

Mark returned to the stables with Jack. 'The police are on their way.'

'Please, I . . . she . . . wanted it.'

'Any more lies and I'll set the dogs on you,' said Fiona. She saw that Burdette was deathly pale. 'Frightened?' She smiled. 'I bet you are. Polly, I hope you're all right and haven't caught any diseases from this lump of sewerage.'

'Don't think you'll get that MBE or whatever it is you were telling me about,' said Mark. 'Instead of going to Buckingham Palace you'll be going to court on a charge of assault and attempted rape. And you'll lose that well-paid job you were bragging about. The cricket club won't want you as its president either.'

The siren sounded.

'That was quick,' said Mark going outside to meet them.

Len Burdette staggered and fell against the wall. Then he slid onto the floor.

'Oh dear, he's fainted – what a coward,' said Fiona.

Jack knelt beside him. 'I think he's had a heart attack.'

'Good,' said Fiona.

Two policemen came into the stables and took over. 'Call an ambulance,' said one, 'but I think it's too late.'

The other one looked at June. 'Are you all right, Miss?'

June nodded. 'My dog saved me.'

'Your lip's bleeding.'

'He hit me.'

Peter saw Rose hurry out of her cottage followed by all the dogs, as he walked towards the house after parking the car. Her expression alarmed him. 'What's wrong?'

'They're all down at the police station – '

'What?'

'A man tried to rape Juju – ' she said breathlessly. 'It was that Len Burdette. Polly attacked him. He's dead.'

'She killed him?'

'Heart attack. They're all giving statements. Fiona's terrified Polly will be destroyed. Why did this have to happen – we were all so happy – things were so good.'

When he had finally felt safe from Urzula's vengeance, Peter felt their life was blessed. Now he felt the luck was draining away.

'You don't deserve this,' said Rose. 'I don't know why terrible things happen to good people.'

'Neither do I, Rose. But it could have been worse. At least he's dead, so Juju will be spared the nastiness of a trial.'

'Ah, here they are now,' said Rose.

Two police cars came slowly down the drive. When they stopped Fiona jumped out, ran to Peter and threw herself into his arms. Anger flooded through him when he saw June's pale face, cut lip and the beginning of a bruise on her cheekbone.

'We took her to the local hospital,' said one of the policemen. 'Just to get her checked. The lip didn't need stitches, but they gave her a tetanus injection and something to help her sleep if she needs it.'

When the police left they all went into the house. Rose told them all to sit in the drawing room while she poured out the sherry.

'There's going to be a inquest,' said June. 'They didn't say anything about Polly, but what if they decide she's savage and want to put her down?'

'I doubt they will,' said Mark. 'She was protecting her mistress. And she didn't kill him, he had a heart attack – probably because he was petrified of being arrested.'

'And having four Rottweilers ready to attack him, would add

to his fear,' said Fiona.

'If the worst does happen we'll hide Polly or say she died or got hit by a car,' said Mark. 'But, if they'd thought she was dangerous they would have impounded her.'

'I told them she saved me – I shouldn't have said anything about her.'

Jack knelt in front of the fireplace. 'The post-mortem will show that he's been bitten, but it's not as if there was blood spurting everywhere or his arm was torn off,' he pointed out as he screwed up sheets of newspaper.

'Thank God we all heard you scream,' said Mark.

'I didn't,' said Fiona. 'I was in the kitchen with Kettle – suddenly his hackles rose, he growled and tore outside as if all the furies in hell were after him.'

'I was turning the compost head – Polly was with me – she was fascinated by the worms,' Jack said as he put logs on top of the kindling. 'I heard a scream, only faintly, but Polly shot off like a rocket, so I followed.'

'You all sit down,' said Rose to Fiona, June and Peter as she handed out the sherry. 'I'll make your dinner. You just relax – you've had a nasty experience.'

'Rose, thanks very much, but if I don't have something to do I'll go crazy,' said Fiona. 'There's not much to do. I was just getting it all ready. Timing is everything, isn't it?' she said slowly. 'I'd just finished braising the cubes of lamb when Kettle alerted me. If I'd been in the middle of braising it the kitchen would have caught fire – I forgot all about it.' She sipped her sherry. 'Would you all like to stay for dinner – it's lamb with apricots and baked apples for dessert.'

'No, I've got a pork chop and you need to be by yourselves,' said Mark. 'But come to my cottage if you need me. Come on, Leader.'

When the fire in the drawing room was burning Jack and Rose went home. Stunned by the events Peter, June and Fiona sat in silence. Peter was pleased to see that the sherry had brought a little colour to June's face.

'I think he would have killed me,' said June. 'Going by what Mark said, he had a lot to lose and he thought I was Fiona, who could have identified him.'

Fiona stood up. 'I can't bear to think about it. I'll go and finish the dinner. Juju, if you want to go to bed I'll bring your dinner up.'

'Heavens no. I'll help – like you I need something to do, but I'm going to have a shower first – I need to get his smell off me. Ugh, I can smell his aftershave.'

Fiona and Peter went into the kitchen. While he set the table Fiona cut up the apricots and poured the stock over the meat and vegetables in the casserole dish. He found the silence uncomfortable, but knew that inconsequential conversation would be intrusive. He saw the Elizabethan recipe book on the worktop and picked it up, hoping Fiona would comment on it, but she didn't. He remembered the day they had bought it.

How happy and carefree we were, he thought. We'll be happy and carefree again, he tried to reassure himself. Burdette's dead, so we don't have to worry about him.

June came into the kitchen in her yellow pyjamas and navy dressing gown. Her hair was wet. Although the bruise on her cheekbone was darker she looked more cheerful. 'Hope it's all right that I'm not dressed for dinner.'

Fiona tutted. 'Really, it's not good enough, is it, Peter?'

Their attempt at humour was forced, but he was pleased that they were trying. He grinned. 'Go and put on your evening dress, Juju. We can't let our standards slip. What do you say to a bottle of wine with dinner?'

'Yes,' said Fiona. 'Red.'

Peter went into the pantry and took a bottle of Merlot off the wine rack. When he returned to the kitchen June was putting wine glasses on the table.

They had almost finished the casserole when Fiona gasped. 'I've just thought of something!'

'What?' said June.

'If it hadn't been for Urzula, we wouldn't have got the dogs. If we didn't have the dogs . . . '

Peter laughed. 'I never thought I'd feel grateful to her.'

June's smile was wry as she raised her glass. 'Thank you, Urzula.'

Fiona didn't know whether to expect Mrs Burdette and Paul for his next riding lesson. She also had no idea what to say to her if she did see her again.

'What can we say?' she asked Mark. 'We have to say something, but to tell her we're sorry would be hypocritical.'

'It depends on how she is. She might have loved him – hard to believe . . . '

'She might not come.'

She did. It was only a few days since her husband had died, but the change in her and Paul was startling. She walked confidently to the tack room and handed Fiona a bunch of flowers. 'I understand if you don't want to teach Paul any more – '

'I do,' said Fiona, thankful that she didn't have to say anything sympathetic.

'I'm sorry about what Len did – '

'Please. Don't apologize. How are you managing?'

'Very well.'

'I'm glad,' said Mark.

She stayed chatting to Mark while Paul had his lesson.

'A merry widow,' said Mark afterwards.

'And a happy child,' said Fiona.

Mark lit his pipe. 'She was very talkative. A bit too talkative really. It's as if the gag's been removed and she's got a lot of catching up to do. She's a rich widow. She's going to buy a smaller house – too many bad memories. She loved him when they got married, but then he changed. She wanted to leave him, but she knew she couldn't support herself and Paul, and she was frightened of his reprisals. He was a convincing liar and her worst fear was that he'd be given custody of Paul.'

'Paul said his father wanted to be a show jumper, but had an accident.'

Mark grinned. 'She told me he was useless in the saddle and

couldn't even have been a show jumper in a local event. She's paid in advance for a year's riding lessons – she gave you a bonus, she said she's indebted to you.'

Fiona smiled. 'For teaching her son or frightening her husband so much he had a heart attack and died?'

Mark laughed. 'Probably both.'

Chapter 47

October

Sebastian was pleased to discover that he had inherited four of his lordship's horses, his Rolls-Royce, two pairs of gold cufflinks, two paintings by Constable, one by Gainsborough and three by Reynolds. Beatrice got nothing. Quentin threatened to contest the will, but Anne and Sebastian knew he did not have the money.

Art didn't interest Sebastian so he decided to sell the paintings, which were still hanging at the hall. There was so much going on with the renovations to the apartments that Quentin and Beatrice did not notice the man from the auction house in London who came to authenticate and value the paintings, and they didn't notice when the paintings were taken away.

Sebastian and Anne went to the auction only out of interest. They stayed in London overnight and were still dazed the following morning when they went down to breakfast.

'It's madness,' said Sebastian, while they waited to be served. 'Six canvases with some paint on them, with no use apart from decoration, are more valuable than the cottage – and not just more valuable – a lot more valuable. I can't understand it.'

'Neither can I. But I'm not going to question it. I don't know much about art or the artists, but I bet a lot of them died poor. If some rich fool wants to pay a fortune, I'm not going to worry about it.'

'There's a man I work with at the bank – his five-year-old son did a painting at school, and because it was his first he and his wife got it framed. The framer put it in the window and someone came in and wanted to buy it – they offered one hundred pounds for it. His parents thought about selling it, but as it was his very first painting they kept it.'

'I would have sold it and got him to paint more,' said Anne.

Sebastian raised his eyebrows. 'Even if it was mine?'

'Yes. Money equals freedom in lots of ways. Where in Cornwall does June live?'

'Between Bodmin and Liskeard.'

'We'd better start house hunting.'

The cottage was sold without Beatrice or Quentin realizing it was on the market. Tucked away, surrounded by trees and out of sight from the main house the people who came to view it could not be seen.

'When do you think we should tell Quentin and Beatrice we're leaving?' said Anne.

'After the way they've treated you – let them find out when we've gone. I'll write them a letter and post it the day before we leave otherwise they might make things hard for the new owners – accuse them of trespassing or something.'

'No. I can't do it like that. I'll tell Beatrice – she's the most reasonable.'

'Reasonable?'

'More reasonable than Quentin.'

Anne found Beatrice in the stables about to mount her horse.

'I've got something to tell you, Beatrice.'

'What now? More nagging? More doom and gloom? I'm about to go riding – I'm meeting friends – I haven't got the time to listen to a lecture. You've got no power here any more, Anne. Quentin's in charge – he is the owner.' She put her foot in the stirrup.

'Wait.' Anne put her hand on the horse's neck. 'There'll be no more lectures from me – I just wanted to do you the courtesy of informing you I'm leaving.'

'Leaving what?'

'Here – Aylington Hall.'

'For how long?'

'For ever. This is my resignation.'

Beatrice kicked her foot out of the stirrup. 'You can't.'

'Why not?'

Her imperious expression changed to dismay. 'This is your home – you've always lived here – you were born here – you can't leave.'

'Since your father died it no longer feels like home. I'm fed up with your and Quentin's malevolence, abuse and – '

'What about Sebastian?'

'He's leaving too.'

'What are we going to do?'

Anne waved her hand in a vague gesture. 'Whatever you like. You've never taken any notice of my advice before – '

'Please, Anne.'

'I've said it all before. Cut down on your spending – be more frugal. Sell the flat in London.'

'We can't sell the flat – where would I stay when I go to London? It's all right for Quentin – he's got his club.'

'Bed and breakfasts.'

'I can't stay in a bed and breakfast! I can't give parties for my friends in London if I don't have the flat.'

'Don't give parties. Don't go to London. What's wrong with Chichester?'

'There's no Harrods in Chichester. Anne, please you can't do this to me.'

'Neither of you want me here – '

'I do.'

'You have a strange way of showing it. Your hostility – '

'I'm sorry. Can you forgive me?'

'It's too late. I'm sorry it's ended like this. I've always regretted that you turned against me.'

'It was Quentin. He said all sort of things . . . '

'And you listened and believed.'

'I was a child!'

'But you're not a child any more. You were the one who demanded the jewellery back – '

'Quentin told me to. He said we were desperate for the money.'

'So you lied when you said it was because they were family heirlooms – he would have sold them and gambled the money away.'

'He needed it to pay off his gambling debts at the club. He's my brother. Please don't go – I need you.'

'Yes, I know you do. But not for myself – just for the work I do, which you don't appreciate.'

'I do. Anne. Please, can't we start again?'

'No.'

'What's going to happen to Aylington – '

'With any luck the National Trust will take it over. If they're not interested it will have to be sold to pay off your debts.'

'Anne, if I tell you something, will it change your mind about leaving?'

'No, but tell me anyway.'

She looked around furtively before saying, 'Quentin told me that if I didn't go against you he'd make me leave Aylington Hall when our father died. He told me I'd be on the streets. He had the power – I don't suppose you believe me.'

'Yes, I do. I understand now. One day you loved me the next you hated me. I never could work out why. But you were nasty even when Quentin wasn't around. Take today for example – he's not anywhere nearby – '

Beatrice snorted. 'Are you sure? He creeps around like a panther. Anyway, you would have suspected something – you might have said something in front of him and given me away. I couldn't go against him – what else could I have done?'

'You could have told me.'

'What good would that have done?'

'I would have told your father – '

'Exactly – and Quentin would have punished me.'

'No. I would have asked your father not to tell him. I would have insisted that he make provision for you in his will.'

'He left me nothing – what makes you think you could have persuaded him to do anything different?'

'He left you nothing because he assumed that you'd still live here with Quentin. If he'd known otherwise he could have left you the London flat or one of the cottages – it's only the house that's entailed. Or he could have stipulated that you have an apartment in the house for your lifetime.'

'Thank you for believing me. Please stay.'

'No. My mind's made up.'

Beatrice burst into tears. Anne forced herself to walk away.

The phone rang when Anne and Sebastian were having dinner. Anne answered it.

It was Quentin. 'Come up to the house immediately.'

'No,' said Anne, putting the receiver down and pulling out the cord, so he couldn't ring again.

Twenty minutes later he arrived at their cottage and banged on the door.

Sebastian opened it. 'No need to knock the door down.'

Quentin pushed past him. 'What's this I hear about you leaving?'

Neither of them answered. Anne could smell the stale cigar smoke on his clothes from the other side of the room.

'It it true?'

'Yes,' they said together.

'You can't.'

'Yes we can,' said Anne. 'You should be pleased.'

'Who's going to do all the accounts and the tax?'

'You.'

'I don't know how – '

'Hire an accountant,' said Sebastian.

'We can't afford – '

Sebastian grinned. 'Of course you can't, because you squander all your money on drink, gambling and cigars and spending nights in London at your club, and your debts are gathering interest every day.'

'You snivelling bastard! I have no illusions about where you come from.'

'I'm not snivelling – but you look as if you're about to.'

'You turned my father against me you – '

Anne shook her head. 'Even before Sebastian was born your

expulsion from school for being caught in a compromising situation with another boy infuriated your father, as did your failure to pass any exams. Your refusal to do any work around the estate that you were going to inherit – '

'When are you leaving?'

'None of your business.'

'It is my business – this is my land. This is my cottage.'

'Get out, Quentin.' Sebastian grabbed his arm and pulled him to the door. Quentin struggled, but he was too unfit and overweight. Sebastian shoved him outside and banged the door shut.

'Beatrice can't have told him I own the cottage,' said Anne.

'Maybe she didn't believe you. They tell so many lies themselves and can't believe the truth when they hear it. They haven't noticed the paintings have gone yet.'

Dear June,
My mother and I want to move to Cornwall. I remember you saying that you have a holiday cottage on your property. Could we rent it for a week while we look around? I have four horses. Would it be possible for me to pay you to stable them if you have room?
I look forward to seeing you again.
Sebastian

Dear Sebastian,
How exciting. Yes, of course you can stable your horses here – we have plenty of room. We had a bit of an upset. One of our old horses died – he was a favourite with the children. A week later one of the mares slipped in the mud and broke her leg and had to be put down. We won't charge you for the stabling if we can use the horses in the riding school. I assume they are suitable mounts for teaching? If not we can come to some arrangement.
Fiona's husband Peter is an estate agent and he is willing to help you. I've enclosed a list of dates when the cottage is free.
Can't wait to see you.
June

Dear June,

Three of the horses are suitable for teaching children. One is more frisky, and would suit a more experienced rider. I will pay for all their food, but I've got all their saddles, which you are welcome to use.

See you soon.

Sebastian

Chapter 48

Sebastian was coming down the stairs with a clothes basket full of washing when he saw Beatrice standing in the doorway.

'Do you want something?' he asked politely.

'Can I come in?'

Normally she would have marched straight in and her cautious manner was so alien he almost laughed.

'Of course.' He went into the kitchen and pushed the sheets into the washing machine. He said nothing while he waited for her to speak.

'Please don't leave. I know I've been ghastly – '

He put powder in the dispenser and closed the door. 'You haven't only been ghastly, Beatrice. You've been odious, rude and vile.'

'Yes, but I've been thinking hard and I know I was wrong – '

'Too late,' he said switching on the machine.

'The cook and the cleaner are leaving. There's no sense of loyalty these days.'

'They know that when we leave you'll forget to pay them.'

'What are we going to do?'

'Cook and clean for yourselves.'

'Sebastian, please stay.'

He shook his head. 'I've outgrown this place.'

She looked stupefied. 'How can you outgrow – '

'I want and need something different.'

'What?'

'I want somewhere where I've got neighbours next door, where I can walk to the shops, see people in the street and chat to them – I can see you think I'm crazy.'

She smiled slightly. 'I do. How are you going to be happy in a terraced house in a town?'

'You'll think this strange, but I used to envy my friends at school – '

'What? Surely you mean they envied you?'

'No. When I was a little boy I used to lie in my big room at night and wish I shared it with someone like the other children at school. I was lonely, and Quentin used to terrify me with stories of ghouls who'd come down the chimney and drag me up the chimney and cook me alive and eat me. In the morning when he saw me, he'd look surprised and tell me that maybe they'd come tonight.'

'I hated it here too – till my mother was killed – then I liked it. I'm sorry for all the ghastly things I said – '

'You only want me to stay because you know you and Quentin won't be able to cope on your own. If I gave in your pleas and stayed it wouldn't be long before you reverted to being nasty.'

'I've changed. Please believe me.'

He filled the kettle with water. 'Even if that's true I doubt Quentin has. Anyway, my mother and I will be going away for a week. We'll be looking for a house – we've changed the locks so don't even think about coming in and looking for my mother's jewellery – it won't be here, she's taking it with her.'

'I wouldn't do that – once I would have, but I've changed.'

'Quentin would search the place if he could get in. Warn him not to, Beatrice, because this cottage belongs to my mother and if there is any sign that's he's broken in I'll call the police.'

'Have we really fallen so far apart?'

'Yes.'

'Where are you going?'

'I don't know yet. We're going away to look for something.'

'You will keep in touch?'

'No. And we will be out of your lives forever. You won't even know where we live. Why so despondent, Beatrice? You can live your lives without any interference.'

'You and your mother are right.'

'You've only just realized that? You didn't have to side with Quentin – if it had been you, me and my mother against him, we might have been able to curb his excesses.'

'Do you really own the cottage?'

'I don't – my mother does. If you don't believe me go to the solicitors – '

'I do. Are you going to sell it?'

'It's sold.'

She looked aghast. 'Already?'

'Yes – hopefully the new owners won't sully your ears with their accents.'

'What am I going to do?'

She sounded so defeated Sebastian felt sorry for her. Remembering what his mother had told him about Quentin's threats to throw her out of Aylington Hall when he inherited it, he said, 'I can give you some advice, but you probably don't want it.'

'I do.'

'I can get you a power of attorney form – '

'Where do I get one of them? What do I do with it?'

'I'll get you one tomorrow then I'll explain and help you fill it in. Come here for dinner.'

'What time?'

'Seven. I'll see you then.'

He turned on the radio and Liebestod from *Tristan and Isolde* filled the room.

Sebastian gave Beatrice the form after dinner. 'I've checked out the financial status of the flat. All the debts are on the house – the flat's safe and there's no mortgage on it. But it's in Quentin's name, so you need to get him to sign this. When he's done that you can put the flat in your name so Quentin can't sell it or gamble it away.'

Beatrice read the form. 'He's never going to sign this.'

'He's so drunk most of the time he'd sign his own execution warrant without realizing,' said Anne. 'Tell him it's something to do with the council, or some bill or television licence or the electoral roll. Then put the flat in your name and go and live in London.'

'Leave here?'

'Beatrice, I'll show you the books tomorrow,' Anne said.

'Unless you can persuade Quentin to keep the house open for visitors and rent the apartments for holidays – how do you think you're going to get money? This place will have to be sold – you'll be forced to sell it – your father's death duties have to be paid . . .'

'Go to London,' said Sebastian. 'And change the locks – you don't want Quentin living with you when Aylington Hall is repossessed.'

'He's my brother,' Beatrice whispered.

'Yes, a brother who threatened to make you leave the home you loved unless you did what he wanted. Your misplaced loyalty to him will make you homeless. Do you want that?'

'No. How did we get into this state?'

'By refusing to listen to reason,' said Anne. 'If we had all worked together this place could have been – not a goldmine, but we could have made enough money to be comfortable and financially secure.'

'Quentin's not going to let you take the horses away.'

Sebastian shrugged. 'He has to. They belong to me.'

'He said he'd shoot you before he let you take them.'

'It's not that he wants them,' Sebastian said. 'It's more that he doesn't want me to have them.'

'I'll find out when he's going to London next so you can arrange for them to be loaded up and transported when he's not here.'

'Thank you, Beatrice,' said Anne.

'Will you let me have your new address?'

'We haven't bought anything yet,' said Anne.

'But when you have – I'd like us to keep in touch.'

Anne nodded vaguely.

'Are you staying in Sussex?'

'No.'

'Where are you going?'

'Cornwall,' said Anne.

'Can we trust her?' Sebastian asked his mother later. 'What's in it for her?'

'She knows Quentin's serious about resorting to violence – whatever her faults she doesn't want you shot or the horses harmed. And she knows that he might drunkenly shoot the wrong person. We have to trust her.'

'We'll have to arrange our departure and the transport of the horses on the same day. He usually spends a couple of days in London at a time.'

'Don't be too hard on Beatrice – '

'She's been hard on you. I don't trust this sudden change in her.'

'I do. It all makes sense. I remember when she turned nasty – it was just after Quentin discovered that he had to inherit – that his father couldn't leave everything to you because it was entailed. Suddenly he was no longer the despised son, he was the heir. He had power and he used it. He'd been bullied and abused at school, and by his mother. His father emotionally abused him – no wonder he hated you so much – you were a threat to his future – when you no longer were he triumphed.'

'So why wasn't he just satisfied with that? I can understand why he hated me, but why turn Beatrice against you?'

'I suppose he thought that I was behind it. He saw us as the enemy. He was in a house full of enemies – he had to have an ally – Beatrice would not have been a willing one so he ensured her loyalty to him by threats. The Beatrice we're seeing now is the real Beatrice.'

'I hope you're right, but I doubt it. If she really was pretending to hate us why didn't she tell you what was going on? She could have been nice to you when he wasn't around.'

'She has no imagination – such crafty behaviour would never have occurred to her.'

'Don't tell her our address.'

'It seems . . . well vindictive not to.'

'Maybe, but at least it's safer. Quentin's threats to shoot me – '

'He won't go all the way to Cornwall.'

'Why not?'

She sighed. 'Maybe you're right.'

'If you really want to keep in touch you can phone the flat. You can go and visit her in London – just don't tell her our address. Quentin might bully it out of her. The last thing we want is for that lunatic to turn up with a gun.'

Chapter 49

November 1974

'Juju, I'm sorry – we've got a snag,' said Peter.

'What's happened?'

'Sebastian is a Gordon-Seymour. I only discovered when he wrote his name on the form in the agency.'

'Hell,' said Fiona.

'He can't be,' June said. 'He lives in a cottage. If he was one of them he'd live in the house. Anyway it's not as if we stole the jewels – all this happened over a hundred years ago.'

'You'll have to tell him,' said Alex.

'Maybe we could give them back,' said Virginia.

'What if they sue us?' said Fiona. 'They've got enough proof. We knew they were stolen and we knew who they were stolen from. They might argue that we should have given them back the day we went to have a look at – '

'But we've hardly got anything left,' said Virginia. 'Just the tiara, Margot's got the ruby and diamond brooch and some pearls. Keith sold the sapphire and diamond ring when we were trying to buy Acacia back.' She looked at Peter. 'Could they sue us?'

'I don't know. I could find out. It might be okay if we offer to give back what we've got. In any case you didn't have the things here – they were in Australia when we went to Aylington Hall – you could say you intended to give them back . . . '

'Sebastian's not going to want to go out with me now,' June said in despair.

'Are you really that fond of him?' asked Virginia.

'Yes!'

'I'm very pleased you are, but it does complicate things. Is it possible to keep it a secret?'

'Possible, but not decent,' said Alex.

'Together again,' Virginia mused. 'Our families were separated by over a hundred years and eleven thousand miles. A journal's brought us together again.'

'In the worst possible way,' said June.

'Talk to Sebastian,' said Peter. 'I think it's best to tell the truth – all of it.'

Sebastian was baffled. Yesterday, when he and his mother had arrived at Trelawney, they had been warmly welcomed. After they had unpacked they had been given afternoon tea, shown around and invited to dinner that evening. Fiona had prepared a delicious three course meal and Rose had cleared the table between courses and washed the dishes. Also present were Alex and Virginia, who had just returned from a trip to France, Switzerland, Germany and Italy, and Mark the previous owner of Trelawney.

Seeing their mystified expressions when June called Alex and Virginia uncle and aunt and Fiona called them mum and dad, they had explained the tangled family relationships, which, Sebastian said to Anne later, made the circumstances of his birth seem simple. The atmosphere was relaxed and they were invited to dinner the following night. Anne was delighted when they discussed the possibility of her living in the holiday cottage permanently and helping Mark with the management. She had wanted a job, but doubted she would be able to find one. She certainly hadn't expected to find something so suitable or so soon.

'The riding school's expanding,' Mark explained. 'We're branching out into teaching show jumping as well as riding. If you did all the admin work that would leave me free to teach and look after the horses with June and Fiona.'

Now it had all changed. When they went over to the house the tension was unmistakable. Sebastian tried to work out what had caused the difference. Did they all have an argument before we arrived? he wondered. Have they decided they don't want to employ my mother and don't know how to tell us? He could see that his mother and Mark were as uncomfortable and bewildered as he was.

Rose had just cleared away the soup bowls, when he asked, 'Is something wrong?'

June looked stricken.

'Have we, or I, done something to offend you?'

Fiona shook her head.

'Then what's the matter? You all seem – '

'It's something that happened a long time ago,' said Virginia.

'How long ago?' he asked.

'Over a hundred years.'

'Why is that a problem now?' asked Anne.

Fiona pushed back her chair. 'I'll go and get it.'

'Get what?' asked Sebastian.

She grimaced. 'The problem.'

They all sat in silence until she returned holding a tiara.

She put it in front of Sebastian. 'This belongs to you.'

'No it doesn't – I don't go around wearing tiaras – what you think I am – a drag queen? I've never seen it before.'

'It belongs to your family. Our ancestors stole it.'

'Ah – Ellen Ingram!' exclaimed his mother. 'She was your ancestor?'

Virginia nodded. 'I'm afraid so.'

'We didn't know you were a Gordon-Seymour until you filled in the form at the estate agency,' said Peter.

'You can have it back,' said June.

He shook his head. 'I don't want it. It wouldn't suit me.'

His mother was convulsed with laughter. 'This is hilarious,' she spluttered.

'I'm sorry, Sebastian,' said June. 'We only came to Aylington Hall to stickybeak.'

'I'm glad you did. If you hadn't I would never have met you.'

'Yes, but – '

'Redistribution of wealth – that's what it was,' Sebastian continued. 'Your ancestors worked hard, while the Gordon-Seymour family had a life of leisure and indulgence. As far as I'm concerned they deserved the riches and I'm glad they got away with it.'

June's eyes widened. 'Really?'

'Yes.'

Anne took a handkerchief out of her handbag and wiped her eyes. 'Really. In fact your family didn't steal from the Gordon-Seymour family – it was the other way around.'

'How do you mean?' asked Virginia.

'When my mother and I were going through the servants' records we discovered that for the first year they weren't paid for their work because they were training – as if it takes a year for someone to learn how to wash floors and scrub pots and pans.'

'Your sister thinks differently – very differently,' said Fiona.

'They were a rotten family – still are.'

June looked disconcerted. 'But you're one of them.'

'No, I'm not. My real father was an Australian who was killed in the war.'

'I married Lord Gordon-Seymour before Sebastian was born. I didn't know what else to do.'

'Did you love him?' asked Fiona.

'Fiona, don't ask questions like that,' Virginia protested.

'It's all right,' said Anne. 'I loved Sebastian's father, but I didn't love Lord Gordon-Seymour.'

'Neither did I,' said Sebastian. 'He loved me and was good to me, but I always felt there was something wrong. It was inevitable that his older son hated me – his father was always comparing us and I remember him telling Quentin in front of me that he wished I was the older son. Even then, I was only about seven, I thought that was cruel.'

'Yes, it was,' Alex agreed.

'And he always made a huge fuss about my birthday – never about Quentin's. Often he even forgot his – or pretended to forget.'

'Do you think we should give the tiara back?' asked Virginia.

'Heavens no,' Anne replied. 'Quentin would only sell it and gamble the money away. This Ellen Ingram – was she in league with Nathaniel – what was his surname?'

'Saunders,' said Virginia. 'Yes, and Sarah Brown. He kept a journal – I typed it all out – would you like to read it?'

'I certainly would.'

'So would I,' said Sebastian.

'I'll have it,' said Sebastian when he saw the view over the Fowey Estuary.

'But you haven't seen the rest of the house yet,' said the estate agent.

'I don't care – the view is so magnificent.'

June nudged him. 'You're almost as bad as I am – I hadn't even seen the house at Trelawney and I wanted it.'

'I'll get a survey of course – if it's got dry rot or anything terrible then I won't buy it.'

It was in dire need of redecorating, new carpets and a new kitchen and bathroom, but to Sebastian these were minor things.

'You can stay with us till it's ready,' said June.

The house was in the town and the following day he and his mother explored the area with June, Virginia and Alex.

His mother loved the Trelawney cottage and looked forward to moving in. When they went back to Sussex Sebastian requested, and was given, a transfer to the bank's branch in Fowey.

'Everything's working out perfectly,' said Anne.

He frowned. 'We've got to get ourselves and the horses safely out of here.'

'Beatrice will – '

'I don't trust her.'

When Beatrice told them the date Quentin would be going to London Anne booked the transport for the horses. On the day, Sebastian took the precaution of making sure Quentin's car was not in the garage. If it had been he would have cancelled the transport for the horses. He was surprised and relieved when Beatrice proved herself trustworthy. He and his mother and the horses arrived in Cornwall unscathed.

Three weeks after Sebastian and Anne left Aylington Hall Beatrice and Quentin had their first argument. When Anne had shown her the books she was appalled by how much money they owed. She tried to persuade Quentin not to cancel the lets on the holiday cottages, but he ignored her.

'What are we going to do for money?'

'We're Gordon-Seymours – they can't touch us.'

'They forced us to sell our London house. Being Gordon-Seymours didn't help us then. We need the money – we've got to keep the house open – we've got to let the cottages – '

He yawned and picked up the whisky decanter. 'All will be well. Going to the club tomorrow night – '

'Quentin, please don't gamble.'

'I'm in a lucky mood – '

'We haven't got any money – '

'Don't need money – got this place.' He took a gulp of whisky. 'You sound just like Anne.' He glared at her. 'I hope you're not going to turn into her.'

Trying not to burst into tears of terror, she watched him swig down the whisky and refill his glass. Forcing herself to smile, she said, 'No fear of that. I didn't mean to nag.' She went to her room and found the power of attorney form Sebastian had given her. She waited an hour and then went to Quentin's apartment. He was asleep in his chair. She gave him a gentle shake. 'Sorry, I almost forgot. This came last week – can you sign it – I've written the cheque – it's for the TV licence.'

He yawned, took the pen from her and signed it.

Amazed at how easy it had been she went back to her apartment and planned her escape. She packed her clothes. Desperate to rescue at least some of the family possessions before the creditors came to value everything, Beatrice packed the best china, silver and crystal into suitcases lined with blankets. She went to the garage and put everything in the largest car and drove to the flat in London, which came with lock-up garages. It took her an hour to get all the cases up the stairs, but when she finally shut the door her sense of relief was so profound she decided not to return to Aylington Hall.

Part 3

Revenge

Chapter 50

Urzula's father helped her find an administrative job at the university. She lived with her parents and was determined to save enough money so she could move away and be free of their questions and petty rules. She had forgotten how stringent the communist regime in Poland was. Used to England and their freedom of speech she found herself in serious trouble when her colleagues reported her because she criticized the communists. Her father was furious and told her he was sorry she had come home. Her mother refused to speak to her. She lost her job and in spite of her tears and apologies her crime was considered so serious she was sent to jail for a year.

I should never have come back to Poland, she thought as she scrubbed the toilet block. If I had not been in such a panic I could have thought properly. I would have gone to France, Germany or Italy and got a job as a courier there. Even if I had stayed in England and the police had caught up with me I may not have gone to jail, and even if I had an English jail would be better than this. It is all Peter's fault. When I am free I will go back to Cornwall and get my revenge. He thought he was so clever pretending that he was living in Australia, but he is not as clever as I am.

Chapter 51

January 1975

'Sebastian,' said Anne when he got home from work. 'Have you heard the news?'

He pulled off his coat, shook the snow from it, and hung it in the hall. 'No.'

'Quentin gambled away Aylington Hall.'

'Inevitable really.'

'It was sold to a developer who's going to turn it into apartments. Quentin refused to leave. When the bailiffs came to evict him, he shot and killed one of them – then he shot himself. He died in hospital.'

It shocked Sebastian that he cared so little that Quentin was dead. 'Anything about Beatrice?'

'No. I'll go to London and see her. Lucky she wasn't there – he might have shot her too.'

Anne went to her bedroom and opened her jewellery box. One by one she took the items out and laid them on her dressing table. She pulled off the engagement ring that her husband had given her. He had put it on her finger and she didn't even look at it. She had just thanked him politely. She and Harry had not had time to buy a ring. She had told him she didn't want one. All she had wanted was him.

Her husband had given her the diamond eternity ring when Sebastian was born. He had come to the hospital armed with flowers, champagne and chocolates. He had put the ring on her finger, but while the nurses exclaimed and told her how lucky she was, she had scarcely glanced at it. All she had been interested in was her baby. She hoped the ring would not scratch him. She took it off as soon as he left. Privately she called the baby Harry. She disliked the name Sebastian, but felt that as her husband had given her respectability and saved her from the shame of being an unmarried mother the least she could do was let him have the name he wanted.

On their first wedding anniversary he had given her the pearl and diamond earrings. On her birthday a few months later he gave her the pearls. Every Christmas, birthday and anniversary he presented her with necklaces, brooches and bracelets with rubies, diamonds, sapphires and emeralds. She wore them to parties, balls and when he took her to dinner at The Ritz or The Savoy.

'I didn't want any of them,' she said to herself. 'I still don't. They are a reminder of the past.'

Beatrice picked up the phone.

'Hello. It's Anne.'

She was so surprised she didn't know how to respond.

'Your stepmother.'

'Yes, I know.' She wondered if Anne had rung to gloat. 'I never expected to hear from you again. I suppose you've heard about Quentin.'

'Yes. That's why I'm ringing. Are you all right?'

'I suppose so – I'm alive. The flat's safe from creditors.'

'I'm in London. Can I come and see you?'

'Why?' Beatrice asked nervously.

'Not to argue with you or demand money. Are you free tomorrow?'

'Yes, it's my day off.'

'You've got a job?'

'Yes – I'm a sales assistant at Harrods – go on, snigger.'

'I've got no intention of sniggering. Do you like it?'

'Yes, actually I do – terrible pay, but I get a good staff discount and I eat in the staff canteen. Yes, come tomorrow – in the afternoon.'

In the morning she went to the Harrods food hall and bought a cake. She set the table in the kitchen with the china she had taken from Aylington Hall then changed her mind and took everything into the dining room. When Anne arrived the first thing Beatrice noticed was that she looked years younger. She also looked happy. After cautiously greeting each other they stood awkwardly in the hall.

'I'm glad you're all right, Beatrice.'

'Would you like some tea?'

'Yes. Thank you.'

Beatrice led her into the dining room.

'I'm glad you managed to rescue the china,' she said.

'Why did you want to see me?' Beatrice asked as she poured the tea.

Anne opened her handbag and took out a large velvet box, which she handed to Beatrice. 'To give you these.'

'What is it?'

'Open it and see.'

Inside were the jewels Beatrice had demanded after her father died. The diamonds sparkled in the sun shining through the window. Too amazed to smile she said, 'Why?'

'If it hadn't been for Quentin I would have given them back to you before we left – they are yours.'

'Thank you, Anne. I really appreciate it.'

'Are you going to buy one of the apartments at Aylington Hall?'

Beatrice shook her head. 'No. I never want to see it again.'

'Oh. Yes, that's understandable – it was your home and it would be difficult seeing strangers – '

'No. That's not the reason.' She closed the jewellery box. 'Funny – I didn't want to leave it, but when I settled here I realized I didn't want to go back. None of the memories are good. I hope the people who buy the apartments will be happier than I ever was. It was a bleak place for Quentin too – and for you as well, Anne, I suspect. How's Sebastian?'

'Very happy. He's got a lovely girlfriend.'

Beatrice cut the cake and put a slice on Anne's plate. 'Good. Give him my love. What are you doing now?'

'I'm an estate manager at an equestrian centre.'

'Lucky you. Congratulations. You look happy and well.'
'I am.'
'Can we stay in touch?'
'Yes.'

Chapter 52

May 1975

'Juju, do like the surname Johnson?' Sebastian asked as they were setting up the jumps for the gymkhana lessons.

'I don't know.' She raised the bar on the jump. 'Why?'

'Have you got a middle name?'

'No. Do you think this is too high?'

'Slightly – put it one notch lower. June Johnson – how does that sound?'

'Who's she?'

'No one yet.'

'Sebastian! Stop being so mysterious. What's all this about?'

'It's a marriage proposal.'

'You're asking me to marry you?'

'No – I'm asking the barmaid in the pub in Fowey. Of course I'm asking you.'

'Well, it's the strangest marriage proposal I've ever had.'

'How many have you had?'

'One. What's all this Johnson stuff?'

'I'm going to change my surname to my real father's – it was Johnson. Do you like the sound of Sebastian Johnson? Or do you prefer Gordon-Seymour?'

She kissed him. 'Definitely Johnson.'

'So will you marry me?'

'Yes, Sebastian Johnson, I will.'

Anne was writing a list of people to invite to the wedding. 'What about Beatrice?' she asked. 'It's up to you, but I think we should invite her.'

Sebastian frowned. 'No. I don't want her there.'

'It would be a gesture of goodwill – '

'I don't feel much goodwill towards her.'

'And actually,' said Fiona, 'there's another problem – photographs of me wearing the tiara. And Juju's going to wear it too.'

'No. I'm not. I'll wear a circle of flowers,' said June.

'You can if Beatrice isn't coming,' said Anne.

June shook her head. 'I've been thinking, and as it's not up to me alone I have to ask what you reckon. You're going to think I'm absurd, but our family stole it from the Gordon-Seymour family. Ellen and Nathaniel didn't get married, so she never wore the tiara, even though she was the one who stole it. Sarah wore it on her wedding day and her husband was bitten by a snake and died. I don't know who else of our ancestors wore it, but my mother – I mean Eleanor – wore it and Jonathan was killed in a fire. Virginia wore it and she couldn't have children, which caused turmoil. Gabby wore it and her husband died. I was supposed to wear it and then found out that Keith and I were brother and sister.'

'But you didn't wear it,' said Fiona.

'I put it on my head when I was trying on the wedding dress. Fiona, you were wearing it when Urzula interrupted the service with her lies and the wedding had to be postponed.'

'And Francesca,' said Fiona slowly. 'She wore it too – I've seen the photos of her wedding.'

'And Francesca is?' Anne asked.

'Our real father's first wife. She had an asthma attack and died at the end of the war.'

June looked relieved. 'So you don't think I'm mad?'

'No,' said Fiona. 'Gabby and I talked about this a while back – in Australia, after I left Eumeralla. So you won't wear the tiara when you get married. If I'd thought about it I wouldn't have worn it either. Thank heavens that when we did eventually get married, I wore a suit and a hat.'

'I propose that we give it back to the family – Beatrice,' said June.

Anne's smile was wry. 'And pass on the bad luck to her?'

'No! It's only unlucky for us because it's stolen – if it was returned to its rightful owner . . . '

'I agree,' said Sebastian. 'Now that Quentin's dead there's no danger of him selling it or gambling it away. I'm sure Beatrice would appreciate it. She goes to lots of balls and banquets – well she used to. I suppose she still does.'

'Contact Gabby and Virginia and see what they think,' said Anne. 'If they agree I'll take the tiara to Beatrice. Are you certain you don't want to invite her to the wedding? She might be hurt.'

Sebastian smiled. 'I'm sure the tiara will alleviate any hurt feelings.'

'And we did a tour of Aylington Hall with Beatrice – we asked some awkward questions – she's sure to recognize us – and there're photos of me wearing the tiara – she'll guess the truth.'

'Anne, did you ever contact Sebastian's grandparents?' asked June.

'No. Until recently I kept his real father a secret.'

'They might like to know about him.'

'They might be dead,' said Anne.

'And they might be alive. Did Harry have any brothers or sisters?'

'A sister . . . she was six years younger than he was. I wouldn't know how or where to start searching. They lived in Adelaide. Johnson's not an unusual name.'

'No, but at least it's not Smith or Jones,' said Fiona. 'Adelaide's a city, but it's not like London. Would you like me to write to my parents and they can go to Adelaide and look up the Johnsons in the phone book . . . that's if you want them to.'

Anne looked wistful. 'Meeting Harry's parents . . . I'd love to. He talked about them a lot – they sounded lovely. I was looking forward to meeting them.'

'We might be able to get their address from the War Office or the Air Force – his parents would have had to be informed when he was killed,' said Sebastian. 'Let me write to them. That would be easier than Virginia and Alex searching through the Adelaide phone book.'

'But they might not live there any more,' said Fiona. 'Do you know their Christian names?'

'No. He just called them mum and dad or his parents.'

'But the War Office might have their names,' June said excitedly.

'Bound to,' said Sebastian. 'They were his next of kin.'

Ω Ω Ω

'How do you feel about it, mate?' Tom asked when they were setting the table for dinner.

Keith straightened the tablecloth. 'About what?'

'You know what.'

'Okay. I do. Juju getting married. I'm happy for her – he looks like a good bloke.'

'What about you and Sophie?'

'We're going well – different to me and Juju, but good.'

'All love's different . . . I assume you do love her?'

Keith nodded.

Tom slapped him on the shoulder. 'Are you going to marry her?'

'She might not want me.'

'So you haven't asked her?'

'No.'

'When are you going to ask her?'

'When the time's right.'

'Gabby, how do you feel about having a honeymoon in England,' Tom asked when they were tidying the tack room.

She looked at him in surprise. 'Us . . . you and me?'

He grinned. 'Yeah – get married here and go to Cornwall in time for Juju's wedding.'

'I'm going to give Juju away,' Tom announced when they were having dinner that evening.

'I thought she was getting married in England,' said Greg. 'Has she changed her mind?'

'No. Gabby and I are going to England for our honeymoon.'

Eleanor dropped her fork. 'You're getting married?'

'Come on, Mum, didn't you guess?' said Neil.

'Er . . . no. Well, I knew something was going on, but . . . ' She smiled. 'Congratulations. I'm very pleased.'

'So am I,' said Keith.

'You've never been out of Australia, Tom,' said Greg doubtfully.

'Okay, Gabby and I can stay here and you can go to England and give Juju away.'

Greg looked horrified. 'And go on a plane – little more than a tin can. No thanks.'

'Now when are you two getting married?' asked Eleanor.

'As soon as possible,' said Tom.

'Nothing elaborate,' said Gabriella. 'Just a small wedding with relatives and neighbours and a few friends.'

Tom looked at Neil. 'Will you be my best man?'

Neil grinned. 'Sure.'

Ω Ω Ω

'Sebastian, you don't want us to live in Fowey when we get married, do you?' June asked.

'Funny, I was going to talk to you about where we should live. Where do you want to live?'

'Trelawney. The house is big enough and we've got two bathrooms. Is that okay?'

'Yes. I'll rent out my house and that'll give us more income. That is if . . . '

'What?'

'Will that be all right with Fiona and Peter?'

'Yes, They're taking it for granted.'

Ω Ω Ω

Dear Anne and Sebastian,
We were overwhelmed with joy to receive your letter and the photos. Harry's letters were full of you, Anne. We did hope to hear from you after his death. We had no idea that you were expecting his baby, and we understand what a terrible position you were in. How we would love to meet you and our grandson. We have two granddaughters. We come to England about once every four years. We came last year, but to meet you and our grandson and come to his wedding we will make a special journey.
Michael and Agnes Johnson

Ω   Ω   Ω

Rather than driving to London Anne caught the train at Liskeard. As she stared out of the window at the view she was aware of the plastic carrier bag at her side. No one would suspect that there was a tiara worth thousands of pounds in here, she thought. Maybe instead of armoured security trucks vast sums of money should be transported by people carrying plastic shopping bags.

Beatrice had wanted them to meet in Harrods, but Anne said she would go to the flat first. 'We can go to Harrods later for afternoon tea,' she said.

Not wanting to implicate Fiona and June's family she had her version of the historical events ready.

Beatrice ushered her into the drawing room. 'You sounded perfectly mysterious on the phone, Anne. What have you got to show me?'

Anne gave her the carrier bag. Looking disinterested when she saw the towel that Fiona had wrapped the tiara in, she pulled it out and unwrapped it. Anne enjoyed her incredulity.

'Is this – is it what I think it is?'

'Yes.'

'Where on earth – how did you – is it real or fake?'

'Real.'

'But where . . . how?'

'Some visitors who did the tour at Aylington Hall recognized it. They wrote to me and sent a photo. I went to visit them and told them it was the stolen tiara. It had been in their family for years.'

'Did you have to buy it back?'

'No. They gave it to me.'

'I suppose their ancestors must have bought it not knowing it had been stolen. I'll wear it to the Queen Charlotte's ball,' Beatrice said excitedly. 'Now, I'll take you to Fortnum and Mason's and we'll celebrate.'

'I've got some news. Sebastian's getting married.'

'I'm pleased for him. I don't suppose he'll invite me.'

'No, I'm sorry.'

'I don't blame him.'

'He's changed his surname to Johnson.'

Beatrice wrapped the tiara back in the towel. 'Because of the scandal surrounding Quentin?'

'It was the name of his real father.'

'Ah. What happened?'

'He was killed in the war.'

'Oh, Anne, how beastly for you. I'm sorry. Did you love my father?'

'No. I hope that doesn't hurt you.'

Beatrice grimaced. 'I didn't love him either. If you'd said you loved him I'd have thought you were lying or demented.'

Ω Ω Ω

'Juju, do you want to wear my wedding dress and I'll wear your bridesmaid's dress?'

'No.'

Fiona looked at her in surprise. 'I thought you said you wanted a traditional wedding.'

'I do – but I'll wear my own dress. You're not offended are you?'

'Heavens no. It's just that, knowing you, I thought you'd want as little fuss as possible – you hated all the fittings for the bridesmaid's dress. Are you going to buy one? I suppose you could hire one.'

'No. I'll ask Rose if she'll make it for me.'

'But what about the fittings? You grouched the whole time – '

June laughed. 'I know. I think I'm turning into a sophisticate. With all the balls we go to we'll need lots more long dresses. Don't fret, Fiona, I haven't changed too much – I want something simple like yours with no train or fussy bits.'

'Er, can we go shopping for patterns and materials and shoes and things?'

'Of course.'

'I think I'm going to faint. If you start saying you enjoy shopping I'll – don't know what.'

'I haven't changed too much,' June said with a giggle. 'I'm not going to wear any jewellery.'

'Oh. I was going to lend you my pearls for your something borrowed. What are you borrowing?'

'I'm not doing any of that nonsense.'

'It's supposed to be lucky.'

'Huh. You did the old, new, borrowed, blue superstitious stuff on your wedding day – that didn't stop Urzula turning up. If it was lucky she would have got lost on the way to the church and the wedding would have been over by the time she arrived. And I was going to do all that when I was marrying Keith. So no, I'll dispense with that tradition.'

Chapter 53

Anne and Sebastian waited in the arrivals hall at Heathrow. The Qantas plane had landed an hour earlier.

'They should be through soon. Are you nervous?' Sebastian asked.

'Not really – a little anxious – I hope they like me. I wonder how they're feeling.'

He squeezed her arm. 'The same, I guess.'

'I've always known, but this – you – is new to them.'

'We don't know what they look like.'

Anne smiled. 'They'll have no trouble recognizing you.'

Sebastian saw a couple walk through the doors. Their faces lit up when they saw him. The woman stopped. The man put his arm around her. They walked up to Anne and Sebastian.

'Harry. Harry,' they said together.

'Are you all right, Fiona?' Mark asked. 'You seem a bit – '

'I'm okay . . . well actually I'm a bit . . . worried that something will go wrong.'

'Like what?'

'I suppose it's because of what happened at my wedding, I can't help feeling gloomy.'

He smiled reassuringly. 'I'm sure Sebastian hasn't got a vengeful ex-girlfriend – '

'Not that sort of wrong. His grandparents are elderly – one of them might have a heart attack or something – it'd be tragic. They only just found him.'

'They both look healthy and they're thrilled and excited about the wedding. And now you've given the tiara back to its rightful owner . . . '

Sebastian and June's wedding at Lanhydrock church was the most moving and surprising Anne had ever attended. As she and Sebastian's grandparents and Mark sat in the front pew waiting for June and Tom to arrive, she recalled her dread at her own wedding. Far from being happy that their daughter was marrying an earl her parents had tried to talk her out of it. She evaded their questions. Now she wondered if her mother had guessed she was pregnant even before the wedding.

'You don't have to marry him,' she had said when she came to help Anne dress the morning of the wedding. 'It's not too late to back out.'

'It is,' was her bleak reply.

'Why?' her mother had asked sharply.

It was the tone that made Anne lie. 'He'll be furious – he might sack you. You'll have to leave the cottage.'

'Don't worry about us.'

She tried to smile. 'But I do worry about you.'

If her mother had asked her if she was pregnant and if her voice had been softer and more gentle Anne thought she might have confessed.

All those years ago she had thought that the truth would horrify them. Now she wondered if she had misjudged their tolerance. She and Harry had been engaged. It was not as if he was a casual boyfriend or a one-night stand. Her parents had come to London to meet him and had been happy about their engagement. When she returned to Aylington Hall devastated by his death they had been loving and sympathetic and she was too afraid of their shame to tell them when she discovered she was pregnant.

For the first three months of her marriage she was terrified she would have a miscarriage. When Sebastian was born her happiness was clouded by the worry that her husband would know that Sebastian was not his son. His unquestioning belief in Sebastian's paternity still confounded her. Her parents never said anything direct, but she knew that they guessed the truth when Sebastian grew up. He was too like Harry. She had never brought him to Aylington Hall. If she had, the Earl would have known the truth as soon as Sebastian got older.

'I never thought that such happiness could come from such inauspicious beginnings,' she thought as the wedding march began and June walked up the aisle with Tom.

She wore the most beautiful dress Anne had ever seen. June's only stipulation was that it had have a full skirt and be plain. The sweetheart neckline emphasized her long neck. She wore no jewellery. The white circle of gardenias on her head and in her bouquet was her only adornment. Fiona and Gabriella wore similar dresses in the same shade of deep green as the gardenia leaves.

During the vows she almost dropped her book in surprise. She heard Agnes gasp.

'I Harry take thee, June . . . '

'You all know me as Sebastian,' he said at the reception, which was held at the Lanhydrock Hotel. 'But I never felt like a Sebastian – and I got teased about my name at school.' He looked at his best man. 'Especially by you.'

Everyone laughed.

'At Heathrow when I met my grandparents for the first time and they called me Harry it felt right, and I knew that was who I wanted to be. Sorry for the shock during the service, but I wanted it to be a surprise.'

'It was,' said his best man. 'I thought the vicar had got your name wrong!'

'Anyone who still wants to called me Sebastian can.' He sat down.

'No,' said his best man, getting to his feet. 'You look more like a Harry, Harry. One of the things he told me was that I was to keep my speech as short as possible. I won't bore you with a catalogue of his good points and a long list of his bad ones. Let us all drink a toast to Harry and June for their future happiness. And to Anne, Harry's mother. And finally to two special people who have flown all the way from Australia to see their grandson for the first time – Agnes and Michael.'

June stood up. 'Can we also remember a young man who was

killed fighting for his country – Harry's father.'

'I should have brought more hankies with me,' Anne said to Mark as June raised her glass and everyone stood up. 'I knew it would be an emotional day.'

When June and Harry went onto the dance floor Mark asked, 'Will you have any problems calling him Harry?'

'No. I've always thought of him as Harry . . . never Sebastian, which was a Gordon-Seymour family name. Are my eyes red?'

'You look beautiful.' He squeezed her hand. 'Anne, will you marry me?'

Fresh tears flooded her eyes. 'Yes.'

For a wedding present, Fiona and June gave Mark and Anne the deeds to the cottage. They married at Lanhydrock church.

Ω Ω Ω

When Tom and Gabriella arrived at Brisbane airport, Keith was there to meet them. 'Sophie and I are getting married,' he said.

Not caring about the crowds Gabriella gave a whoop of joy.

'A quiet wedding – no fuss,' he said.

Keith's idea of a quiet wedding was very different to Sophie's and her family. Over one hundred guests were invited and the reception was held in the homestead at Acacia. They had their honeymoon on the Great Barrier Reef. When they came home two weeks later Tom and Gabriella met them at the airport.

'We've got something fantastic to show you, Mate,' said Tom.

Keith saw Sophie and Gabriella exchange conspiratorial smiles. 'What?' he asked.

'Your wedding present,' said Tom.

'Did you wonder why no one in our family gave us a wedding present?' asked Sophie.

'No – I didn't even notice. I thought the reception was our wedding present.'

Gabriella laughed. 'Far from it.'

Keith's mind whirled with possibilities. A horse? he wondered. Two horses – a breeding pair?

He was unprepared for the surprise that awaited him. After driving into Acacia Tom took a left-hand fork. Five minutes later he stopped in front of a house. Virginia and Alex were on the veranda.

'Welcome home,' said Virginia when they got out of the car.

Sophie put her arm around him. 'Do you like it?'

'Is it for us?'

Tom nudged him. 'Who else would it be for, you drongo?'

'How did it get here?'

'We all contributed for it to be moved from a place a hundred miles away,' said Gabriella. 'You do like it, don't you?' she asked anxiously.

Keith grinned. My dreams have come true, he thought. 'I reckon,' he said. 'Thanks, thank you all so much.'

Chapter 54

December 1975

Peter was concerned when Fiona started crying when they were having dinner with his parents at their cottage.

'Darling, what's wrong?'

She found a hanky and wiped her eyes. 'I don't know.'

'Don't you feel well?' asked Lynette.

Fiona's sobs increased and she left the table. 'Sorry.'

Peter was about the follow her, but his mother said, 'She's gone upstairs – I think she wants to be by herself.'

Lynette looked at him accusingly. 'Have you had an argument?'

'No. She was all right when we left home.' But he realized that she had not been herself for days. She had been distant and introspective. The news, a few days earlier, that the Australian Prime Minister Gough Whitlam had been sacked by the Governor General had infuriated her, but surely it would not have caused her tears.

After five minutes she came back into the dining room. 'I'm really sorry about that,' she said. 'I don't know what's wrong with me.'

When Fiona's emotional state persisted through the week Peter sought Charles's advice. 'I'm worried she's having a breakdown,' he said.

'Not a breakdown,' said Charles. 'It's probably a reaction.'

'But why now? Everything's calm – going well.'

'She's had a lot of upheaval in her life. Even though everything is all right now there's bound to be some rebound.'

'Why? I don't understand. Yes, she had a few traumatic experiences – '

'Just a few?'

'Well more than a few, but – '

Charles grinned. 'Her troubles really began when she came to England and met you. Sorry – not funny. Look, Urzula messed things up on your wedding day, and then Juju was nearly raped. That's a lot of upheaval in a short space of time. I bet very few girls have ever had their wedding postponed by a false allegation.'

'She must be unhappy – she cries all the time.'

'All the time?'

'Well at least twice a day. She says she doesn't know why. We're all worried about her – Juju, Sebastian, Rose – '

'She should see a doctor. Does she sleep all right?'

'Yes.'

'Is she tired?'

'Yes. Very. She sleeps a lot.'

'It's probably nothing – but it's best to get it checked. She might have an iron deficiency.'

'She shouldn't. She eats lots of fruit and vegetables – '

'Sometimes iron doesn't get absorbed properly.'

As he drove home Peter tried to think of the reason or reasons for Fiona's unhappiness. Maybe she thinks that I have married her for her money, he thought. But I pay all the bills, I refuse to have my name on the deeds. I paid for the new bathroom for June. It's not money. It can't be. What then? Has she fallen in love with another man?

That situation was too terrible to contemplate.

Peter became even more worried when Fiona, as well as being emotional, began to look pale and ill.

'Stay in bed in the morning and I'll bring your breakfast up,' he told her.

'I'm all right,' she insisted, switching on her alarm clock. When he came back from the bathroom she was asleep. He turned off her alarm. In the morning his alarm did not wake her, and she was still asleep when he left for work.

'Did you go to the doctor?' Peter asked when he arrived home from work a few days later.

'Yes.'

'What did he say?'

'He did some tests.'

'What sort of tests?'

'Just tests,' she replied vaguely.

One evening when he came home she was waiting at the front door.

'Some women get very grumpy,' she said.

'What?'

Her eyes swam with tears. 'Some woman get very emotional – like me. It makes some women sick. It doesn't affect some women at all.'

'What doesn't?'

She smiled. 'Being pregnant.'

'I thought she was,' said Charles when Peter told him.

'Why didn't you tell me? I've been worried to death. She was so pale I wouldn't have been surprised if she'd told me she only had two weeks to live.'

'Because it might have been something serious – I didn't want to raise your hopes.'

'You did the opposite – I was drowning in pessimism.'

'I'm surprised you didn't suspect.'

'If she'd been sick every morning then I would have. She didn't even have any odd cravings. She didn't have a clue herself until the doctor asked her if she could be pregnant.' He laughed. 'She didn't tell me until the tests came back – she didn't want to get me excited in case it was something else.'

The baby's room was furnished with mahogany furniture and white cotton bedding. When the baby was born the walls would be painted pink or blue. Fiona's wedding veil that was edged with satin ribbon was arranged over the cradle to keep out flies and insects. Rose and Anne made baby clothes and knitted jackets, booties and shawls. Virginia and Alex planned to come over for the christening.

Their baby was born in the middle of August.

Peter held her in his arms marvelling at her perfection and the mass of dark wavy hair on her head. 'Hello, Ruth,' he whispered.

Chapter 55

Urzula's parents' life was governed by routine. Nothing had changed since she was a child. They went out with friends every Friday and Saturday night. As soon as Urzula was released from jail she waited until Friday night and broke into their house and stole money from the tin under the sink in the kitchen, which was where they had always kept it. She went back to England. She had lost a lot of weight, and with her brown hair she doubted that anyone in Liskeard would recognize her. When she saw her reflection in the mirror she hardly recognized herself. They had hacked off her hair in jail. Although distraught at the time, now she was pleased how much it changed her appearance. To her surprise her natural hair was shiny. She hadn't realized how dyeing and perming it had made it so dull.

When she arrived in Cornwall she booked into a cheap bed and breakfast hotel for two nights, which was all she could afford. It was October and the tourist season was over. She looked at the register and saw that she was the only guest. They put her in a single room, which was clean and comfortable and had a bathroom next door. She made conversation and learnt that the couple who owned the hotel lived next door. The next morning she caught the bus to Bodmin and got the key to the front door and the key to her room cut.

She went back to Liskeard and checked the electoral roll. With a jolt of triumph discovered that she was right. Fiona and Peter still lived at Trelawney. June's surname was now Johnson and she and her husband also lived there. So many changes in such a short space of time, she thought when she saw that Mark Bolitho now had a wife. She looked up the address where Peter had lived before his marriage. As she expected Lynette, Yvonne and Charles no longer lived there. I wonder if any of them are married, she thought. She knew that Yvonne worked at Liskeard Hospital. She may have moved to another hospital, but when Urzula knew her she had loved her job.

She lay in bed that night planning her future. First revenge, she thought. Then I will go back to London and get a job with a tour company. An exclusive tour company this time where they stay in expensive hotels. What will make Peter and Fiona suffer most? I do not want to kill anyone so what can I do? I cannot risk watching their house. Peter goes to work during the week, but June and Fiona do not. And Mark Bolitho is always around with the horses. And the gardener and cleaner are there during the day too. Even if they do not recognize me they will be suspicious. Whatever I decide I will have to do it at night. It has to be something that I cannot be suspected for. Vandalism? No, that will make too much noise. Burn down their house? Yes. But how can I make sure they are not in it? October – they used to go away in October before he met Fiona. Will they still go? Fiona gets on well with his family – better than I ever did. But what about June and her husband? Would they be happy to all go away together?

Images of the house burning and destroying all the valuable china, crystal, silver and photographs occupied her mind until she fell asleep. When she woke the next morning she thought how Peter and Fiona would feel when they saw the burnt wreckage of their house.

When she went into Liskeard she saw one of her old colleagues going into a bakery and she stood next to him. When he didn't recognize her she felt more confident. She walked past the solicitor's office where Lynette was a legal secretary and saw Lynette come out at five o'clock. Lynette didn't recognize her either. She hadn't sought out Peter and had tried to avoid him, but when she passed him the next day and there was no glimmer of recognition in his glance her plans took shape.

She waited outside Liskeard Hospital. Yvonne came out at five thirty. Keeping a safe distance away Urzula followed her. Her new address in a smaller house was half a mile away. She saw Lynette's car parked outside.

'Now I know where you all live,' she thought, 'I can begin to make plans.'

She drew a sketch of the position of the house at Trelawney in relation to the cottages. I will have to go to the back, she thought, to the conservatory, which cannot be seen from the cottages. She tried to remember whether the floor of the conservatory was wood or tiles. I hope it is wood – tiles will not catch fire. The curtains will burn well – and the plants, but if the floor is tiled the fire will not spread. There is a door with stained glass between the kitchen and the conservatory. I know the cottages can be seen on one side of the house, but there is nothing on the other side where the drawing room is. The curtains, sofa and chairs will burn well. I will buy petrol and candles.

She picked up her cigarette lighter and flicked it on. She watched the flame and smiled.

Polly rushed into the bedroom growling. Anne and Mark got out of bed.

'Something's wrong,' Mark said softly. 'I'll have a look.'

Anne pulled on her dressing gown. 'It might just be a fox.'

But her heartbeat increased when Kettle tore up the stairs. They put Polly and Kettle on leads and hurried outside.

'What about Barker ?' she asked.

'He's more likely to welcome a burglar than frighten them off.'

Polly strained on the lead and dragged them to the side of the house, just as they heard breaking glass. Immediately they saw someone throw a lighted candle through the broken window of the drawing room. There was an explosion of fire. Mark let Polly off the lead. The intruder saw them, and from the light of the fire, Anne saw the arc of liquid land on Polly, followed by a candle. Polly burst into flames. Anne screamed. Kettle howled and almost pulled Mark off his feet.

'Ring – ' began Mark.

'Stay where you are! Do not move!'

'Urzula!'

'Yes. If your wife leaves here to ring the police I will set you on fire just like the dog.'

Anne tore off her towelling dressing gown and threw it over Polly. 'It was a marriage of convenience,' she shouted. 'It's not convenient any more – I hate him, so if you kill him you'll do me a favour.' She turned and ran, almost tripping over the hem of her nightdress.

She saw the door of the Haynes' cottage open and Leader and Digger ran out. 'No!' she yelled, catching hold of their collars. 'Polly's been killed – fire.' She grabbed Jack's arm and whispered. 'Take them round the other way – it's Urzula. Be careful – she's broken a window and set fire to the drawing room. She's got petrol, or something, and candles.'

She rushed into their cottage and dialled 999. 'Fire, police and ambulance,' she gasped when they answered. She gave the address and ran back outside. She reached Urzula in time to see Digger hurl himself at her back and bring her to the ground. Barking furiously Leader joined him.

Mark let go of the lead and Kettle ran forward. Anne picked up the can of petrol and the cigarette lighter.

'Kettle, Leader, Digger, here!' Mark called. They ran to him. 'Stay right where you are, Urzula, or I'll set the dogs on you again.'

Jack tipped a bucket of water over Polly. He knelt beside her and pulled back Anne's dressing gown. 'She's still alive. Oh, God.'

Chapter 56

'You are charged with five counts of attempted murder, Miss Luk,' said her lawyer when he visited her in prison. 'Other charges are animal cruelty – '

'It was going to attack me.'

'It was defending – '

'I was defending myself from it. It was only a dog.'

'The British take acts of cruelty to animals very seriously, Miss Luk. The dog had to be put down it was so badly burnt. Things are looking very bad for you. There were not only four adults living in the house, there was a baby.'

'A baby? I knew . . . nothing about the baby. Is it Peter's?'

'Yes.'

Her eyes flooded with tears.

'The case for the prosecution is that you set fire to a house knowing that there were four people and – '

'I knew four people lived there, but I also knew they were on holiday.' She pulled a crumpled tissue out of her pocket and wiped her eyes.

'You have to convince the jury of that.'

'No. You have to convince the jury of that.'

'Miss Luk, Mr and Mrs Bolitho saw you set fire to the house. They saw you deliberately set fire to the dog.'

'Listen, you stupid man, I am pleading guilty to setting fire to the house. I am pleading not guilty to attempted murder. I am pleading self-defence about the dog. If it had not growled and rushed at me I would not have had to protect myself. Is that beyond your comprehension?'

'Do you want me to defend you or not?'

'No. I want someone better than you. You could not even get me bail.'

'Unless you can pay for a lawyer and not depend on legal aid you have no choice. No one offered to pay your bail and as you have no money yourself, releasing you before your trial was not considered. If you are not satisfied with me you could defend yourself. So, do you want me to defend you or not?'

'You look as if you are just out of law school, but it seems that I have no choice.'

He opened his briefcase and took out a pen and pad. 'Then tell me how you knew that Peter and Fiona Yelland and June and Harry Johnson were on holiday.'

'I followed them. I found out where Peter's sister and cousins lived and I watched their house. They all used to go on holidays together at the beginning of October when the weather was cooler and the tourist season was over. On the first Saturday in October I saw Lynette, Yvonne and Charles bringing their suitcases out of the house. Charles and his girlfriend – '

'How did you know it was his girlfriend?'

'I had never seen her before, but I suppose it was his girlfriend, but whoever it was they put their cases in his car. Then I saw Fiona and Peter arrive in the Land Rover – '

'Who was driving?'

'Peter. Fiona was in the passenger seat.'

He wrote it down. 'Go on.'

'Fiona's twin sister and her husband were in a Rolls-Royce behind them.'

'What colour was the Rolls-Royce?'

'Burgundy. Why does it matter?'

'The more you can accurately describe the more you will convince the jury that you saw them leaving. Most Rolls-Royces are black – '

'Yes, I understand now. Yvonne and her boyfriend got into the Rolls-Royce and Lynette got in the Land Rover. So that is how I knew they were on holiday and that their house was empty. I am not a murderer. I did not want to hurt them.'

'Weren't you worried they would see you?'

'No. There is a park opposite their house and I watched from there – behind some bushes. I know their holiday routine. They all go together and stop off for lunch at a pub. Their parents go with them too. They rent a big house somewhere in the country and go for walks. That is how it was when I was Peter's girlfriend – nothing has changed. They are so boring and predictable.'

Ω   Ω   Ω

Polly's body lay on a white sheet. The vet had told them that the other dogs had to understand that she was dead. At the surgery she had been washed to remove all the smell of petrol. Her blanket was folded beside her and would be buried with her. Fiona, Mark, Harry and Jack led Kettle, Barker, Digger and Leader to the graveside. Kettle sniffed her body and whimpered. Barker nudged her as if trying to make her get up. Leader looked bewildered. Digger howled. Ruth started to cry and Peter, who was carrying her, stroked her head. Mark and Harry pulled the sheet over Polly and lifted her into the hole Jack had dug. When the hole was filled in Jack planted a Rosemary bush on her grave. They all went back to the house where Fiona had made sandwiches and scones.

The windows of the wrecked drawing room had been boarded up and the door was closed, but they could still smell smoke and burnt wool from the carpet. The curtains hung in blackened tatters.

The damage can be repaired, thought Anne, but our spirits can't. Will the miasma of evil ever fade?

Rose made the tea and sat down next to Jack.

'I want to go home,' whispered June.

Harry took her hand. 'Where's home?' he asked gently.

'Australia.'

Mark was sitting opposite Anne and the sight of his distress almost made her cry. She knew her son would have no qualms about living in Australia, because even before he knew about his real father, he had wanted to go there.

When they returned to their cottage, Anne put her arm around Mark. 'Are you all right, Darling?'

For the first time since the fire he smiled. 'Apart from my wife hating me and our inconvenient marriage? How did you think of that bluff so quickly?'

'I read it in a novel – different circumstances – the hostage was being held at gunpoint. I was terrified she'd know it wasn't true, but once I'd gone, she wouldn't have gained anything by killing you.'

'I don't know – she was trying to kill Fiona and Peter and Juju. One more death would not have mattered to her. She knows there is no capital punishment. She may have thought that if she killed me she could escape. She didn't know about the other dogs. Rose and Jack are elderly. She must have expected to get away with it. She would have too, if we didn't have the dogs. I was fast asleep. If Juju goes back to Australia Fiona might want to go too.'

'Yes. I know. But we can visit them.'

He sighed. 'Trelawney will have to be sold.'

'The new owners might be nice. The cottage belongs to us now.'

'What about Rose and Jack? They might not be wanted. And you'll miss Sebastian – I mean Harry.'

'I will. But he has to live his own life – and as I said we can visit.'

'Or . . . we could go too – all of us. Jack and Rose too if they want to.'

'Are you serious?'

'Yes. What do you think?'

'I think we should wait. June might feel differently later on.'

Chapter 57

Urzula's legs were shaking so much she was glad they offered her a chair. Because she was guilty of arson and killing an animal she had thought she would be made to stand. Remembering her interrogators in Poland she was surprised by the courtesy. Even the prosecution barrister had been polite, although his questions had made her seem unreasonably vindictive. After he had finished she sensed that the jury was not on her side. She was relieved when her barrister stood up. She had seen him making notes during her cross-examination.

He smiled encouragingly at her. 'Miss Luk, when did you feel Peter Yelland was losing interest in you?'

'Just after he met the twins. On my birthday we went to a restaurant and he talked about them all evening.'

'Can you remember what he said?'

'He was derogatory. He described one as being as prickly as a hedgehog. He said the other one looked dazed.' She contemplated saying that when she had seen them in her agency she thought one of them was on drugs, but knew that this allegation could be disproved and would make her look even more vindictive. She contented herself by saying, 'He was not flattering about them. He looked triumphant. He told me that they were rich enough to buy Trelawney outright and have money left over. I knew he was not interested in them – he was interested in their money. He talked about their money more than he talked about them.'

The prosecution barrister stood up. 'Excuse me, my lord, but we are trying to establish whether or not the accused is guilty of attempted murder – the conduct of her ex-boyfriend is irrelevant.'

'My lord,' said her barrister, 'I'm trying to show that it was Peter Yelland's callous behaviour that made Urzula Luk act as she did. There is also the aggressive action of Fiona Lancaster towards Urzula Luk that has to be revealed to the jury.'

'You may continue, but please be brief,' said the judge. 'The object of this trial is to prove or disprove whether the defendant knew the owners of Trelawney were on holiday when she tried to burn it down.'

At the end of the first day Urzula felt that the only thing that had been gained was that the jury now knew that Fiona had attacked her and would be prepared for the details.

When Peter was called to the witness stand the next day his confident manner and expensive grey suit, crisp white shirt and burgundy silk tie, unsettled her. Already unnerved she had to fight back her tears, then thinking they might soften the jury's attitude toward her, she gave up and let them pour down her face. As her barrister shuffled his papers she wiped her eyes.

'Mr Yelland, when did you discover how rich Fiona Lancaster was?'

'The day I met her.'

'And her money attracted you.'

'No. It surprised me. Her beauty attracted me.'

'Yet you were involved with Urzula Luk?'

'Involved with – not living with, engaged to or married to.'

'Did you love her?'

'No. I – '

'Yet your relationship was sexual?'

Peter looked cornered. 'Yes,' he said after a pause.

'Are you in the habit of starting a sexual relationship with someone you do not love?'

'I liked her – '

'Enough to use her for sex, but not enough to consider marrying her.'

'I didn't use her for sex – or anything else.'

Urzula was pleased to see that Peter was rattled. His respectability is being punctured, she thought. The jury see a good looking man – my barrister is showing that he is scheming and married for money not love.

'When you imagined that Urzula was a threat you bought four guard dogs – Rottweilers, which are capable of extreme savagery.

Is that correct?'

'Yes. But they – '

'Thank you. I have no further questions.'

Urzula wondered how the prosecution would counter the damage.

'Mr Yelland, were the dogs bought solely as guard dogs?'

Peter looked relieved. 'No. Initially they were deterrents, but they were also pets. From the beginning two lived with us, one lived with Mr and Mrs Hayne and one lived with Mr Bolitho. Our two had their baskets inside – the others also slept inside the cottages.'

'Were they trained?'

'Yes. Mark Bolitho trained them.'

'Did he train them to kill?'

'No. He trained them to obey commands. Sit, heel, no, come here, stop – that sort of thing.'

'You have a baby. Were you worried about the reaction of the dogs to the new arrival?'

'No. They're very good and gentle with our neighbours' children. When one had a baby in a pram they were interested, but not aggressive. They were also gentle with toddlers. Once a little boy ran up to Polly and tried to climb on her back – she didn't mind at all.'

'Thank you, Mr Yelland.'

'Miss Luk, when Fiona Lancaster came into your office and attacked you, were there any witnesses?'

'Yes, my colleague.'

'She threw the coffee over you first and then the contents of the ashtray, is that correct?'

'Yes.'

'Where did the cigarettes and ash land?'

'On my face, in my mouth, in my eyes, and in my hair. My eyes were inflamed for a week.'

Fiona, dressed in a navy linen suit and a white blouse with a high collar with a cameo brooch at her neck, looked devastatingly innocent as she went into the witness box. Urzula knew that the jury would have no trouble understanding why Peter had been attracted to her. More than ever she was aware of her own lacklustre appearance.

'Mrs Yelland, did you go into the estate agent's office where Urzula Luk worked and throw coffee over her?' asked her barrister, seemingly unmoved by her beauty.

'Yes.'

'Even though you could have scalded her?'

'The coffee wasn't hot.'

'How did you know?'

'There was no steam.'

'If there had been steam would you have thrown it?'

Fiona hesitated. Urzula saw that she was floundering. Her cheeks were flushed and she was chewing her lip.

'Or were you in such a bad temper you wouldn't have cared?'

'I'm not sure.'

'Not satisfied with ruining her clothes, you then tipped an ashtray full of cigarette butts and ash over her head. Is that true?'

'Yes.'

'Was this because Urzula had warned you that Peter Yelland was after your money?'

'Yes, but she lied. She – '

'An extreme retaliation. Are you normally so violent?'

'Peter overheard her lies and broke our engagement. I was upset.'

'Did he break your engagement because he thought you believed her?'

'No, but he thought her allegations would spoil our relationship.'

'Did it ever occur to you that he was after your money?'

'No. Never. I wanted to put his name on the deeds – he refused. He – '

'Thank you, Mrs – '

Fiona interrupted him. 'Peter pays all the bills. He works full time – if he was after my money he would have given up work! We don't even have a joint bank account because – '

'Thank – '

'He refused!' she finished.

Urzula saw that Fiona was on the verge on losing her temper. She wanted her barrister to provoke her, but to her annoyance he finished his questioning. The prosecution barrister stood up.

'Mrs Yelland, on the morning that Miss Luk told you that Peter was after your money had you invited her to visit you?'

'No.'

'Did she write or phone to tell you she was coming?'

'No.'

'Did she knock or ring the doorbell?'

'No.'

'She just came in?'

'Yes.'

'How did she get in?'

'The door was ajar.'

'Did she call out?'

'No. The first thing I knew she was in the kitchen.'

'So she trespassed?'

'Yes.'

'Did you ask her to leave?'

'Yes.'

'Did she leave?'

'No, not then.'

'How many times did you tell her to leave your house?'

'I can't remember.'

'More than once?'

'Yes.'

'When did she eventually leave?'

'When Peter came into the kitchen.'

'Thank you, Mrs Yelland.'

'Mr Jovanovics, how would you describe Urzula Luk's capabilities as a courier?' Urzula's barrister asked.

'Excellent.'

'What was her attitude?'

'I'm not sure what you mean.'

'Did she seem happy, sad, depressed?'

'Happy.'

'Did you understand that she was making a new life for herself?'

'Yes.'

'In your opinion was she a threat to Peter and Fiona Yelland?'

'Not any more.'

'And yet you took the trouble to write to them? Why?'

'I wanted to know if she was the Urzula Luk who had caused their wedding to be postponed.'

'Why? What was it to you?'

Stefan hesitated.

'Did you like Urzula?'

'Yes.'

'Enough to start a romantic relationship with her?'

'Perhaps, given time.'

'But in spite of being attracted to her you wrote to Peter and Fiona. Why?'

'I wanted to find out if it was her before I started anything. I didn't want to have any sort of relationship with someone so vindictive.'

'But you considered Urzula was no longer a threat to them. She was beginning a new career – and she excelled at it. You not only wanted to find out who she was, you told Peter and Fiona Yelland what company she worked for, their address and when she would be returning to Dover. A more compassionate man would have left those details out. A more compassionate man would have allowed her to continue with her new life as a courier. A more compassionate man would have known that she had found happiness and fulfilment.'

Urzula's expectation that the jury would believe that she was not guilty of attempted murder disintegrated when the veterinary report on Polly was read out and the photos of her body were shown to them.

Even if they do believe me, she thought as she watched their horrified expressions, they will find me guilty anyway – just because they have this stupid love of animals.

Another good-looking man, thought Urzula as June's husband entered the witness box.

Urzula watched as her barrister got to his feet and stared at his papers, looking perplexed. What is the matter with him? she thought. We will not win this case if he stands there looking dim-witted.

'You are known as Harry Johnson?' he finally asked.

'Yes.'

'But your name is actually Sebastian Gordon-Seymour.'

'It was. It's now Harry Johnson.'

Their case is unravelling, Urzula thought gleefully. He is a criminal. Why else would he change his name?

The prosecution barrister stood up. 'My lord, please may I have a word in private with the witness?'

'Five minutes,' said the judge.

How did he discover that juicy piece of information? Urzula wondered, regretting that she had initially doubted her barrister.

She looked up at the gallery. Lynette and Paul's parents were looking unconcerned and her expectations that he was a convicted criminal faded. When the prosecution barrister returned and explained the situation she saw that the members of the jury looked either sympathetic or interested.

A war hero father, she thought. That is all I need. They will discount the fact that he is illegitimate.

Her barrister resumed his questioning. 'Did you also marry a girl for her money, Mr er . . . Johnson?'

'I don't understand the question.'

Urzula's barrister looked taken aback. 'I don't understand why you don't understand the question.'

'You said 'also'. I've only ever married once. Your question implied that I have been married before.'

'Then – did you marry June Clarkson for her money?'

'Certainly not. I married her because I loved her. And Peter married Fiona for the same reason – love.'

'But you live in a house owned by June and her sister – a big house.'

'June not only lives at Trelawney she works there. She gets up at six every morning to see to the horses. I have plenty of my own money. I own a house in Fowey – I rented it out when I married June.'

'You gave up your job at the bank when you married June.'

'Yes.'

'Why was that?'

'The riding school was expanding. I work with the horses and help teach children show jumping. I work longer hours and harder than I did at the bank.'

Urzula expected the prosecution barrister to object to the questions, on the grounds that they had nothing to do with the trial. That he didn't made her realize that he was not concerned about the answers.

'Your living arrangements are unusual.'

'Are they?'

'Yes. You and your wife live in the same house as Peter and Fiona Yelland. There is an empty cottage on the property. Why do you not live there?'

'Trelawney has five double bedrooms – there is plenty of room for two couples. And it's not as if we are all casual acquaintances.'

'Do you each have separate kitchens?'

'No. We share the kitchen, the drawing-room and the dining-room.'

'Do you share a bathroom?'

'No. There are two bathrooms.'

'What about the bedrooms – do you share them?'

The barrister for the prosecution leapt to his feet. 'Objection – '

Harry laughed. 'I am happy to answer the question, my lord.'

The judge looked at Urzula's barrister. 'Please remember that

Mr Johnson is not on trial. Limit your questioning to relevant matters – the morality of the victims of this crime is not an issue. I will let him answer as he has requested.'

'Peter and Fiona Yelland go alone to their bedroom at night. June and I go alone to our bedroom at night. I believe in monogamy and so do Peter and Fiona.'

Looking crestfallen her barrister said, 'No further questions.'

'The bites on the back of Miss Luk's neck – were they severe?' the prosecution barrister asked a sister from the accident and emergency department.

'No. They were superficial – they bled, but they were not serious.'

'Did it look as if she had been attacked by a savage dog?'

'No.'

'Did they need stitches?'

'No. The worst cut was to her cheek where she had fallen and hit her face on the gravel.'

'Did she require hospitalization?'

'No. Her bites and cuts were cleaned, antiseptic ointment and a dressing were applied and she was given antibiotics and a tetanus injection.'

What little sympathy I might have gained has been wiped out, Urzula thought.

Battling her impulse to argue Urzula listened to the prosecution's summing-up. Succinctly he had listed her actions which, he told the jury, had escalated as her obsessive jealousy had grown. The vicar had given an account of her interruption at Peter and Fiona's wedding and the subsequent search through the marriage registers, which proved she had lied. Her threatening letter to Peter had been read to the jury. Although her lawyer had made much of the incident where Fiona had gone into the estate agent's office and thrown coffee and cigarettes over her the prosecution barrister had, in turn, made it sound like a reasonable act. She hoped that the six women on the jury would resent Fiona's beauty.

She knew the six men would admire it.

She wished she could run out of the courtroom, but forced herself to listen as he continued his damning summary.

'Peter Yelland had not asked Urzula Luk to marry him. They were not engaged and had been going out together for just over a year. He ended their relationship before he began dating Fiona Lancaster. There was no betrayal, yet Urzula Luk was determined to seek revenge through a series of well-planned and calculated acts. It is significant that she has no character witnesses. Not one person has come forward to attest to her good character, but many have come forward to condemn her, including the estate agents with whom she worked.

'She has admitted her guilt to all but one of the offences. With all the witnesses she could hardly do otherwise. You have to decide if there is enough evidence to support her story about knowing the house was empty at the time she tried to burn it down. Her claim that she knew that the four occupants of the house were on holiday is based on her knowledge that one October they all went on holiday when she and Peter were going out together. She was so obsessed with revenge that she followed Peter's cousin Yvonne home from the hospital where she worked so she could find out their new address. She claims to have watched their house.

'She said she saw them come out their front door with suitcases. She saw a Land Rover arrive and assumed it belonged to Peter and Fiona Yelland. Yes, they own a Land Rover, but so do many people. She saw a Rolls-Royce arrive. From where she claims to be standing in the park, spying on them, she would have had difficulty seeing their faces. They did not get out of the car. Yes, Lynette Yelland got into the Land Rover, but as she was Peter's sister and as there was a baby in a carrycot on the back seat, that she went with them, while Yvonne Pascoe got into the Rolls-Royce, was an obvious conclusion.

'And did the Rolls-Royce and the Land Rover have banners flying, proclaiming that they were going on holiday? No. Did one of them leap out of their car and shout that they were going on holiday? No. So why was the accused so sure their house at Trelawney would be empty? Did she see their suitcases? No, because they were in the boot out of sight. The only suitcases she saw belonged to Peter's sister Lynette, their cousin Charles and his girlfriend, and their cousin Yvonne. They could have been going on holiday and Peter could have been driving to the airport to see them off.

'Urzula Luk is a proven liar. She set fire to their house with the intent to murder, not just the man she imagined had betrayed her, and not just the woman he had married, but their baby daughter and June and Harry Johnson. But although she claims that she knew nothing about the baby, Fiona Yelland was often in Liskeard with a pram. Miss Luk lurked around the town, spying on them. With her prison-cropped hair and extreme weight loss she was unrecognizable. But they were not. Unfortunately for Urzula she had no idea that, because of her threats, the occupants of Trelawney had bought dogs to protect themselves – and protect them they did – one to the death.'

Urzula studied the jurors' faces. They believe him, she thought. They will find me guilty. His repeated use of the words 'claimed' and 'obsessive' will colour their minds. My barrister will have to do better than that.

She felt sick. Her heart was pounding so rapidly she wondered if she would have a heart attack or faint.

I do not suppose anyone would care if I did have a heart attack, she thought.

Her barrister stood up. 'Urzula Luk was heartbroken when Peter Yelland, the man she loved very deeply, ended their relationship. Had it not been for his spiteful act in contacting the police when he received the letter from Stefan Jovanovics Urzula would today be a successful courier, his dog would not have been killed and his wife's drawing-room would not have been destroyed.'

Urzula saw Peter's look of outrage. Clever, she thought. Good way to remind the jury that he married Fiona for her money.

'Why did he do it? He knew she had found a new job and was

no longer a threat to him or Fiona. He knew that for most of the year she would be in Europe. Urzula's actions caused Peter's wedding to be postponed. Peter's actions caused Urzula to be sacked from the job she enjoyed and excelled at. Terrified that she would be arrested she went back to Poland. Unfortunately she had forgotten how intolerant the communist regime is. In a conversation with colleagues she made a minor criticism. She was reported, arrested and spent a year in a brutal Polish prison. Her head was shaved and she lost so much weight none of the people she knew in England recognized her when she returned.

'As you have heard, Peter Yelland is no innocent. He knew how wealthy Fiona Lancaster was when he met her. In Urzula's opinion he was after Fiona's money and he ended their relationship to begin one with Fiona. It hurt Urzula that no matter how intelligent she was and in spite of her many talents, she could not compete with Fiona. She tried to warn Fiona. But instead of being grateful for the warning from someone who knew Peter well, Fiona retaliated by storming into Urzula's workplace and throwing coffee and cigarette butts and ash over her. Consequently she was unable to keep an appointment with prospective buyers. Her colleague went instead and secured the sale. Urzula lost a good bonus, which would have gone a long way to solving her financial problems.

'A lot of emphasis has been put on the victims in this case. But Urzula was also a victim. Instead of trying to sort things out with her fiancé, who had broken their engagement, Fiona was in such a bad temper that she attacked Urzula. But this was not the only time Urzula was the victim of a physical assault. You have all heard Lynette Yelland admit that she followed Urzula out of the church and struck her across the face with a bridesmaid's bouquet. Not satisfied with that, Lynette pushed Urzula so hard she fell over and badly grazed her knees and hands. Until she tried to burn down the house Urzula had never attacked anyone. She had never hit Fiona or Lynette who had both attacked her. No wonder she was so aggrieved that she sought revenge.

'Her declaration at Peter's wedding was caused by her desire to damage Peter, who had callously dropped her when he became interested in a rich girl, and to inconvenience Fiona who had publicly attacked her, the result of which was financial hardship and inflamed eyes. Knowing that she would be hounded out of Liskeard Urzula went to London. Unable to find a job desperation drove her to write to Peter. All she wanted was a reference so she could continue her career as an estate agent.

'Urzula has admitted to killing the dog. But this was no ordinary dog, ladies and gentlemen. It was a Rottweiler. A guard dog. How many of you seeing such a powerful and fierce dog rushing to attack you, would not have defended yourselves? Peter and Fiona had, not just one Rottweiler, but four Rottweilers. Four savage dogs capable of killing or seriously injuring a human. Urzula used the only weapon she had – fire. She did not plan to hurt the dog, because she had no idea that Peter and Fiona owned savage dogs. Mr Yelland says the dogs were not savage, but we only have his word for it. Perhaps he tells the truth and they are not savage with people they know and are used to, but they got the dogs, on their own admission, for protection.

'Urzula is not a murderer. She knew that Peter and his family went on holiday together in October, but she took the precaution of making sure that things had not changed now Peter and Fiona were married. She found out where Peter's sister and two cousins lived. She saw a Land Rover arrive at their house. A Land Rover *did* arrive at the house she was watching. She did not know what sort of car Fiona's sister's husband owned, but she saw a Rolls-Royce – not just any Rolls-Royce but a burgundy Rolls Royce.

'Urzula said she knew they were on holiday. Fact – they *were* on holiday. Their house *was* empty. Urzula tried to burn down an *empty* house. Urzula did not assume they were on holiday. She *knew* they were on holiday. Because she did not want to harm or kill anyone she went to the trouble of making sure they would be away.'

The jury deliberated for two days. When they delivered their verdict of not guilty, Urzula burst into tears of relief.

She hugged her barrister. 'Thank you. I am sorry I was rude to you in the beginning.'

He nodded.

'Will you visit me in jail?'

'No.'

'I thought you were my friend.'

'No, Miss Luk, I was your barrister.'

Chapter 58

Peter felt his reputation had been seriously damaged. He could cope with being called spiteful and petty, but what he found hard to face was the defence's case that he had married Fiona because she was wealthy. The day after the trial he and Fiona invited his parents, Lynette and Yvonne to Trelawney for dinner. Charles was on night duty at the hospital. While Fiona was putting Ruth to bed June, Rose and Anne prepared a large saucepan of spaghetti Bolognese. Mark poured everyone a drink.

'Perhaps he's right,' Peter said as they sat in the kitchen.

'Right about what?' asked his mother.

'That I am petty and spiteful.'

'Stop being ridiculous,' said Lynette. 'Why should you have let Urzula get away with it?'

'If I hadn't contacted the police she'd still be a courier. Polly would still be alive instead of dying such a hideous death.'

'How could you know what she'd do?' asked his mother.

'I knew she was unhinged.'

Yvonne, who was setting the kitchen table, put her hands on her hips. 'So you should have let her get away with wrecking your wedding day?'

'As Fiona said she wrecked our wedding, but not our lives or our future – if I'd just shrugged it off . . . '

'Peter,' said his father, 'it's useless going over what you did. You did it. I think you did the right thing. Not out of spite, but because you wanted her to be punished for her actions. It's what I would have done.'

'It's what most people would have done,' said Lynette. 'The law was on your side. People who get away with one thing think they can get away with anything.'

'It's not just that – all that stuff about me marrying Fiona for her money – I feel tainted by the accusations.'

'No one who knows you would believe that,' said his mother.

'And if they do,' said Yvonne. 'Their minds are as nasty as Urzula's.'

Only Mark went to the court to hear Urzula sentenced.

'Four years,' he told them when he returned in the afternoon. 'She'll be out in less if she behaves. And the time she has already spent in jail will be deducted. We have to think about what to do. Because of her instability I'd guess she'll blame all this on you. She'll leave jail with a criminal record and be unemployable. In my opinion she'll want revenge.

'She might even find someone in jail to help her. I can't see her character improving in prison – if anything it will get worse. Unless she's deported she won't go back to Poland. I've been thinking,' he continued. 'Since you moved here there has been one upset after another. It's not a happy place any more. And when she is released she'll be more of a threat.'

Fiona lifted Ruth into her high chair and spooned pureed carrots into her mouth. 'What do you think we should do?'

'Leave here – all of us – you too, Rose and Jack,' said Mark.

'Where would we go?'

He smiled at Anne. 'Australia. Buy land in the country – start a riding school and – '

'Australia?' said Lynette in dismay.

'Australia,' echoed Fiona. 'Whereabouts in Australia?'

'South Australia.'

He saw June's radiant smile.

'I've always wanted to go to Australia,' said Rose. 'It was just a dream, but now . . . '

Mark saw that although Lynette was looking upset her parents were looking enthusiastic. 'You could come for holidays,' Peter said to her.

'I suppose,' she said doubtfully.

'You could move there,' said June. 'You could live in Adelaide and visit us at weekends. Lots of sun.'

'And snakes and bushfires,' said Lynette.

'Not in the city,' said Fiona.

Ω   Ω   Ω

'Alex,' said Virginia waving Fiona's letter. 'Wonderful news. They're all coming home. And June's pregnant.'

He smiled. 'How long are they staying?'

'For ever. They want to live here – they've decided on South Australia. Sebastian's, I mean Harry's, grandparents live in Adelaide. I'm so excited – Anne and Mark and Rose and Jack are coming too and Peter's parents. You'll be busy. They want to buy land somewhere and Fiona asked if you'd design their houses.'

'How many?'

She looked at Fiona's letter again. 'A big one with separate wings for me, Peter, Juju and Harry,' she read. 'A house for Mark and Anne, one for Rose and Jack and one for Peter's parents. And another cottage for guests. Lynette, Yvonne and Charles will visit for holidays and who knows? They might even decide to emigrate. Maybe we should have two cottages for guests! We want it all to be the same as now except that we'll be in Australia not Cornwall. I am surprised that Peter is so willing to leave as he's close to Lynette, Yvonne and Charles, but he said that there are too many bad memories and Trelawney no longer feels like home. We are bringing the dogs. We spoke to the vet and he said that although they will have to spend time in quarantine it would be kinder than finding them a new home, which might be difficult, because people usually want puppies.'

'I'm glad they're coming home – I know Urzula's in prison, but they'll be safer here,' said Alex. 'The only things they'll have to worry about are snakes and spiders.'

'I'd rather deal with them than Urzula. Where are you going?'

'To my study to start designing all those houses.'

I've given you a choice, wrote Alex. *You'll need lots of land for paddocks and orchards and vegetable gardens, so to save space plan A is a terrace of five two-storey houses, identical in layout, each with three double bedrooms. Plan B is single storey houses in a terrace. Plan C is detached two storey houses. Plan D is detached single storey houses.*

For the main house, I based the design on Trelawney and added a veranda – all the doors will open onto it like at Kingower. It's got six double bedrooms and two bathrooms with a shower room downstairs.

Peter spread the drawings and plans out on the dining-room table. 'These are superb. They look Victorian – lots of character. Love the lacework on the verandas.'

'Dad's an architect,' said Fiona.

'Is he?' said Anne. 'I thought he was a property developer.'

'When he left university he hated being part of a team that was destroying Sydney – Victorian buildings were torn down and replaced by skyscrapers, so he started his own property development business.'

Anne picked up one of the plans for the cottages. 'Beautiful.'

'Look at the stable block – your father's really put a lot of work into these,' said June.

Mark studied the drawings and plans. 'Because of our ages it would be best to have single storey houses. We can all manage the stairs at the moment, but when we get older we're bound to find them more difficult.'

'A terrace or detached?' asked Anne.

'A terrace . . . as Alex said it saves space.'

'Alex, what do you think about moving to South Australia?' asked Virginia.

'Whereabouts?'

'Well, they've got all that land . . . '

'You mean moving into one of their houses?'

'Yes.'

'You know how you and Fiona used to quarrel all the time.'

'I've changed. We got on very well when we were in England and we were staying in her house.'

'Yes, but it was temporary. Besides our lives are here – our friends – '

'I want to be close to Fiona. To watch her children grow up – to have them call me Grandma.'

'Why can't we just have holidays there?'

'I want more. Do you think I'm being selfish?'

He shook his head. 'Misguided. Their property is remote.'

'Acacia was remote.'

'You were a child when you lived there.'

'We've got a car. We can drive.'

He went to the window and looked over the harbour. 'I'd miss this view. I'd miss Sydney.'

'So would I. But you'd have another view. You've missed Fiona – people are more important than places.'

'True, but what about my work?'

'It's time you retired.'

'I can't sit about all day drinking tea and doing nothing.'

'There'll be plenty to do. You love riding. You're good with horses. You like Mark. He might appreciate having a man his own age around.'

'He'll have Peter's father.'

'You could help him and Anne with the management of the riding school.'

'They might not want my help. Fiona is sure not to want us living so close.'

'Me living so close, you mean. Why don't we ask her?'

'Virginia, that would put her in an awkward position.'

'Peter's parents are moving onto their property. You're happy designing a house for them, but not for us.'

'Virginia, I don't want us to argue over this.'

'I'm not arguing. You pointed out that I never got on with Fiona when we lived in the same house, but I wasn't the one who said I'd punch Peter on the nose – '

'I was upset. And I did apologize.'

'Only after being prompted by Fiona. I'm upset now. Upset that my husband won't acknowledge that I've changed because I learnt from my mistakes. I'm upset that you think Fiona doesn't love me enough to want me near her.'

'I didn't say that.'

'You didn't have to.'

Dear Mum and Dad,

What a hoot! Lots of people came to look at Trelawney and a really nice family offered the asking price, which we accepted. A few days later someone put in a higher offer – a much higher offer. We couldn't remember who they were so they came to meet us. None of us liked them. They were status-conscious and not interested in the horses, so we turned down their offer. Kettle growled at them, and that's when I decided that there was something wrong with them. They were jabbering on about how much they could rent the cottages out for and how rich they would be. Their two children were sulky brats. The first people had three children who adored horses and the dogs liked them.

Knowing how well you got on with Mark and Anne we were hoping that you would like to move onto our property. You can build your own house if you want to. You probably don't want to leave Sydney, but it would be terrific if you decided to move. If you don't we hope you'll visit us a lot. The dogs are going to be taken away tomorrow ready to fly to Australia. Michael and Agnes have promised to visit them when they are in quarantine.

Juju and Harry are very excited about the baby. Funny that her pregnancy is so much more serene than mine was. She did have morning sickness, but she wasn't an emotional wreck like I was!

Love
Fiona and Peter

Fiona took off Ruth's wet nappy. 'Wonderful news, darling. You've got a cousin – his name's Michael after his great-grandfather. He was born an hour ago.'

Ruth smiled and gurgled.

'I know you can't understand a word I'm saying, but you like it when I talk to you, don't you.'

Ruth kicked her legs. Fiona secured the clean nappy and pulled a white nightdress over Ruth's head.

'We exchanged contracts yesterday and soon we'll be moving to the other side of the world. Won't that be nice? Michael and Agnes found us some land and Dad has designed houses and they are being built now. When you're old enough we'll teach you to ride – but you don't have to if you don't want to. Ruth,' she said solemnly, 'I promise I'll be a good mother. I won't fuss – at least I hope I won't.'

She heard Peter came into the nursery and turned. He put his arm around her. 'You are a good mother.'

'I'm so afraid I'll get it all wrong – being a parent.'

Peter picked Ruth up and put her in her cot. 'You will get some things wrong, and so will I. But we'll get lots of things right too.'

Fiona gave Ruth her rattle. 'I hated my mother when I was younger.'

'So you'll do things differently. You won't be possessive – you'll let her be independent and – '

Fiona put her head on his shoulder. 'I want her to be happy. I want her to love me.'

'She will. She's got two parents who love her and each other. We'll all be happy. We will, darling. We will.'

Chapter 59

February 1978

Before leaving the hospital in Brisbane for the long drive home Tom went into the cafeteria and fortified himself with two cups of strong coffee. His back ached from sitting by Gabriella's bedside for so long. He had tried to ring Eumeralla, but there had been a severe storm, which had brought power lines down. His journey was delayed by fallen trees across the highways. When he drove up to Eumeralla the bushes and trees were heavy with rainwater that sparkled in the sun.

His parents, Keith, Sophie and Neil gathered on the veranda when they heard his car. He'd cried at the hospital, but was determined not to cry now.

'What is it – I mean what are they?' asked Keith.

Although exhausted he ran up the steps. 'Boys!' He grabbed his mother and hugged her then flung his arm round his father's shoulder. 'You're grandparents. Mother and sons are well. They'll be home in ten days.'

'What are their names?' asked Keith.

'Laurence and Gregory.'

'Boys,' said Greg. 'Boys for Eumeralla.'

Also by Joanna Stephen-Ward

Vissi d'arte – A novel about love and music

Eumeralla – A family saga

The Doll Collection – A crime novel

Suspicion Points – A detective novel

These books can be downloaded as a Kindle eBook or a paperback print-on-demand from www.amazon:- .co.uk or .com.

Printed in Great Britain
by Amazon